# $ix Days to Midnight
## Part of the K-Cycle Series

Kat Duncan

ISBN: 0615438431
ISBN-13:978-0615438436

# DEDICATION

To Dave.

# PROLOGUE

With an explosion of dirt and hooves, Mirza whipped her mount toward the starting line. Embroidered blue velvet and black silk leggings revealed a figure that should have belonged to a girl forty years younger. A young man, also in the traditional blue of the Kazakhs, waited for her to pass, then drove his horse forward. The centuries old Kyz Kuumai race had begun. The Kazakhs, with a tradition of riding that spanned thousands of years, took their games seriously. This 'Chase the Girl' race being the most gentle. His goal, to steal a kiss before she could cross the finish line. If not, then it was the lady's turn. But not for a kiss.

Mirza held a firm lead at the first turn. They now rode due north, Kazakhstan's towering Tian Shan mountains looming before them. Past the peaks lay Siberia. To the east, Mongolia. Everywhere else, nothing.

Except for the small staff of on-lookers, there was not another person for hundreds of miles. She looked back, her long black hair, streaked with silver, flowed around her face. With a glint of glee in her sparkling brown eyes, she slowed ever so slightly to let him close the gap.

The second turn brought them past a small air-field, dotted with several very modern jets, their only viable mode of transport in the desolate countryside. Beyond that, the main building of the compound jutted from the rocky plain. As the finish line approached he came alongside, and leaned toward her. With a quick slap of her stout riding whip, her horse surged forward. She crossed the finish line still un-kissed. The first half of her victory.

Now, the race reversed. As he fled for the safety of the starting line, she became the pursuer. Even the cool desert air couldn't keep the sweat from glistening on the horses' necks. With only a hundred yards to go, she again whipped her horse forward. As the starting line approached, a look of victory, and relief, broke across his face. Then a sharp crack of her whip across his shoulders brought him flying to the ground. Dust and stone flew as he rolled to a painful stop.

She pulled her horse around, and dismounted. As he spit dirt and blood, she pulled him to his feet.

"Well done, Abay," she praised. "Perhaps next time I will let you take the kiss."

"Yes, madam," he spoke, bowing slightly.

"Then again, perhaps not." With casual neglect she pulled off her riding gloves.

An older man approached. A black rimless cap adorned his head. A carefully embroidered brown vest over a white shirt covered his rotund form.

"There is a telephone call for you, madam."

She glanced at the caller ID, then pulled a dangling earring from her left lobe.

"Anton, what a pleasant surprise to hear from you," she said, switching to German. "You are up so early. It is still very dark in Zurich." It didn't bother her that an American satellite recorded her every word.

"Or up so late, my dear Mirza. There is so little time left, I hate to waste it sleeping." His voice was strong, firm, and in control.

"I am very disappointed with you, Anton. Keeping secrets from me."

"I would never lie to you, my dearest."

"Neither would you ever speak the truth." She let the words hang in the air. "I have dispatched my men to deal with this Thompson girl."

"She is no one."

"Too many people have already read her dissertation. She is sending it to everyone looking for a grant. I want her stopped." She slapped her thigh with her gloves.

"Delicacy is needed, Mirza."

"I do know of this word, delicacy, but you know its meaning too well. Always maneuvering in and out of shadows. No one knows your methods or your goals. The whole world knows mine. Action. Conquest. Nothing less."

"My dear Mirza. You would mold a tea cup with a hammer."

"The hammer is to forge the sword." She paused. "Perhaps you like your women to be young."

"I am too old for such thoughts. For you or any woman."

"Judging by your last visit to me, I would say that is hardly the case."

"You flatter me."

"When will you visit me again?"

"I don't intend to become the male Black Widow. I know when to leave and when it may be safe to return."

The line went dead. She tossed the phone to the servant. A sparkling Range Rover pulled up and the driver scrambled to open the door. A frail man inside stared at her through thick glasses. He slunk deeper into the vehicle as she slid in next to him.

"Has the money been transferred?" She now spoke in English.

"Yes, Ms. ul-Beg. The one point six billion is now in Grand Rapids."

"Good. Everything is ready. Except for one remaining detail."

\*\*\*

The gleaming Lear 60 business jet pulled to a halt on the tarmac, far from the distant terminal.

"Lass den Motoren laufen," the only passenger instructed in his native Swiss German.

The pilot nodded, leaving the engines idling, ready for what was coming.

The man stepped down the stairs and pulled off his sunglasses. He scanned the area. Good, her jet had not yet arrived.

The man looked up into what should have been a brilliant blue African sky, now splotched with billowing acrid yellow and black bruises from the sudden impact of riots that engulfed the city during the night.

A rusted shuttle van pulled up to the Lear, and an elderly guard stepped out.

"I am being welcoming you, Herr Dr. Mahler." the guard struggled in broken English.

"When will she arrive?"

"Patience, my friend, patience."

A blue and white airport security vehicle pulled up and waited a distance away. Through the tinted windshield, Mahler couldn't see the driver clearly, but he appeared to be wearing a chauffer's uniform.

"Who is that?"

The guard squinted. "I am not knowing. Shall I..."

Mahler shook his head.

He pulled a photo from his pocket. A woman, American, twenty nine, long strawberry blonde hair, high cheek bones, sparkling green eyes. Janet Thompson. Her research paper had been brilliant to the point of naiveté.

"You'd think she'd have more sense," he muttered. He looked back once more at the mysterious security car, pulled in a stiff breath, stood rod straight tall, and walked with the guard to the shuttle van to wait and watch.

# CHAPTER ONE

Janet Thompson suppressed an exhausted yawn as the aircraft broke through a layer of high cloud to reveal the hilly African terrain outside of Harare. She'd been unable to catch even a moment of sleep on the long trek from Tulsa. Every connection had been full to capacity, except for this last one from Johannesburg. She was one of a mere six passengers. Odd she thought for an aircraft that could hold several hundred. Even with all the extra room, she'd been too tired to sleep.

She pulled the e-mail from her purse and stared at it again. SBU, Swiss Bank United, the logo read. Her research grant had come from one of the largest banks on the globe. Anton Zelman, the Director General himself, had signed it.

She craned her neck to better see the country she had so intently researched. Like Oklahoma, the land was neatly divided into perfect rectangles of farmland. But even from this altitude something looked wrong. The colors weren't the same as the farms back home. Instead of uniform greens and browns, there were irregular splotches of tan and black. Weeds and brush must have taken over. Zimbabwe, once the breadbasket of Africa, was starving. She was here to prove why. And with luck prevent the instability from spreading.

As the aircraft descended, farmland gave way to clusters of small houses. Then the capitol came into view. A long plume of acrid black and yellow smoke streaked across the city. There must have been a fire. As they approached the airport to the north east, more streaks appeared until they blended and blurred into a solid mass that roiled and bubbled toward the airport. Tones of alarm came from several passengers as they spoke in the lilting whistles of their native Shona language. In the blink of an eye, while she traveled, an evil cloud had descended over the city she had studied in such detail.

Only the approaching runway quieted them. The wheels touched the ground and the seatbelt tugged at her waist as the aircraft slowed. However, instead of turning toward the terminal, the aircraft turned away and parked on a remote section of pavement.

As the engines spun down she glanced out the window. A neon yellow billboard caught her attention. 'SBU Swiss Bank United, your personal bank in a hundred countries' the caption read. Splashed across the sign was the handsome smiling face of Anton Zelman. Tufts of thick salt and pepper hair showed beneath his outsized American style black cowboy hat, complete with a silver and turquoise concho brooch studded in its center. His gray blue eyes blazed with trust.

Odd hat for a Swiss Banker, she thought. But who was she to question the patron who had made this trip possible?

A motorized stairway and a rusted shuttle pulled up to the jet. An elderly guard entered and began a long incomprehensible explanation.

"Excuse me, sir," Janet spoke when he finished. "What is happening?"

The guard fumbled with his papers for a moment. "Ganit Fompason you?" he mumbled in broken English.

"Yes."

"American, yes?"

"Yes."

"Patience, American my friend. Patience."

Patience was not a virtue she had yet mastered.

She glanced at her watch. Dawn back in Tulsa. Marcie, the perennial lark, would be up. She pulled out her cell phone and pressed speed dial. A few breathless moments, then she heard ringing. A sigh of relief spread through her that her new cell phone was working as promised in this distant country.

"Hey you, big sister. How is Zimbabwe?" Marcie bubbled.

"I'm stuck in the airplane. They're not letting anyone off. If I don't get through soon, I'm going to miss my ride."

"Jan, what was the plan?"

Pulling the e-mail from her purse Janet continued, "Director Zelman's chauffer was supposed to meet me outside of customs and take me to the university."

"Do you have any phone numbers?"

"Just Zelman's office number in Zurich."

"What happened to the always over-prepared assistant professor I used to know?"

"I left her back in Tulsa."

"Jan, I guess being in Africa proves you're serious about this whole research thing, doesn't it?"

Janet knew there were a thousand questions buried in the one. "Marcie - I needed to get away. I..." Janet paused trying to form the words she needed to say.

"Was I that much of a burden?" Marcie interjected into the silence.

"Marcie, no. That's not it at all. I love every minute we are together."

"Miss," the guard adjured in broken English. "Cell phones no in jet."

"Marcie, I have to go."

"Yeah, I heard. Call me," her sister spoke as Janet closed her phone with a worried sigh.

Eight years sacrificed. Not a shred of resentment over raising her kid sister. But with Marcie sailing through her senior year in college, Janet was free to pursue her dream. Across the field of runways and strips of grass was the terminal. Only a few hundred yards remaining and she'd come to a dead stop. So close, yet so far.

One by one the guard called out five names. One by one she watched them file down the stairs and into the van. She stood in anticipation of her name to be the sixth and last.

"Please you down sitting. Another moment."

Janet's heart pounded. Why would she be singled out? "What is going on?"

"Being to you okay," the guard reassured. The guard looked around, stroking his chin in worry. "City very much danger. Being you careful. A man coming to protecting you."

"What man? Who?"

A tall man ducked to enter the aircraft. Straightening, he made a quick scan of the empty airliner. He forced a smile at her.

"Ms. Thompson? Welcome to Africa. I am Brandt Mahler." His English was crisp, precise and very European. He extended his hand in greeting as he walked toward her.

Janet knew of Mahler, having used many of his papers in her research. She never expected to ever meet the famous Swiss economist. Yet, here he was, looking nothing like the mental image she had conjured. Instead of a wizened sage, before her stood a thirty year old. Not more than a year older than her. He stepped toward her with elegance and grace. His smile was warm and disarming. Too disarming, carrying a tinge of discomfort that alarmed her.

If he was not mentioned in Director Zelman's e-mail, then he shouldn't be here.

"Dr. Mahler? Why are you meeting me? Did Director Zelman send you?" Her tone was skeptical and wavering as she ignored his outstretched hand.

He looked down at his rejected hand and with a cough he dismissed her rude gesture.

"Zelman? Uh, no." His voice paused a moment longer than it should. He stepped deeper into the aircraft, just past her, facing the door and forcing her to turn in her seat to look at him. His eyes repeatedly darted to the door as if expecting someone. The hairs on the back of her neck prickled.

"There has been an unfortunate change in circumstances," he continued. "It would be best if you came with me."

"But Director Zelman was very explicit in his e-mail," she said wielding the document in club-like defense. "I'm to meet his driver and he'll take me to the university."

"Well, I'm here now, and you can come with me." He flashed her a warm magazine cover smile.

Standing, she faced him. She hadn't just come nine thousand seven hundred and seventy two miles to be derailed by a conceited man, short on answers. She placed one hand on her hip.

"No."

Mahler blinked at the word he was apparently unaccustomed to hearing. It took him a moment to recover.

"Uh, we shouldn't be standing here." His gaze again darted to the door.

As her sense of fear rose, her voice broke into a surly swagger.

"I'm sorry, but I'll need to speak with-"

In the flash of a second, Mahler's eyes widened as he focused on something at the door.

"Get down!" He lunged for her, forcing her head down.

A deafening gunshot exploded in the cabin.

Janet screamed.

The old guard spun around and fumbled with the gun still in his belt clip. Two shattering pops jerked him backwards. His face and chest erupted in streams of red. Then he crumpled.

Janet choked out another scream.

Mahler grabbed Janet and pulled her deeper into the aircraft. Trapped. His eyes darted, looking for a way out. His hand grabbed a red handle. Out came the small emergency exit door. A bullet pinged off Mahler's temporary shield. Before the air-slide even had time to spring outward he pushed her. Another bullet whizzed behind her. She landed face first on the inflating rubber and rolled head over heels onto her back. Mahler dove out and slid with her to the ground.

Bullets tore through the slide as he pulled her under the aircraft and into the van filled with gaping people. Heart pounding, she jumped into the passenger side. The old engine ground to life only to sputter and die.

"Verdammt!"

A second try and the engine choked to a halting rumble. He pulled the shift into drive. The rear window exploded, spraying shards of glass over everyone. Screams filled the van and Janet put her head between her knees. Stomping on the gas Mahler hurtled the old vehicle down the runway. He barked a set of German instructions into his cell phone.

"What in God's name is happening?" Janet screeched as bullets pinged off their vehicle.

"Janet, please remain calm," he suggested.

Dazed by adrenaline surging through her veins, she shuddered agreement as the van serpentined side to side making it as difficult a target as possible. He slid the shuttle to a screeching sideways stop inches from the door of a business jet. Sleek and powerful, it was the perfect getaway vehicle. Its engines whined with impatient power.

"Get in! Move!" Mahler commanded, herding her up the short steps.

Janet scrambled up and leaned in through the small door. She took a seat and clasped the buckle in a frantic motion.

"Schnell! Schnell!" Mahler ordered the pilot as he grabbed the door handle. He was still yanking the door shut when the jet blasted off down the taxiway. The pilot pivoted the plane onto the main runway. As the door closed and sealed shut Mahler slammed against the side-facing divan. He clawed at the leather to pull himself up, and lock his seat belt.

Out the cockpit windshield, Janet spotted the gunman racing toward them in an airport security car. The jet gained speed as it hurled head-on toward the car in an ultimate game of chicken. Too close. The car was too close. In excruciating slowness, the nose of the jet lifted. Janet felt the lift as the tires left the concrete. Then the landing gear slammed against the car's roof, making the jet heel over to the right. A shower of sparks spewed from the wing tip as it touched the concrete runway before the pilot righted the aircraft. A sickening lurch swung them to the left as the jet fought to grip the air. In agonizing slowness, the jet teetered, deciding to which side it would find death. Then with smooth power, they angled to the sky and left danger behind.

"By the way, I enjoyed your PhD dissertation very much," Mahler spoke over the wailing engines. "As you can tell, it has impressed a number of people." He casually groomed his rumpled clothes.

"Who is shooting at us?"

"Not us. You. It's Zelman."

"That doesn't make sense. He is the one who gave me the grant to come here."

Mahler huffed out a quick laugh of disgust at his new guest's gullibility. "Well of course he sent you the money. It was the only way he could get you here."

"I don't understand. Director Zelman was kind enough to give me the money I needed to come study the Zimbabwe economy and finalize my dissertation."

"No, Janet. Completing your work is not why he approved your grant." His gaze bore down on her, his tone a hard reprimand. "He and his partner think your paper was far too accurate, and you might figure out their next move. They decided to block your research. Permanently."

Her head thumped against the cold window frame.

"Zelman brought me here to kill me?" she puffed out.

"Too bad you didn't write your paper a year earlier. Zelman would have made you rich. Now he needs you dead."

"All I did was write my doctoral thesis on the collapse of the Zimbabwean economy."

"That is not all you wrote. You concluded that the collapse was contrived as an experiment in depression economics."

"Yeah. My computer projections show that Zimbabwe's downturn was more than just another recession. Someone may have intentionally destroyed the local economy to test what would happen."

"Did it not occur to your overly abstract mind that this hypothetical someone might have a keen interest in keeping their little experiment a secret?"

Despite the fear that still gripped her, she gritted her teeth at his insolent tone. "Nothing I wrote could have led to being shot at."

He heaved a sigh of exasperation.

She turned away, staring out the window to the smoke that choked the city. "What happened here?"

"This is what is left after a night of food riots and fires."

"This can't be real," she mouthed in disbelief.

"Janet, the mathematics in your dissertation are brilliant. But, no matter how bland and bloodless your numbers may seem back at your university in Tulsa, they have very real meaning in this world." A smug self-serving smile broke across his face.

She didn't respond. The collision of the brutal reality around her with her abstract paper left her speechless.

"You could say thank you for my compliment," he cajoled.

She spun around to face him. "Look," she said lacing him down with arms crossed, "I've just dodged God knows how many bullets, real bullets mind you, I haven't slept in thirty two hours, and right now I am desperately trying to ignore a man who, up until two minutes ago, I would have given my eye teeth to meet. So back off!"

He raised a palm in truce and broke from her strong gaze.

"By the way, where are you taking me?" she asked.

"I am not taking you anywhere. We are simply traveling together. I was thinking Brussels might be nice."

"Brussels? I don't want to go to Brussels with you."

"Perhaps you'd rather stay here? You seem to be quite popular."

"No thank you. Brussels is good. Tulsa would be better."

"I have a bit of business to conduct here in Zimbabwe, and then I'm headed for Brussels tonight."

"Okay. Brussels then Tulsa. I just want to get out of this crazy place." She glanced around noticing the aircraft's interior for the first time. "Uh, Brandt...thanks for saving my life."

"You are welcome, Janet. I'm very happy to be of service to someone who so eagerly reads and cites my work."

Her breath caught as she looked into his eyes. They were a blend of polished sapphire and crystalline steel with a mirroring depth that cascaded into eternity. She had to look away.

"How did you know I was about to be shot at?"

"Your faculty advisor, Professor Jones, is a good friend of my boss, the Director of the World Monetary Fund. We've been monitoring Zelman for months. When Jones mentioned Zelman's sudden grant to you, we knew something was up. I had you paged in Johannesburg, but you didn't respond. Fortunately I was already in the area, or else you and I would be having this conversation in the morgue. Nasty place. Besides, I think you are much prettier with your head still attached."

Janet sighed to cover her irritation. And fear.

"But why?" she asked. "Why would Zelman want to experiment with the destruction of nations?"

"It is a warm up exercise for a larger prize. Next to Zimbabwe, can you tell me in which country Zelman is most active?"

"No. Where?"

"The United States."

Her jaw dropped. "He wants to destroy America like he did Zimbabwe? Why?"

Brandt didn't answer. Instead he lifted his briefcase to his lap and pulled out a sheaf of paper.

"The Counter Manipulation of Economic Inflectives in Zimbabwe," he read, "by Janet S. Thompson. Stimulating title."

"I mimicked your papers."

"For what does the S stand?"

"Nothing. I never use it," she said turning away.

"Tell me, or I'll have to start guessing."

"You'll never guess," she said in a curt tone.

Brandt softened his voice. "Then tell me. Please..."

She held his gaze for a long moment, interest warring with trust. "Solterra."

"Solterra," he mouthed, letting the word roll from his tongue. "Sol. Terra," he repeated, "Sun and Land, as in Oklahoma."

"Clever, huh?"

"Did it come from your mother?"

She gave him a sideways look, not eager to confide more. "My Dad. Janet came from my Mom, Solterra from my Dad. He always had a whimsical flair." A faint smile moved across her face in memory. "My Mom was the plain Jane type, hence Janet."

"Does he call you Solterra or Janet?"

"Neither. He's gone. So is she."

"I'm sorry."

"Thanks."

"What kind of work did he do?"

"He was an oil field repairman covering Texas and Oklahoma."

"Big territory."

"Yeah. The only way to get around was in our little Piper Cub. He was always taking me along on emergency repairs, letting me bunk school. Drove my Mom crazy." The glow of pleasant memories spread across her mind's eye. "He called me Salty. He said a little bit of me made everything taste better. But too much was hard to swallow."

"I can agree with that!" Brandt chuckled.

"Hey!"

"A lot of you certainly comes through in this paper," he said. "It's brilliant. Appallingly lacking in pragmatics, but still quite brilliant. Where did you get such an unusual concept?"

"Oh, nowhere in particular."

"There must have been some source for the inspiration."

"Well, yeah..."

"Then what was it?"

"You," she said, daring to look at those blue eyes again.

That infuriating thin-lipped smile broke across his face, making Janet's gut twist. He was breaking through her defenses, and she shouldn't allow him any closer. But he seemed to understand her theory.

"Your papers describe so many real world situations," she continued.

"Yes, unlike academic theoreticians such as you, I write about real solutions to rebuilding real economies. However, I don't see the connection between my work and yours."

"I found the common mathematical thread in your papers, inflectives."

Brandt looked genuinely puzzled by her analysis of his work.

"Don't you see it?" she asked. "The underlying theoretical connections among all of your practical experiences?"

Brandt continued his incredulous stare.

"One night I fell asleep reading your papers. When I woke up the next morning, I knew precisely what I wanted to write. I understood how it all fit together."

"So you're saying my papers put you to sleep. Thanks a lot!"

"No," she half-chortled. "You know what I mean." So much for understanding her theory. It was impossible to have an in-depth conversation with such an exasperating man. "Didn't you say you had business to attend to here in Zimbabwe?"

"I do, but not in Harare. I'm here to talk with Michael Madibara."

"The rebel commander?"

"I prefer to call him opposition party leader."

"Why do you need to talk to him?"

"He's about to become the new Prime Minister. He is negotiating WMF loans contingent on his take-over."

"How much is he borrowing?"

"Five billion."

Her brows ticked together at the amount. "You handle that kind of money?"

"Not often. Usually it's more."

With a short tisk, she turned away.

Her cell phone rang. She suppressed a horrified look thinking she'd broken some regulation banning phone use on aircraft. She went to silence it, but paused at the caller ID.

"It's Zelman," she whispered to Brandt.

# CHAPTER TWO

"Go ahead, answer it," he said as he leaned in to listen.

As the heat of his body surrounded her, her voice wavered into the phone. "Hel-lo."

"Tell me, Ms. Thompson, what did you think of my cowboy hat?"

His voice was strong and firm, with the lightest trace of an accent that was hard to identify.

"What?"

"My black cowboy hat on the billboard. Surely you didn't miss it. I purchased it in your hometown of Tulsa."

Janet made a huff of disgust. "A Swiss cowboy? Couldn't you do better than that?"

"It's amazing what a few billboards can do. One third of Zimbabweans now believe Switzerland is a part of the United States. Very successful advertising campaign. I'm using the same hat in my present American campaign. It's working even better. Fifteen percent of Americans think Switzerland is a part of Canada. Never underestimate the power of stupid people in large numbers, Ms. Thompson."

"It takes one to know one."

"Very true, very true. By the way, you can trust Brandt. He doesn't know he is working for me any more than you do."

"I'd never work for you."

"You have no choice because you have only six days to Midnight."

"Midnight when?"

"Midnight is not a when. It is a what."

"Is Midnight the reason you're trying to kill me?"

"Oh, that. It wasn't me."

"I don't believe you."

"It is true, Ms. Thompson, because my people don't miss. It's been a very pleasant conversation, Ms. Thompson. Brandt, I know you're listening. You really should have mentioned that your very well appointed jet was a gift from me." The line went dead.

"What kind of a bizarre conversation was that?" Janet asked. "I'm not working for him. If you are then you and I have a problem. And what does he mean by six days to Midnight?"

"Zelman loves mysteries. Midnight must be a clue to his plan. And instead of wanting you dead, he has selected you to solve it."

"Well, he selected wrong. I'm not solving anything."

"I see." His bland tone indicated doubt.

"But if Zelman didn't do the shooting, who did?"

"The person he works with must disagree with his strategy, preferring a more, shall we say, direct approach."

"Who is this person?"

"A powerful person."

"You didn't answer me."

"You are correct. I did not."

Brandt lapsed into silence, withdrawing himself from further questions. He began to study her paper, probably hunting for the common threads in their work.

Janet closed her phone and put it away. Brandt's dismissive statement left her with the sick feeling that her problems were just beginning. No one could make her do this. She didn't come here to solve a madman's riddle and she didn't have to stay.

Midnight or no Midnight.

As Janet watched Brandt sweep his long, elegant fingers down the page, the armrests of her seat began to shake. At first she thought it was turbulence or something wrong with the aircraft. Looking down in puzzlement she noticed it wasn't the seat, but her own hands trembling. The aftershock of trauma took hold of her.

She looked to Brandt to be sure he hadn't noticed, then stood and stepped to the lavatory, closing and locking the door. She put her hands on the rim of the sink and stared at the person in the mirror. A slender heart shaped face looked back with an expression of worry. She looked young, too young to be shot at, too young to be lying dead in some horrid morgue. The woman's eyes began to bunch together as tears ran down her face. She was sobbing and piling her two hands over her mouth to block the heaving sounds of her crying.

Only then did Janet connect with reality. She was the person in the mirror.

Her hands shook horribly, yet she managed to fumble the phone out of her pocket and press speed dial.

"Marcie?" Janet croaked through her tear tightened throat.

"Jan, how is everything going?"

"Not - so - good," Janet managed to get out before the choking sobs started again.

"Jan, what happened? Are you okay?"

"The guy - then shots, and I - the guard - I screamed," Janet babbled.

"Jan. Slow down. Get a grip. What happened?"

"He - he shot at me."

"What? Who shot at you?"

"I don't know," her voice trailed off as her sobs started again.

"Are you okay? Are you safe?"

"Uh-huh."

"Jan, where are you now?"

"In his jet." She wiped at her eyes.

"Whose jet?"

"Mahler, Brandt Mahler."

"Did he shoot at you?"

"No, no. He...uh...saved me. And now I'm in the bathroom of his jet."

"Who is this guy Mahler? His name sounds familiar."

"He's the guy whose papers I used in my thesis. He's taking me to Brussels."

"Why Brussels?"

"So I can go home. I want to go home," Janet slurred as the post adrenaline crash swept over her. "I'm so tired. I have to go home." She glanced in the mirror and the sight of puffy red eyes made her start to cry again.

"Jan, we'll get you home. So let me get this straight. You know this guy, he saved you, and he is giving you a ride to Brussels so you can come home?"

"Yeah."

"Do you feel safe with this old man economist?"

"Yeah, I feel safe with him."

"Good, so it sounds like you're okay for now. Mahler will take you to Brussels, then you'll fly home."

"Yeah, home. But - he's not old. And he's handsome."

"He's handsome? Mahler, Mahler. I know that name. Yeah, I remember now. I read about him in a magazine. Hold on."

The phone crackled loudly in her ear. Janet tilted her head away from it, making tears trickle sideways over her nose. She sniffed as she reached for a tissue to wipe her face.

"Here it is. Wow! He is handsome. Says he is the most eligible bachelor in Europe. I wouldn't mind being rescued by him."

It felt soothing to hear Marcie's jovial voice, trying to lighten Janet's spirits. Marcie spent way too much time fantasizing about famous men. If she only knew what he was really like.

"Yeah, he is kinda cute, when he's not being pompous."

"Cute? He is drop dead gorgeous!"

There was a knock on the door.

"Janet, we're landing. Time to fasten your seat belt."

"Marcie, I gotta go. We're landing."

"In Brussels?"

"No, at a rebel base. Love ya. Bye."

"What?" Janet heard as she closed her phone.

She splashed cold water on her face, patted it dry with a towel and stepped out.

"Are you okay?" Brandt asked.

"I'm fine. Great. No problem." She brushed past him and took her seat.

The Lear had only been airborne for half an hour when it banked and circled in an approach to a grass airstrip. As the jet tilted Janet got a glimpse of their destination, an extensive golf resort. The opulent country club sprawled over hundreds of acres. The flowing layout of the fairways and the clusters of guest buildings was swank and inviting. A second glance and a closer scan revealed derelict military vehicles littering an overgrown fairway. Several buildings had collapsed and others stood with sections missing. The entire area was in ruins. How recently had there been fighting here? In bizarre contrast, a lone tractor was frantically trying to hack down and clear brush off the nearest fairways.

"What *is* this place?"

"Michael's opposition party headquarters."

"You mean rebel camp."

"I wouldn't call it that, if I were you," Brandt said with narrowed eyes.

18

The jet leveled for descent. The pilot carefully eased the aircraft onto the soft earth. Despite his expert efforts, the plane jarred and bounced along the rough ground. Janet gripped the armrests of her seat until the jet finally came to a bone rattling halt.

Brandt unclipped his seatbelt, bounced up, and grabbed a plain cardboard box. He pushed down the jet's door, forming a short stairway to the ground, and charged out. A rusty open jeep pulled up to the base of the stairs, the remnants of its broken tailpipe belching blue smoke.

Janet followed Brandt, but balked at the sight of two rugged men sitting in the front seats, AK47 assault rifles slung over their shoulders. She shrank back into the Lear, stifling a choking cough.

"It's okay," Brandt assured from the bottom step, "Michael is waiting for us."

"I'll just stay here."

"That would not be wise. You'd best come with me." He reached to take her hand.

Janet took a gulp and stepped from the jet. The jeep's driver leered through broken teeth as Brandt helped Janet into the back while carefully balancing his package. The driver ground the spent vehicle into gear, and it lurched forward.

The area surrounding the resort was beautiful. Verdant rolling hills were dotted with patches of trees and heavy underbrush. A gentle breeze blew fragrant warm air from the countryside. However, the area they headed toward was far less comforting. Piles of cement rubble stood in untended disarray. Burned scars of underbrush cut across the craters and ruts that passed for a roadway.

Scattered around the complex were men lounging or walking about, each with a rifle at the ready to answer any threat. All eyes fixed on the new arrivals as the jeep careened toward an impressively ornate but decaying central lodge building. Battle holes peppered its red tile roof and the few carved shutters that remained hung at odd angles.

"What *was* this place?"

"It was once a gorgeous golf resort. It's been abandoned for years, ever since the original land owners fled the country."

The jeep seized to a halt in front of the lodge building. Brandt hopped from the vehicle, offering his hand to Janet, his package in the other. Janet sat in motionless fear.

"We should get inside," he urged.

Janet sat, frozen in position by TV images of war-torn Africa.

"Janet, this is not a time to dawdle or show fear. This is a very rough place. We need to move quickly, and everything will be all right." Brandt seized her hand, and hauled with un-gentlemanly assertion, forcing her out of her trance.

She looked around as Brandt drew her along by one hand. Formerly landscaped walkways and flower beds had been trampled to caked mud by thousands of careless boots. The wooden stairs leading to the massive front entrance groaned in protest as an ominous welcome. Inside the dark cavernous main room, beams of sunlight blazed trails in the steamy air. From high in the vaulted roof they streaked laser-like through holes of odd shapes and sizes, revealing damp festering piles of fallen ceiling plaster. Clusters of iridescent purple birds flitted about, chittering like school children on a field trip. The fetid odor of rotting wood and animal dung assailed Janet's nostrils as she reluctantly moved forward into the gloom.

She startled when a uniformed figure emerged from the shadows.

"Brandt!" came his warm voice. "It is so good to see you, my friend!"

The tall muscular man spoke with a crisp Cambridge accent. He was remarkably handsome, with a dark African complexion, high cheekbones and gleaming eyes that viewed the world from beneath a distinctive angular brow. The two men greeted each other with fraternal hugs.

"Michael, you are looking fit. It must be the easy life you are now living."

"Ah, yes. Luxury at every side," Michael joked gesturing to his squalid surroundings. He turned to Janet.

"And you must be Janet Thompson. Your dissertation on my homeland is brilliant."

"How did you get it?"

"There aren't many papers written about Zimbabwe. My people thank you for your insight. Too bad it could not have come in time to avoid devastation."

Janet's mouth hung open, no reply seemed forthcoming.

He turned back to Brandt. "Do I dare ask what is in the box? Could it be?"

Brandt handed the gift to his friend, who snapped his fingers at an aide. Michael gingerly opened the box, and lifted out one of the bottles of bronze liquid.

"Scotch! My friend, you are indeed welcome here anytime."

Michael pulled the corked stopper from the bottle, and poured the precious libation into each of three glasses on a tray the aide had produced. The men each took a glass. The aide pressed the third glass into Janet's hand.

"To Zimbabwe!" Michael saluted, and the three clinked glasses. The two men took cheerful swallows. Janet merely dipped her upper lip into the poisonous fluid and retreated, huffing away the powerful fumes.

"So, Janet - may I call you Janet?" asked Michael.

"Yes, of course."

"Janet, I hear you have had your first encounter with Anton Zelman." She cleared her throat. "Yes. My first and my last."

"Oh, I doubt that very much, Janet. Zelman does not work that way. Once you have been selected, he will be very reluctant to release you."

"I'm not his prisoner," stated Janet with as much conviction as she could muster, setting her whiskey back on the tray.

"He called her on the flight here," Brandt informed. "He said he didn't shoot at her."

"Then, it must be so. He never lies. But, who then did shoot?"

"I have my suspicions."

"Mmmmm. Your friend Mirza?"

Brandt gave a resigned nod. The two men locked worried eyes.

"This sounds very serious, very serious indeed," said Michael.

"Who's Mirza?" Janet asked.

"Don't you read the newspapers?" Brandt replied.

"Apparently not the same ones as you. Talk."

Neither man answered. Then Michael broke the silence.

"Mirza ul-Beg is a Pakistani-Kazakh woman who made a fortune as a nuclear arms trader. She is bent on a Jihad with America. The WMF suspects Zelman is working with her to start a new recession then push it into a full-fledged depression and destroy the American economy."

"Why?"

"She wants to create heaven on earth by destroying the evils of modern society."

"Why would Zelman be helping her?"

Michael shrugged.

"I think that is the point of his Midnight riddle," Brandt answered.

"Zelman didn't shoot at me. ul-Beg did. But they are working together. This doesn't make any sense."

"Think about it, Janet," Brandt lectured. "Do you think the world's greatest capitalist and the world's greatest anti-capitalist are going to see eye-to-eye? No. They are opposites temporarily joined by a common need. What that is, I don't know."

"Why don't you arrest them?"

"Not enough evidence. Besides, Kazakhstan is not exactly cooperative, and we don't know where Zelman is."

"You've lost the director of one of the largest banks in Europe?"

Brandt nodded. "Actually, his entire conglomerate is now the largest banking empire in the world. And, yes, we can't find him."

"Who is this we?"

"Besides the WMF, the European Union's President's Office."

"The EU president himself is gunning for Zelman?"

"Big time. He wants him bad."

"What about the Americans?"

"They think Zelman is great. He's pouring in billions to bail out failing banks. They think he is their savior. We think he is collecting ways to manipulate worldwide markets, what you call inflectives."

"How do you know all this?"

Michael waved his hand at the destruction around them.

"Your paper explained it all." He gave Janet a penetrating look. "You have exposed Mirza's plan, and she needs to..." He stopped mid-sentence and gave her a smile tainted with a twinge of pity. "Perhaps we should talk of more pleasant topics. The future of Zimbabwe perhaps?"

"I thought you would never ask," Brandt replied. "Let's go."

Puzzled, Janet followed the two men down a dim hallway to a small room containing a vast collection of golf club sets. The aged leather bags were splotched with the white lacework of mildew, the clubs tarnished to the limits of usefulness. Brandt and Michael each selected a bag and stalked away, leaving Janet standing alone in the musty room. Determined not to be discounted by two know-it-all egotists, she hefted a bag and followed after them. In the main hall, aides had taken the bags from the men, who were headed toward the front door. With distinct neglect, they left Janet to carry her own.

Scurrying with the heavy bag over her shoulder, she caught up with them just as Michael swung into the driver's seat of the ancient jeep. Brandt climbed in next to him. Neither of them took note of Janet, they were busy swapping quips and jokes. She dropped her bag and stood with uneasy patience, waiting for a gentlemanly hand.

Where were Brandt's elegant manners now? This was a picture that would never make it into one of Marcie's magazines.

Janet huffed out a stress busting sigh, pitched her bag into the back seat, then clambered in beside it. It took several tries before Michael was able to resuscitate the vehicle and rattle off toward the freshly cleared fairway.

As the jeep approached the first tee, the men's jovial mood shifted ever so slightly. They had serious business to discuss, and golf was the proper gentlemen's venue. They exchanged some world-wide news, avoiding comments on the local political situation. Apparently, women were not a part of the tradition, as Janet discovered when her back-seat contributions were studiously ignored.

Michael shut off the jeep and vaulted out, hefting his bag over his shoulder. Brandt followed suit, not even glancing Janet's way as she sat, arms folded, in the rear seat. She dragged herself up behind them as they were assessing the first hole. Michael was letting Brandt tee off first.

"How far?" Brandt asked.

"Two-hundred-twenty yards."

The previously gentle breeze turned stiff and hot, assaulting the three of them on the open fairway. The sun had climbed higher and threw its heat down at them in waves. Janet wished she'd remembered to pack a hat. She had sunscreen in her luggage, but that was only an abandoned memory.

Brandt pulled his five wood from his bag. With precise care he straddled the ball. He squared his broad shoulders and made an expert swing. Janet held a hand to her forehead to block the sun's glare. The ball sailed high into the air, heading directly toward the cup, then hooked and landed in an un-mowed section.

Michael also selected his five. His swing was sharper than Brandt's, but despite his extra power, he too hooked and landed badly. The two men started back to the Jeep.

"Hold on there. We're not done here yet," Janet insisted. She pulled the driver from her bag, and readied for her swing.

"Janet, a driver will hook worse than we did. Use your five," Brandt chided.

She ignored him, aligned her shoulders and hips, and swung. Her driver kept the ball low, out of the wind, and her expert swing had no hook at all.

Brandt watched in unbelieving silence as her ball sailed a perfect trajectory, bounced once and rolled onto the green.

"That is how we do it in Oklahoma," Janet said as she swaggered past the astonished men to the jeep.

As the trio worked their way down the course, the two men gingerly began the discussion of the WMF loan. Janet cupped her ear now and then to try to catch every word.

"The original landowners must be given back their rightful property," Brandt explained.

"Brandt, you know I could never do that. The land has already been reallocated to the soldiers who fought for independence. Politically, I could never take that from them. My government would collapse within days."

"Michael, you can't have a proper government if all the land is owned by former soldiers. That's no more legitimate than it was before the conflict."

"My friend, I hear what you are saying. We are a nation made up of many kinds of people. How can I possibly please them all?"

Despair colored the tone of Michael's words. He was in a tenuous position, not yet in charge of his vast territory and liable to be toppled from power if he made the slightest wrong move. Brandt was pushing him to find the right answers.

"Agreed. A strong economy is the long-term goal, but in the short term you may have to make some unpleasant choices."

"Ah, yes. Then as the famous saying goes 'The surgery was a success. Too bad the patient died'."

Back and forth the discussion went as they played their way down the course, trailing behind the relentless tractor, churning through the overgrown brush, clearing a barely playable swath for them.

Janet's occasional helpful comments sputtered and failed like dirty spark plugs. She could hear the aggravation growing in Brandt's voice. Despite his arrogance, she could tell he had a great passion for justice and deep convictions about how to promote economic success in these desperate circumstances.

This was so very different from her hypothetical discussions back in Tulsa. Chalk dust was the worst outcome there. Here the goal was to avoid more riots and warfare. People would die if Michael and Brandt couldn't succeed. She could imagine how hard it would be to control the broken-toothed jeep driver if a solution couldn't be found. The economic ruin of the resort spoke for the need to re-engage the former land owners. But to please everyone seemed impossible.

Down the course they played. Each hole they completed brought them one step closer to failure. The last hole was a difficult par five with a severe dogleg to the right. The mood degenerated to frustrated resignation. However, Janet spotted a clear path through the tangle of political turmoil. She placed her tee into the earth. Instead of aiming down the fairway, she angled her aim over the trees to bypass the dogleg.

"You can't allow non-farmers to squat on the land," said Brandt. "It will continue to stay useless that way. You've got to get it into the hands of productive people."

Janet swung.

"I can't just give it back to the previous owners, nor can I sell it off to the highest bidders, much as I could use the cash."

Her ball sailed high over the trees then dropped steeply.

"Why not do both," Janet interjected as she landed her ball in perfect alignment in the side branch.

"You can't have your land and eat it too," Brandt chided, as he took an extra shot to catch up with her.

"Give everyone land credits that can be used to buy land from a central pool." Janet chipped her ball onto the rough-hewn green where it quickly skidded to a halt. "That way everyone will feel as if he's had a fair chance to get land."

Brandt glanced at Michael, then turned to Janet with a puckered frown. Janet broke into a grin because Michael's brows raised with interest.

"Janet," Brandt condescended with school master repulsion, "if you give credits to two people for the same land, you haven't solved anything."

She had to let the two men take their shots ahead of her since they were further from the cup. Feeling far too comfortable offering such crucial advice, she stood leaning on her putter, gesturing in the air with her free hand.

"Make the credits redeemable for cash. Many would opt for the money, leaving enough land to go around."

"That would cost a fortune, more than the WMF could loan," Brandt rebutted as he sank his putt for on par.

The men stepped back to give her access to her ball. She tilted her head to one side, eying an impossible twenty foot putt.

"Make the credit's cash value a fraction of the value of the land, say ten cents on the dollar. Arrange the credits so the land buyer must contribute another ten cents on the dollar. Most people would take the money and only people who are serious about farming would actually get the land. It's self-funding and affordable. Everyone gets something, and the land becomes productive."

With a firm tap she smacked the ball forward. It rolled directly into the cup, for a two under par eagle.

The two men stood looking at her for a brief moment, then faced each other. Brandt's face was blank, but then one side of his mouth turned up as he considered her words. Michael grinned openly, showing a flash of white teeth. His large hand reached out to Brandt. As they shook hands Michael leaned back and let out a deep-chested laugh of victory. The wind seemed to catch his heavy note of relief, carrying away the remaining tension.

"By George, I think she's got it!" exclaimed Michael.

Sitting in the rear of the jeep as Janet drove them back to the jet, Michael and Brandt talked with rising excitement in their voices.

"Now I understand why Zelman selected you to solve his riddle," Michael spoke as he assisted Janet to step out of the driver's seat.

Brandt stood, too busy examining clumps of dried earth on his shoes to notice Michael's complement, or his manners.

"My people are indebted to you, Janet," Michael continued. "I hope you and Brandt can join me at my inauguration ball."

The image pleased her. She would look good on Brandt's arm, making a grand entrance into the ballroom, flash cameras popping. They'd dance together and give loads of photo ops to the fashion magazines. Then she saw Brandt's scowl.

"Thank you, Michael, but I'm going back to Tulsa as soon as possible. I'm sure Brandt will be able to come, and I'm certain he will be able to find a suitable escort to accompany him." Janet sent a glare in Brandt's direction just to emphasize the point.

Michael looked back and forth between his two guests, then nodded his head in resigned understanding.

"Good luck, Brandt. She's a handful."

"She'd be a lot less of a handful if she could learn to keep her theories properly locked up in her ivory tower," quipped Brandt.

Janet made a scowl as the two men exchanged fraternal hugs in the fading afternoon sun, while an aide snapped pictures. Then she stomped off to the Lear. She took a quick look back at him. For a brief moment she thought she caught a look of admiration in Brandt's eyes. He covered it with his signature smirk and followed that with a little wink, just for good measure. Janet resumed her haughty march to the jet. Minutes later they were airborne again.

"Brussels, then Tulsa," the sleep deprived Janet muttered, dropping her head against the seatback.

"You can put your seatback down," said Brandt. "You look exhausted."

The richly appointed cabin was foreign to Janet who had never traveled outside the American mid-west. She pushed the release on the arm rest and was surprised that the seat converted into a perfectly flat sleeping bed. She closed her eyes and tried to let her mind drift.

Just a few feet from her, in the fuel tank, an air pressure switch slowly expanded as they gained altitude. Set to international cruise altitude, it would detonate a charge that would use the aircraft's own fuel to trigger self-immolation. The short flight from Harare hadn't triggered it. The longer and higher flight to Brussels would. The jet slowly gained altitude as Janet drifted off into much needed sleep.

But she couldn't seem to settle down to sleep. Something wasn't right, and her mind wouldn't release its hold on her consciousness. She opened her eyes when she realized her cell phone was ringing. She reached into her pocket and retrieved it. Again, it was Zelman.

"Now what do you want?" she snapped.

Brandt leaned over to listen and Janet tipped the phone toward him.

"Ms. Thompson, testiness does not become you. I was merely calling to congratulate you on a spectacular round of golf. Your Thompson Accord was brilliant. I am confident I selected the right person to solve my riddle."

"I am not solving your riddle! Why does everyone keep saying that? And how do you know about the golf?"

"I have my methods, Ms. Thompson."

"Why on earth would you congratulate me for undoing your destruction?"

"I was getting bored without a challenge. Oh, by the way, there is an altitude bomb in your starboard fuel tank. Good day."

Brandt unclipped his seatbelt and scrambled to the cockpit. The engines abruptly slowed, and the aircraft began a gradual descent.

When Brandt returned, Janet was sitting up, wide-eyed with fear. "That's it. I'm grabbing the next flight out of Brussels. I've had it with that psychotic maniac!"

"Well, I am sorry, but Brussels might take awhile. We'll need to stop before then. We can't risk carrying a bomb for eight hours."

"Whatever. The next flight out of anywhere. I really don't care as long as it is far from Zelman - and you!" She pointed an accusing finger.

"Salty, I am hurt," Brandt mocked, pushing out his lower lip. "I have always viewed myself as an excellent traveling companion. Besides, I can't let you do that. Too many flight connections on the way back to Tulsa, too dangerous. And face it, even Tulsa won't be safe. You'll be traveling with me until I'm certain you'll be safe."

"Great! First I'm hoodwinked to Zimbabwe, shot at, dragged off to a rebel base, bomb threatened, and now I've been kidnapped. Absolutely wonderful!"

"The day is still young."

"Where are we stopping?"

"Kenya. Go to sleep. You'll feel better."

"No!"

"Go to sleep, Salty."

Janet's gaze drifted toward the ceiling. Her father used those same words when she couldn't sleep as a kid.

"My name is Janet, not Salty." She harrumphed back onto her flattened seat with a stony scowl. A minute later she was asleep, her face soft and angelic.

He watched her sleep for several minutes, then gently covered her with a blanket.

\*\*\*

Janet's eyes popped open and she sat bolt upright. How long had she been asleep? She rubbed her eyes trying to push consciousness into her hazy mind.

White gauzy curtains were gathered at the posted corners of her huge bed. Above her head, mock canvas walls sloped tent-like at multiple angles. The room, decorated as an opulent safari tent, was illuminated by bright sunshine pouring through a wall of plate glass with a panoramic view of a vast open plain.

A vague memory of her short but exhausted walk from the jet to her bed surfaced in her mind. Then the memory of the bullets and the broken toothed man followed. Her throat tightened.

No. That was yesterday. This is today. Today she was going home to Tulsa.

She scanned the room. Earth toned tiles formed the floor, covered here and there by brilliantly patterned scatter rugs. Janet set her feet on the cool tile. Through a carved wooden doorway she could see a marble bathroom. The room was meticulously decorated with tastefully understated care. Such a spectacularly beautiful room, especially compared with her dorm-like apartment at the university. She had no idea there was richness like this in Kenya.

She scrounged the room but couldn't locate her suitcases. Then she remembered her scramble out of Harare. All she had were her passport, wallet, and phone. Nothing else from Oklahoma remained.

Turning with a sigh, she noticed a radiant white sundress, strappy sandals and wide brimmed straw sunhat laid out on the end rail of her brass-framed bed. New clothes. How long had it been since Marcie dragged her on a shopping spree into the city?

The clothes were lovely, exactly her size, and given the low neckline, obviously hand-picked by Brandt. Still dressed in her plain clothes from Oklahoma, she stood and held the dress against herself, admiring the way it flowed as she spun around. Bright, vibrant, alive. She couldn't wait to try it on.

She padded to the luxuriant bath and started the shower. As she waited for the water to warm she thought of Brandt. He knew there would be bullets, yet he was willing to rescue the girl from Tulsa.

As she undressed she felt as if she were shedding an outworn skin from the past so that something exciting and new could emerge. If she let it. Warm grassy air blew past the pale cotton drapes that blocked the view of her new world. She pulled them back.

Inches from her window was a giraffe's face so close she could count its individual chin hairs. The towering creature, with its dark round eyes, stuck its enormous head through her window.

She screamed, long and loud.

Brandt burst through her door. She screamed again, grabbing at a skimpy hand-towel to cover herself. The giraffe looked to Brandt who chuckled at the situation.

"Betty, you don't belong in here." He stepped to the window to ease the animal back out.

"Neither do you!" The stinging impact of a shampoo bottle hit him in the back of the neck.

"Autsch!"

"Get out of here!"

He grabbed his neck with one hand while continuing to push the bovine as it nibbled at the front of his shirt.

"Just let me get this window sh–"

He barely ducked her second missile. It smacked against the frame of the window, startling the giraffe, which pulled back its head. Slamming the window shut, Brandt lunged toward the door, but slid on spilled shampoo and fell flat. Struggling in the sudsy pool, he raised himself up to a scrambling crawl, then slipped prone again. A bar of soap ricocheted off his back as he franticly slithered out of the room and slammed the door.

"Don't ever do that again!" she screamed.

"Believe me, next time I won't try to rescue your attacker," he assured through the closed door. "By the way, Betty is harmless. She's the resort's pet giraffe. She's been here since she was injured as a calf when poachers killed her mother."

"Oh," she replied, her voice meeker. "Where are we?"

"I told you, Kenya."

"Obviously. I mean this place."

"Okonkula Safari Lodge. Do you like it so far?"

"Yeah, nice. But it lacks privacy."

"Sorry."

"I'll bet you are." Janet stepped to the window and closed the drapes, letting her blood cool by blowing out a long breath. "You okay?" she asked.

"Yeah."

"I can tell."

"How?"

"You're smirking."

"How can you know that? You can't see me."

"Because you enjoyed that too much."

"Yeah, I did." She imagined him ducking reflexively as another bar of soap thudded against the closed door. "Breakfast is ready whenever you are." She heard his sudsy slogging as he moved away, muttering, "Boy, she's something."

Goosebumps raced over her skin as she thought of the handsome knight who had come to rescue her. And of his admiring gaze when he glimpsed her nakedness.

***

Janet emerged onto the dinning patio in her new clothes, feeling like a new woman. Before her lay a grand expanse of grassland, covered by a big blue sky. A warm gentle breeze fluttered the fringed edging of an umbrella that covered one solitary table. Beneath it sat Brandt alone, guarded from the brilliant sun. Janet's dress swayed around her long legs and the breeze lifted her silky waves of red hair making it bounce and shimmer in the African sun. Brandt looked up and hiked in a sharp breath.

She walked up to the table. He rose, took her hand by the fingertips, and without a word, led her to her seat.

Her last meal had been a bag of airline pretzels twenty two hours earlier. But she wasn't hungry. She wanted to drink in the radiance splashing around her, and enjoy Brandt's attention. For at least one day she could pretend she was worthy of male admiration. Never before had a man given her looks of that caliber.

Hiding a delicious shiver, she glanced over at their jet a short distance away on the simple runway that serviced this very exclusive resort. It must still have the bomb in its fuel tank. Were they within its kill radius? She let the thought pass.

Several zebra grazed near one of the wings, their tails swishing back and forth as they casually moved together. Beyond the zebra, cloud crowned Mount Kilimanjaro dominated the view of the plain.

Brandt poured her orange juice from a glass pitcher. A waiter with a linen towel draped over one arm, poured steaming black coffee into an elegant porcelain cup. She buttered a croissant and savored a small bite.

Words weren't used.

Brandt didn't take his eyes off her. She tried not to let it fluster her, but her heart refused to cooperate. She knew much about the intellectual side of Brandt from his many papers, but nothing about him as a person. Who were his parents? Who were his friends? Who were his girlfriends? It didn't matter as long as his focus was on her. At least for today.

"No boyfriend?"

"What?"

"You heard me."

"Whatever."

"When did you two break up?"

"What are you talking about?"

"You must have a boyfriend. Or had."

"What is this, twenty questions?"

"Thirty if need be." He flashed his signature smirk.

"Ough." She put her croissant down in exasperation. "You are impossible." She looked away, then back.

"So, no boyfriend."

She didn't answer, just yanked her fruit bowl toward her and stuffed a strawberry into her mouth. He continued his stare.

"Oh!" She pushed her bowl away and crossed her arms.

"Why do you keep looking at me?" he asked.

"What?"

"You keep looking at me. Like you can't believe your eyes."

"Look. I've studied your writings for years. I never thought to look behind the name on the paper to find out who you were. Then poof you come dancing into my airplane, dripping good looks, and rescue me from a madman. I think I've earned a little staring, all right? You happy now?"

"Thank you," Brandt said. "I was beginning to worry you hadn't noticed how handsome I am."

The dissonant squawk of a two-way radio came into the patio. Janet stared as a hulk of a man ambled up to them in a slow waddling shuffle. He was dressed in greasy gray coveralls, unzipped to his navel, showing his blubberous pink torso. Flaming red hair exploded from his head. A matching five day stubble spread across his face.

"Brandt, my man!" he said in affectionate California surfer twang.

Brandt stood, and they clasped one hand, delivering identical pats on the back with the other.

"Jimbo, good to see you, man."

"Dude, I heard you got a problem with your bird."

"Yeah, an issue in the starboard fuel tank."

"Hey no problem, bro." Jimbo turned to Janet with a broad grin. "Say, who's the chick?" The man awkwardly bowed to take Janet's hand. "Hellooo. I'm Jimbo Wilson, aircraft mechanic. And whooo are yooou?" he intoned in his most romantic voice. He bent to kiss her hand.

"Ah, Jimbo. She's with me," Brandt said, rescuing Janet from his amorous advance.

"Oh, yeah. Gotcha, man." He winked and clicked his tongue at Brandt. "Nice catch."

"Thanks."

"Well, let me take a look at your bird." He dropped a walkie-talkie on the table, then ambled off to examine the jet. Janet watched as a brand new Mercedes panel van drove out onto the runway. With zero sense of urgency or alarm, Jimbo pulled out some equipment and started working under the right wing.

"Who is that guy?"

"James Bradley Osgood Wilson, III, best aircraft mechanic in this part of Africa. Black sheep of a very blue blooded Connecticut family. Thrown out of the American Air Force. He does great work, especially if you need discretion. He has a long clientele list."

"Yo, bro," the walkie-talkie squawked. "I got the video on it. You want it out quick, or you want it out safe?"

"How long for safe?"

"Two days."

"Quick works for me."

"Gotcha, man." Jimbo walked back to the van, gathered up some more equipment then returned to the jet.

From her distance, Janet watched in detached fascination as the improbable man twisted and turned under the wing, manipulating some mysterious device in hopes of snagging the bomb.

"Got it," Jimbo said a few minutes later. "Hey, and I didn't destroy your bird." He held up an object in one hand for them to see.

"What is it?"

"I.E.D. A terrorist bomb."

"Al Qaeda?" Brandt asked.

"I don't think so. Too sophisticated. Not their style. This is professionally engineered. Probably in Europe."

Janet watched as Jimbo casually turned the bomb over several times. Even from this distance Janet could almost see his eyes gleam in fascination at the exquisite prize in his hand.

"Yep. Definitely European. You have some very serious people mad at you, bro."

"Not me. The girl."

Jimbo looked up from his jewel, focusing his gaze on Janet.

"Gotcha." Walkie-talkie in one hand, the bomb in the other, he ran his greasy sleeve across his bristled chin in puzzlement. The scratch of whiskers across rough cloth rang clearly through the radio. "And she looks so innocent. You want it as a souvenir?"

"No. Get rid of it."

Jimbo strolled off into the savannah, bent down into the high grass for a moment, then slowly ambled back and climbed into his van. A moment later there was a sharp explosion. Janet jumped and screeched. The zebra startled and ran. The waiter stood unflinching.

The van pulled up to the patio, and Jimbo sauntered out. He lit a cigarette with his jet fuel saturated hands and winked at Janet. She picked up her coffee and tried to ignore him.

"How much do I owe you?" Brandt asked.

"Brandt, my man, you're my friend."

"How about a hundred grand?"

"Euro?"

"Yeah, euro."

"That'll do."

Brandt wrote out a check.

"Nice meeting you," Jimbo said to Janet. "Good luck with your friends." Turning to Brandt, he said, "Say hi to your Dad for me."

"Will do."

Jimbo glanced back at Janet. "And she looks so innocent." He shook his head in bewilderment, picked up his walkie-talkie, walked to his van, and drove away.

"Brandt. A hundred thousand euro for twenty minutes of work? That works out to half a million dollars an hour. Does the World Monetary Fund have that kind of money?"

"Of course not. That was from a special fund."

"What kind of a *special* fund?"

"From Zelman."

"You have access to Zelman's money?" Janet set down her coffee cup with a hard clack onto the saucer. "Whose side are you on?"

# CHAPTER THREE

"Salty, it's not like that."

"What is it like?" she asked pointing a finger toward his chest. "A hundred thousand euro of Zelman's money with the flick of a pen. Traipsing around Africa in Zelman's luxury jet. All while you think his buddies are shooting at me. Explain this in a way my *simple* American brain can understand. And don't call me Salty. I'm Janet."

Brandt ran his fingers through his hair, searching for words. His glittering grey-blue eyes flitted from the canopy to the table.

"Zelman has always been a generous donor to the WMF. Especially for special projects. As a banker he needs the stability the WMF provides. As for me, officially, I am supposed to be chained to my desk, writing research reports. Unofficially, I talk to people. Convince them to do this or not do that. Hence the jet. Sometimes things get, well - messy. Like the bomb. That is where people like Jimbo are needed. Zelman prefers discretion in these matters, and would insist on proper compensation. The WMF also prefers discretion, as long as official funds aren't used."

"So you *do* work for him."

"No," he insisted.

"So you think." She gave him an acid look of reproach. "And what about the bomb? Professionally engineered in Europe. Let me see..." She mocked, scratching her chin in feigned thought. "Who do we know who lives in Europe? Could it be your beneficent patron - Zelman?"

"No. He wouldn't plant the bomb, then tell us about it."

"Then who? That ul-Beg woman?"

"Yes, Mirza. Nice lady."

35

"You know her?"

"I've been to her compound a number of times. Very clever and innovative woman. PhD in nuclear physics. You'd like her."

"Like her? She's trying to kill me!"

"Don't take it so personally."

Janet crossed her arms and looked away with a huff. Then she turned back and leaned forward, both palms on the table.

"Well, somebody has to stop the two of them."

"Somebody is."

"Who?"

"You."

"Oh, no," she said, wagging her finger. "I've already told you. And your buddy Zelman. No riddles. You can pass the message along to Mirza as well, next time she stops by for a little chat with another one of her gifts."

"Janet, it doesn't work that way."

"Don't tell me how it does or does not work. I said no."

Brandt paused as if thinking through his strategy. "I suppose you think you could sit back in your academic cloister in Tulsa, analyze your way to an answer, and stop them by writing a paper? This is the real world."

"Yeah, your world, not mine."

"You academics are all the same. It takes real world experience to stop people like Zelman and ul-Beg, not theoretical mathematics."

"You know something, Brandt, I think you're right. And Zelman is so unbelievably stupid to pick me to solve his riddle and not you."

"So you'll go back to Tulsa where you think you'll be safe."

"Yeah, safe. As in anywhere but here."

"I see," Brandt said, signaling his disbelief. "By the way, the EU president wants to meet you."

"Me? Why?"

"Because he believes you hold the keys to Zelman's arrest."

"Why would he think that?"

"Because I told him so."

"You told the EU president I would help him arrest Zelman?"

Janet couldn't believe the gall of this arrogant man. She stared at him in fist-tightening fury, unable to even think of one word to speak in rebuttal.

"We'll leave this afternoon and meet him in Brussels." He stood. "Meanwhile, let's have some fun. Go get changed."

Brandt walked away, cutting off her protests. She was trapped. Trapped with an infuriating man who ordered her around like he owned her. He was delaying her on purpose. She would be perfectly safe in Tulsa.

Fun. Right. She was so angry she didn't even care to ask what he had in mind. Alone at the table she sulked and ate every crumb on her sparse plate. Was there no such thing as a decent breakfast anymore?

When she returned to her room there were a pair of khaki shorts, sneakers with white socks, a New York Yankees tee shirt, and a bicycle helmet laid out on her bed. The savannah was not a place she imagined bicycling. Perhaps they'd ride around the compound. That didn't sound like much fun, but maybe she could exercise off her anger.

She slipped off her sundress and put on the shorts and tee shirt. Sitting on the bed she pulled on the socks and sneakers. A pony tail would keep her hair in order.

He had to believe in her theory if he was willing to take her to the EU president. Huh. Funny how getting shot at added credibility to her theory. Not that she thought it was worth the risk. She checked herself in the mirror. Her theory was the reason he'd come to rescue her. That is what he wanted. She grabbed the helmet and opened her door.

Brandt was waiting in the hall. His pupils widened as soon as he caught sight of her in her casual sport clothes. The thrill of his ever-so-subtle reaction zinged through her. He stood motionless for a moment, just looking at her. She managed to stop the most eligible bachelor in Europe dead in his tracks. It made her feel – beautiful. She felt her cheeks tinge red as she stood agape at his stare. She made a few mock modeling poses along with some not-so-polite faces, anything to cover her embarrassment. And to prolong his admiration.

"You look great," he finally said, letting his wry smile overtake his lips.

"I'm glad you think so. Where are we going? Around the compound?"

"Uh, no," he said recovering from her stunning impression and meeting her eyes. "Up on Kilimanjaro."

Janet's brows contorted together. "What?"

Without answering, he led her outside to a helicopter that was idling in the savannah. Two metallic blue mountain bikes were strapped to its landing skids. Brandt opened the copter's door, and the astonished Janet clambered in. The engine revved to a deafening level as they lifted off the quivering grass. Janet covered her ears as they swung off toward the mountain.

A vast plain of grass lay below them, punctuated randomly with small herds of animals. Grazing in unperturbed ease, they seemed accustomed to the beating sound of the machine that flew high over their heads. Janet wanted to ask Brandt exactly what they were doing but the whining tumult of the engine prevented conversation. If she could speak, she would demand answers. Logical, sensible answers. Answers that a controlling, possessive man would be loath to give. Because if he did, he wouldn't be able to control.

Fifteen minutes later they were alone on a high ridge, watching the helicopter descend into the distance. The upwelling of air from the plain below was noticeably cooler and moister than it had been at the compound. The rocky soil held small windblown scrub that provided an unblocked view of the open vista. A few tall plants with bushy brown trunks and several vertical branches, each with a tuft of pulpy green leaves were the only plants of any size.

"Seneco," Brandt explained as Janet stared at the odd plants. "At night it drops below freezing here so the tuft of green contains a special antifreeze. Some of these plants are hundreds of years old."

"Plant-based antifreeze, amazing."

Despite the chilly air, the equatorial sun was blazingly hot on her exposed arms and legs, and she was glad she had remembered to apply sunscreen. The only problem was the brim of her helmet. It wasn't wide enough to shield her eyes from the sun. She turned it over in her hands, then set it on her head anyway. Brandt handed her a pair of sunglasses. Clothes, helmet, sunglasses. He planned everything. And all the right size. How did he do it? She nodded in grateful acceptance and put the sunglasses on.

"And where are we...?"

"Just above the base of the mountain. We've crossed over the border into Tanzania. Kibo," he said, turning and pointing southeast toward the cloud shrouded volcano, "the main peak, is about ten miles from here. Let's go." He snapped his helmet in place and his signature smug smile broke across his face. He anticipated giving her a hard time on the trail. Adjusting his sunglasses and pushing off, he headed along a steep gravel path.

"Brandt, wait up, I've never mountain biked before," she called.

Down the jarring trail they descended. There is nothing like this in Tulsa, she thought as she struggled to keep from sprawling onto the ground at each turn or drop. Despite the cool air, she broke into a sweat as she strained to keep up. Within minutes the air grew warmer and the vegetation more dense and tropical. Low leafy trees provided mottled protection from the stinging sunlight. Brandt maintained his lead on her, but never let the distance get too great. As she adapted her skills to this new experience, she studied him, eyeing his moves and learning his technique.

When Brandt slowed at a sharp turn, Janet seized the chance and swung to the inside. With one foot down for balance, she made a sliding turn, spraying gravel over her startled host.

"Yee-haw!" she yelled in Oklahoma cowgirl pride as she passed him.

Caught off guard, he faltered for a moment, then recovered. "Oh no you don't," he replied, answering her challenge. Brandt had nearly caught up when she stopped to admire a breath-taking view ahead.

"I thought you said you hadn't mountain biked before," he said between gulps of air.

"Mountain biking, no. Moto-cross, yes. It's very popular in Oklahoma. I made a lot of guys angry when I passed them."

"I'll bet you did," he said with admiration. "But tell me, was it Janet who passed them, or Salty?"

She tilted her head. Brandt had made a keen observation about her. Ever since her father died, she'd reverted to being Janet. Salty was the moto-cross cowgirl, not Janet. Janet was the plain-Jane with no boyfriend and an analytical mind. Salty was the adventuress, the one who could causally sip orange juice within the blast radius of a bomb.

Janet was her mother, Salty her father. But there was a third person within her that was uniquely her. That person added something new. She was a romantic, a flirt, a seductress. That was Solterra. Janet intended to keep a close eye on her. Especially with someone as handsome as Brandt so near.

"What is it you Americans say? Last one down is a rotten egg."

He pounded off down the trail.

"Alrighty. Bring it on!"

They twisted and turned down the rugged course, each taking the lead, only to lose it again moments later. Janet was invigorated by the downhill rush. She found a second wind and didn't even feel short of breath.

This was so very different from anything she had experienced before. She liked being able to throw Brandt's challenge back at him. Judging from Brandt's face, he liked it too. Wasn't that a refreshing new experience?

Brandt suddenly pulled up short. Ahead was a small plateau. A dining canopy had been set up, with a table complete with linen table cloth and fine china. The trees were taller at this altitude, and one branched over the canopy. A few waitstaff stood ready to serve a mid-trail refresher. Past the tent was a glorious view of the Amboseli plain. They set aside their bikes.

"Would you care to join me for lunch?" He extended his crooked arm, and she looped her arm through his.

"Don't tell me. Zelman is paying for this too?"

"No," he said in a husky tone, "This is from me."

The blue of his eyes glowed like the sky overhead. Janet thought for a moment he was going to kiss her, and that she would have let him. Instead, his expression seemed to be one of longing. Of seeking. Whatever it was, he drank her in thoroughly before he led her under the dining canopy.

The lunch was quite the statement. But what was it he was trying to state exactly?

Pop. Liquid foamed from a bottle of champagne. A champagne flute was placed in her hand. She held it American style, with her hand around the cup.

"To Kenya," she toasted.

"To Salty," he returned.

They clinked glasses with a dull thud.

"Like this." He moved her hand down the stem to hold it European style. Electricity sparked along her arm.

She adjusted her grip and the slender glasses chimed together with a bright ringing sound. Effervescence tickled her nose as she sipped her drink. She swept her gaze across the limitless horizon.

"Africa is an amazing place," Brandt mused. "I've been coming here since I was a kid, but I never cease to be amazed."

"Yes. This is so - incredible." She leaned closer to him until her head hovered against his shoulder. Then, just as quickly, she pulled back and straightened.

Brandt chuckled as if he knew Janet had just pulled in Solterra's reins.

He guided her to the table and offered her a seat. The air at this elevation was heavy and warm. The canopy and the foliage provided a grateful break from the blistering equatorial sun directly overhead. A waiter placed lemon slices into a tumbler, then poured water while another placed a bowl of soup in front of her.

A perplexing array of utensils adorned her table setting, with a total of four spoons. Which to use for the soup? She quickly eliminated the small spoon with a fork at the top of the plate, as well as the smaller spoon on her right. She glanced to Brandt. He picked up his round soup spoon, of course, and placed its far edge into the soup, spooning away from himself before bringing it to his mouth. She followed, but nearly gagged on the unexpectedly cold liquid.

"Do you not enjoy gazpacho?" he asked.

"The only time I eat cold soup is from a tin can."

"Tin can?"

"Yeah, you know, can opener, tin can, spoon. It's cheap and fast. Easy cleanup, too. I keep one in my purse in case I have time to eat before teaching class."

"Really."

"You ever eat soup cold, right out of the can?"

"No. I can't say that I ever have."

Clearly, Brandt was accustomed to a different lifestyle than she. A refined world where one did not eat soup from a can. Where one knew how to hold a champagne flute to make it ring and which spoon to use for each purpose. Janet tried harder to mimic his spooning technique.

"Brandt, how did you become interested in economics?"

"I come from a long lineage of bankers. I've been engaged in economics since I was born."

"Where did you go to college? Did you get scholarships or loans?"

"My grandfather donated the economics building to the University of Zurich."

"Oh. I guess you didn't need loans. Boy, do we come from different worlds."

"Perhaps. They might be more similar than you might realize."

"Like how?"

"Who taught you moto-cross?"

"My Dad."

"Sounds like he taught you a lot of things."

"Yeah, he did."

"And you bunked school and traveled with him a lot, on emergencies?"

"Yes."

"My father taught me many things too. He took me out of school to travel with him during emergencies. Sounds similar to me."

"But you are so refined compared to my backward country ways," she said in a half-mocking tone. Just as she was about to place the overfull spoon into her mouth a splash of tomato dropped onto her shirt.

"And you, Janet, how did you become interested in economics."

"I had Professor Jones as a lecturer as a sophomore. Everyone thought he was so dry and mathematical. I found him to be so pertinent. I mean, this stuff was real. It affected everyone. We would talk after class and he became my mentor. A year later, when my dad died, Professor Jones helped me get scholarships that allowed me to stay in school. We were struggling, my sister and I. I almost dropped out so I could earn more money."

"How old is your sister?"

"Marcie is twenty two, a senior at the university. She's even a sorority sister and everything," Janet spoke in maternal pride. Memories flashed in her mind's eye. "When Marcie was born we had a big family. Even my great-grandmother lived with us. But by the time I was a freshman in college it was just the three of us, Dad, Marcie and me. I was so sick of funerals." With a smooth scoop she finished the soup. "I became the Mom. Then Dad got sick and he went so fast. I needed a surrogate father. Professor Jones fit the bill, and economics became my life."

The waiter removed the soup and placed a full dinner plate in front of her.

"This isn't wildebeest or something, is it?" she asked.

"It's Beef Wellington."

"Is that some fancy French dish?"

"No." He chuckled. "The French would never eat anything named after the man who defeated Napoleon."

"Right. I knew that, of course."

"But it is similar to the French filet de boeuf en croûte."

"Oh, right." She nodded sheepishly at the foreign words.

"The beef is coated in pâté then baked in a pastry shell."

"And what is pâté?"

"Puréed fatted goose livers."

Janet couldn't prevent the disgust that curled her lips.

"Don't ask questions if you don't want to know the answers."

Janet shook her head in a slight no. "You know, Brandt, we were having a nice conversation, and then you go and say something that is downright annoying. You'd be far better company if you weren't so condescending and difficult."

"Am I as difficult as Zelman?"

"I'm beginning to think you are both the same."

He chuckled brightly at her. Picking up his champagne glass, he took a sip and raised his brows at her in a provocative expression. He was clearly enjoying their little series of parries. She smiled, feeling a flush of pink cross her cheeks.

She could learn to enjoy Brandt's attention. Maybe the new Janet should cut Solterra a little slack. A bold seductress would be just the thing to handle haughty Brandt and his subtle games.

When they finished their meal they returned to their bikes.

"How much farther?" she asked.

"We're at about three thousand feet above the plain. Maybe a little over half hour or so."

"I wonder what Zelman's next move will be? I half expect him to show up any minute."

"I don't think he could track us up here."

"I just have a feeling..." She scanned the trail ahead, already planning how to beat Brandt. Sitting on the dirt just to the side of the trail was a black cowboy hat with a turquoise concho brooch in the center. She picked it up. It was just her size.

"Zelman," she said.

"How do you know?"

"It's identical to his. Even the concho is the same."

"How did he find us up here?" Brandt glanced around.

She paused, half afraid and half intrigued. Then she shrugged.

"Who cares!" She pulled off her bike helmet, and put on Zelman's gift. "Yee-haw!" she whooped as she scrambled down the trail with Brandt in hot pursuit.

***

"You have just enough time to clean up," Brandt said as they stepped from the helicopter back at the compound and swatted clods of dried mud from their legs. "Wheels up in an hour."

As Janet stepped into her room she noticed the white half sleeve seersucker blouse with a breezy floral pull-on skirt.

"Oh, my."

These clothes were much better than anything she had lost in Harare. She dismissed the twinge of discomfort she felt over a stranger buying her expensive clothes. She glanced at her cell phone and decided Dr. Jones would be awake by now.

"Janet, how is my star pupil enjoying Zimbabwe?"

Janet explained what had happened since they last spoke.

"My," was all he managed to say. The quintessential academic could easily interpret the abstract economic aspects of Janet's story. But the hard reality of the shooting and the bomb was beyond his comprehension, so he simply ignored it.

"What do you know about Brandt Mahler," she asked.

"He's asked for my help a number of times. He is very well connected with numerous world leaders. Sort of a world-wide ombudsman. He has a way of getting difficult tasks done. His research papers present very interesting concepts. But, they lack mathematical rigor."

There was a crash on Dr. Jones' end of the line, and Janet knew it was pointless to ask what had happened. She hoped it wasn't his ink well again. She waited until Dr. Jones' phone fumbling finally ended.

"What about Anton Zelman?" she asked.

"Colorful man. He's the director of SBU, but he probably controls assets beyond that. He's been bailing out a number of failed American banks, and is very popular in Washington."

"Sounds like he could be a wolf in lamb's clothing."

"That could be. He has been embroiled in a number of banking scandals, but he always manages to come out unscathed. Some people say he is terrible. Others claim he is wonderful."

"What is your opinion?"

"About what?"

"If Anton Zelman is good or bad?"

"I don't know. I've never thought about him like that."

"Thanks. It'll probably take a day or two for me to get back. I'll see you then."

"Sure thing, Janet. By the way, University Housing is very angry with you."

"Why?"

"Because of the way you left your apartment. I didn't realize you were such a terrible housekeeper. It was quite a mess."

"But, I didn't leave a mess. It was neat as a pin, as always."

"I went and saw it myself. You should be ashamed of yourself. The place looked like you'd had a frat party in there. Please be more considerate in the future."

"Uh, I will," Janet said, her brow tightening.

"Good. And I didn't think you were taking your desktop computer."

"I didn't. It wouldn't make sense for me to take a desktop computer."

"Well, it wasn't on the desk in your apartment. Did you lend it out for a friend to use?"

"No. It should be there where I left it."

"Well, don't worry. It will turn up. Anyway, we'll discuss this when you return. Stay away from fruit. You might get air sickness on the way back."

Air sickness? What about shot or blown up?

"Will do, Dr. Jones. I'll be careful. Bye."

Was it Zelman or ul-Beg? Someone had broken into her apartment and stolen her computer. They were going to be very disappointed. Whatever they were looking for didn't exist. She didn't care about the computer, it was old. And all of her research was backed up on the university server anyway.

She bit her lip, picturing what her ravaged apartment must look like. She'd seen the aftermath of a few frat parties when she was an undergrad. Smashed furniture and dishes, food everywhere. A queasy bubble of anger popped in her gut. Her photo album dating back five generations, Dad's scrapbook from the Vietnam war, a few cherished pieces of her grandmother's set of good china, collected piece by piece from laundry soap boxes. They were all she had left of her family. And her precious antique books, once neatly cataloged, must now be scattered about. She gritted her teeth, hoping they were okay. More than ever she wanted to get back to Tulsa.

She picked up the hat Zelman gave her, and grimaced at recalling what he looked like on the billboard: handsome, authoritative, and trustworthy. About as trustworthy as a rattlesnake. And now he was following her everywhere, first her apartment, then Zimbabwe, and now even up the slopes of Kilimanjaro. Who knew how dangerous he could be? She shouldn't keep the hat.

She fingered the turquoise concho stitched to the front. It was surprisingly well attached. She flipped the jet black hat over and looked inside. The label read: Midnight by the Tulsa Hat Company. Strange name for a hat, even if it was midnight black. Another frustrating clue that led nowhere. On the inside of the hat, behind the concho, was a tiny flaw in the felt. She picked at it and uncovered a small hole. She unraveled a bit more.

There, carved into the back of the turquoise stone was a miniature radio transmitter.

# CHAPTER FOUR

Janet looked around for a tool and found a pair of nail clippers on the night stand. She knelt on the bed, opened out the handle and went to gouge out the evil device. But she didn't. Instead, she smiled, put the hat down, and folded the clippers. Keep your friends close, she thought, and your enemies closer. Janet Thompson could learn to fight back. She didn't need Brandt to rescue her.

When she stepped from her bathroom, a chambermaid was packing her few new belongings neatly into elegant luggage. She noted the luggage had ample room for Brandt to make later additions.

Her phone rang and she looked at the caller ID.

"Anton, thanks for the hat," she said in a flip tone.

"I'm glad you like it, Ms. Thompson."

"I especially like the concho. It makes me feel so - connected - with you."

"Yes it does," he chuckled. "I understand why you are Dr. Jones' star pupil," he said duplicating Jones' exact words. She remembered that the phone had been delivered by currier from SBU moments before she left for the airport. "What does Brandt think of the hat?"

"Hmmmm...He seems to like just about anything I wear."

"I can imagine."

"I don't like what you are doing. I'm not going to solve your puzzle, no matter what you do. You can't manipulate me."

"I see," he said.

"Do all you Swiss say 'I see' when you'd rather not answer?"

"I'm not Swiss, and no, not all of us. Good day."

Janet wondered if all of Zelman's conversations were so brief. Perhaps he lived his life one minute at a time, and that particular minute was up.

She dressed and found Brandt enjoying the breezy afternoon under the canopy on the dining patio, reading Le Monde. She should tell him about the bug in the hat. But not just yet. He put down his newspaper and gave her an admiring once-over.

"Do you approve?"

"Oh, yes. Very much."

"And what about Zelman's hat?"

"Well, I don't think it goes too well with the outfit I chose for you, but you do wear it well."

The sun had inched past its mid-day peak, baking the surrounding plain with shimmering waves of heat.

"It's time to go." He stood, and offered his arm. She hesitated, torn between her irritation of him, yet attracted by his gentlemanly manner. His signature wry smile and a gentle nod of his head coaxed her into accepting his arm. They strolled to the aircraft, walked up the steps, and left Kenya behind.

"Please excuse me, but I need to do some work," said Brandt moving to the front of the aircraft.

Janet pulled out her passport and idly flitted through the empty pages. Amazing, she thought. She'd been to three countries and didn't have one stamp to show for it. She put her passport away and pulled out her phone.

"Janet! I got your message. Are you still alive?" Marcie asked, breathless.

"Yep. They haven't gotten me yet," Janet joked.

"And how is Don Juan?"

"Irritating. He is constantly needling and pushing my buttons."

"I imagined him as the suave romantic type."

"Oh, he is that too. Sometimes he's so handsome, courteous and attentive I could just fall for him. Most of the time I want to choke him though, because he doesn't appreciate my intelligence."

"Explain that."

"When we talk about economics, we clash. He tells me I'm too analytical, that I live in an ivory tower, and that I'll never have the experiences he's had in the real world. I think it is a cover up because he is intimidated by my academic ability."

"But you said he was a world renowned economist. Why would he be intimidated by you?"

"Because I was able to pull out the central mathematical theory behind his papers, and he didn't. My inflective theory is stealing his glory."

"And what are the other buttons he's pushing?"

"He is so seat of the pants. He doesn't stop to think things through. He ignores half the details and just makes decisions before he has all the information he needs."

"Left brain, right brain," Marcie commented.

"Huh?"

"You are detail oriented, abstract, analytical. He is a generalist, looking at the big picture, working through people to accomplish his goals."

"Working through people or manipulating people?"

"Is he hurtful?"

"I don't think he means to be. Not really."

"Then what you call manipulating, other people would call working with people."

"Marcie, where on Earth did you get all of this stuff?"

"Jan, I'm a psych major, remember."

So much like Mom.

"But he didn't see the pattern of inflectives in his own research papers. How could he be a big picture thinker if he couldn't make that leap of logic?"

"Maybe he has. He intuitively uses your theory without making an overt academic recognition of it."

"I don't understand how you can say that."

"I didn't think you would. You should've taken more gen-ed classes. When will you be coming home?"

"We'll be flying to Brussels tonight, and I hope to fly back to Tulsa tomorrow."

"Good. I'll see you then."

"Love ya, Marcie."

"But, Andy," she heard Brandt say into his phone, "you need to compromise with Nikolai." He bent forward, angling the phone as if he were lecturing a defiant child. "No! You can't stop the Russian army from..." He pulled the phone away from his ear and with open jawed frustration stared at the suddenly silent device.

"What's wrong?" Janet asked.

"Oh, my friend Andy, an oil minister in Azerbaijan, is playing hard ball with Nikolai the Russian Foreign Minister. And now Nikolai is pushing back, threatening war. The recession is agitating everyone."

"I saw on the news that the Russians are in Georgia again. That's right next to Azerbaijan."

"Yes. An invasion would be very easy for Nikolai, and politically advantageous."

"Can't you talk logic to them both?"

"Wouldn't that be nice. I guess if I could, I would soon put myself out of a job."

Brandt closed his phone and tucked it away. "By the way, we're going to make a quick stop in Dubai then meet the president in Brussels."

"Dubai? Why Dubai? That's not what I would call on the way."

"True, but it's only out of the way by a few hours. We will just make a quick stop for a meeting with someone who may be able to help. It'll be fine."

"No, it will not be fine. Not with me. I'm not playing, have I mentioned that? I've had enough bullets and bombs. I'll get a ticket to Tulsa in Dubai."

"Janet, you're not going to get a decent connection to Tulsa from Dubai."

"I'll wait in the terminal until I can work out the connections."

"Obviously you're not a world traveler. Fly with me to Brussels and you'll be far better off, not to mention safer."

Janet huffed, folded her arms and stared out the window at the sea of clouds. It wasn't as if she had much choice.

A few hours later the afternoon sun bore down on an arid landscape below. Off the left side of the aircraft the Persian Gulf came into view. As the Lear began the arc of its final approach into Dubai, they passed over a cluster of islands. Janet's jaw dropped when she recognized the pattern they made as a map of the world, each continent its own cluster of islets. The channels between them were filled with luxury boats of every size and style. As they passed over the city itself, Janet looked down the length of Sheikh Zayed Road, the glitzy sky-scrapered highway that ran through the heart of Dubai City's financial district. A place she'd only read about.

"I don't understand why we have to come all the way to the oil-rich Persian Gulf for advice."

"Janet, first of all Dubai is not an oil rich country. Only a very small percentage of their economy is now based on oil. Finance and tourism are far larger."

"So, fine. They are not oil rich. Just rich."

"They are a very clever people, and invested their short lived oil money well. A man named Sheik Mohammed bin Rashid Al-Falasi is a major reason for their success. Secondly, Rashid is the man who first proposed Zelman's plot to me. His analysis is based in reality unlike your theoretical inflectives."

"Inflectives are not theoretical," insisted Janet. "They are real."

"You misunderstand. I believe there are what you call inflectives in the economy," Brant continued. "There are definitely small events that have very large impact. I disagree that they are best described with mathematics."

"Okay," she said with a waiver of doubt. "Explain that one."

"For example, in 1973 Johnny Carson told a joke about America running out of toilet paper."

Janet looked at him like he had three heads.

"Within hours there was a run on toilet paper. Super market shelves were emptied, America's toilet paper supply was devastated. Hundreds of tons of toilet paper was stolen from public restrooms. Millions of Americans went un-wiped."

Janet let out nasal guffaw. "Small event. Big impact. Inflective..."

"Yes, but listen. Efforts to ration backfired, only serving to validate people's worst fears. Carson publicly apologized. People interpreted it as just the opposite, as a ruse to cover over a real problem. Even the great Johnny Carson couldn't stop the panic. It had taken on a primordial life of its own. A black market in toilet paper flourished. Only the privileged could wipe themselves."

Janet covered her mouth to hold back the belly laugh.

"Delivery trucks were hijacked," he continued. "Riots broke out. People all over the country were injured and hospitalized."

Janet's eyes grew serious at his words. This wasn't so funny.

"It took three weeks for the fire to burn itself out. Finally, the unfounded shortage was over. But people had horded so much that the nation now faced a massive glut. Paper mills shut down, thousands of innocent people lost their jobs, families lost their homes."

Brandt held her gaze with his. "There never was a shortage. None. Just a simple twenty second joke that mathematics could not have predicted. In normal times, the joke would have been just that, a joke. A few chuckles, and a minute later it would be forgotten. But this was during the second Arab oil embargo. Fear had gripped the American people. They were willing to believe the worst. The joke became a short lived inflective, a point of inflection that changed the direction of the economy. Carson just happened to stumble on to it. Had it occurred at any other time, nothing would have happened. But at just the right moment, a very small thing had a huge impact."

Brandt paused to let his words soak in.

"Fear and panic, not arithmetic, caused this. Now explain the need for your advanced mathematics."

Janet was silent.

"Carson never intended for anything bad to happen. Now, imagine what would have happened if Carson was Zelman and he wanted a catastrophe."

Brandt's gaze bore into Janet's. She blinked.

The sound of the Lear's tires screeching contact with the runway brought her back to reality. They rolled into a private hangar. The sheik's limo was waiting for them. Still wearing her cowgirl hat, Janet rode through the ultra-modern city feeling like a cowpoke on his first trip to town after a long winter of isolation.

"Quite an impressive city, don't you think?" Brandt asked.

"Ostentatious is what I was thinking."

When they stopped in front of the sheik's office building, a doorman walked to their car and opened Brandt's door.

"Good afternoon, Dr. Mahler," the doorman said as he held the door open, first for Brandt, then also while Janet sidled out after him.

Janet strained her neck looking up at the immense structure.

The doorman cleared his throat. "This is the Burj Dubai," he explained. "The world's tallest building. It is a half mile tall with 160 floors."

"It's," she paused, "extravagant."

"Thank you. It is a modern stylized version of traditional Islamic architecture. The floor plan is based on the hymenocallis flower."

Janet rolled her eyes back up at the edifice as they walked. He led them through the lobby to a large mirror and chrome elevator, then left them alone for their ride up the towering building to the sheik's office.

"Nice digs," Janet mused as the elevator gracefully hurled them skyward.

"Yes. At four thousand dollars a square foot, it should be."

"Who can afford that?"

"Zelman is the second largest shareholder."

"Wow."

"Mirza is the largest."

The elevator chimed and the doors opened.

"Brandt, my young friend, welcome."

"Rashid, it is good to see you!"

The two men exchanged traditional cheek kisses. Janet raised a brow because she'd expected the sheik to be wearing a turban. Instead, she saw a man in his late fifties wearing light slacks with a cotton shirt and loafers. Even with his casual attire, his slow graceful motions bespoke years of authority and power.

"And you must be Janet Thompson," Rashid said, extending his hand for a European handshake. "I am very impressed by your dissertation."

"Thank you. How did you get it?"

"Economics is a very small world. Please, both of you come in, come in."

They passed through a foyer of secretaries and stepped into a massive inner office overlooking the city, the sparkling blue gulf in the near background. The office was richly decorated in blond oak paneling. Priceless antiques were on display in glassed cases. A sweeping Arabian scimitar with a handle of gold and faded green tassels hung prominently. Below it was its matching scabbard. Next to the pair was a pitted and worn bronze star navigation astrolabe, probably used to guide the caravans across the deserts.

Numerous hand inked maps lined the walls, each protected behind sealed glass. Janet couldn't read the Arabic inscriptions, but assumed they must be hundreds of years old.

Rashid gestured to two leather armchairs opposite his large desk. Brandt sank into one with comfortable ease. Janet tried to copy him, but the enormous chair in the cavernous office made her feel like a schoolchild called in to see the principal. She edged forward and braced herself against one of the armrests.

"How is your father holding up under all the economic pressure, Brandt?" Rashid asked.

"He is very busy lately. And yours? Is he enjoying his new retirement?"

"It is kind of you to ask. He is struggling, wanting to rejoin the fray. He would enjoy all the financial battles the recession has brought. He is thoroughly enjoying those few I allow him to play with. Part of that enjoyment is keeping track of your career. You have been very active lately." The kindly man smiled at Brandt with fatherly admiration. "I wish I could offer you both a drink, but as a minister, I am bound by Sharia Law and alcohol is forbidden in my office."

"I brought this," Brandt said, revealing a pocket flask of his signature twenty year old Scotch Whiskey.

"Oh, my favorite," the sheik enthused. "And is it still alcohol free?"

"Absolutely."

"Then it is not a sin for me to drink it, since even if it did have alcohol I would not be aware of it, and it would not be a sin."

A secretary instantly produced glasses, ice and water, apparently in anticipation of Brandt's gift. The three raised their glasses to each other. The sheik pulled in a whistle of air after his first painful shot. Janet palmed her glass, and returned it full to the tray. Rashid eyed his glass in admiration, and smiled.

"Now, how may I help you, my friend?"

"Rashid, do you think you could explain your observation that Zelman is working with Mirza ul-Beg to destroy the American economy? Please keep it simple. Ms. Thompson has very little pragmatic experience."

Janet glared at her nemesis.

"You must forgive my friend," Rashid apologized. "Brandt is very much like me. We both have much experience, and unlike a learned academic such as yourself, we prefer to work directly with people to solve problems. My analysis of Zelman is based on experienced suspicion rather than computed statistics and high-level mathematics."

Unable to determine if the man had praised or insulted, Janet tried to soften her scowl and listen.

"Ms. Thompson, are you familiar PBEC, Persian Basic Enterprises Company?"

"No. I have never heard of them," she was forced to admit.

"They are on the New York Stock Exchange, a multi-national corporation headquartered in Grand Rapids, Michigan. However, their actual operating center is in Riyadh, Saudi Arabia. PBEC is a holding company that owns controlling interest in hundreds of exclusively American companies."

"It's not unusual for companies to have a legal office in the US, and an operational headquarters elsewhere."

"Yes, Ms. Thompson. That is very true. But PBEC has some unusual reasons for doing this. Their mission statement is to unify small Arab and American investors to promote peace and harmony between the two cultures. Millions of people in the Islamic world are being attracted to invest in America, especially now, due to the weak American dollar."

Janet relaxed a bit and shifted back in her seat, crossing one leg over the other. "I understand, but why does this draw your suspicion?"

"There are two problems that PBEC solves. First, Muslims are forbidden by Sharia Law to engage in usury, charging interest for loans. PBEC has very carefully structured its portfolio so it receives no usury interest. Second, PBEC cuts through the fog of American business culture, providing safe and comforting investments for Muslims."

Janet shrugged. Business was business. "That does not seem worthy of any suspicion."

"PBEC also provides an excellent investment opportunity for Americans. Their rapid growth has made them the darling of Wall Street. They are buying American companies on a daily basis."

"Sounds like a win-win situation. I see nothing at all wrong with what they are doing."

"Yes, one would think. Please, Ms. Thompson, come to my computer and look at their financial statements."

She stepped around his desk and sat in his seat, a privilege, she suspected, not granted to many women. She surveyed the graphical display of information, then clicked the mouse a few times to review the underlying data.

"These financial statements all look normal."

"Do they, Ms. Thompson? Look at how much debt they have."

"Hmm...I don't see the overall debt anywhere."

"Exactly. Their general level of debt is well hidden. Each of the companies within PBEC has borrowed money using another PBEC company's assets as collateral. It is a circular debt structure. In other words their debt is supported by other debt. Just like your notorious Enron company. They are actually drowning in debt."

"That is a very poor way to run a company. If any one company were to encounter a financial problem, the whole house of cards could come falling down. Obviously, they have very poor management."

"Or very good management. Perhaps it was intentionally engineered to collapse."

"That makes no sense at all." Janet pushed away from the computer to follow Rashid's movement to the window.

"Ah, but it does. You see, Ms. Thompson, Mirza ul-Beg is very sophisticated. I believe she wishes to destroy the American economy by turning the American dollar against itself. She has money, an estimated two hundred fifty billion dollars of personal assets. That gives her control over trillions. But this is only a tiny fraction of what is needed to trigger an economic collapse. She needs to leverage what she has."

"How do you know Mirza is involved with PBEC?"

"It is public record that Mirza ul-Beg is on their Board of Directors."
So open, yet so concealed. Hidden in plain sight.

"I believe," Rashid continued, "she is the mastermind behind PBEC. Her financial empire is very extensive. Large enough to keep her ultimate plan well hidden."

"Yes," Janet agreed, "Brandt was telling me of her investments in this building."

"Mirza is very wealthy, now the wealthiest women in the world. I believe she provided PBEC with seed money and then promoted Arab investment. She has probably done this with a dozen other companies. Her goal is to destroy each company as part of a well orchestrated collapse. Such a well timed collapse of so many large companies will cause a panic. What is the word? Snowball. It is known in your country, yes?" He turned from the window and gestured with his hands, one tumbling over the other. "As the snowball rolls down the hill, it gets bigger and bigger."

"But, even that is not enough to disrupt the entire American economy," insisted Janet, slowly wagging her head.

"I agree, Ms. Thompson. That is where Anton Zelman comes in. He has essentially done the same thing by cross linking European and American banks. The actual monetary loss is one thing. The effect of panic is another. A tightly coordinated collapse of their mutual companies would cause a huge panic. It would greatly amplify the losses."

"But Zelman would be destroying his own wealth. What would be his motivation to do that?"

"I predict he will move his assets out just before the collapse. After banks across the world collapse, Zelman would emerge as the last man standing, dominating the new banking system that would rise from the rubble. He would be wealthy beyond imagination."

Janet was quiet for a few moments, trying to mentally convert Rashid's general observations into analyzable numbers. At last she shook her head again.

"The collapse of Zelman's banking empire, along with PBEC, is still not enough to bring down the entire US economy. It would take something much bigger than that."

"Or something much smaller."

"Smaller?"

"It could be, as we Arabs say, a straw that breaks the camel's back. Indeed, it could well be something very tiny, and by itself insignificant. But delivered at the right moment, it would be devastating."

Janet's thoughts raced. An inflective? "What could possibly be so small, yet so crucial as to cause economic disaster?" she asked, shifting her hat back off her forehead.

"Ah, this is still unknown to me. It is the missing miniature piece to the puzzle."

Janet frowned. The minister's suspicions seemed plausible, but not very well-founded in facts.

"Rashid, when do you think this collapse might happen?" asked Brandt.

"I've been monitoring PBEC closely. It has been traded very heavily in the last week. I predict something will happen within the next few days," Rashid calmly answered.

"When I spoke with Zelman yesterday," Janet said, "he told me I had six days until Midnight. Only I don't know what he meant by Midnight."

"Midnight could be the missing puzzle piece. What it is exactly, I don't know. But apparently, Zelman does. In five days we will find out. Unless you can find out what Midnight is before then, and stop it."

"The American government is already taking desperate steps to climb out of this recession. I'm sure that will help," offered Janet.

"Yes. But governments don't produce wealth. They tax wealth, and borrow wealth, and print paper. Only the private sector can truly end the recession. And Mirza and Zelman now dominate the private sector." Janet couldn't believe that was true. No one was that powerful. She shook her head.

"You see, Ms. Thompson, there are still seventy trillion dollars in toxic Derivatives and Credit Default Swaps that have not washed out of the world economy. That is equal to the Gross Domestic Product of the entire world. Until these toxic assets are removed, the world economy will be very vulnerable. All it will take is a very small match tossed into this very large pool of gasoline. If this Midnight piece is thrown into the present situation, it could have long term effects that will be far worse than the Great Depression."

The Sheik's words conjured the voice of Great-grandma Thompson telling her stories of the Dust Bowl. She'd come through the Great Depression with barely the clothes on her back. Great-grandpa Thompson had been forced to abandon their farm after the crops failed. For nearly three years they wandered, moving from one Hooverville to another, begging, or worse Janet suspected, before Grandpa could find work.

"Did you see much of Harare?" Rashid asked. "Is it as devastated as the news reports suggest?"

"We flew over," Brandt explained. "Smoke everywhere. The fighting had to have been brutal."

"That was just the dress rehearsal for the play Mirza wants to present across America. That is her vision for your Tulsa. And a hundred other American cities."

An icy silence descended over the room, broken only by the rhythmic tick of an antique American grandfather clock. Janet watched its pendulum slowly swing back and forth, counting down the seconds to disaster. Yes, she decided, it could happen to America again. And this time it would be worse.

The sheik quaffed his drink in two invigorating gulps, then cleared his throat. "Well, thank you Brandt for another delightful non-alcoholic beverage."

"May I leave you the bottle?"

"Thank you, no. The last time you did, it spontaneously fermented, and one of my wives found it. A very difficult phenomenon to explain."

"I understand. Thank you very much for your help, Rashid."

"Brandt, you are very welcome. And Ms. Thompson, I wish you sincere success in finding the solution to stop Zelman. I pray that you will continue to survive any assassination attempts. Stay close to Brandt, he will keep you safe."

"Thank you. I guess," said Janet, frowning at the oddly-silent Brandt.

Rashid walked them out through the foyer to the elevator. As they waited for the elevator to arrive, Janet's cell phone rang.

"Dr. Jones, how are you?"

"This is Dr. Jones. I thought I would call during my coffee break to see how you like it in Zimbabwe."

"I'm actually in Dubai just now, with Sheik Mohammed bin Rashid Al-Falasi discussing Zelman's plans to destroy America's economy."

"Oh, how very nice."

The elevator's broad doors opened, and Brandt guided Janet inside.

"It was very good to meet you," Janet said to the sheik, receiving a gracious nod in response. Brandt pressed the lobby button.

The elevator doors began to close, and she heard a crackle on her phone.

"Are you still there, Dr. Jones?"

"Yes, I'm still-"

The signal faded as the wide metal doors closed, blocking reception. Annoyed, Janet hit the door-open button and Dr. Jones' voice returned.

"-there, Janet?"

"Yes," she said, hopping off the elevator to avoid losing the connection.

A distant crackling pop, like a short burst of Chinese firecrackers, went off in the elevator shaft above them. Poised on the elevator's threshold, Brandt hesitated. With a whoosh, the elevator disappeared, leaving a gaping dark hole behind the wide open doors. There was an inrush of air as the falling elevator sucked in everything behind it.

Brandt teetered on the edge, flailing his arms against the inductive down draft. He was being drawn backwards into the gaping maw.

# CHAPTER FIVE

Janet grabbed for him, fisting his shirt. With a sharp yank she pulled him to her. They stumbled a step away from the elevator doors. In one smooth motion Brandt steadied them by clutching Janet into a dance-like turn.

A moment later the elevator's massive counter weight careened past the open cavity. A whipping sound followed as its severed cables tore at the air in their downward acceleration. With sudden force, a ragged cable end lashed out at them, snapped at Janet's feet and disappeared down the hole.

"Ahhh!" she yelled, looking down, half expecting her toes to be gone.

Instead a wedge had been gouged out of the marble at her feet, and the arrowhead shaped missing piece stung in her shin. A moment later a loud double crash reverberated up and down the empty elevator shaft. Echoes continued for many seconds as the three of them stood in stunned silence.

"Janet? There's noise on the line. Are you still there? I think I lost you..."

"Dr. Jones, I have to go. I call you back later."

She closed her phone as Brandt knelt to examine her leg.

"You're lucky," he said, cleanly pulling the fragment out, leaving only a small trickle of blood. "If you hadn't pulled me back, you'd have to do this all by yourself." He pulled a band-aid from his wallet and applied it to her shin.

Rashid stood motionless, his jaw agape at the near miss he just witnessed, and, Janet suspected, at the cavalier attitude of his guests. But she was too stunned to feel anything except an odd giddiness.

"I'm very sorry about your elevator," she said.

"Yes, I think we should try the stairs," said Brandt.

Rashid reached into Brandt's inside coat pocket and pulled out the flask. He took a hard pull, and placed it back with a gentle pat.

"We'll see ourselves out, Rashid." Brandt pointed inquisitively toward what appeared to be an Arabic emergency exit sign. Rashid nodded, and the two ambled away along the hall then down the long series of stairs.

"The only reason you brought me to Dubai was to get Rashid to lure me to stay to work on the Zelman riddle," Janet puffed as they worked their way down the exhausting stairway.

"That's not the only reason."

"For coming to Dubai?"

"No, to get you to stay." He grinned for a moment then glanced at his watch. "We'll fly to Brussels overnight. Meanwhile we have a few hours to kill. Let's relax on one of Dubai's world famous beaches, then grab some dinner."

"No. I want to go. Give me one good reason why we can't go now," she continued.

"Because you are hungry and your legs will be very tired by the time we reach the bottom."

"I'm not hungry."

"That's not true, is it?"

Janet's voice grumbled in protest. Then her stomach followed, giving away her secret.

"Brandt, I don't have a swim suit for the beach."

"Not a problem."

They emerged at ground level into a small covered courtyard. The limo stood waiting. Brandt held the door for her as she slid in.

Janet glowered out the window as the limo wound its way through the streets, then across a small causeway. It dropped them off at a five star hotel on a small island in the gulf. Except for Rashid's office building, it was the tallest building she had ever seen. Its gently curved structure swept skyward forming the shape of a massive spinnaker sail.

"The Burj Al Arab," Brandt explained. "It is said to be the world's only seven star hotel." He led her inside and they walked up to the concierge desk.

"Janet Thompson," Brandt announced to the man.

"Yes, Ms. Thompson. This is for you. You may change over there."
The man handed Janet a small box that contained a two piece swim suit.

"How did they know I was coming?"

"I called."

"Before I even agreed to this?"

"Yes."

"Don't you think that was a bit presumptuous of you?"

"Not at all. I was right, wasn't I?"

"You're infuriating."

"Some - mainly the inexperienced - may call it that. Others refer to it as being prepared."

Janet narrowed her eyes at him. It did nothing but cause his blue-grey eyes to blaze, daring her to challenge him further. Brandt took a box of his own, and left to change.

As she walked to the changing room she passed a magazine rack. On the front cover of Les Potins, a French gossip magazine, was a picture of Brandt with some unknown blond bombshell on his arm. She couldn't read the caption, but could clearly read the enjoyment on both of their faces. A pang of unexpected jealousy gripped her. She flipped the magazine open. Inside was a picture of the glamorous couple in a bright red Maserati, tooling around a corner, smiling for all the world to see.

The most eligible bachelor in Europe. Marcie's words echoed in her mind.

Eligible, yes. Trustworthy, no.

By tomorrow Brandt Mahler would just be a memory. A mysterious and intriguing memory, but a memory just the same. Humph! Why not enjoy the memory while it lasted?

Inside the changing room she was not surprised that the bathing suit fit her perfectly. The tiny yellow suit with black piping trim and black string ties flattered her flat stomach and long legs. It also clearly outlined curves she normally kept concealed. She slipped on the thin, flat sandals, and topped her head with Zelman's hat.

When she emerged, Brandt had also changed. Now it was her turn to take in a breath. His broad muscular chest, tinted with tight black curls, rippling abs, and taut, sinewy legs made even her latent libido kick start.

They strolled out to the palm tree studded beach dotted with small cliques of people. All were obviously glitterati from around the world. She recognized one man, a star from a movie she had seen, but couldn't place his name. He waved a warm greeting to Brandt who nodded recognition back. The sun was to the left, low near the water which was a lovely turquoise blue.

The light breeze made few waves. Instead the water sloshed all about as if it were a giant bathtub. The white, hard-packed sand was hot. Even through the sandals, Janet's feet heated as she and Brandt made their way out to a cabana. The air was thick and humid and the sun strong. Janet was glad when a host offered them iced juice, which was thankfully alcohol free.

"Isn't this relaxing after a hard day escaping assassins?" Brandt quipped.

"Yeah, great," she said, trying to sound casual. "So tell me about Mirza. Did she come from money or acquire it?"

"Ah...both. She came from a wealthy Pakistani family. As I told you before, Mirza is very intelligent. Like you, she is great at mathematics. Hiding her secret hatred of the West, she took a PhD in nuclear physics in the '70s from the Catholic University of Leuven in Belgium. She became a lead scientist in Pakistan's nuclear weapons program. After a falling out with conservatives who didn't share her bent for nuclear Jihad against America she found a welcome in Iraq as head of their nuclear program."

"So what?" Janet asked. "Iraq's weapons of mass destruction program never went anywhere. It was a flop."

"That is what the public was told. Mirza succeeded in building the ultra high speed uranium tetraflouride centrifuges needed for the long process of making weapons grade uranium. But in 2003 the Americans invaded Iraq. She needed a new sponsor and her precious centrifuges needed a safer location. A few days later there was a deposit made to a numbered Swiss bank account. The amount was 1.2 Billon US dollars. The account number was 19720521, the date Mirza received her PhD.

"The next day she loaded her centrifuges on an airplane headed to North Korea. But the Americans received a secret tip off, and the aircraft was shot down and crashed into the Persian Gulf." He gestured toward the water. "Just a couple of hundred miles north east of here. Desperate to prove Saddam had Weapons of Mass Destruction, the American Navy expended a huge effort and recovered thousands of pieces and reassembled the aircraft. The centrifuges were not on board. They had never been loaded."

"Where did they go?" Janet asked.

"Well, two weeks later there was another deposit to Mirza's bank account. This time it was for 2.3 billion, coming from the Islamic Republic of Iran."

"She sold them twice?"

"Yes, and Mirza was the source of the false tip off to the Americans. They fell for it and conveniently provided a cover story for her."

"How do you know this?" Janet asked.

"Anton told me."

"Do you have these conversations with Anton and Mirza often?"

"Not often. It not like the North Koreans would let them walk the streets of Paris with the paparazzi snapping pictures."

Janet shook her head in dismay. This was too tangled a web for her to be caught up in, but she was curious.

"So Mirza went to work for the Iranians?"

"No. She changed her tactics," Brandt continued. "She realized that an economic Jihad was much more powerful than a nuclear one. Mirza wanted to use America's own dollar as the ultimate Weapon of Mass Destruction."

"So that's how she hooked up with Zelman."

"In more ways than one. The story is that she fell in love with him, but he didn't return her affections."

"Why not?"

"I don't know."

"You know, Brandt, you seem like a nice guy, but you seem to be awfully friendly with some very shady people."

"It's not that I'm friendly with a lot of evil people, it's just that I'm friendly with a lot people. Some more evil than others."

"Who told you about Mirza being in love with Anton?"

"Rashid."

"How long have you known Rashid?"

"I was just a small boy when I first met him on a business trip with my Dad."

"I can't imagine your life. Jetting around the world meeting sheiks and presidents ever since you were a child. I feel out of my depth everywhere we've been."

"Well, Janet, you seem to be making an impressive life for yourself as a brilliant and creative economist."

"Did you actually forget yourself and give me a compliment?"

He smirked. "Your problem is that you are smart, but overly analytical. You won't be able to solve any real world problems until you get to the level of experience that I have."

She turned away, weary of his taunts, yet wanting to throw his words back at him.

"But your experience is with people. Especially female people, right?"
She sensed that Brandt was calculating a response without success.

"Let's go for a boat ride," he said.

They walked to the water's edge to a small sailboat that was pulled
up onto the shore. The flat little twelve foot boat with its bright red sail
looked cute and inviting. Brandt pushed it into the water, and Janet sat on
its flat surface while Brandt pulled up the small sail. Soon they were
underway. Janet enjoyed the relieving breeze as they headed out into the
bay.

"Do you like this boat?" he asked.

"Yeah, I guess so."

"How about that one?" Brandt pointed to a massive multi-deck
yacht, complete with helicopter pad.

"Uh Brandt, you're getting kind of close to it."

"Yes, I am."

One of the yacht's crewmen stood on a small platform at water level,
looking at them. As they approached, he spoke.

"Herr Dr. Mahler. Welcome. Your dinner is ready."

He grabbed their small boat and held it steady while taking the hand
of the astonished Janet to help her step off. She followed Brandt as they
walked up the short gangway to the main deck. A staff of five people
waited for them to take their places at the outdoor table. The young
couple sat in their swim suits as the low Persian sun slowly sank toward
the water, leaving a welcome coolness. The yacht began a slow cruse.

"Ms. Thompson," a waiter asked, "may I serve you a Caesar salad?"

"Uh, yeah. Yes, sure."

The waiter began the tedious process of hand grinding anchovies.
Janet sat mesmerized by the warm ruddy sunlight sparkling off the water.

"Tell me this isn't better than spending the night in the Dubai airport
waiting area," said Brandt.

She glanced at his face and flicked an errant strand of tousled hair
over her shoulder. He'd done this for her. Lunch on Kilimanjaro, dinner on
a yacht on the Persian Gulf. All this for her.

"Brandt," she said after the waiter finished preparing their salads and
stepped back, "you continue to astonish me."

"Good. That was my intention."

They ate in silence for several minutes, enjoying the glistening colors
playing across the waters of the gulf.

"Brandt, what about the other women in your life? No girlfriend?"

He put down his fork and looked her directly in the eyes.

64

"Salty, uh Janet. It feels good for me to be pursuing a woman for a change, instead of the other way around."

"Oh?" she questioned, picking up her salad fork with precision. "Who are you pursuing? What's her name?" She pursed her lips and sat in wide eyed innocence waiting for his answer for a moment before the two of them burst into laughter.

When they finished the waiter approached. "May I recommend fish for dinner?" he asked.

"Perhaps not for a girl from Oklahoma," suggested Brandt.

"We have fish in Oklahoma," protested Janet. "Bass is my favorite, with trout a close second."

"Very well," the waiter replied. "I would recommend the sea bass along with a truffle risotto."

"What is a truffle risotto?"

Brandt gave a snort.

"Risotto," the waiter explained, "is short grain high starch Arborio rice that becomes creamy when cooked. We prepare it in broth with cheese. Our chef prefers to use Carnaroli, a special Arborio hybrid rice from northern Italy. It is slightly firmer than Arborio. He tops it with a very strong tasting mushroom known as truffle. The mild risotto contrasts well with the pungent truffle. It would seem an unlikely pairing, but it tastes like perfection."

"It sounds good. I'll try it."

"What do you have for a Riesling?" Brandt asked the waiter.

"We have an Riesling Engelgarten from Alsace by Deiss Marcel. It has a heavy apple nose, but is otherwise very light, easy drinking. Perfect for a warm evening."

"Yes. That would be perfect."

The waiter withdrew to obtain their wine.

"I don't appreciate that snort, Brandt. I may be a working class girl who never had your opportunities. That doesn't mean I deserve scorn. Unlike you, everything I have I've earned, the hard way."

"Scorn? Scorn comes when I don't snort. Janet, tell me, who is the vintner of the wine we are having?"

"Deiss Marcel."

"And from what type of rice is risotto made?"

"A special Arborio hybrid, Carnaroli."

"And which is the correct direction to spoon soup?"

"Away."

"Explain why you are studying me and everything I do, desperately trying to learn about my world."

"I am not studying you," said Janet. "I just happen to have a good memory for detail. In this case, simply trivial, and for me pretty useless, information." She made a dismissive wave of her hand for emphasis.

"I don't think that explains it."

"Look, I don't understand your world, Brandt, or why you would choose to live in it, because you obviously have all the choice imaginable to do whatever you please. Expensive rare wine, yachts, fast cars. It just doesn't make sense to me."

Brandt chuckled. "Let me guess your next thought, fast women."

The waiter poured a wine sample. Brandt swirled, sniffed, tasted, and nodded acceptance.

"We taste the wine first to assure the cork is still good."

"What has the cork got to do with anything?"

Brandt opened his mouth to reply, but Janet cut him off, angry with his airs.

"Brandt, how do you do it?"

"Do what?"

"Keep up your pretenses. Do you enjoy it that everyone bows and scrapes to you? Do you actually enjoy it that the public is watching your every move? You have no privacy, no life you can call your own."

Plates of steaming sea bass were placed in front of them.

His eyes sparkled at her attack. He breathed in a voluminous whiff of the fragrant dinner.

"Ah, sea bass. Don't you just love it?"

She placed her fists on her hips and grunted exasperation.

He laughed.

"To answer your first question — I have been bowed and scraped all my life." He smirked at his twist of her words. "It's normal for a man in my position. The answer to your second question is the same. I was raised for this job since birth. I have always been in the public eye. I was groomed and tutored, given a level of experience few can match. My mother calls it raising the public."

"Don't you resent that? Even sometimes?"

"Of course not. I am Swiss. I deplore everything but resent nothing."

Janet couldn't help but laugh at his self-deprecation. The waiter lit a candle to displace the descending evening. Janet tasted the bass and the risotto. She did love it. It was delicious and she wanted to eat it all. Brandt ate several bites in rapid succession, savoring the unique flavors. He put down his fork and looked at her.

"My job, and my choice, is to teach the public how to be civilized in the twenty first century. To me this means doing good while enjoying life. It is the same as my role in the WMF. To provide cool civilized judgments in a very harsh world. It has been the destiny of the men in my family for generations. Have you ever heard the French term 'noblesse oblige', the obligation of those of high birth? That is the noble tradition that I can never break."

"Should I now call you Prince Brandt?"

"Oh please do! It has a rather pleasant ring, don't you think?"

She rolled her eyes. "I could never do what you do."

"I agree."

She crossed her arms and glared at him. But she couldn't maintain her stare against that contagious grin. They both burst into laughter.

"I like you, Janet Solterra Thompson. I like your probing, self-invented style."

He raised his glass.

"To you!" he saluted.

"No. To you, the man who would teach the world style and grace."

They clinked glasses with a clear undulating ring.

"Dr. Mahler," the head waiter said, "I am loath to interrupt, but your schedule requires you to finish."

He glanced at his watch.

"Yes, thank you. We need to go." The waiter led them down to the main bedroom, and closed the door behind them. Their clothes from the hotel were laid out on the bed.

Janet put one hand on her hip and wagged a finger from the other hand at Brandt.

"Oh, no you don't."

Brandt chuckled. "Sorry. They must think we are traveling together in the broader sense of the phrase." He grabbed his clothes and made to leave.

"No, that's okay. Just, uh, turn around. And no peeking!"

As Janet pulled off her suit, she heard the rustle of his clothing. An electric tingle moved across her skin, knowing that Brandt was so close, and also so very naked. For a moment, she wanted to turn around, then got a grip, and quickly put on her clothes.

"Are you decent?" he asked.

"Yes. But how are we going to ride the little sailboat back now?"

Brandt just chuckled as he led her from the room. A second later the sound of the turbine engine of the helicopter started up. She should have known. He was prepared. Always prepared.

As the helicopter gained altitude, Janet watched the illuminated white vessel drop away against the night-black water. What kind of a life was this? There were people starving in Zimbabwe while she and Brandt had burned through a small fortune just to eat one meal that they didn't even finish. Once back on the plane, Brandt resumed his endless phone calls. The idea of wasteful extravagance continued to nag at her as the Lear pushed Dubai behind them. During a break in his calls she pressed him.

"Brandt, how can we justify spending so much money on dinners, clothes and planes while there are people starving?"

"Janet, you know the answer. How many people would have been fed if we hadn't eaten dinner on the yacht? None. How many people will be starving if we don't stop Zelman? Millions. Billions."

"But it doesn't seem right. Don't you care about people?"

He looked stung. For the first time, genuinely angry.

"Why do you think I've been working for the WMF? For the glamour, fame or the incredible salary the WMF pays me?" He gave her a hard stare. "Because I really do care. But I know what it will take to really help people. First to stop Zelman. Then to straighten out the damn economy. Without that, all the self denial in the world won't help at all. Not one child more will be fed."

"But personal sacrifice is the hallmark of..."

"Perhaps you think I should be Gandhi and spin my own thread while I work toward world peace. Even his gains weren't sustainable. India fell apart when he died. And now, fifty years later, India and Pakistan are pointing nuclear weapons at each other. That is not the answer." He sat across from her and hunched over his shoulders and pointed his finger. "Self denial doesn't work. It is up to you and me, right here, right now, in this jet, to do something that results in more than feel-good platitudes." He punched a fist into his open palm.

"You seem so angry."

"I am. I've been in the cars while protesters throw eggs and decry the work of the WMF. I've begged ministers not to squander money while their people starve. Not millions, but billions. And now with the old international monetary systems breaking down because of fears of another depression, people are making mistakes in the trillions. Do you have any idea how many people could be fed with a trillion dollars? It would obliterate world poverty for a century. That is a lot more important than giving up our dinner."

Janet watched the furrows on his forehead deepen. An inexplicable pang echoed deep in her gut. What was it? Empathy? Understanding? Or something more.

"I've been there," he continued. I've lived it. It's discouraging. But I'm still putting my neck on the line to fix these problems. But, I can't do it all by myself."

She looked into the liquid depth of his eyes and realized what was going on. Brandt was asking her to stay. Not just because he wanted her to stay, but because he actually needed her help to solve real problems. He was a generalist who needed her analytical abilities. A shiver crossed her shoulders and buzzed down her arms. He needed her.

"I'm sorry. What can I do to help?"

"Stop Zelman!" Brandt's jaw clinched tight as he stared out the window into the nothingness of the dark sky. With a huff of pent up frustration, he pulled out his briefcase and started reading a report.

What could she do to stop Zelman? She debated the question, then checked her watch. Lunchtime in Tulsa.

"Hello."

"Do you think Zelman could use inflectives to bring down the American economy?" she launched without preamble.

"Oh Janet, is that you?" Professor Jones spoke, unable to use the caller ID. "Uh, let's ponder that." Janet could imagine the whirring inside the man's mind. "I don't see how. The American economy is just too large. Even with perfect manipulation of several of your inflectives there is just not enough amplification of the impact."

"But even before my paper, Zelman was able to use inflectives to bring down the Zimbabwean economy. He proved that inflectives can be used to change the course of entire economies."

"Zimbabwe with its weak economy was one thing. The United States is another. The American economy is thousands of times larger and stronger."

"I hoped my inflectives could be used to steer economies through difficult times. Zelman proved they can. But in the wrong direction."

"Janet, he can't use inflectives to bring down the whole US economy."

"Then what does he want me here for?"

"I cannot imagine. You should come back soon so we can get to work on the data you've collected so far. There are important people in Washington who are interested in your theory."

"Brandt says Zelman saved me from the bomb to solve his Midnight riddle."

"I like riddles."

"Yes, Professor Jones. I know you do. I don't see how I can solve it or even why it needs solving. Midnight must be an inflective. Rashid said something about a tiny straw that breaks the camel's back. Do you think there is such a thing?"

"I'm confused, Janet. Such a thing as what?"

"Let's call it a super-inflective, Dr. Jones. It would be something very small and normally insignificant. But at just the right moment it could be used to trigger an implosion big enough to destroy the US economy. If I research the numbers, and come up with an algorithm I might be able to find it."

Brandt sauntered past her on his way toward the back of the plane. The dark slacks he wore couldn't hide the smooth ripple of muscles on his thighs. Janet bit her lip and tried to suppress images of him in his swimsuit.

"Hmmm...very intriguing concept," Dr. Jones replied. "But Janet, even if a super-inflective did exist, it would be unpredictable. It would change from day to day, hour to hour, depending on the details of the situation. It would take a huge super-computer to make a prediction. Even then it would only be valid for a few hours."

"I guess you're right. Too unpredictable and impossible to find in five days."

"Speaking of days, did you do any interesting sightseeing today? I have heard that Africa can be quite thrilling to visit."

"Brandt and I went mountain biking on Kilimanjaro. We stopped half way down for a champagne brunch overlooking the Amboslei. Then we had dinner in Dubai on a luxury yacht on the Persian Gulf."

"He seems like a nice boy," the detached man said.

"Yeah, he does. Irritating sometimes, but nice."

"What was all that noise I heard on the phone when I called earlier?"

"Nothing, just our elevator being destroyed by agents working for Mirza ul-Beg."

"Oh."

Brandt returned from the back of the plane, dressed in formal business attire.

"I have to go, Professor Jones."

"Good bye, Janet."

"The bathroom is all yours if you'd like to shower and change before bed," Brandt said.

Even though it was early, she was exhausted. Janet checked her suitcase. She knew Brandt planned her clothing and she half expected to find a very skimpy teddy for nightclothes. Instead, there was a full flannel night shirt that draped to her ankles, and a thick white terrycloth house coat with black lapel accents, and a matching pair of slippers. She took the items to the lavatory.

The closet sized facility was as well appointed as the rest of the jet. Utilizing every cubic inch of possible space, it had a full shower and efficiently comfortable changing area.

As the warm shower water trickled over her skin her thoughts drifted to Brandt. What was he to her? Rescuer, friend, potential lover? As she lathered shampoo into her hair she couldn't help but dream of what it would feel like if Brandt's fingers were doing the work.

Dressed in her night gown, robe and slippers, she emerged from the lavatory, her wet hair wrapped in a towel. Brandt was sitting in front of the jet's large video monitor. The familiar face of the US President moved on its digital image. The president was making a firm statement about the economy. Brandt looked up and smiled at her, making her heart skip. She moved to the couch and sat next to him, rubbing the towel to dry her hair.

"Watching the evening news?" she asked.

"No. Video conference."

"Good evening, Ms. Thompson," The president stated. "Brandt tells me that you did some very good work in Zimbabwe."

Janet stopped rubbing the towel into her hair.

"Uh, Mr. President, I uh didn't realize, I mean I wouldn't, I uh..." Clasping the robe's collar around her neck, she stood. Flashing daggers from her eyes at Brandt, she moved to the back of the cabin.

Brandt chuckled.

"Beauty and brains," The president commented with a smile.

"A devastating combination," returned Brandt.

"Brandt, you were explaining why the United States should bail out the banks in Iceland."

"Yes, Mr. President."

"Brandt, you've known me for years. Can't you just call me John?"

"No, Mr. President. Not for another three years. Hopefully seven. As I was explaining, after congress approved the seven hundred billion dollar bailout plan, the Treasury went ahead and borrowed the first five hundred billion. Within minutes the banks in dozens of small countries went broke as all the liquid capital around the world was sucked into the United States."

Janet, despite her anger, couldn't help being drawn into eavesdropping on their conversation.

"Brandt, are you saying that the US Treasury shouldn't borrow money?" he asked.

"No, not at all, Mr. President. All I am saying is that the Treasury must move in coordination with other countries. There needs to be a world central bank to coordinate global borrowing to minimize negative effects on world markets."

Absorbed by the conversation, she tried to ignore the jingle of her cell phone. Finally, its persistence pulled her away.

"Don't you find it amazing," Anton began, "that a country as large as the US thinks it is the only country in the world and that it can do whatever it wants without worrying about other countries?"

"What do you mean?"

"What John is talking about with Brandt."

"How do you know what they are saying?"

"It is my airplane. The US Treasury just borrowed half a trillion dollars in one massive move. Who lent it to them?"

"The financial sector."

"Yes. That would be me. As Rashid told you, I am now the financial sector. And where did I get the money?"

"From the normal pool of assets that everyone borrows from on a daily basis."

"Yes, a pool that when splashed empty by one oversized swimmer leaves everybody else high and dry."

"So what is Brandt's plan going to do?"

"He will bail out Iceland for two billion, and The Ukraine for twelve, and so on for the other countries. But he needs to borrow the money from somewhere."

"Where?"

"The US."

Janet watched Brandt's graceful hands gesture in the air in an animated conversation with the president.

"But isn't that going to put the same money right back where it started?"

"Almost. With that much money ricocheting back and forth across the Atlantic several times, I get to keep a couple of billion. Not bad for a day's work."

"You are awful."

"Thank you."

"You must be stopped."

"Yes. That would seem appropriate. You could tell the president of the United States. You could tell the World Monetary Fund. Neither action would be particularly difficult at the present moment."

"Oooo. You are so exasperating!"

"Thank you."

He paused. For the first time he didn't hurry the conversation to an abrupt end.

"Are you in love with Mirza?" she asked trying to catch him off guard.

"No," he replied, surprising her with his quick candor.

"Is she in love with you?"

"Yes."

"You are such a strange person, Anton. Why do you have such an odd relationship with her?"

"Mirza and I are opposites that attract. Mirza wants to create paradise on earth by destroying the world's wealth. I want to create paradise for me by having the world's wealth. In the short term we need each other. We have the same tactics for achieving opposite ends."

"What about the long term."

"She will have to kill me."

"Why?"

"There is a bit of a long term compatibility issue between us, don't you think?

"Then why does she love you?"

"The words 'why' and 'love' in the same sentence? Odd question. There is no why to love, Ms. Thompson. Surely you know this."

"You're not answering my question, Anton."

"Mirza and I are opposites that attract. Just like you and Mirza. You are so much alike, and also so opposite."

"Well, I'm never going to find out how opposite we are. I'm going back to Tulsa."

"Ah, Ms. Thompson. The blush of youth. You wear it well. So innocent. It is so unfortunate that only one of you will be able to survive. Sleep well, Ms. Thompson."

# CHAPTER SIX

She puzzled over Anton's words as she closed her phone and looked to Brandt. A fight to the finish with Mirza? This was not happening to her. No, she had nothing to do with Mirza. She was going back to Tulsa. Leaving this whole mess far behind. She shook her head to clear away Anton's dire warning, and turned her attention to Brandt's conversation with the president.

"I hope you have a good afternoon, Mr. President," Brandt spoke.

"Good night, Brandt. Thanks for the advice. I will consider your proposal."

The video monitor went blank. Brandt turned to Janet and smiled.

"You're wrong, Brandt," she said, walking forward and resuming her seat next to him. "The treasury needs to borrow so it can spend to restart the economy."

"Not entirely true. Borrowing solves some problems but creates others."

"But government borrowing is factored in the paper economy. It's not a part of the real economy," she lectured.

"Tell the people in Harare their problems weren't real. Explain the concept of the paper economy to the fisherman in Iceland with a fishing boat empty of fuel, and an ocean full of fish laughing at him. There is one world economy, we all share it, and it is very real."

"But government spending is how Roosevelt ended The Great Depression," said Janet, sitting on the edge of the couch and working a brush through the tangles in her damp hair.

"That is not what ended it," said Brandt, following the strokes of the brush with his eyes. "On March 12, 1933, the greatest moment in modern economics occurred. After only a week as president, Roosevelt gave his first fireside chat. Close to ten thousand American banks had failed and people were pulling their money out at a meteoric rate. The very foundation of society was rapidly crumbling. Those were desperate times filled with desperate people. Yes, Roosevelt did turn to his advisors and turned on the printing presses. But more importantly, he turned to the people." Brandt took a hard swallow when she swooshed her hair to the other side.

"Yes," Janet interjected, "he told the people not to withdraw their savings. But, that wouldn't have made much of a difference." Janet continued brushing, then stopped and tried to separate a tangle with her fingers.

"Let me help," Brandt offered. She handed him the brush. Brandt's eyes were transfixed on her luminous wet hair. He held his curled fingers under her hair so he could support it and brush without pulling.

"Roosevelt explained in ordinary terms why he was printing money and why he had ordered a national banking holiday," he continued in an unwavering voice, his brush strokes slowly becoming longer as he undid her tangles.

"He clearly outlined his well thought out reasons. But most important, he asked for the confidence of the people."

Brandt stopped, then succeeded in penetrating a tangle and resumed brushing in long, languid strokes. Janet's eyes closed in pure pleasure.

"Americans had to work together or they would fail together. He told the people there was 'something more important than currency, more important than gold, and that is the confidence of the people themselves'."

Brandt's hand had worked its way up her hair, his warm knuckles grazed gently against the base of her neck. His voice became huskier as he continued.

"The next day people lined up at the banks to redeposit their money. Three hundred million dollars, a huge amount in 1933, poured back into the banks. Not imaginary money borrowed or printed by governments. Real money, earned with real work by real people."

His brushing slowed until Janet could barely feel it. Until she realized that he was combing without the brush, just using his fingers.

"It was leadership, not paper and ink, that saved the world. This is as true today as it was in 1933."

Janet struggled to understand Brandt's point. His closeness threw her mind off its track and it was hard to gather herself back to coherent thoughts.

"Hum," she replied. "You make quite an interesting point." She let him finish the brushing. "But, I'm not convinced. I'll have to run a computer simulation to see if you are correct."

Brandt burst into laughter. "I can't imagine two people more opposite than the two of us."

"Finally we agree on something," she chuckled back.

Brandt finished his work and reluctantly handed the brush to her. She stood and her bare feet padded to the rear of the aircraft. Instead of moving directly to her bed she stopped at the Brandt's small office next to the galley. Scanning an array of his pre-printed essays she selected one along with several high-lighters. Her housecoat slipped from her shoulders and she lowered herself onto the bed Brandt had previously converted for her, complete with pillows and turned down sheets and blankets. Brandt lowered the cabin lights as she pulled the bed covers over herself. It was still early, but he knew she was tired, so he slid to the far end of the couch to continue his work without disturbing her. But instead of going to sleep, she turned on her light.

"What are you reading?" he asked.

"One of your papers." She didn't look up as she studiously worked the paper.

He walked back to see.

"What are all those colors?" he asked.

"I'm highlighting each of your different idea threads in a different color."

"Idea threads?"

"Yeah. See, this thread about deficits is in yellow, and starts here. It restarts again down here."

Brandt shook his head in bewilderment. "You poor thing," he said as he walked back to the front of the aircraft.

Marcie was right, they were indeed opposites. But being an opposite could mean completing the missing pieces in the other person. Assuming the pieces were meant to fit together. She looked at Brandt as he sat down. A smile came to her face as she remembered the touch of his fingers against the back of her neck. She ran her fingers along Brandt's paper without reading it. She wanted to touch his words, to feel his thoughts, not about economics, but about life. She closed her eyes, replaying their brief time together since yesterday.

She was just dozing off when he woke her with a gentle whisper.

"Janet. Change in plans. We're going to Baku in Azerbaijan." He took a seat opposite from her.

"Baku? What about Brussels?"

"My friend Andy Topnazarov, the oil minister I told you about before, has uncovered a plot to disrupt the STC Pipeline."

"What?" She sat up.

"The Sangachal-Tbilisi-Ceyhan pipeline. It runs eleven hundred miles from Sangachal on the Caspian Sea, through Tbilisi in Georgia to Ceyhan on the Mediterranean in Turkey. It carries two percent of all the world's oil."

"That's impressive, but what does it have to do with Brussels or even Zelman and inflectives? Don't tell me Zelman bought it for you."

"No." Brandt laughed. "Don't be ridiculous. It cost billions. He bought it for Andy.

"Andy's people discovered explosives at a remote section of the pipeline. We'll fly with Andy to the site for a first hand inspection. Blowing up the pipeline would mean a massive spike in oil prices and an extreme deepening of the recession."

Brandt stared at her for a long moment, waiting. He maintained a wry smirk as he stepped to the cockpit to tell the pilot. After a moment Janet realized his smirk was because she wasn't protesting the latest delay in getting to Tulsa. He was slowly winning. And she was letting him. The airplane banked to the right and headed north.

She felt herself being drawn in by him. Not by his glamour, money or fame. By how he viewed life, by what he was trying to accomplish, trying to civilize a brutal world, trying to help the poor and by stopping exploitation.

When she first met Brandt, she thought he was just a man of privilege, but without purpose. But Brandt was so much more. He was a man of true power. Even though he held no official worldly position or title, he was a person of world leadership. Just because of who he was and nothing more.

"Brandt, I've been thinking," she commented when he settled next to her after returning from the cockpit. "Zelman needs to find or create a super-inflective. Without it, his plan will fail. That's why he saved our lives. That's got to be his purpose for the Midnight puzzle."

"Super-inflective? Explain that one."

"Zelman doesn't have enough ordinary inflectives to trigger the self-destruct of the American economy. Even if we assume he is working with

Mirza and will destroy PBEC and his own banking empire, he still doesn't have enough. A super-inflective is a very small, short lived opportunity that can have a very large impact. It might last for only a few hours and is nearly impossible to predict."

"I don't recall any mention of super-inflectives in your dissertation."

"Of course not. I invented them just now to get one step ahead of Zelman."

Brandt's eyes blazed with interest. Janet's heart leapt as heat raced up her neck.

"What would it take to predict a super-inflective?"

"It would take a very large super computer."

"How about a Cray XT5?"

"You have one?"

"Yeah."

"Don't tell me. Zelman bought it for you."

Brandt just sheepishly shrugged agreement.

"Now I know what he meant by you working for him without you even knowing it."

"The WMF has a computer lab at its headquarters near my apartment in Zurich. We'll fly there tomorrow after we meet with the EU President."

"You make it sound so casual. We'll just saunter into the EU President's office, have a friendly chat, hop on your jet, use your super-computer and save global civilization."

"That's about it."

"I don't think I will ever understand your world."

"Maybe you already understand it better than I do." He sat looking at her for a moment. That same look of recognition he had at the lunch on Kilimanjaro swept across his face. Again, she thought he was about to kiss her. Instead, he stood and returned to the front of the aircraft.

She lay in bed for a few more minutes before getting up to get dressed. She opened her suitcase and set out her newest set of clothing, a red-and-white striped blouse with blue and red ruffled trim, grey pin-striped slacks and a cute little matching jacket. As soon as she had it on she wished Marcie could see her in it. She dialed her cell phone.

"Marcie, what time is it in Tulsa?"

"After lunch. Where are you now?"

"Headed to Baku."

"Jan, I thought you were headed home. You live in Tulsa, not Baku."

"Yeah, but there is some trouble there that Brandt needs to deal with."

"Well tell him to drop you off at an airport and he can deal with all the trouble he wants."

"I think he wants me to help him."

Silence.

Janet waited for the inevitable analysis.

"Jan. I don't like the sound of that. He wants you to stay?"

"Yeah."

"Why?"

"I think he likes me."

Silence.

"Jan, flirting with a cute guy is one thing. Getting used by a playboy is another."

"I know. But there is something else."

"What's that?"

"I think I like him too."

Silence.

"Jan, you two are not compatible. You both think in very different ways. Don't fall for this guy. It will only be trouble."

"Hey, we're opposites. Opposites attract."

"They also clash. Tell me you are not going starry-eyed for some magazine cover playboy. Jan, I don't want you to be hurt."

"But can't we just..."

"Jan!" Marcie cut off. "Don't do it. It simply won't work. He's the globe trekking economist. Let him solve the world's problems. You need to come home."

"When did you become all big and grown up?"

"Four years ago. You just never noticed. And you. You need to come home."

"Okay."

"You don't sound convinced."

"I'll come home."

"Good. Call me from the airport. I'll pick you up and cook you dinner."

"Since when do you cook dinner?"

"Trevor taught me."

"Who is Trevor?"

"You'll have to come home to find out," the younger girl teased, and then hung up.

"Alrighty, then," Janet said to mute phone.

Janet frowned at the new-found image of maturity Marcie was flaunting. She suspected it would evaporate as quickly as it came. But then, Marcie was right. Despite the physical attraction growing between Brandt and her, and the thrilling prospect of playing a part in solving the world's economic problems, Brandt was a playboy whose lifestyle troubled her. Especially the women and money. She didn't even want to know about the women.

It was ten p.m. when the lights of Baku came into view. From the airport they rode in the oil minister's sleek Bell 310 helicopter with dramatic green and red accents splashed across its blue fuselage, the colors of the Azerbaijan flag.

"Andy's estate is about twenty miles from here, south of the city. It's a very impressive ancient building overlooking the Caspian Sea."

They landed on a pool of brightness that illuminated the round patch of asphalt with the universal H in its center. Brandt slid open the exit door, and stepped out. Waiting for them at the edge of the glow was a tall woman, blond hair lifting in the strong breeze from the rotor. Janet instantly recognized her as the bombshell from the French magazine in the Dubai lobby.

"Hello Andy!" Brandt enthused.

The woman walked up to Brandt, and without saying a word wrapped her arms around his neck and gave him a long hard kiss on his lips. Brandt struggled for only a moment before his resistance faded and he clasped his hands onto her slender waist.

"Ahem," Janet interrupted.

"Oh, Andy. This is Janet Thompson. Janet, this is Anechka Topnazarov, STC Pipeline Minister."

"Ah, Janet," Andy said. "Welcome to Baku. I am very pleased to meet you."

"I'm, uh, pleased to meet you as well."

"I'm sure you are," Andy spoke with cat-like challenge. "I enjoyed your dissertation very much."

"Thank you, *Andy*. And how did *you* get a copy of it?"

"I always keep track of Brandt's latest interests." Andy batted her lashes at Brandt.

"Oh yes. Brandt has a lot of interests, doesn't he?" Janet asked, twisting her lips together and glaring at Brandt.

"Come, let us refresh ourselves after your trip."

They turned toward the house. Carved stone arches, illuminated by lights placed around the sprawling building, formed a sweeping curve that focused attention on the unseen sea in the darkness below the rocky cliffs that skirted the shoreline. The large building was an impressive backdrop for the expansive sea. Each of the stone arches formed a small nave containing a unique statue. Andy caught Janet's eye sweeping the building.

"Every one of those naves describes an event in the long history of my country. Constantine himself once had a villa here. This building is a recent addition to the site. It is only six hundred years old. You'll notice that all the stonework facing the sea is very heavy. Baku means 'pounding wind'. The storms that come off the Caspian can be quite impressive. In fact, you arrived just in time to enjoy one tonight."

The challenge in Andy's voice told Janet that she had an entirely different idea of what enjoyment might be. Janet looked back behind her to see workers attaching steel cables to the helicopter in anticipation of the storm.

"You can see the lights from Baku to the north. The beginning of the pipeline is just eight miles from here at the Sangachal terminal. Iran is fifty miles down the coast."

Andy led them into the building to a fully enclosed courtyard with a flowing pool of steamy water. The pool was an irregular shape nestled into the ancient bedrock with stairs and seats cut into the natural stone. The water bubbled up from a hidden underground spring, and spilled off through a small channel chiseled into the stone. Beneath the crystal green water the stone was polished smooth from millennia of use.

The inner walls of the room were solid stone blocks with a carved wooden dome ceiling overhead. The carvings showed historical events and were at one time painted, but now only persistent flakes spoke of its past glory.

"This is one of many natural mineral springs in the area. The water is very comforting, especially if you are trapped here during a cold windy storm. Isn't that right, Brandt?" said Andy, shifting her shoulders up in feminine provocation.

Brandt's gaze was locked on Andy and a suppressed smile passed over his face at some pleasant memory. Janet's eyes narrowed. Brandt and Andy had been lovers.

They passed through the spa's courtyard, back outside to a sweeping alcove overlooking the vast Caspian. The early winds of the fledgling storm were already toying with Janet's long hair, tossing it around in a swath of red streaks. The dark sea was alive with the colored lights of oil rigs. A flotilla of boats moved about in a bee hive of activity.

"So many oil rigs," Janet commented.

"Of course! My people invented the oil business twelve hundred years ago. Azeri Light Crude is the best oil in the world. But the Caspian is a land-locked sea, ninety feet below sea level. For years we were blocked out of world markets. Now that the exploiting Russians are finally gone and we have our pipeline, my country is growing again."

"You sound angry about the Russians. Isn't Topnazarov a Russian name?"

"Don't remind me."

"Andy doesn't like the Russians," Brandt spoke. "There are two other smaller pipelines that start at the Sangachal, one through Georgia and the other through Russia, both going to the Black Sea. Andy shut off the oil through the Russian Transnov a year ago."

"And now the Russian army is only twenty miles from my STC pipeline," Andy sneered.

"Nikolai is mad at you."

Andy spoke something in Russian, and Brandt gave her a scolding look of admonition.

"Andy, don't be so stubborn," he said. "You need to talk to him, and re-open the Transnov." Andy pouted and twisted her head, encouraging Brandt to continue his coaxing. But he didn't.

"Come, let us return inside before the wind gets too strong."

They sat at a small café table next to the hot spring. A waiter approached with a tray of drinks, offering Andy first choice of the three small glasses of clear liquid.

"Na zdorovye," she saluted as she downed the beverage in a single pop. Brandt followed suit. The two raised their empty glasses, then slammed them rim down onto the table. They turned to Janet. She cautiously raised her glass, and took a half-hearted swallow.

The incendiary liquid immediately sprayed out of her mouth as she took choking gasps for air. The waiter offered her a glass of ice water. She used it to extinguish the burning pain in her throat, interspersing the ice cold water with frantic gulps of air.

"Swallow hard and it only hurts once, we say," Andy advised with a self-satisfied smile.

Janet sat contritely nursing her ice water. She stared at Andy, trying to assess her rival. But with Janet now safely neutralized, Andy turned her full attention back to Brandt.

"I see your father has been very busy. You must tell him that I miss him very much."

"I will. I'm sure he misses you as well."

Andy's eyes winced ever so slightly at the rebuff. Good. She wasn't getting Brandt to warm up to her overtures.

"So, tell me what's happening with the pipeline," Brandt said.

"My men found some terrorists with dynamite. They shot two, but two got away."

"Could they have been outside agents?"

"No. They were locals. It is best if I show you. We will go tomorrow. It is too late and the storm is coming."

Janet could already hear the whispers of the coming gale as it whistled around the edges of the building. Andy's eyes gleamed as she spoke of the storm. She leaned toward Brandt, revealing even more cleavage through her loose blouse. Uhgg! She was trying to seduce Brandt right in front of Janet.

"Come. Let us enjoy the spa," purred Andy.

Janet's eyes bolted wide thinking about how she might be expected to dress for such an occasion. Would she measure up in a non-swimsuit competition next to the Azeri Barbie?

"Do you have a swim suit?" Andy asked Janet, appraising her body up and down.

Had her Dubai suit been packed? She looked to Brandt who subtly nodded yes.

"Yes, I do," Janet answered with little relief in her tone.

"Good. Let us retire to our rooms, then reconvene here."

Servants led them to separate rooms. Janet was quite certain that there had been a time when Brandt's room had not been so separate. She also suspected that time was recent.

Janet's room was an impressive assembly of ancient stone and modern convenience. The walls were cold stone, but the floor was warm. She'd read about Roman style heating systems. Plenums must undergird the floors here. Tapestries hung from the walls, depicting a variety of historical events, their delicate colors enhanced by artful modern lighting. A four poster bed with a diaphanous canopy held her bag, already opened for her immediate selection.

It took her only a moment to change. She didn't want to give those two a chance to be alone together. It could be embarrassing barging in on a romantic interlude, or worse, a full seduction. Janet felt like a third wheel as it was. As soon as she emerged from her chamber, a servant led her back to the spa. Andy and Brandt had beaten her back, and were already in the water, laughing and talking of old times. Thankfully, they were not locked in an embrace. Janet stood there biting her lower lip. A brief zing of fear blasted through her. Was Andy nude? It took a moment for Janet to realize that the effect came from the fact that Andy's skimpy bikini was taupe colored. Even though she was under the water, Janet could see her runway model body. She sighed. No point in even trying to compete with that.

Janet approached the carved pool and dipped a toe. The water was a perfect warm temperature allowing her to easily glide in. Just as she sat down on the underwater ledge, a strong gust of wind pounded the building. The lights flickered once, then went out. Servants immediately began lighting candles about the room.

With the warm flickering glow of candlelight Janet imagined herself transported back several millennia in this very spot, which undoubtedly would have looked very much the same. Emperor Constantine sat in this very same water. The pinnacle of luxury had not changed at all after so many long centuries. Janet tried to absorb that thought.

She was slammed back to modern times when Andy giggled and slid closer to Brandt, her slim legs interweaving with his under the warm crystalline water. Brandt did nothing to either entice her to continue or to repel her, but he clearly enjoyed her attentions. Sitting nearly across from them, Janet could only watch as Brandt's shoulders relaxed and his eyes half-closed.

Janet's lips pursed together and twisted into a frown. She suspected that Andy had something to do with the electricity breakdown. It was unlikely that the main power and the emergency generators had both failed simultaneously.

Under the water, Janet's fists tightened. Her eyes narrowed, riveted on Brandt's reaction. If he wasn't going to stop Andy's advances, she would do it for him.

# CHAPTER SEVEN

Janet had little ammunition to work with, only her suspicion that Andy and Brandt had once been close, but had a falling out at some time. Over what, she didn't know.

"Andy," Janet spoke, disrupting the blonde's light touches playing over the curls on Brandt's chest, "I saw you on the cover of Les Potins earlier today when Brandt and I were in Dubai together." She emphasized the word together. "When was that photo taken?"

A gust of wind pounded the heavy wooden door, and a cold sizzle streamed under it along the stone floor blowing a chill over the water. The candles flickered, and several blew out.

"Brandt was here with me two weeks ago." Andy's voice was hard and pointed, with dagger-like sharpness.

The ground itself seemed to rattle as a burst of concussions hit the building. Andy's words seemed too carefully chosen.

"Oh? Do you two get together often to ride around in the Mazerati?"

Andy didn't answer. Bingo. Janet had hit a nerve.

"Andy and I ran into each other by accident at the yearly Baku oil conference two weeks ago. The Mazerati photo had been taken months before that. Wasn't it Andy?" Brandt replied with a soothing coax.

Again Andy didn't answer. Instead her face took on the faintest quiver of a sting. Brandt had apparently not told her that he planned to come to conference. Andy withdrew a few inches with a pout, but managed to keep Brandt's hand in hers. She forced her pout into a smile and held her eyes level with Janet's.

When a series of gusts slammed against the shuttered windows, Janet almost bolted up out of the spa. The sound was identical to the Harare bullets splattering against the shuttle van. But the shutters held as they had for hundreds of years. The sturdy walls reverberated for several seconds after the blast ended. Janet swallowed, and re-gathered her courage.

"Too bad you aren't still together," said Janet. "You seemed like you were such a handsome couple on the magazine." Janet spoke firmly, finally evening the score after Andy's vodka trick.

The wind was now a constant fusillade, its pounding blending into a steady whistle that seeped through the gaps in the doors, rattling the hinges. It seethed around the rafters of the building, but its fury couldn't penetrate the walls to get to Janet.

Andy released Brandt's hand. Janet couldn't quite tell from his wry grin whether Brandt approved of her interference in the situation or not.

The wind seemed to abate, but Janet knew better than to think the storm was over. Andy could still be very dangerous. It probably wasn't really a good idea to be on her bad side.

"This pool is magnificent, Andy. How long has it been in use?"

Andy didn't answer, her lips narrow and taut. The steam rising from the water swirled around Andy's face as if she were withholding her fuming breath, banking her fires for later. A dragon biding her time.

"At least five thousand years." Brandt filled in. "Probably much longer." The power and danger outside continued in all its fury, but Janet now had confidence that the stony defenses around her would protect Brandt and her.

"It is absolutely beautiful here. Andy, you must be very proud of this estate."

Janet could see Andy's face change to an expression of deep-felt pride. The stalemate was broken, however briefly.

"I am. It is an important part of my nation's history, and I am very proud to be the one to get it back again and protect it. My ancestors have owned and lost this property many times over the centuries. But always it comes back. Now it is my turn to care for it."

Some forlorn piece of wreckage crashed against the outer wall with a thud. A brief silence held them for a moment. No one seemed inclined to investigate. The servants didn't move and the wind soon resumed its howling.

"How were you able to get it back?" asked Janet, trying to distract her thoughts from past memories of dangers of twisters on the Oklahoma plains.

"Since the Russians left, Azerbaijan has gone through major changes. Even though my country is not entirely, what you might call democratic, we have undergone stable privatization, and have won high marks from the WMF for economic progress. With Brandt's help I was able to negotiate billions of dollars of foreign investment in my pipeline. My nation is very proud of the pipeline I built for them. My reward was the return of my family estate."

"No one protested the handover of such a valuable estate to a private citizen?"

"Humph! Not at all. I am adored by all the people. There is not an Azeri within a hundred miles who would not gladly lay down his life to protect one hair on my head."

Janet had her first glimmer of why Brandt broke up with Andy. Such pride led to arrogance. Of course, Brandt had his share of it, too. But he was able to temper it better than Andy.

"How old were you when you secured the money?"

"Nineteen."

"Wow," enthused Janet, "so young for such a large project."

"I usually get what I want," Andy said, looking at Brandt.

The tempest outside had moderated, but continued whistling and pounding the building, yet leaving the three warm and secure, safe in the heavy stone cocoon that had protected bathers for hundreds of years.

"Do you remember getting what you wanted from Alistair Wadsworth?" asked Brandt in a genial tone.

Andy broke into laughter. "Yes, I do remember."

"Andy and I were sophomores in college and decided to negotiate the STC Pipeline. I had known Paul Uster, the CEO of Royal Petroleum since I was a kid, so I arranged a series of meetings. There we were, two teenagers, sitting in the RP Board Room, negotiating billions of dollars in contracts with Paul and this guy Alistair the bean counter. Andy had proposed a series of water and school projects for the villagers along the pipeline to win their loyalty and protection for the pipeline. But Alistair was tearing apart every dime. 'I'm sorry' he told us, 'but I simply cannot justify these costs.' He shook his head in rejection, closed his ledger and crossed his arms finalizing his decision. Andy glared at him. She looked down, sucked in her cheeks and puckered her lips for a moment of thought. She reached over, grabbed him by the tie and slammed him onto the table. 'You need me more than I need you. The projects stay.' She then spat on the table in front of him, and pushed him back. Paul smiled and gave us everything we wanted."

Andy beamed at Brandt. The memory of her victory was theirs to share.

"How did you two meet?" asked Janet.

"We both were students at the university in Zurich. Andy told me about her dream of building the pipeline. I mentioned it to Zelman who immediately jumped on board with the idea. With his seed money secure, and with my connections, Andy and I were able to interest a number of investors, mostly large oil companies."

"I imagine you two have had a long history of adventures," Janet commented.

"Yes we have," Andy replied. "Haven't we, Brandt?"

Brandt's generous smile at Andy said more than Janet wanted to know.

A waiter brought a tray with three small glasses of dark red liquor.

"This is Azeri-Nar, a pomegranate cognac from the Gyandja-Tovuz region in northwest Azerbaijan."

They each took a glass.

"To Alistair Wadsworth," Brandt toasted.

Andy laughed as they clinked glasses, but Janet was reluctant to try hers.

"Don't worry, Janet," Andy assured. "It is strong, but not like the vodka. Sweet, and very good for the stomach and heart. Sip it if you don't believe me. Drink it all and you will sleep well tonight."

Janet took a sip. She wanted to sleep well, but not if it meant that Andy and Brandt would be able to be alone together. Never mind! She shouldn't think about that. She drank a healthy swallow. The cognac was indeed as good as Andy had promised. The pounding wind, now powerless to do harm, the warm water, the cognac and the flickering candlelight all swirled in Janet's exhausted mind.

"We should retire," Brandt said.

They finished their glasses, and stepped from the pool. A servant handed Janet a huge towel. She wrapped it around herself quickly even though she could see that Brandt was now staring at her and not Andy.

Andy led Janet to her room, walking at her elbow like a warden. Janet felt ordinary and plain next to the lithe beauty. There was simply no way Brandt would be interested in her after having that to gaze at.

Despite her fatigue, Janet lingered in her doorway a moment to assure herself that Brandt entered his room alone. He did. Andy stalked back past Janet's door with a smug smile.

"Sleep well, Janet," said Andy, the false note of seduction returning to her voice.

Janet retreated into her room and glanced at the bed. Her cell phone was blinking a message from Marcie. Janet checked her watch, four o'clock in Tulsa.

"Jan, where are you now?"

"I'm in an ancient stone villa overlooking the Caspian Sea."

"How'd you get there?"

"It is owned by one of Brandt's girlfriends."

"Oh? Former or current girlfriend?"

"Former, at least for the moment."

"And how are you and Casanova getting along?"

"Good, I guess."

"And that means what?"

"I don't know. I guess I feel like I have to compete with his previous girlfriends, and I'm not convinced they are still previous."

"And why would you want to? I thought you agreed that you were coming home, that you and Brandt couldn't get along."

"Oh, yeah. I forgot."

"You forgot! Jan, don't tell me you're actually thinking of going after this guy."

"No, 'cause I think he is going after me."

"Is he coming on to you?"

"No. Yes. Kind of. He keeps doing these sweet romantic things that make me think he likes me. Then he says something that infuriates me. I don't know."

"Jan, repeat after me. Tulsa. Tulsa is my home."

"Marcie. No."

"Jan. Say it."

"Tulsa...Tulsa is my home," Janet droned. She lay back on the bed and sighed. "G'night, Marcie."

"Good night. See you soon! In Tulsa!"

"Yep. Tulsa. Home."

Janet closed her phone and her eyes followed. Could home be wherever Brandt was? And how many more Andys were there?

\*\*\*

Morning sunlight poured through Janet's window. The storm had ended, and workers outside were pulling back the heavy wooden shutters that had protected her room during the night. Andy was right. Janet slept perfectly. She felt fresh and more alive than she had in years. As she had come to expect, clothes were laid out for her, a plain blue cotton shirt with long sleeves, lightweight jeans, hiking boots and a construction helmet with a SOCAR logo on it, the A shaped like a slender oil derrick and smaller English words: State Oil Company of Azerbaijan.

A maid directed her to an outside patio overlooking the Caspian. The sheltered portico protected them from the otherwise cool breeze. The brilliant ball of the sun rose over the glittering water, filling the morning with a clean, fresh sense of renewal. Then, Janet's bright mood darkened when she saw Andy and Brandt sitting at a small café table, speaking in Russian and laughing. Andy gestured expressively with her hands, which always seemed to come to rest on Brandt's. Brandt stood as Janet approached. He pulled a chair out for her.

"Janet," Andy spoke, "I do believe the Azeri-Nar did agree with you. You look very well rested."

"Yes, it is hard not to sleep well in such a comforting location, with such an attentive hostess," Janet replied, her voice carrying a sharp edge of resentment.

Both Andy and Brandt had only small plates in front of them. There was pitifully little food on the table, a small round loaf of bread, plain yogurt, and a heavy rind brie cheese. Only Americans knew how to breakfast. Brandt broke off a hunk of the bread for her. Its hot yeasty steam made her mouth water. She watched as Brandt spooned some yogurt for himself, and applied a dollop of fig preserve to its middle. Janet mimicked him as a waiter poured her espresso into a miniature cup. The yogurt was fresh and warm, with a sharp sour bite that played against the sweet fig. Perhaps this breakfast was not as bad as she first suspected. What it lacked in substance, it made up for in flavor.

"Andy and I were just laughing over my first encounter with Nikolai Brosnarov. Nikolai had once been Russia's governor of Azerbaijan and occupied this very villa."

Andy winced melodramatically at the thought, as if she had just chomped into a sour lemon.

"Andy's family has had a centuries-old blood feud with the Russians and with Nikolai in particular."

Andy crossed her arms and nodded deeply at the virtuous history of her family.

"We met Nikolai during the construction of the Transnov pipeline, when the STC was still in planning. There was an ancient church slated for demolition by the Russians, and we flew to Moscow to plead with Nikolai to save it."

"I didn't plead," Andy reminded. "You did."

"You should have," Brandt scolded before turning back to Janet. "As you might imagine, the meeting lacked warmth. Nikolai wouldn't budge, and the church was leveled."

"But, I made my point," Andy bragged.

"Yes, indeed you did. But that was all we accomplished. We were lucky Nikolai let us out of the country."

"What did you do, Andy?" Janet asked.

"Not much. Same as in London. I spat on the table in front of him."

"Andy, Moscow is not London. Nikolai is not Alistair. The church is gone."

Andy crossed her arms and turned away. "Now Nikolai's precious pipeline is empty," she retorted.

"And Nikolai has Russian tanks twenty miles from your STC. Andy, it is far past time to learn when to compromise. Reopen the Transnov pipeline. It has only a fifth the capacity of the STC. That is not much, and will cost you nothing, absolutely nothing. But it will assure the security of the STC, your STC, that you worked so hard to build. With the western world in recession, and Russian oil revenues down, the Russians are very nervous. Their collective trigger finger is getting very itchy. It would help Nikolai politically if you would bend just a little."

"Tochno! Exactly! That is why I won't."

Brandt raised his two hands in exasperation, then crossed his arms like Andy, and turned back-to-back with her in a futile stalemate. Now Janet understood why they broke up.

Letting out a long harsh breath, Brandt was the first to break his stance and return to breakfast. Janet sighed and looked out over the lawn to the helipad where workers were unshackling the helicopter from its storm moorings. She glanced around the lawn, noticing the copious amount of debris strewn about by the fickle wind. An old man pushed a small handcart along the grass, collecting smaller pieces of flotsam, while two younger men in a golf cart cleared away larger items.

"So, what are our plans?" Janet asked.

"We'll fly to the site where the terrorists were found. I doubt we will need more than a few hours. We will be back here in time for lunch," said Brandt.

Janet nodded acceptance of the simple plan.

When they were finished, Andy waved her hand for the dishes to be removed. Simultaneously, the helicopter engine started.

She led them across the now pristine lawn to the helicopter. The three sat together behind the pilot, with Brandt strategically placed in the middle. The engine revved and the aircraft lifted and smoothly arced away from the glittering Caspian. Within a few miles, signs of civilization faded, giving way to a rugged landscape of gray and brown, broken by an occasional patch of greenish grassland.

They spoke via headphones to be heard above the engine noise. The conversation was almost exclusively in Russian. Andy and Brandt laughed and joked, with Andy's hand often on Brandt's knee. At particularly funny points, her hand slid upward dangerously without Brandt's protest.

Janet was green with spite. How could he continue to let her flirt with him when they had broken up and were obviously not a good match? She yanked off her headphones and tossed them on the seat, staring out the window at the rugged landscape.

"Sorry, Janet. We didn't mean to exclude you," he tried to say over the engine. Unable to hear clearly, Janet shook her head no, crossed her arms, and fixed her stare outside.

It seemed like an eternity before the helicopter descended into a clearing, and the engine octaved down to deafening silence worsened by the lingering ringing in her ears.

The rugged landscape of bleak hills covered with grass and low scrub was cut by a naked swath of dirt road. A hot, dry wind blew in occasional gusts, bringing swirls of grit and dust along with it. Janet shielded her eyes from the sting of sand and the caustic smell of something she couldn't identify. The air was alive with the chirrup of crickets and the buzzing of insects in the grass. A small grouping of black birds, flitted up, twisted together in the air with loud cries and then floated down to land confetti-like and search for food.

"We've crossed the border into Georgia," Andy explained.

"Where is the pipeline?" Janet asked, shielding her eyes with her hand and looking about for something resembling a large cylindrical shape.

Andy laughed. "The pipeline is right here, buried for its entire length to protect it from terrorists. This part of the world is not like your gentile Oklahoma."

A scruffy, heavyset foreman approached with two scrawny younger assistants in tow. The foreman had a Kalashnikov rifle slung across his chest. In rapid fire unintelligibility, he spoke to Andy.

"What's he saying?" Janet asked Brandt.

"I don't know. It's in Azeri."

They followed the foreman to a small hand-dug pit a short way from the road. As they neared it a putrid odor wafted across Janet's face. She looked down. At the bottom of the hole were two fly ridden corpses. Janet revolted away as Andy explained in English.

"My men found them digging this pit over the pipeline, and opened fire. The others got away."

Next to the hole was a small wooden box with several sticks of dynamite. Andy picked up one of the sticks, fingered it for a moment, then snapped it in half over her knee. She tossed the pieces aside and signaled the foreman to continue.

They followed the foreman and his men to a small stand of skinny scrub trees. Brush and additional cut saplings helped to hide a Praga transport truck. Russian army, complete with a dust dulled red star on each door.

"Russians?" Janet asked.

"The truck is Russian, but not the terrorists," Andy replied. "There are Russian occupation troops just twenty miles from here in South Ossetia. They hate my pipeline," spat Andy, "and could easily bomb it if they so chose. But so far, they haven't. They would certainly enjoy looking the other way while any of a number of terrorist groups took the truck and fulfilled their wishes. Then they would laugh while they claimed innocence."

The foreman led them to a rusty metal tank sitting on the open truck bed. He opened a valve, and let some of the brown-black liquid splash onto his fingers. He held it up for Andy to smell.

"Crude oil," she said. "Not Azeri Light. Not from around here."

"Coals to Newcastle," Brandt said. "Why would they bring crude oil here?"

"Is there enough dynamite to actually damage the pipeline?" Janet asked. Andy translated for the foreman.

"He thinks no. The pipeline was built to withstand attacks of this nature."

"So why?" Brandt asked.

"Perhaps they didn't want to actually damage the pipeline," Janet speculated. "Instead, they only wanted to create the image of disaster. They would explode the charge, fill the hole with oil, light it on fire, and send back some satellite phone videos for YouTube. You don't have to actually stop the oil to create a world wide panic."

Brandt nodded understanding. "Mirza's goal is to create capital flight from the United States. All they need to do is to make oil prices surge, sucking more money out of American stocks. Zelman and Mirza are working both sides of the equation. They are brilliant."

"This isn't Mirza or Anton," Andy retorted, dismissing their joint theory.

Without warning a sharp rifle shot pinged off a nearby stone. Brandt pushed Janet to the ground, falling down beside her, shielding her with his body. His hand pressed down on her helmeted head, keeping her still and giving her a firm signal not to move a hair.

She pressed her lips shut, trying not to scream and draw more bullets toward them. A thickening wad of fear silently gurgled up through her throat as she remembered the gun shots in Harare. Breathe. Forcing herself to take halting shallow breaths made her long to fill her lungs with relieving air. Her heart thumped, loud and heavy, in her chest as she mentally assessed every part of her body. She had not been hit. She hoped no one else had been either.

Forcing her eyes open, Janet's gaze darted from bush to bush, tree to tree trying to find the sniper. The foreman had his rifle poised in front of him, slowly scanning it in aimless directions.

She was tempted to speak, if only to ask what they were planning to do. The utter silence of those close by was as eerie as waiting for another shot to be fired. There wasn't even a whisper amongst them. It had only been a single rifle shot. One sniper against six others? Of course, only one was armed. Would the helicopter pilot send for help?

They were pinned down in an exposed position out here in the middle of the barren hills. Any movement or sound would draw more fire. But they couldn't just keep still forever. A fly fizzed over her and landed on a blade of grass. A gust of wind drove sand up her pants leg, shirt sleeve and nose. Janet gritted her teeth. She turned her face toward the ground and snorted it out. Brandt made a low sound of disapproval. He pressed his hand down harder, driving her face against the ground. The taste of dirt in her mouth made her force her head to the side to spit out a burst of air so she could breathe.

Brandt made a short hiss just as a series of three shots rang out, whizzing overhead. The sniper was trying to flush them from the meager shelter of the uneven rocky soil and scrub brush. No one moved. Janet heard nothing besides the metallic clatter of sand blowing against the truck. Not even the cries of the birds or the chirp of the crickets could be heard. Not a good sign. Maybe there was more than one. Was this the kind of real world experience Brandt told Janet she lacked?

Another burst of shots pinged into the side of the army truck. A few landed with more thud than ping. Janet shifted her eyes up to the Russian truck. Oil began to gurgle down the side of the rusted tank.

The foreman focused on the direction of the gunfire. He shouted intentionally drawing a staccato of gun shots in return. A shot pinged below the truck, sparking a stone. The oil burst into flame. Poisonous black billows rolled skyward from the truck. Realizing what was about to happen, Brandt rolled over Janet. Crawling away from the truck, he dragged her with him. He pushed her down flat and lay half over her.

Silence. Just the roar of the fire. Brandt said nothing. Janet breathed in the tang of distant gun smoke mixed with the sweeter aroma of fresh oil and bitter smoke. She tried to muster some saliva to coat her parched throat, but her mouth had gone dry. She worked to suppress a cough. She felt Brandt shift above her. Slowly she raised her head until she could just peer over the grass.

The foreman lay flat on the ground, the surrounding saplings providing no protection. Two tan lumps beyond him were his men. Their heads were down, but moved slowly right to left, scanning the horizon. Janet swiveled her eyes trying to spot the shooter. She couldn't see Andy.

The foreman spoke something in a low growl, then popped up and fired off a series of shots. Janet jerked at the sharp sound and despite Brandt's protection cringed with her arms wrapped around her helmet.

She blinked then stared wild eyed as a distant figure broke from the tall grasses and ran toward a dense clump of trees. The foreman pumped off two more rounds, but the man kept running.

Andy stepped from nowhere in front of Janet's view and wrenched the rifle from the foreman's hands. With graceful ease she stood straight and tall in full view and tracked the figure. The fuel tank of the truck exploded, but Andy didn't flinch. She slowly squeezed the trigger. The man dropped.

"This is my pipeline," Andy sneered. "I built it. No one will stop my oil."

Ignoring the burning truck, the men scrambled forward looking for more snipers.

"All clear," Andy called a few moments later.

Brandt eased Janet up from the ground.

"Are you okay?"

She nodded.

Andy barked out orders and watched while the men went forward to the sniper's body. She gestured at the men to put the new body into the hole. Walking with Brandt to the hole, Janet winced as the dead man's head bounced over the rough stone in unfelt pain as he was dragged by his feet to the rim of the hole. In horror, Janet gaped at the vacant face of a boy not more than twenty years old. One foot on the dead man, Andy posed gun in hand while one of the aids snapped her picture with the burning truck in the background. With a shoving foot Andy rolled the still oozing body into the pit, where he landed on his rotting friends. She said something to the foreman, and the men lined up around the hole, and urinated on the corpses.

"Good. Now they can guard my pipeline forever," Andy spat.

The men shoveled dirt as Andy, Janet and Brandt walked back to the helicopter. On a dry crack of mud Janet took a misstep and nearly fell. Her head swirled as the images of the dead men drained the blood from her face.

"Are you sure you're okay?" Brandt asked.

"Yeah, I'm fine."

She believed that. Until her stomach convulsed. Leaning into the low brush she retched the tension from her gut. Brandt stood at a protective distance.

"Sorry, I just..."

Her stomach roiled again and she discharged the last of her anxiety.

Andy shook her head in dismay and continued walking to the helicopter.

Brandt helped Janet stumble along behind. He helped her inside and strapped her into her seat. He planted the headphones over her head. The helicopter engine started, idled for a few moments, then accelerated, covering the shoveling men in a dusty cloud as it lifted off.

Andy seemed to be in a jovial mood as the helicopter made its way back. Janet could imagine the glorious headlines and front page photo in tomorrow's Azerbaijan newspapers.

"Brandt, can you stay for a few days? We haven't done any sightseeing for so long."

"No. Janet and I are already late for Brussels. The halls of power won't wait."

"You'll at least stay for lunch."

Brandt glanced at Janet's ashen face. "No thanks, we need to get directly to the airport."

"Oh, are you sure?" Andy pouted.

Brandt nodded yes.

Back at the airport the helicopter touched down in front of the Lear. Out on the tarmac Andy repeated her greeting kiss, long, slow and passionate. But this time Brandt's steely stance cooled her passion. After Andy finished, Janet followed Brandt up the narrow steps into the plane. He unceremoniously turned and closed the door behind them without even a wave good-bye to Andy. Janet eased into her seat and clipped on her seatbelt. She glanced out the window and watched Andy as she stood on the tarmac, a fist on each hip. One look at Andy's scowl and Janet realized this would not be her last encounter with the mistress of the STC.

***

The nose of the jet was pointed due west as it climbed to cruising altitude. The familiar safety of the Lear provided the comfort Janet needed to recover. Her mind was a turmoil of thoughts. Brandt seemed so cavalier about the shooting and the rotting men in the hole. On the way to Baku he professed to be working for the good of mankind. Yet, he seemed so detached from the corpses who were once real people and he made no comment at all about the young sniper.

"Brandt, doesn't it affect you when you see people dying right there in front of you? I don't understand. How can you be so cold?"

Brandt's jaw clenched tight at Janet's accusing tone. Then he softened.

"Janet, it must be hard, seeing people die for the first time. I still remember the horror of my first time. I was eight, traveling in the Congo with my Dad. Our convoy was ambushed. The fire fight lasted over ten minutes before the rebels were pushed back. It seemed like hours to me. I wasn't so worried for myself, but I didn't want my Dad to die. Six of our people were killed. I was so relieved when I finally saw him coming toward me to find out if I was okay.

I didn't lose my Dad that day, but a good friend of my Dad's died right next to me. It was the first time I'd seen anyone die. I was so terrified that even back in Switzerland I continued to have nightmares."

Janet dropped her gaze to the floor, trying not to picture the scene. It was all too real. Especially for an eight year old.

"But, as an adult I have to face these things. I have to go where people shouldn't go, trying to solve problems others don't care about. I can't avoid seeing these sorts of things. If I let it get to me I would have to stop going. I could stay safe at home. It would be an easy life. Without danger, or *purpose*."

That made her look up at him. He did have a sense of purpose. She admired that in him more than she cared to admit.

"Cold?" he continued. "Cold is when you don't care. I do."

Weary of thinking about it, Janet slumped in her seat, placing her arm over her eyes.

"As I said before, I couldn't do what you do," she said.

"Janet, the STC situation could become a real problem. We need to divert from Brussels. We need to go talk with Nikolai in person."

"Do you always have this much trouble staying on task?" she huffed.

"Now that you mention it, yes," he quipped with a snicker.

"And where is Nikolai?"

"At a Russian airbase in Krasnodar in southern Russia. It's not far out of our way, but I'm not certain how well Nikolai will welcome us."

"You've already made the arrangements, haven't you? Before we even landed in Baku."

Brandt shrugged as he glanced at his watch.

"Excuse me, but I need to make some more calls." He stepped away from her, pulling out his phone.

Purpose. Just three days ago she craved purpose. Oklahoma was too small, too confining. She wanted to be involved in the shaping of world events. To make a difference to people. But this? Was this the definition of purpose?

"But Mildred," Brandt spoke into his phone, "the problem is there isn't enough international coordination. The old international monetary system is breaking down."

Mildred? US Secretary of State...?

On the other hand, Brandt's world was *too* big. And its purpose was all too real. The fate of nations pivoted on what he did or failed to do. It was a dizzying world with responsibilities she might not be able to face.

After he finished with his call, he sat pondering whatever it was that had been said. She could tell he was contemplating his next move because he was tensing his right foot, making the muscles of his leg jump.

"How did your call go?" Janet asked.

"Okay. Sometimes it is slow going. I've been working to increase the level of international cooperation. I believe it is the key to ending the recession." His eyes darted over her features. "What is left of the old Bretton Woods system is just too weak to solve today's problems. Assuming Mirza and Anton don't obliterate our economies entirely."

He stopped scanning her face and settled on her eyes. It made her heart flip flop.

"Are you okay now?" he asked.

"Yeah."

Brandt nodded and got up. "I've got a videoconference set up in fifteen minutes. I need to change."

As he headed to the back of the Lear, Janet sat back in her seat and speed-dialed.

"Hey, Marcie."

"Jan, hey. Are you still in Baku?"

"No, we're headed in the direction of Brussels."

"It's about time. Wait a second. 'In the direction of...' Do you mean directly to Brussels. None of Brandt's diversions?"

"Well, we just have to stop at a Russian air base and then..."

"Jan! You're scaring me. I don't want to hear it."

"Sorry."

"Jan, why? Why aren't you running back home as fast as you can? As a matter of fact, I don't understand why you left in the first place."

"That makes two of us." The drone of the airplane filled the silence. "Marcie, we need to talk."

"It's about time. So talk already."

"I love my job as an assistant professor at the university. But, I need more. I want to do things, not just study them or write about them. I want to get involved in the action."

"Jan, I'm not the one you need to say that to. It is yourself. You want to do things? So do them. What is the problem?"

"You're not mad at me for leaving you behind in Tulsa?"

"Jan. I love you, but you can be a bit over the top sometimes. Don't you think? You always seemed to think you had to out-mom Mom. Frankly, I could use a break from you."

"Oh." Out of the mouth of babes...

"But, what you are doing now is crazy. You need to come back. Now."

Brandt emerged from the lavatory dressed in a three piece suit. He looked amazing. So sophisticated and elegant. An hour ago they we lying in the dirt dodging bullets. Maybe he really was a prince. He dialed his phone and started a conversation in French. She watched Brandt's expressions as he expertly wove his conversation.

"By the way, how is the playboy?" Marcie asked. "He make any moves yet?"

"No, he has been a perfect gentleman. But, I tell you, the way he looks at me sometimes. It makes me..." she said, her voice trailing off in a sigh.

"How does he look at you?"

"I don't know. Those eyes, they look right through me and I melt. I feel safe with him, even when we're being shot at."

"Jan!"

"Sorry. Oh, and Brandt keeps buying me these beautiful clothes."

"You actually like the clothes he picks? You always hate it when I pick stuff for you."

"I've never really paid attention to fashion. You know that." Janet took a breath. "But Marcie, he has impeccable taste, and I love what he picks. Everything fits me so perfectly and I think I look great. At least he says I do."

"I don't understand you, Jan. You are letting him run your life. He's even dressing you now."

"Well, I would pick my own clothes, I'm pretty sure he'd let me, but I don't know how to pick the right things. You know fashions, but I don't."

"You're worried about the proper fashion to wear while being shot at?"

"Very funny, Marcie."

"Get his credit card. I'll use it to teach you all about fashion when you get back."

They both chuckled.

"When are you leaving Brussels?"

"I don't know. I'll let you know if I leave."

"You mean when you leave."

"Yeah, that's what I said."

"No, you said if you leave."

"Whatever. I'll call. Love ya."

"Love you too."

Janet appraised Brandt in his suit. He wore a plain white shirt, no tie, and left the two top shirt buttons undone. His only accents were a red handkerchief in his breast pocket, and Swiss flag pin, red with white cross, on his lapel. So conservative, yet so trendy. Outspoken, yet politically neutral. He was bridging worlds torn apart by narrow-sightedness and national self-interest. Only Brandt could do that.

"I can't meet the Russian Foreign Minister looking like this," she said with worry, gesturing to her jeans and boots.

"Of course not. I already selected your clothes and put them in the lavatory. Hurry, now."

She thought of Marcie's words about Brandt running her life. It wasn't true. She could make decisions for herself. But just now there was little choice but to change into what he provided. Right?

In the lavatory hung a classic sleeveless little-black-dress with thin strap shoulders and low neckline. Silky hose and shiny black high heels adjoined it. An American flag pin declared her identity. Well, what of it? Unfortunately, Marcie, as usual, was right. Brandt was dressing her up. So? She could do with a bit of dressing up. With chagrin, Janet changed and stepped back into the cabin. At least the black outfit went with her cowgirl hat. She let it hang across the back of her shoulders.

He looked up from his papers and a smile of admiration broke across his face. She spun around flirtatiously for his benefit, swaying her hips and shoulders. She was rewarded by watching his eyes grow.

"How do you always get my clothes to fit so perfectly?"

"I study women."

"I'll bet you do."

He signaled for her to be quiet, and straightened his suit. On schedule, prominent leaders of four nations appeared on the aircraft's cabin monitor. Besides the American, representatives from The United Kingdom, Israel and Azerbaijan also appeared. Janet watched in amazement as Brandt casually assembled the elite group of statesmen and worked his magic.

"Thank you all for joining me," Brandt spoke to the group. "I am concerned that there may be misunderstandings regarding the presence of the Russian army so close to the STC Pipeline."

"Yes, that is of major concern?" the Brit asked.

"There's no misunderstanding. It's clear they want war!" shrilled the Azeri.

"There are some people in my country," the Israeli spoke with a practiced cadence, "that think the Russian goal is to threaten the pipeline in order to block Israeli plans for a reverse flow trans-shipment terminal to bring Caspian oil to the Far East."

"The Russians aren't your biggest problem," said the UK representative. "If the Azeris will just re-open the Transnov pipeline the

Russians won't care. You should be more concerned because you have to wait for the money to build your terminal."

"The US cannot provide funding for the Israeli trans-shipment terminal until the recession ends," the American explained.

"The Russians must be pushed out of Georgia," the Azeri fumed.

"Yes, something needs to be done about this aggression. The Russians must agree to retreat. If not, there will be retaliations," said the Israeli.

"There will be more than retaliations if the Russians can't get their oil through. Other nations besides the Russians have an interest in keeping oil lines open."

"Gentlemen, please," Brant soothed. "Quentin, you've developed good relations with the Russians. You also, Hadar. Can either of you offer Nikolai anything to delay his plans?"

Janet's cell phone rang.

"Are you enjoying the talking heads?" Anton said.

"Actually, yes I am. But it is all so complex and confusing. I don't know how Brandt can know so many people and keep track of them all."

"Yes, Brandt is very good at what he does. But I worry about him sometimes."

"Worry? Why, because you keep trying to kill him?"

"No. He can handle that. I worry because he knows so many people, but he has no friends."

Anton's words made Janet think he was joking at first. But he was serious. He worried about Brandt?

"Who *are* you Anton? Why do you do what you do?"

"Only four days left to find Midnight, Ms. Thompson. Use them well."

Yet again the phantom vanished.

"Thanks to all of you for your time," Brandt spoke to the electronic meeting. "I hope to visit each of you in the near future." Brandt closed the connection.

"Man," Brandt said to Janet as he slipped off his jacket and undid his cufflinks, "the recession has everyone so edgy. I am beginning to understand just how easily Zelman could leverage the tension to pull off his plan."

"Brandt, tell me about your best friend."

"Huh?"

"Tell me about your best friend. You must have a best friend."

"I have a lot of friends."

"I can see that. I mean a best friend, not someone you know because of business or politics."

"Michael Madibara was my best friend in high school. We could talk about anything. But after he went to Cambridge we drifted. It is not the same anymore."

"I thought he was from Zimbabwe. How did you manage to be in the same high school?"

"He was an exchange student at a private high school in my home town."

"How about now? Is there someone you confide in all the time?"

"I guess that would be my Dad. I talk to him all the time, almost every day. We were together a lot when I was growing up. We traveled together, several times a month."

"Did you play baseball together?"

"Janet. I'm Swiss."

"So, does that make you genetically incapable of comprehending baseball?"

Brandt snorted out a sudden laugh. "Yeah, I guess it does." It was good to see his smile again.

"What about other sports, how about...umm..."

"No, we didn't play football, what you call soccer. But we did meet a lot of world leaders."

"But you didn't do anything outside of business and politics?"

"No. Why would we?"

Janet understood Zelman's concern.

"Dr. Mahler," the pilot announced over the jet's speaker system, "we are entering Russian airspace."

Janet glanced out the window, and her jaw dropped.

"Brandt, look!" she croaked in near panic.

Brandt's gaze followed hers. Outside the window, inches from their wingtip, was a Russian MIG fighter jet, its wings laden with a bristling array of rockets.

The MIG was so close that when its pilot raised his visor, she could read the stern determination on his face. She spun around, and an identical warship guarded their other wing.

"Oh God."

"It's okay, Janet. Nikolai is just making a statement."

Had he said that to calm her panic, or his own?

He took her elbow and led her to her seat. "Buckle in for the landing."

The two resolute sentinels escorted them the entire distance to the airfield. As the ground approached, the Lear passed over a column of tanks returning from maneuvers. A long rectangle of soldiers jogged along behind it. A platoon of men threaded its way through a crowded obstacle course. Smoke puffed from a howitzer on an artillery range. The Russian forces were on high alert.

The MIGs continued to track them with undeviating precision. Just as the Lear's wheels touched the runway, the two MIGs peeled off.

"I don't think Nikolai is very happy with our visit," Janet spoke, stating the obvious.

"He is very unhappy with my association with Andy."

"You can tell him all about your breakup. That should help."

Brandt's lips twisted into a frown.

The Lear taxied toward a hangar, halted in front of an arc of jeeps, and its engines pitched down to silence. The gaps between the jeeps were filled with soldiers, their shiny buttons gleaming against their crisp green uniforms. Each cap held a bright red star. They stood at attention, their bayoneted rifles at their sides, implying immediate readiness to kill on command.

Brandt pushed down the door and emerged. Janet followed in his shadow, so close she nearly bumped into him as he stepped off the bottom stair and stopped.

A rotund man in his sixties emerged from behind the soldiers. He wore a plain gray business suit, white shirt and black tie. A cuff of white hair circled his balding head. He stopped and glared at them, his feet spread, his two fists placed on his hips in angry determination. Images of Nikita Khrushchev played in Janet's mind. His displeasure was palpable. She swallowed hard.

# CHAPTER EIGHT

He moved forward, bulldozing toward Brandt. At the last moment he stepped past Brandt and stopped in front of Janet.

"Janet Thompson," he boomed, "You I am very pleased to meet." A warm smile broke across his face, and he took her hand between his two ham sized palms. "Your dissertation is brilliant."

"Thank you, Mr. Minister," the startled Janet replied. "How did you get it?"

"New ideas travel fast these days. And please, call me Nick. I also am pleased to see Dr. Mahler has made such dramatic improvement in his selection of personal friends. Please tell him I am almost ready to forgive him for last visit with me."

Janet blinked at the Russian. She turned to Brandt who stood with stolid calmness, staring straight ahead. Just as she opened her mouth to deliver the minister's words, he faced Brandt.

"Brandt, good to see you again!" he boomed, then laughed with upwelling gusto. Throwing his arms around the off-guard Brandt, he squeezed. Brandt's face turned red and looked like it would pop like an over-pressured tube of toothpaste.

"Good to see you again also, Nikolai," Brandt strained, trying to keep his lungs from collapsing.

"Please, come my friends. Let us move inside."

They walked into the hangar and then to what appeared to be an office the Foreign Minister had temporarily commandeered. The floor was bare cement, as were the blank walls. In the center of the room stood a large wooden desk with an enormous leather chair behind it. Two sturdy metal chairs faced the desk.

Nikolai swept his hand across the seating. Brandt tilted his head at Janet and she sat in one of the seats, he in the other. Nikolai wriggled onto the leather seat, shifting his weight to settle himself in like an eagle settling on its brood of eggs. He reached into a drawer and pulled out a bottle of clear liquid with a small stark black label. Scooping into the drawer a second time, he produced three shot glasses. With practiced precision, he poured.

"Na zdorovye!" he saluted.

"Na zdorovye!" Janet and Brandt repeated. Janet adroitly hefted her glass in salutation, then joined the men as they thumped the glasses down, hers upright and still filled.

"What may I do for you, my young friends?"

"I am concerned about these military exercises of yours, so close to the STC pipeline."

"Why would that be of any concern, my young friend?" he asked, lifting a white brow.

"With America and Europe in such a deep recession, some people would view the Russian military presence as destabilizing to world oil prices. That could dramatically worsen the recession."

"Heh, heh, heh." The man's deep throated laugh reverberated. "You are so much like your father. So direct. So honest. I admire you. But not your Anechka Topnazarov! She is thorn in side of Russian Republic. Tell her this for me: I want Transnov pipeline opened."

"I have, Nikolai."

"Tell her again."

"Nikolai, I have."

The minister's eyes grew hard, and his face stern. With one powerful blow he slammed the desk top with the palm of his hand. The glasses danced. Clear liquid spilled from Janet's glass. The desk groaned and bent under the power of the man, the wooden legs grinding against the cement floor.

He held his two huge hands up before him, turning his wrists and admiring his hands like a sculptor.

"These two hands build Transnov. They are not happy it is without oil. They do not want Anechka to open it. They want to go there and reopen it themselves."

He gestured, turning a huge imaginary valve wheel to release the black gold once again into his pipeline, a satisfied smile overtook his face as he worked.

Then he leaned his weight back into his chair, its wooden frame strained to the limit, creaking like a ship under heavy sail. He rested his two huge feet on top of his desk.

"I've missed my old villa on Caspian Sea." He closed his eyes in dreamy rapture. "Janet, you have chance to enjoy spa?"

"Yes, I did. It was very lovely."

"Yes," the man intoned, his voice sliding into a comfortable sigh. "I will enjoy having my old villa back."

Janet tried to imagine which would be worse, sharing the spa with Nikolai or Andy. It would be equal she decided. They were both the same. Two people divided by a common personality.

"Nikolai," Brandt pleaded. "Your army must not move on Azerbaijan."

"Why?" the man roared. "Give me one reason why I should not."

Brandt's eyes darted back and forth, knowing the man had every reason to invade, and none for restraint.

"Your men. Do you want to risk Russian lives?"

"If American recession gets any worse, my men will need target practice Azeris will provide."

Brandt licked his parched lips.

"Nikolai, please," Brandt spoke in desperation. "Give me two weeks. I will get the Transnov reopened without the Russian army."

"Two weeks without Russian army. Two days with Russian army."

"Nikolai," Janet interrupted, "what about your legacy? Do you want to be the one who is remembered by history as the man who was duped by Mirza ul-Beg and Zelman to destroy America?"

Nikolai sucked in his cheeks contemplating Janet's words.

"One week. You deal with Zelman and relieve ailing economy, or I deal final blow to she-wolf Anechka. But, I promise nothing," he said, standing to end the meeting. "Now go."

A military aide stepped up to the couple. They rose and followed him to the office door. Janet paused and looked back at the stubborn man.

"I promise nothing," the Russian repeated.

*** 

The landscape below was fading to nightfall as the Lear finally cleared Russian airspace and entered the relative safety of the Ukraine.

The bright red glow of sunset still lit the MIG escorts as they suddenly broke their wing hold and zoomed away like two giant hawks looking for new prey.

Janet breathed a sigh of relief. She moved to the front of the cabin, and sat on the sofa style divan. Tucking one leg up under her made her appear relaxed in the safe haven of the Lear when in reality she was tempted to fold up in the fetal position and try not to think. Brandt sat next to her.

"How serious is Nikolai about invading Azerbaijan?" Janet asked.

"Very serious. He is under a lot of political pressure from Moscow to act. I'm surprised he gave us a week."

"If Andy would just reopen the Transnov would Nikolai stand off?"

"Yes. But Andy won't. She's too obstinate. Economically, none of this makes sense. The Transnov is far smaller than the STC. The Russian Republic doesn't need the relatively small amount of oil it would carry. Likewise, the Transnov would not create significant competition to the STC."

"Then why are they fighting?"

"Two reasons. One is internal national politics. The second is pure bull headed entrenchment."

"You know Andy. You're still close. Can't you talk to her?"

"Andy and I were very close once. There was a time when I could talk to her about anything, and she would listen. Until we broke up."

"Tell me about your relationship with her."

"Not much to tell," he said.

He stood and moved to the small galley, obviously uncomfortable with the topic. He poured water into the coffee maker and set a pad of coffee into the holder.

"Did you date her?"

"Yes."

"Are you dating now?"

"No."

He pushed a button, and the coffee machine started to sputter and percolate.

"What about the French magazine? The one with the two of you on it."

"What about it?"

"Brandt, I'm not going to play twenty questions with you!" Janet snapped. "Answer my questions or not. But don't toy with me."

He paused for a moment thinking about what he wanted to say.

"Andy and I started dating in college. We had some pretty wild times together, the STC Pipeline being just one. We soon had a worldwide reputation and were a hot item in all the gossip magazines up until a year ago. Then we broke up, and haven't dated since."

He went to pour himself a cup of coffee. "Do you want some coffee?"

"No. Why did you break up?"

With a huff he set down his cup, and pushed the decanter back into place instead of pouring.

"Coffee's ready," he said to the pilot through the closed cockpit curtain. He sat down next to Janet again. He looked at her for a moment, then his shoulders slumped and he stared at the floor.

"A number of reasons. The main one was that our relationship had grown to the point where we should have started talking about getting married. She wanted to, but I didn't."

The pilot came out. "So, Mirza has gone nearly an entire day without another assassination attempt. She is really slipping," he quipped as he filled a cup with coffee and stepped back into the cockpit.

"Are you against marriage in general, or just to her?"

"Someday I'll get married, definitely not to her," Brandt wagged his head slowly.

"Why?"

"There was something missing. A big part of it was her intolerance. She is hard, and just can't bend. I am a person of compromise. I believe a person needs to grow and change."

"Do you ever think you will get back together?"

He met her gaze again, but his eyes were muted - almost sad.

"There is always speculation in the tabloids that we will. A few weeks ago at the Baku oil conference, Andy and I sat next to each other. The press went crazy. It was good to see her again, but as friends."

"Tell me you didn't like the way she handled the terrorists," Janet pushed.

"I won't deny it. Yes, I like it that Andy is a strong woman. But, she doesn't have a soft side to offset it. If she's changed at all, she's only grown more stubborn."

"Brandt you can't have it both ways, strong and soft."

"Oh, no? I think you're wrong."

For a long moment he fixed her in his bright blue-gray gaze. Then he flashed his signature wry smile and retreated to the rear of the plane to continue his endless calls.

Another reference to her? She wasn't strong like Andy, surely he could see that. She looked at Brandt punching buttons on his phone. Was he really thinking about her? She needed to know. Decision time was nearing. Brussels was almost here. Brussels, then home. Home without Brandt. Too many decisions to be made. Not enough information.

"How much longer until we land?" she asked in frustration.

"We should be approaching Brussels soon. You certainly may ask the pilot." He broke into a conversation in French.

Janet stepped to the cockpit. The pilot sat slouched, asleep in his seat while the aircraft hummed away on auto-pilot.

"Hey, what are you doing?" she scolded the derelict man, nudging his shoulder to wake him up. He slumped forward against his seat straps.

"Brandt, come quickly!" She felt his neck for a pulse.

"What's wrong? What happened?" he asked, crowding into the tiny cockpit, trying to assess the situation.

"His pulse is fine, but he's totally unconscious." She noticed the pilot's empty coffee cup and sniffed. "Chloral hydrate."

"How long will he be out?"

She glanced at the fuel gage.

"About an hour longer than our fuel."

"How do you know so much?"

"I read a lot," she said sitting in the empty co-pilot's seat and clipping herself into the seat harness.

"What are you doing?"

"Preparing for our landing."

"You have a pilot's license?"

"We don't bother with formalities back in Oklahoma. My Dad let me fly his Piper."

"This Lear is a long way from a Piper."

"Hey, two wings and a tail. How complicated could it be?"

She switched off the auto-pilot and the jet immediately went into a dive. She pulled up too hard, and Brandt went flying onto the floor.

"Whoa, there," she muttered as she roller-coastered up and down. It took several stomach lurching tries before she regained control. Then she looked at Brandt sprawled on the floor.

"Hey, you look just like other morning, only no shampoo." She put on the headphones, and found the airport card the pilot had dropped on the floor. She tuned the radio to the correct frequency. "Brussels Tower, this is LJ60 for approach."

"LJ60, Brussels Tower. Negative on approach. We're putting you into hold."

"Negative on hold. Pilot has medical issue and is unconscious. Unlicensed pilot in command."

"What? You can't fly!"

"Well, if you think you can do a better job, you're welcome come on up and get to it."

"Identify yourself."

"Ja..." she caught herself short. "Salty Thompson."

"American?"

"You bet your Belgian waffles I am." She quickly checked the dizzying array of computerized instruments. There was a jumble of words over the radio as the flight controllers discussed how to handle the situation. "Hey, I suggest you start giving me some instructions. I'm only fifty miles out."

"Negative. Too much altitude. Suggest you attempt to circle."

She pulled the throttles back, and nosed the jet down severely.

"LJ, what are you doing?"

She pulled on the air brakes.

"Getting rid of altitude."

"You can't do that!"

She leveled out at approach altitude, pushed the air brakes off, and gave a little throttle.

"Well I just did. Now start talking landing instructions." She pulled on her cowgirl hat and turned to Brandt who had managed to sit up and hold himself there by clinging to the pilot's seat. "The captain has put on the seat belt sign. Please return to your seats and put your seatbacks and tray tables into their fully upright and locked positions."

Brandt smirked as he gingerly stood and complied with her instructions.

Salty scrambled to familiarize herself with the alien craft's bewildering instruments and controls. Everything was computerized. Gone were the old familiar mechanical dials and gages from the Piper. Replaced with touch screen flat panels. There was too much data to absorb quickly enough to do any good. Brandt was right, the Lear was a very long way from her dad's Piper. Deadly right.

While she struggled, Brussels Tower had her make several moves as they vectored her into position. She sensed they were testing her abilities to follow their instructions. Or buying time. Her hope brightened when the distant sight of blue runway lights appeared on the black horizon. But when the red runway end markers came into view her previous bravado evaporated. Janet started to panic, her heart making her chest thump. Her mind flashed back to the first time she landed a Piper.

"You can do it Salty," her father told her.

Time slowed to a crawl as the runway inched closer and her mind surged into overdrive. "You can do it Salty," she repeated to herself. The runway end markers grew larger and larger, then suddenly they flashed beneath her as the Lear passed over the runway and she inched the unfamiliar jet down.

"LJ, you're too high, too fast. Pull up, pull up!"

Cold sweat prickled on Janet's forehead as she stared at her white knuckled grip on the control yoke. Her courage wouldn't hold out for a second pass. It was do or die. At a hundred and eighty miles an hour she was burning up runway fast.

"You can do it Salty."

Her grip loosened. The plane flowed forward in a smooth relentless rush. With deft precision she throttled back the engines, applied flaps and air brakes, let the aircraft flare for a moment to blow off excess energy - then brought her down.

"Yee-Haw!" she yelled as she made a perfect three point landing, not knowing she was heard in five million households listening to the late breaking news.

But the runway markers at the far end were too close. There wasn't enough runway left to stop. She clamped on the wheel brakes. The tower was right, too high, too fast. The brakes groaned and protested as the wheels chattered and bounced along the evaporating runway. The jet swerved right then left as she fought with the foot pedals to keep the struggling jet on the runway. Still the end markers charged toward them. She yanked the brakes harder with both hands. The harsh resonance from the overstrained brakes rattled the entire aircraft and reverberated throughout the cabin. Her shoulder straps stretched taut as the jet rolled over the last of the warning stripes. Then with an ungraceful backward lurch, the jet stopped.

Silence.

The only sound was the low idle of the engines and a metallic ticking sound as the overheated brakes cooled. She breathed, then whistled out a long breath.

"Brussels tower, LJ60. Taxi instructions," she said trying to keep her wavering voice level.

"Negative. Throttle down."

"I can take her off the runway."

"I said throttle down!"

"Okay, okay. Boy you Belgians are an edgy lot." She lifted the bright red finger guards from the two engine switches, and snapped their silver batons down. The engines faded. Within seconds the jet was pummeled with fire foam. "Hey, what are you doing?"

"Standard procedure."

She straightened her cowgirl hat and skipped past Brandt who was struggling to unclasp his tangled seatbelt. She pushed down the door forming the short stairway to the ground and stepped out into a frame of surrealistic foam.

They were surrounded with flashing red lights. Then they were bathed in white glare from nearby TV news trucks, their antenna poles stretched skyward, beaming live signals throughout Europe.

Video cameras zoomed in and flash cameras popped dazing the bewildered novice. But only for a moment. Then Salty Thompson smiled and blew kisses to the world, and made several victorious fashion diva poses. A gentle breeze put the foam into a swaying motion behind her and flipped her long hair up, exposing her bare shoulders and the decadent neckline of the black dress. With one hand behind her head she made a pert little turn as she made Marilyn Monroe winks. Her cowgirl hat and American flag pin left no doubt of the origin of this brash beauty. Taking the hand of a fully suited firefighter, she eased her long legs down the stairs, pointing her high heeled shoes and looking more like a movie star being welcomed on the opening night of her premier than an impromptu and unlikely pilot. The press corps pushed forward.

"Is this the first time you ever landed a jet?"

"How did it feel to be trapped in a run-away airplane?"

"Who designed your dress?"

"Is that your rodeo hat you use in America?"

Answering as many of the reporters' questions as she could, she was led away to a rescue ambulance.

The stairway was vacant as Brandt stumbled out, the pool of light and attention moving away from him. Never before had the limelight been stolen from him so completely. An angry scowl moved across his face. But a moment later his chest heaved up a few chuckles and his lips changed into a smile of admiration. He had finally met his match.

And he liked it.

He caught up with her just before the vehicle drove away.

"You were amazing!"

"Yeah. That was fun. Let's do it again!"

Brandt burst out laughing, then kissed her in the glaring camera lights. Salty put her arms around his neck and pulled him in. She knew who would be on the cover of next week's magazine.

Then the doors closed and the Janet part of her pushed him away.

"No, no more," Janet said, stiffening with embarrassment at what her flirtatious third side had done.

"Janet!" he scolded.

Salty giggled, then pulled him back for a proper kiss.

\*\*\*

The sun was barely up the next morning when the smell of coffee awakened her. She slipped a deep-pile bathrobe over her shoulders and stepped into the central suite area that separated her bedroom from Brandt's. Dressed in a matching hotel robe, Brandt sat at the dining table reading the morning newspaper.

The zeal of his smile left no doubt as to what he thought of how she looked in her robe.

"Good morning," he said, standing to offer her a chair. He poured her some coffee and placed his paper in front of her. There on the front was a half page photo of her cowgirl hat pose.

"You are an overnight celebrity."

"Wow. I'll bet Andy never made the front page." A wave of pride went through Salty's body. Her Dad would have loved that photo.

"No, she didn't. The best she ever did was page four."

"Where is the picture of us kissing?"

"Page *two*."

A clear note of pride came through Brandt's voice. A thrill tickled across Janet's gut as she sat down. "What are you eating?"

"Croissant."

"No, that goop."

"It's Bircher Muesli. A mixture of cereal, fruit and yogurt."

"Yuck."

Her cell phone rang. It was Zelman.

"What did you think of my cowgirl hat?" she asked, mimicking his first words to her.

While she was distracted by Zelman, Brandt put a cup of muesli in front of her.

114

"You were fantastic!" Anton proclaimed. "You are on the cover of every major newspaper on the planet. Le Monde has the best photo, but Milano has the best headline. 'Cowgirl Lands Bronco Jet'."

Brandt put a spoon in her hand.

"Half of Italy is in love with you. The other half is jealous. The entire cover of The London Sun is your photo and 'Yee-Haw!'. If you survive the next three days, I'm going to make you my media chief."

She idly twirled the spoon and stuck it into the cup.

"Thanks, Anton. It's comforting to know I have such a bright, if tenuous, future."

"A word of advice, keep the Mirza problem quiet. She has quite the reputation. It's amazing how fast notoriety can turn to leprosy."

The line went dead. For such a horrid man, there was something almost likeable about Zelman.

Brandt pressed the TV remote. A news clip of the Learjet landing appeared. The faint dark silhouette of the jet appeared against the night sky, accented only by its red and green blinking lights.

"Oh my gosh! I forgot to turn on the landing lights!"

Brandt laughed aloud, throwing back his head.

The video showed the jet touching down, complete with her now world famous Yee-Haw, followed by her glamorous exit from the foam shrouded fuselage. It ended with Brandt's kiss. She did look good in Brandt's little-black-dress and high heels. But it was Anton's cowgirl hat that made the scene. Part of her smiled, and part told her that by tomorrow she will have been forgotten. Then the clip started over. Surely the Belgians must have something better to do than admire this vagabond American over and over. She pushed the TV remote and looked at Brandt finishing his muesli.

"How can you eat that stuff?" she asked.

"Same way you do." He gestured to the table with his chin.

She looked down at her empty cup.

"Oh yuck!" she grimaced, sticking out her tongue in disgust.

Throwing back his head again, he broke into laughter so contagious she couldn't help but join.

"So, what is on today's agenda?" she asked after their laughter died down.

"Just to meet with the president."

"What about the Cray computer?"

"Are you accepting Zelman's challenge?"

"Well, maybe spending another day or two won't hurt. And no, I'm not accepting his challenge. I'm accepting yours."

"The computer is at the WMF headquarters near my apartment in Zurich. We can fly there later today. It's yours as long as you need it."

\*\*\*

The Berlaymont, the modern sweeping X shaped building that houses the European Commission, the EU's executive branch, loomed in front of their limousine.

"Wow, the building is huge. So much larger than the US Capitol Building. So much glass." Janet gawked.

"Yes, indeed. The locals call it the Ber-lay-monster. We Europeans lack the efficiency you Americans take for granted."

The guards didn't ask for Brandt's identification as they were guided to a darkened glassed in gallery overlooking the twenty-seven member Council meeting room. Several dignitaries seated in the gallery nodded welcome to Brandt in hushed silence.

Janet was glad for Brandt's fashion sense. The fitted dark suit with its shimmering brocade skirt and silk jacket made her feel as if she fit in with the other well-dressed women. The diminutive print and flowing style of her blouse gave her a refined feminine aspect that turned heads. Or were they gawks of recognition for Cowgirl and her hat? Brandt had said the black hat didn't go with the suit, but Janet wore it anyway. It seemed a part of her new personality.

Representatives from each of the twenty seven European states entered the main room and took their seats at the sprawling oval table. Everyone rose as the president entered and took his seat at the apex. He was a handsome man with broad shoulders and a trim figure that filled his suit perfectly. Salt and pepper hair and blazing gray blue eyes, like Brandt's, told everyone he was a man of authority.

The president spent a moment theatrically organizing his papers then stood. His solemn eyes swept around the table, lingering for moment on each member.

"Here, put these on." Brandt handed Janet a pair of headphones and flipped a switch to English.

"Members of the council," the simultaneous translator spoke over the voice of the president, "I am here to warn the People of Europe of an evil cloud approaching us."

His ominous oration warned of one thing, the economic woes that Anton Zelman was raining over the world. He started with Africa, describing how the fertile land of Zimbabwe was no longer able to feed its people. Then to America, and the dangerous concentration of financial power to one company, SBU. Asia, then his words traveled to Europe, the last bastion of defense against the fires of devastation that were sweeping around the globe. As his description traveled, so did the level of his voice as well as the level of threat he described.

"He makes Zelman sound awful," she whispered, lifting a single headphone from one ear.

"Yeah, he really hates Zelman."

"Why?"

"Many reasons, but mostly because Zelman beat him out of the SBU directorship. It's been open warfare ever since."

"What are they going to do with Zelman?"

"Nothing. This is Europe. We don't actually do anything."

Janet snickered, but quickly covered her lips with her knuckle as she was stared down by one of the diplomatic matrons.

Finally the president finished speaking. Everyone stood and applauded as he left. Janet figured they were all happy he had finally stopped shouting. She removed her headphones and stood with Brandt.

"He makes Zelman sound so evil," she said as Brandt led her from the gallery.

"Janet..." Brandt stopped walking and looked her in the eyes. "These are not normal times. This is not just another recession that will end in a year." His eyes were filled was a serious concern Janet had never seen in the unflappable Brandt. "Zelman and Mirza must be stopped." Then his face lightened. "Come. I'll introduce you to the president." He turned and directed her through a series of halls. A guard nodded to them as they simply strode past him and without knocking went right into the president's office.

"Janet Thompson," the president enthused, standing from behind his massive desk and walking toward her. "I'm so happy to meet you. Brandt has told me so much about you. Judging from your television appearance last night, he has been very accurate in his description. And I found your dissertation to be brilliant."

"You got a copy of it, too?"

"Many things move across my desk." He turned. "You look well, Brandt."

"So do you, Dad."

Janet's gut twisted in a twinge of surprise. She suddenly understood Brandt's casual admiration of the man. She also noticed their common features that extended beyond general good looks.

"Come, Cowgirl. Let us eat. I want to hear all about how you will help me stop Zelman. To finally give me my revenge."

They took an elevator to the top floor which led to a private dining room that overlooked the city. The large oval table could seat twenty eight. Today there were just three. The president seated Janet on the side, then took the seat at the head of the table. Brandt sat across from Janet.

The waiter held a bottle of wine for Brandt's approval. Brandt nodded and the waiter uncorked it, then poured a small amount into Brandt's glass. He took a sip, then nodded his approval to the waiter. Brandt's father also nodded at the waiter. After the man finished pouring their wine he withdrew to obtain their luncheon.

"Do you enjoy seafood?" the statesman asked.

"Why do you ask, Mr. President?"

"Please, call me Valter. Because Americans love to have mussels in Brussels. Even your American president used that line with me. Your people have such a bizarre sense of humor. Although I must admit, even I laughed at your 'bet your Belgian waffles' comment. It's already the latest school boy catch phrase across the continent."

"I'm glad you enjoyed it," Janet beamed, taking in the jolt of pleasure at her unrequested fame.

"And how is Anechka?" asked Valter. The stone silence that followed told him everything he needed to know. "Oh, I see."

"We had a pleasant conversation with Nikolai Brosnarov yesterday. He gave us a week to resolve the Transnov issue."

"That is a pleasant surprise. Not that it will do any good in the end. I am already forming the team to negotiate the Russian withdrawal from Azerbaijan. He must have a logistics problem, and needs the extra time."

"I think not," Brandt mused. "Janet was able to appeal to his vanity by commenting on his legacy in history if he was duped by Zelman."

Valter raised an impressed eye brow in Janet's direction.

"Clever move," he said to her. "Perhaps I should have you join the withdrawal negotiations."

Embarrassed by the comments, Janet said nothing.

Their meal arrived. Valter took up his fork, but waited to see Janet's reaction to her food. The mussels were delightfully cooked in white wine, and lightly seasoned with fresh chopped basil and pepper. Valter beamed when her face reacted to the pleasure of the food. They were delicious and she ate them studiously while listening to the men catch up on personal news.

"Janet and I will be flying to Zurich later to use the WMF super computer to analyze Zelman's activities," Brandt said to change the subject back to business.

"Ah, good. As you just heard, I am trying to warn everyone about Zelman's diabolical plans. But this is a difficult thing to prove with any certainty. Perhaps the computer can provide proof."

"Rashid Al-Falasi thinks Zelman's first move will be to destroy SBU," said Brandt.

"Can you imagine such a thing? I cannot. The director himself destroying his own bank, after he worked so hard to wrest it out of my hands. Dear God, I cannot think of the legacy of the family's bank being brought down to such a low purpose. Did Rashid say how we would know if Zelman is about to do such an atrocious thing?"

"He said Zelman would first move his personal money out of SBU."

"Good. That, of course, is against the law and will allow me to arrest him." Valter looked at Janet. "Please, you must fly to Zurich immediately and prepare to capture Herr Zelman in his own trap."

Janet nodded and bit down on her lower lip. It sounded as if so much depended on her skill with the computer. She had no idea what the numbers would tell her.

"How long do you think we have before we can catch Zelman trying to destroy SBU?" Valter asked.

"Zelman spoke of six days. That was three days ago," Janet informed.

"In less than three days we will have him," said Valter, lifting his glass to offer a silent toast.

Valter stopped short when an aide strode into the room and bent to whisper into Valter's ear. Valter murmured something back, but the aide shook his head in the negative, then he left.

"What is the matter?" Brandt asked.

"SBU has just declared insolvency," the president beamed with a self-satisfied smile.

"Did Zelman pull his money out before hand?"

"No. It looks like his timing was off, and he has shot himself in the foot."

"Well, that should take care of Zelman for good," Brandt declared with conviction.

"He must have overextended the bank," Valter said, "and run out of money before he could complete his plan. Zelman has outfoxed himself. He is done for, SBU is mine, and you Ms. Thompson, are a free woman."

"What do you mean?"

"With Zelman no longer a player in this dangerous game, your new friend Mirza will quickly lose interest in you."

A conflicting array of emotions swept over Janet. She was relieved that she would no longer be in danger. But she was also sad that her unexpected importance was suddenly gone. Valter no longer needed her.

More importantly, neither did Brandt.

# CHAPTER NINE

"Well, I must be going," Valter said. "It was very pleasant meeting you Ms. Thompson. I hope you have a pleasant trip back to the United States. Brandt, see her out for me, will you?"

An awkward chill was left in the wake of Janet's former celebrity status. How quickly she'd gone from 'Janet' and 'Cowgirl' to 'Ms. Thompson'. She suddenly felt as if she'd overstayed her welcome.

Valter stood and exited the room, leaving an empty vacuum behind him. That was it. She was no longer needed in Europe. She wouldn't even be able to finish her dissertation research on Africa. She might have to start her paper all over from scratch. All she had to show for her foolish choices was a wrecked apartment and Zelman's Midnight hat. She should have stayed in Tulsa where she belonged.

"Well, I guess I should head to the airport and see about getting my ticket back to America." She stood and looked to the door.

"Janet, don't go. Why not stay for a few days? I could show you all the sights."

"Brandt, I barely have enough money for a ticket, never mind sightseeing."

"Please, it will be my treat." He walked to her. His penetrating gaze pierced her like an electric jolt, then he leaned in and kissed her, zapping her with a startling energy. "I don't want you to go."

She pulled away, tired of being jolted and shocked. "I don't know."

"Stay for a few days. We'll have some fun."

"I'm not sure I'm interested in your kind of fun."

"You know what I mean. You know who I am."

"Do I, Brandt? I don't really know you at all." Janet couldn't keep the hurt and anger from her voice.

"Three days, eight countries, two shootings, one bomb, one ruined elevator, and one plane with no pilot. I saved your life, you saved mine. No, you're wrong. I think we know each other pretty well."

"How well? What is my favorite color?" she challenged. "Do I like hot dogs with mustard or ketchup? Do I own a cat? No, you know nothing about me or who I am as a person."

"You're right. I know none of those things. But I know something no one else does. I know why you left Oklahoma. To find something you lost when your father died. Yourself. I'm the only one who has ever met Salty or Solterra. No one else saw you sweat trying to land an airplane. Only I heard you choking down your own sobs in the airplane lavatory. No one else felt the kickback from the jealousy that raged within you over Andy. I know you very well."

"You! You make me so angry!" She went to pound his chest with the ball of her fist but stopped. Instead she leaned to him, laid her forehead where she had aimed her blow and started sobbing.

Brandt put his hands into her hair and massaged her head with his fingers.

"Cry," he said, his voice soft. "It's okay. Go ahead and cry."

Janet buried her face into his warm chest and cried. So much had happened. So much that was out of her control. She was out of her element, and out of her league, everywhere she turned. The emotional roller coaster was too much to handle.

"I'm sorry. You must think I'm a cotton headed coward."

"That is not what I think at all." He slid the side of his index finger under her chin and lifted, then softly placed his lips on hers. "That is not what I think at all," he repeated.

He kissed her again, moving his lips over hers and sending waves of heated sensation all the way down to her toes.

"Please stay."

"Okay," she whimpered. "I'll stay for a couple of days."

"Good," he throated with a kiss, enveloping her in his warm arms. Her arms looped around his neck. "I still have time to win you over," he whispered. His lips were soft and light. "I'd like to show you the soft side of Europe. There is a reception at five o'clock this afternoon at the Royal Museum. Then we'll fly to my apartment in Zurich. Let's just walk the city until then. It is a beautiful day. Let's enjoy it together."

Hand in hand they walked away from the Berlaymont and stepped to their limo. A short drive later they emerged and with aimless wandering, entered the city's center. The late August air was warm and still. Music from a small brass band came from a side street.

"Manneken Pis," he said.

"What?"

"That music is from the procession for the Manneken Pis."

"What is that?"

"Come, I'll show you."

They soon caught up with the music as the tiny ensemble approached a small bronze fountain containing the statue of a young cherub boy, his left hand aiming his mock urine flow into the basin below. The group started to carefully dress the statue.

"All this fuss is for a little statue?"

"Oh no, this is perhaps the most important landmark in the city. Legend says that the enemy kidnapped the infant king, Godfrey of Leuven. They placed him in a basket hung from a tree branch to taunt and goad the local army into a losing battle. Just as they were about to attack, the tiny king peed onto the enemies' heads, distracting them and ensuring a victory for his people."

Janet laughed at the idea. "Even baby pee can be an inflective," she joked.

"Yes, I suppose it can."

The cluster of spectators blocked Janet and Brandt's view as the minstrels finished their task of dressing the statue. When they stepped back the landmark was dressed in cowboy clothes, complete with black cowboy hat and turquoise concho.

"Zelman!" squeaked Janet in panic, scanning the crowd for assassins.

"No, no. Manneken Pis has over a hundred outfits. This one has been around for years."

She smiled at the foolishness of her reaction. Zelman was gone. Defeated. Done for. She had nothing more to fear.

Somehow she wasn't quite convinced. She forced herself to shrug off her sense of pending doom.

"They seemed to enjoy dressing that statue," she said watching the procession fade away along the street.

"Yes. It is a long tradition."

"How about you? Do you enjoy dressing me?" She set one hand on her hip.

"What do you mean?"

"Ever since I arrived, everything I've worn was selected by you. You have been dressing me like a toy doll."

"Don't you like the clothes I buy for you?" His shoulders slouched and he made a small adorable frown.

"Yes, I do. That is not the point. I feel like a mannequin in a department store window. I am not a puppet under your control." She raised her arms and shook them up and down, miming strings attached to her wrists. "I want to select my own clothes."

"I'm not stopping you."

"But...I don't know how. Teach me about fashion," she said, hardly keeping the demand from her tone.

"Fashion?" He set two fingers against his chin as he looked at her, measuring his response. "Hmmm...okay." He looked up and down the street, deciding where to take her. He led her around a corner to an upscale boutique.

"Herr Dr. Mahler!" the saleswomen enthused. "Welcome to my shop. I am honored by your visit. How may I help you?"

"My friend would like to learn about fashion."

"Learn about fashion?" The woman appraised Janet in a quick scan. "The famous American Cowgirl, Salty Thompson, already made quite an impressive fashion statement last night."

Janet stepped forward and offered her hand. "Please, just call me Janet. And I really do need to learn."

The woman made a brief handshake and let a smile emerge. "What would you like to learn?"

"Basics. I need basics."

"Hmmm." The woman scanned Janet's features, appraising her attributes.

"Well, first of all, you must consider color. You have red hair with very light cool skin and green eyes. Blacks, like what you have on now will always work for you. So will grays and off whites. Avoid reds and bright orange or bright green. They will clash with your skin and hair. Select earth and autumn tones, darker orange and darker green is good, terracotta, olive, maroon, apricot, gold and golden yellow. Blue will work from the waist down. Never wear pastels, especially pink. Be careful with purple, choose darker shades especially while you are learning. White will also work, especially in the summer."

"Okay, that's a lot to remember. What about the style?"

"You are slender, with a shapely figure, and a light bounce to your step that will complement both slim lines and wide flounces alike. You can basically wear anything, but avoid bland styles. Also, heavy or complex prints won't work well for you. Textures, patterns and clothes that make a statement will always work."

"What would you suggest for today?"

"Let's start with a basic suit. A black wool skirt with a charcoal gray textured linen jacket, perhaps. For your blouse," the saleswoman placed her chin in her hand, scanning Janet, "classic silk with something a little bit bold, perhaps this." She held a sweeping white silk blouse, with abundantly over cut pull ties up to her. "Yes, that works. Would you care to try it on?"

"Yes."

Janet took her clothes to the changing room. A few minutes later she stepped out to a mirror.

"Oh, I like that," the woman intoned. Janet looked to Brandt, whose signature grin told her his opinion.

Over the next hour and a half, the two women selected several more sets, varying the coordinating pieces until they were satisfied with the look. Brandt sat in patient proximity, a contented smile hovering on his face as he watched Janet try on outfit after outfit. At last she settled on her final choices. She decided to wear the linen jacket from the store. It complemented her brocade skirt very well.

"My driver will collect the packages," Brandt instructed as they stepped from the boutique.

"Thank you," said Janet to Brandt. "Especially for letting me win our little battle over clothes."

"Was it a battle? Well, no problem. I'm Swiss. We're all about compromise."

"What do you mean?"

"It's the Swiss way. We try to see things from the other person's point of view. Once in our history we had a civil war, about the same time as your American one. By your standards, it was a small war. But it had a big impact. We realized we needed to get along. We don't even have a common language, yet we manage. A hundred people died in our civil war. Six hundred thousand died in yours. I like the Swiss way of compromise better."

They continued walking. Brandt kept Janet's arm wrapped over his. They wandered along several streets past tall, stately buildings and into a lovely expanse of park. The afternoon air was mildly fragrant with the combined scent of many plantings along the angular paths. Warm sunshine bathed those who had gathered at the park for rest or recreation. Janet admired the casual layout of the landscaped park and enjoyed the peaceful atmosphere. For the first time in several days she felt she could relax and let go of her concerns.

"Do you want to try a treat that even an American can enjoy?" Brandt asked as they passed out of the beautiful park.

"Sure, what?"

He took her hand and swept her into a small hole-in-the-wall diner.

"This is the birthplace of the French Fry. McDonalds, eat your heart out."

The air was heavy with the tang of hot oil and the pungent scent of fried potatoes and salt. Brandt handed her a tiny cardboard basket.

What is this?" she said pointing to a small container in her basket.

"Mayonnaise. You have that in America."

"On french-fries?"

"Of course. What else would you put on them? Ketchup?"

She picked up a fry, blew on it to cool it, dipped it in the mayonnaise with a scowl and tasted it with her tongue.

"Hmm," she intoned with approval. Biting into it, she crunched the crisp outer layer and found the softer texture inside.

"Oh, my. This is amazing."

"Their secret is to fry them twice. With an ample rest in between." Brandt ordered another container, and they continued their walk along the street.

"I love this city. Next to my home in Zurich, this is where I most love to be."

"What about Africa?" she asked.

"I enjoy my work in Africa and around the world. But I never leave Europe for more than a week or two without coming back."

"I guess I've disrupted your life quite a bit, haven't I? You should be back in Zurich, chained to your desk," Janet goaded with an impish smile.

"No! I'm having too much fun with you. Especially now that you're not being shot at."

Janet snorted out a laugh and clamped back onto Brandt's arm.

"How long have Zelman and your father been rivals?"

"Since birth."

Janet chuckled. "No, really. How long have they been fighting?"

"I'm serious, since birth. They were born on the exact same day, in different parts of Europe. They are half brothers, and they have battled ever since they first met."

Janet stopped walking and stared up at Brandt. No wry grin, no devilish sparkle to his eyes. He wasn't kidding.

"Yes, Zelman is my uncle. It's hard to believe, I know."

Janet blinked. Her mind blank.

"You see, my grandfather had a life-long love affair with an actress in Prague, Maria Zelman. That was where Anton was born. My grandfather was the director of what later became SBU, and he traveled often to Eastern Europe. My father was born in Munich, where my grandfather lived with my grandmother. My father's mother was German, and his official residence is still in Munich at his family's original home."

Janet's mind raced to catch up with all the new information and deal with the latest unexpected turn. "Oh. That's how your father can be involved in European Union politics, even though Switzerland is not a part of the EU."

Brandt nodded, trying to gauge her oddly unemotional reaction.

"So, Zelman grew up in a soviet-controlled country?"

"My grandfather brought his other family back to Munich just before the Iron Curtain went up."

Janet raised a brow, trying hard to absorb the twists of fate and the intertwining relationships. "When did your German grandmother find out?"

"Oh, my grandfather was very open about the whole thing from the beginning. Zelman gets that from him. He never lies. Then again, he never tells the truth either. That's why if Zelman says he didn't shoot at you, then we can believe he didn't. But that doesn't mean he won't try tomorrow."

Janet shook her head. It was too much to think about.

"Anyway," Brandt continued, "my father's mother was very jealous of Maria. But my grandfather wanted his two boys to grow up together. Dad was the perfect one, Anton the black sheep. Naturally, they clashed. Dad was always trying to outdo his half brother. But somehow, Anton never failed to find a way to steal victory away from him."

Now Janet nodded. She believed Zelman was capable of anything.

"After my grandfather worked to unite several banks to form SBU, he announced his retirement. My father had been groomed all along to be the new director. Just before my father took the office, Zelman orchestrated a hostile takeover. My grandfather capitulated. I think the reality was that he didn't have to, but was so impressed by his bastard son, that he gave it all to him. My father was livid, and hasn't recovered to this day. His every waking moment is spent calculating revenge. That is why he was so interested in you. I'm sorry he gave you such a cold brush off. It wasn't because he didn't want to be with you. I'm sure he wanted to return to his office to simultaneously gloat about Zelman's ruin and mourn the collapse of SBU. Or plan its recovery."

"What about you? Do you want to gloat?"

"Oh, I don't know. My uncle is very maddening and certainly deserves what happened. But there is also something very attractive about him. I've never been close to Uncle Anton as far as spending time with him. He was never, ever welcome at our home near Zurich. But he has always been a presence in my life. He has a tantalizing and bizarre charm that makes you enjoy your time with him, even while knowing he may be using and manipulating you in the process. He can make you believe you can actually trust him."

Their meandering had led them to the massive stone front of the Royal Museum. Red banners, announcing a travelling exhibition of Japanese art, hung from its bronze statue capped pillars. Once inside, Brandt was waved through the security checkpoint, but a guard motioned Janet off to the side. A short, burly woman began flourishing a metal detecting wand over her, its squealing whine modulating embarrassingly as it passed over her brassiere. When she finished, Janet went to stalk away, but the woman uttered something.

"What?" Janet snapped.

"The hat. The hat stays here," the woman said with hand extended.

Janet looked to Brandt for guidance, but he was turned away, talking to some unknown person. She shouldn't let the guard intimidate her like that. And she didn't want to be without her hat. It had become a twisted source of security knowing such a powerful man was listening to her every move. Reluctantly she handed over her possession, and gingerly stepped away, half-expecting another call back.

She caught up to Brandt in a quick series of steps, but he didn't offer his arm as they walked side by side into the main hall. Obviously she was no longer his escort. They were in public, and the other Brandt had emerged. Now what was her role? How should she introduce herself? Teacher, economist, celebrity, bomb target, guest, friend, cast-away? Her personalities were multiplying.

"Brandt!" an older man greeted them. "Comment-allez-vous?"

"I am well, Francois, thank you. May I introduce my friend, American Economist Janet Thompson. Janet, this is Francois Legrand, the museum's curator."

"Dr. Thompson. Forgive me, but I didn't realize you didn't speak French," the curator apologized taking her hand for a light handshake.

"Yeah, uh sorry. I guess we don't use much French in Oklahoma," she replied awkwardly.

"But, of course." The man turned from Janet to Brandt. "My friend, I am so glad that you could join us today. Your presence is an unexpected pleasure. Did you know that Prime Minister Umigaki is here? He will be most delighted to see you."

"I had not been able to confirm that he was coming. I'm glad he is here. I haven't seen him in several months and there are some things I'd like his opinion about."

Janet followed Brandt's gaze toward a compact man with soft gray hair, a round face and dark eyes. The Prime Minister raised his hand in greeting upon seeing Brandt. The two men stepped toward each other.

"Brandt, it is very good to see you."

"And good to see you, Shiro," he said shaking hands while reaching around for pats on the back. "This is my friend, economist Janet Thompson."

"I am pleased to meet you, Dr. Thompson," he said, with a formal shallow bow to her. Not knowing the proper protocol, Janet awkwardly leaned forward and extended her hand. Offended, the Prime Minister simply stood straight, brushed his suit coat, and turned away toward Brandt.

Janet tried to hide her embarrassment over her lack of social grace by looking up at the ornate pillared arches of the open galleria that looked down upon the main hall. Realizing her provincial gawking was not helping her gain poise, she scanned the room and was quickly rescued by a wine steward who offered her a glass.

Janet took a heavy sip, taking in the sea of elegant visitors over the rim of her glass. A salmon pink kimono clad woman approached, her rapid steps controlled by the high platformed shoes she wore.

"Brandt, I am so very glad to see you." She took Brandt's hand and pressed it warmly between her two hands. "How is your father? I was hoping to see him again."

"He will be here shortly. He has been terribly busy lately, otherwise he is very well."

"Ah yes, your tyrannical uncle has been making everyone's life difficult lately, hasn't he?"

129

"Indeed he has." Brandt took a half-step back, revealing Janet hiding behind him, her lips still poised at the edge of her wine glass. "Fumiko, this is my friend, economist Janet Thompson."

She swung around to Janet, her waist length string of pearls swaying in the open air. Her traditional Japanese makeup gave her face a doll-like sheen of perfection.

"Dr. Thompson, I am most pleased to meet you." She made a brief bow.

"Yes, me too." Janet mimicked the woman's bow and didn't even spill a drop of wine. She was quite pleased with herself. Until panic struck as Brandt was pulled away with the Prime Minister. She faced the Japanese woman with a pasty smile.

"Do you work at the WMF with Brandt, Dr. Thompson?"

"No, not really. I'm just a teacher working toward my PhD."

"Oh," the woman replied. "I see."

The smaller woman's gaze strayed to a cluster of people. Lifting a hand in greeting, she shuffled away, leaving Janet marooned in isolation, contemplating her wine glass. She attracted a few awkward stares as she stepped over to a side table and set her nearly-full glass down next to a tray of hors d'oeuvres.

An uncultured girl from Oklahoma didn't belong in this erudite world, a world in which Brandt not merely thrived but dominated. She watched as he nodded greetings at people a short distance away, even as he spoke earnestly with the Prime Minister. It seemed that everyone there was eager to catch Brandt's eye.

Janet glanced back toward the exit. It beckoned with the enticing promise of freedom. She surveyed a path toward it. She could dodge around the small groupings of conversation. No one was looking her way. She had no possessions. She could simply walk out the door, collect her hat and be gone. She remembered seeing a subway stop near the museum. From the subway, the airport should only be a short distance. In five minutes this tension-filled and confusing world could be behind her. Her cell phone rang.

"Dr. Jones." she said in a low tone, relieved to be momentarily rescued from the condescension that surrounded her.

"I heard that SBU collapsed today. Does that mean you lost your grant money to study in Zimbabwe?"

"Yes, that is one way of putting it."

"Do you need help buying a ticket home?"

"No, I have enough. Brandt, ah Dr. Mahler, invited me to stay a few days in Europe, but I think I will head home sooner."

"That is too bad. You went all the way to Europe. It would be nice to see a few things while you are there."

"Yeah, well, I don't seem to fit in here. I think I belong back in Tulsa."

"I understand. I feel that way sometimes too. I'll see you soon."

"Yes, it will be good to see you. Bye."

Janet closed her phone, stared at the floor for a moment to gather her courage, took a deep breath and started toward the exit. Turning to look back to see if Brandt was watching, she accidently bumped into Mrs. Umigaki.

"Oh!" the woman startled, her pearls swaying wildly.

"I'm very sorry!" exclaimed Janet, her face turning as pink as the woman's dress. "Great pearls," Janet said, focusing on anything that would serve to cover more embarrassment.

"Thank you," replied the woman, pressing the swinging strand against her chest.

"I love pearls. Do you know why?"

"Why?"

"Because they go with everything!" Janet enthused. Was the porcelain face suppressing a smile? Janet glanced at the woman's ears. Two diamond studs graced her tiny earlobes. "Too bad you don't have earrings that match. They would look beautiful on you."

The woman responded with a scowl.

Oh great. "Did I say something wrong?"

"You'll have to ask him about it," the little woman fumed, jutting her chin in her husband's direction.

"What? He wouldn't buy them for you?"

"I've been waiting two anniversaries."

"Well, come with me," the brazen American offered, pulling her new confidant toward the Prime Minister.

"Shiro," she blurted with unrefined authority, "what is this I hear about you not getting Fumiko her matching earrings?"

"Excuse me, please?" the Prime Minister stated, hiding his surprise behind an expressionless face.

Two Japanese gentlemen who had been standing at a discrete distance suddenly took intense interest in the events, placing their right hands under their suit coats.

"You've made her wait more than two anniversaries for the matching earrings?"

Fumiko nodded harsh agreement with her new friend as the Prime Minister stood blinking in incredulous silence.

"Shiro," huffed Janet, "I expect this inexcusable oversight to be resolved as soon as you get back to Japan."

The Prime Minister made a mild snort along with a curt nod of his head.

Taking Fumiko by the arm, Janet led her away. "Now make sure he gets the proper size and color to match the necklace. If he doesn't I want to know about it."

Fumiko giggled at the idea. She was remarkably girlish for an older woman. Janet smiled. The Prime Minister and Brandt gaped as the two women walked away, arm in arm. The two Japanese men relaxed, withdrawing their hands.

\*\*\*

Dusk had settled over the city by the time Janet and Brandt emerged from the museum. Janet twirled her hat upside down by its leather cords as they strolled along. The streets of Brussels were busy with after-work relaxations. Bright neon signs spread colorful light between the buildings. Music drifted from a cafe accompanied by the discordant screech of a karaoke singer.

"Come on," said Brandt as he pulled her inside. They sat at a small table and Brandt ordered two beers while they watched the amateurs' painful renditions.

"Let's go," he said during a lull in the singing, pulling her up to the microphone.

"Brandt," Janet protested, "I'm not good in front of people."

"You'll do fine."

"I won't do fine. Look at what happened at the art museum."

But it was too late. He had already shoved a microphone into her hand and the music started. Janet sheepishly mouthed the words from Shania Twain's "Man, I Feel like a Woman" as they moved across the karaoke monitor.

"Whoa, whoa, stop, stop the music." Brandt gestured to the person next to the karaoke machine to push the stop button. He pulled Janet back to their table. He leaned his head down to hers. "Janet, you stay here. Salty and Solterra come with me." He put her hat on her head, and pulled her back to the microphone. With her hat on, the cafe erupted in recognition of the previous stranger.

"Cowgirl!" they chorused.

The music started again. Salty's heart revved up. Then, in dismay she watched Brandt return to their table and settle down behind his beer.

"Hey!" she shouted at him for abandoning her.

Her voice boomed through the tiny café with the microphone's help. Brandt laughed. Salty's face flushed. Everyone was looking at her. Her eyes scanned the crowd across the little café. With a sudden burst they chorused 'Hey, Cowgirl!' back to her.

The electric beat of the music started. Encouraged by the enthusiastic response, she dove in with the song. "Let's go girls!"

She brought her hands together and bumped the microphone against her palm for tempo. The crowd at the café cheered and joined in. With everyone clapping time Solterra's eyes locked with Brandt's. She didn't need to read the words on the karaoke console.

"I'm going out tonight - I'm feelin' alright," she sang with a clear gusto she never knew she had.

She swung her hips and tossed her hair. The crowd erupted. With one hand skyward, she spun around. Then, pulling off her linen jacket, she swung it over her head. Half the crowd stood to sway along with her, joining in her loose dance.

"The best thing about being a woman..." she continued as a handsome, blonde guy from the crowd came up to her. She put her arm around his waist, and they swung about in unison. To Brandt's horror, the man unbuttoned his shirt and, bare-chested, placed it on Solterra's shoulders in anticipation of the next line.

"Men's shirts - short skirts," she sang as she teasingly hiked her skirt up from mid calf to mini-skirt height. The crowd whooped and hollered.

Brandt's wooden smile failed to hide the unfamiliar pain of jealousy as he rose up out of his seat and stood unmoving. When the song ended, the cafe erupted into applause. The blonde made to kiss Solterra, but she put out her hand to return his shirt. When he took it she turned and bowed to the crowd's on-going applause. It took several minutes before the excited crowd allowed Solterra to return to her table. They applauded and whistled as she blew her now world famous kisses, and returned to the table.

"You don't seem very happy," she jeered to the scowling Brandt.

He frowned as she settled back down at their table. She took a deep draught of her beer. The crowd cheered her on, but she didn't finish the whole glass.

"You're the one who let Solterra out of her cage."

The crowd begged for more of Cowgirl, banging their mugs on their tables.

"Come on. Let's get out of here," he said, standing, turning his back and stomping to the door.

"What's the matter, Brandt?" she asked with sly scolding tones when they were outside. "You don't like getting payback for Andy?"

# CHAPTER TEN

"No," he said glaring at her, his eyes narrowed slits, his lips a thin line.

"Well, at least I didn't kiss the guy. Twice!"

"I didn't kiss her. She kissed me."

"Could have fooled me. It didn't look like you were fighting real hard."

"I didn't do anything wrong. It's over between us."

"Hummph! Looks like nobody bothered to tell her!"

He angled his shoulder away from her, and folded his arms. They stood in silence for a moment. Then his upper body relaxed, and he turned back. He blew a hard breath through his lips.

"Okay, you got me. I can't believe I'm asking forgiveness for enjoying a kiss. But look Janet, I could never live with a woman like Andy. I needed something more, but I didn't know what it was. Until I met you."

His eyes became soft and round. With one brow quirked up he looked vulnerable. When he pulled her to him, she gave in, leaning into him like she was made of warm clay.

"It's not so easy to resist, is it?" he whispered, holding his lips against hers.

He kissed her, a possessive kiss that told her that she could belong to him, that she should belong to him. When he broke the kiss, he put his arms around her, and held her tight. She let out a long sigh. She wanted to hold onto this moment forever.

"Cowgirl!" came a shout from behind them.

Janet turned to wave. Knowing the dangers of notoriety, Brandt kept hold of her waist and turned her away. He hustled her away from the group of men coming toward them. With rapid steps they turned down one street, then another, losing themselves in the darkness and crowds. Gradually Brandt slowed their pace until they were again strolling.

Cool night air invigorated them as they walked into the Saint Hubert Gallery, the century-and-a-half-old glass shopping mall. They sauntered in easy leisurely steps down the length of the building, arms around one another's waists. Just the two of them, alone again.

"Tell me more about your parents," Brandt asked.

"There's not much to tell."

"Well, let's see, you've already told me your father was an oilfield repairman who flew a Piper Cub. What was your mother like?"

"My mother was a perfectionist. As a girl, she always had perfect grades and perfect school attendance. She started teaching Sunday school when she was twelve."

"I guess Janet really is your mother's daughter."

She chuckled softly, but Brandt became quiet, almost pensive.

"Thank you. For staying," Brandt said at last.

"Yeah. I'm having fun," she admitted.

Now that her adventure was winding down, Janet thought about how it would feel to leave Brandt in a few days. Ache sat on her chest, not for more adventure but for Brandt, to see if she really could be his. She wanted him. Wanted to consume him, bring him into her and never let him go. Analytical Janet admired Brandt for his work in economics. Tomboy Salty liked to beat Brandt at mountain biking. And there was something more. Solterra. A whole new portion of her personality was breaking out. And now that she was out, there might be no going back.

The soft glow of the lamps that hung from the gallery walls warmed the night shrouded space. Solterra stopped, pulled Brandt around to her, and holding his face between the palms of her hands, kissed him. At first it was just a light touch of the lips, a soft seductive brush. Then she pulled him closer. Her arms slipped around his neck and a consuming fire flashed across her. The gnawing ache built within her. She finally released her hold on his lips, and raised her chin as Brandt bent to her neck. He attacked the two spots on either side of her throat that sent thrills down her arms.

"Solterra," he murmured.

The third point in her personality triangle was fighting to emerge. But Brandt was the most eligible bachelor in Europe. How many times had he been in this situation with a woman? Probably hundreds. He himself told her he was a student of women. And she doubted that he really knew what he ultimately wanted in a woman. As wonderful as he was, he would soon tire of her. In a few days he would let her go. Back to America. And that would be the end of her time with Brandt Mahler. She pulled away from him.

Brandt's eyes were hungry, but he released his hold.

"Solterra is not ready," he stated.

"Oh, Solterra is ready. It's Janet who thinks you're too smooth." She reached to stroke the edge of his jaw. She made a mild smile.

Brandt caught her hand and held it there. "If you are afraid of getting more involved, I understand."

"Do you, Brandt? You've been here before. Women, money, jets, the media. I haven't. I'm just a simple girl from Oklahoma. I'm completely out of my depth. In a few days I'll go home. And you'll let me. Even Solterra isn't ready for a broken heart."

Brandt held her with his eyes, carefully forming his words.

"You're wrong. You are the most amazing woman I've ever met. I don't know of another woman who could write your theory of inflectives, land a bronco jet, or kiss me like you just did. Janet, Salty, Solterra. Each is spectacular. But to find all three in one woman? That will never happen to me again. No, I'm the simple boy who is out of his depth. And no, I will not just let you go back to America without fighting for you first."

He pulled her in and kissed her over and over with a slow passion that equaled hers. Each kiss was long and unhurried. Finally he broke away.

"It's getting late. The flight to Zurich is short, but we should go."

He phoned the limo driver and they were soon settled in their seats on the jet, preparing to take off. Janet bit her bottom lip when she realized Brandt was staring at her. But then, she'd been staring at him, too. His expression grew into a smile that held her full attention.

The plane's engines revved to a high pitch as they took off. As soon as they leveled out, Brandt unclasped his seat belt. He got up and leaned over Janet's seat, delivering a deliciously warm kiss.

His phone rang. He straightened up and took it out of his pocket, looking at the caller ID. He winced. With a glance at Janet, he stepped toward the front of the plane to answer the call.

"Yes, Mr. President. What can I do for you?"

Janet sighed and unclipped her seatbelt. She sat waiting on the sofa for a short while, but since Brandt was occupied with endless phone calls, she spent the short flight repacking her luggage. She added her new purchases and imagined Marcie's widened eyes as she admired the selections. Janet would be the best-dressed teacher in Tulsa. It took some of the sting out of her failed trip. Before she knew it they had to seat themselves for landing.

It was nearly midnight when she and Brandt took the ten minute train ride from the airport to Bahnhofstrasse. They walked down the twisting narrow brick and cobblestone lanes of Zurich's Altstadt. Even at this late hour there were people milling about the Old Town, perhaps leaving a restaurant or getting home from the theater.

"These lanes are so narrow," Janet commented.

"The original ordinance stated that the lanes had to be wide enough to turn a pig around."

"Small pigs," Janet joked.

The ground floor of Brandt's apartment building was an upscale boutique. The old buildings were plain stucco without decoration and only basic trim. Each building touched the next, forming one smooth seamless façade.

"Some of these buildings are over five hundred years old," Brandt explained after watching Janet's curious gaze.

Such timelessness gave the buildings a depth of character that Janet had never seen in America. The charm and warmth both impressed and invited.

"Nice digs," Janet enthused with a flash of raised brows.

"I love this building. It's old, but so cozy and elegant inside."

Brandt unlocked the wrought iron gate to a cobbled courtyard. Stucco walls jutted at odd angles, bounding the discordant space. Over the centuries, each wall must have had a purpose. Their intent was now lost leaving the viewer to ponder the chaos. Through an inner wooden door and they passed into a small foyer to a tiny elevator. It was barely big enough for them and their luggage, forcing them into face to face proximity.

She looked him in the eyes. Again that achy feeling welled up in her chest. Leaning toward him she put her arms around his neck and kissed him. It was a soft kiss, much softer than the ones Andy gave him. He wrapped his arms around her back, and pulled her close.

The elevator chimed and stopped, breaking their moment. Brandt pushed open the door, and took her by the hand to his apartment. Just inside the door he pushed the light switch. Janet glanced around. On the left was a tastefully appointed kitchen. On the right was a miniature bathroom with all the essentials tightly engineered to fit a space that was built before plumbing had been invented. Past the kitchen were a living room and two bedrooms.

He stepped to the kitchen, and pulled out a bottle of wine. With practiced ease he cut the foil, and pulled the cork. He poured a taste and handed it to her. Giggling, she swirled the wine as she had seen him do, following his ritual with perfect detail. Approval beamed on his face.

They carried their glasses to a narrow stair that lead up to a roof-top terrace. The lights of Zurich spread around them. Below them, stucco and ornamental bric-a-brac cascaded down the small hill to the glimmering River Limmat a short distance away. On the other side a small knot of blue and white trams jostled, scooping late night passengers to their destinations. The ebony expanse of Lake Zurich spread to the horizon, lined with clusters of lights. Brandt eased himself to the railing, and leaned against it, watching her scan his city.

Janet sat on one of several lounge chairs, their umbrellas tightly folded.

"No grill," she commented.

"What do you mean?"

"In America, a space like this would have a propane grill."

"Yes. Americans do have some rather odd traditions."

"Odd? I'll have to teach you the art of the grill when you come to The States. Again." Her eyes blazed with the invitation.

"You're on." He sat next to her, and moved to sip his wine. Instead she took his glass from him and kissed him again. Balancing a glass in each hand, she was defenseless against his counter attack, placing his palms against her cheeks and holding her kiss. After a moment he pulled back, laying a series of gentle brushes of his lips over hers, interspersing these with gentle bites. The bites moved along her lips, then toward her ears.

She reflexively pulled away, nearly spilling their wine. He put them on a glass table and resumed his attack until she surrendered her ears and let the delicious sensation flow over her in waves. When he moved down to her neck, she stretched to give him better access. He made a slow swirling motion with his tongue, raising goose bumps along her arms. She grabbed his shirt below his collar and hung on, arching her back as the charge swept across her skin.

With a deep-throated sigh, he stopped.

She understood his signal. The next move must be hers. As a gentleman, he would not continue until she had selected the path. But what path? As Brandt had told her many times, her inexperience was a shortcoming. Her mind raced to Andy. Rough, fast, nimble. Yes, as a sought-after bachelor, this snail's pace would not suit him for long.

Solterra playfully reached for the top button of his shirt. Her dexterous fingers flexed open one button, then another. Leaving the bottom one done, she pulled his shirt down over his shoulders, pinning his arms and capturing him in a hold that he did nothing to resist. An inviting grin spread across his face. She pushed to turn him around, and he fell backwards onto the couch. She knelt over him, straddling his body, and released the last button. She placed his hands on her buttons, and coaxed him to release her.

When she bent over him, her hat slid from her back and landed on Brandt. Horrified that Anton was listening, she quickly broke off, and scanned the patio.

"What's wrong?" he called.

"Nothing. Just one minute..." Darting to the door she spoke quietly into to the bugged pendant. "Sorry, Anton. You can't listen to this part. By the way, too bad you lost. But thanks for the hat." She clopped down the stairs and tossed the hat in the bathroom. Half way back to Brandt her cell phone chimed a text message.

"ms t, y wd u think i lost?"

Tossing the phone aside with a shrug, she bounded back to Brandt. A light hop landed her on his chest. She smothered it with rapid, open-mouthed kisses.

"Whoa," he said "slow down."

"Slow down?"

"Yes, let's take things slow. I want to savor every part of you."

"But...I thought you preferred wild and fast."

"What makes you think that?"

"Andy."

His deep breath and harsh sigh made her rise then fall. The heat of his skin penetrated to her bones.

"Andy never understood. Slow is far more satisfying." A tickle of fingers ran up her spine. After his one-handed expert tug, her bra strap hung loose. "I intend to see that you are completely satisfied."

He reached beneath the loose bra and circled her nipples with his thumbs. She arched against the pain caused by her teeth crushing her lower lip. Sensation sung along her body all the way to her toes.

"Slow is good," she breathed through clenched teeth.

Unable to hold herself up, she sank back onto his chest. While she recovered her breath, he drew off her bra and skimmed his large hands over her skin. He gathered her hair to one side and slid his fingers into it, crushing its softness in his hands.

Solterra enjoyed his slow petting. She was in no rush and was delighted to be the focus of such avid attention. With languid, deliberate motions he drew off every piece of clothing she had on. Each item was tossed aside with a rapid flourish and a flash in his eyes that exposed his underlying passion. The moment she was completely naked he sat back and admired. Solterra enjoyed being on display. She pointed her toes and stretched her arms back behind her head, reclining so he could see everything he wanted.

Brandt groaned out a long breath of anticipation. "You are so beautiful."

He leaned to kiss her, beginning with her belly and working his way down each leg. When he finished that he reached for a foot, massaging away any remaining doubts Janet might have had. His focus changed and he came to lie down alongside her. She clutched him, welcoming the heat of his body against her cooling skin. Warm, taut muscles urged her to dig her fingers into them.

Her hands rippled down his back and got caught in something. He still had his pants on. That would not do. Reaching into the space between their bodies, she fumbled and tugged until she'd opened them. She reached inside. He was warm there, very warm. As she stroked him his mouth met hers. They moaned together, mouths and tongues seeking to merge and play.

She broke the kiss so she could remove his pants, but he leaned into her and maintained the kiss while he wriggled out of the rest of his clothes. He leaned over her, shifting her thighs apart until he could sink between them. His body was solid and warm and fit her perfectly. She arched her hips, but he didn't enter her. Instead he bent his head and nibbled at her ear.

All sense of time and place was driven away with each delving kiss, each delicate caress, or nibbling bite he delivered. He moved from her neck to her breasts, sweeping his tongue around and popping her nipples out through his soft lips.

Solterra's desire built and her moans grew louder. He ignored the demand in her tone and let his lips roam over her shoulder and down her arm. She responded by increasing the pressure of her fingernails against his back. When she could no longer stand the wait, she lifted her legs and wrapped them around his back in a tight hold.

Giving in at last, he arched back against her legs and drove himself inside her with a smooth satisfying stroke. Pent up desire flowed through her. Her heart raced. She pressed her hands low against his back, urging him to thrust deeper and faster. He resisted at first, taking his time and making her almost whimper in protest.

She could feel him growing inside her. A mass of molten fire. His hips moved in rhythmic motions, his orgasm mounting along with hers. All at once she shattered. Her breath gone. Her heart stopped. She heard a low, drawn out growl and then he leaned down over her. His arms were shaking as he tried to hold himself up. She grasped his sweat-sheened back and pulled him down on top of her.

"You okay?" he gasped in her ear.

"I don't know yet. I'm numb all over."

A short chuckle puffed against her ear. "Good."

\*\*\*

Janet drifted awake. A gentle pattering of rain and wind blew against his bedroom window, lulling her back into half sleep. After they had made love, he had covered them against the night chill with a warm blanket until the rain started. Now in the soft cocoon of his bed, she pulled the quilt up to her chin. She loved the rain and her thick haze of pleasure was hard to shake off. A smile moved across her face at the thought of lazing all morning in bed with Brandt. She'd slept solidly, enveloped in Brandt's arms. For the first time in a long while she hadn't dreamt. Because dream had become reality? Time to wake up and see if it held true. She stretched her legs under the coverlet and arched her back, bumping against him.

"Mmmm, good morning," she murmured.

No answer. She rolled over to wrap him in her arms. Instead, all she encircled was a stray pillow. She sat up and looked around.

He was gone.

A moment of panic gripped her, wondering if he had abandoned her, if his impression of their first night together could be so different from hers. Then she caught the aroma of coffee. She slid out of bed and stood. Something bright lay against the dark coverlet. A bathrobe. It was spread out, waiting for her. She slipped it on and pointed herself in the direction of the coffee.

"Morning," she said brightly, seeing Brandt seated at the table.

"Morning." He replied without looking up from his newspaper.

She walked toward him planning a warm kiss, but when he continued his self indulgence she took the seat next to him. He looked up and smiled absently, then lifted the pot of coffee and poured her some. Her gut twisted at his cool greeting.

"We made the papers again," he spoke.

"What page this time?" She blew on the coffee and sipped, trying to hide her hurt.

"The article starts on page one, but continues on page four with a photo."

He flipped open the paper to reveal a photo of Michael Madibara and Brandt shaking hands in agreement with Janet behind them.

"What does it say?"

"The headline reads, 'Financial deal struck at luxury resort'."

Janet let out a guffaw. "Luxury resort! Who do they think they are kidding?"

Brandt smiled a bit, warming to Janet's laughter.

"Let me translate some more for you. 'Michael Madibara, Zimbabwe opposition party leader and Brandt Mahler of the WMF struck a loan deal worth five billion dollars. The plan, dubbed the Thompson Accord, was drafted by Dr. Janet S. Thompson, Senior Economist for the WMF."

They both couldn't help chuckling at the continued inaccuracies.

"So I got my PhD and a job all in one fell swoop. Wow, am I good or what?"

"Seriously, Janet, you are good. Your plan will be the future of the country. You have given them a chance to lay a firm foundation that will affect many lives for years to come. You may have even averted another civil war, saving thousands of lives."

"Oh," she replied with an uncomfortable shrug.

Brandt just smiled and went back to reading the paper.

Janet shook her head. Thousands of lives saved by playing golf. She couldn't believe it. Neither could she accept his cold praise. How could he shift from the passion of last night to his aloof distance of this morning? It was as unfathomable as his shift from constant needling to praise. She was uncomfortable with it and didn't trust it. Just like she knew she couldn't trust Zelman.

She was even more uncomfortable with the mantle of responsibility implied by Brandt's praises. It was one thing to be the abstract academic throwing out suggestions and ideas here or there. It was another thing entirely to have the fate of a nation full of hungry people teetering on her ability to resolve a thorny issue. For the first time she had a glimmer of why Brandt harped so incessantly on the need for experience.

Her cell phone rang. It was Zelman.

"Now you are a rock star, too!" Zelman said with joviality in his voice.

"Huh?"

"I'm watching a cell phone video of you singing at the club last night. It's all over YouTube. You were great. You have a hundred thousand hits already."

Janet furrowed her brows. Again, it was one thing to flirt for the cameras. It was another thing, an unwelcome thing, to have them follow her around. Celebrities have no control over their lives. What was it Zelman had said about notoriety turning to leprosy?

"You don't seem very upset about losing SBU," she commented to change subjects.

"Of course not. I don't lose."

"The great Anton Zelman never loses?" she mocked. "Can that really be true?"

Anton was silent for a long moment. Janet looked at her phone to be sure she hadn't lost the call.

He answered with a single terse word. "No."

"Tell me then, when have you ever lost?"

"It was a long time ago, almost thirty one years now. She was my Heidi and I lost her to another man."

"I can't imagine you in love, Anton."

"Oh I loved her. I still do. And I always will."

"I'm...sorry," Janet spoke quietly, feeling empathy for the evil man who she suddenly realized was a real person. "Who did you lose her to?"

"Valter. Enjoy your day. It will be busy."

The line went dead.

Janet's mouth hung open.

Anton was in love with Brandt's mother? Thirty one years. That would be about a year before Brandt was born. Janet stared at Brandt, focusing on his eyes. He sensed her stare and looked up from the paper. She smiled at him. Her heart raced as his eyes blazed into her. Eyes that were exactly the same color as Anton's on the billboard in Zimbabwe. Not only that, he had that same intense look. The look that insisted on trust even though you knew you shouldn't.

"What did my uncle Anton say?"

"He told me to enjoy my day because it would be busy."

"Huh. That's a strange comment," he said, spooning his muesli. He offered her a bite of it, but she shook her head. Reaching to a small plate, he offered her a tiny hard roll and some butter.

"Don't you have any eggs or fried potatoes or anything?"

"For breakfast?"

"Never mind," she sighed, taking two of the rolls. "So, what are today's plans?"

"I thought we would tour my city today."

"Sounds wonderful," she replied. She gave him a small kiss on his cheek. "Brandt, what is your mother's name?"

"Adelheidis," he answered, "Why?"

"Oh, just curious." It took a moment for her to recognize the Heidi buried within the larger name.

"Brandt, is Zelman really such a bad guy?"

He put his spoon down and looked into her eyes.

"I don't know. I've known him all my life. At times I've viewed him as merely mischievous. Albeit on a grand scale, but never hurting innocent people. But, he has ruined whole companies without any sign of compunction. Lately it is different. You saw Harare. It's almost as if he was possessed or something."

"So he has changed. He's more dangerous than before. I'm worried about what he might do next."

"Janet. Zelman's empire is gone. He is no longer a player. The problem is behind us."

She should tell him about the hat. About never losing but once. "But, Brandt..."

"Janet! Enough. You're talking nonsense," he scolded.

Janet's face dropped at his rebuff.

"Hey, I'm sorry," he apologized. "I guess we've all been stressed out. I guess I'm just having trouble adjusting to the calm after the storm."

"The expression is calm *before* the storm."

"What?"

"Nothing."

"I wonder how the stock markets did overnight," Brandt said. "There will probably be some degree of fallout in the aftermath of the SBU failure."

He turned on his television to a German business channel. Even without him providing a translation, Janet could tell there was trouble in Asia. Big trouble. The Nikkei 225 was down 12%, and the Han Seng down nearly 18%.

"Looks like the collapse of SBU has triggered a domino effect on other banks," Brandt said, his eyes darting across the numbers plastered on the screen. "The contagion is spreading and Europe will be next. Now we know why Anton warned that our day would be busy. We need to get you on to the Cray to see if your mathematics can overcome your inexperience and stop Zelman from pulling down the world economy."

So much for the city tour. So much for I told you so.

Soon they were dressed and walking the crowded streets. Situated directly on Bahnhofstrasse the WMF building was only a few minutes' walk from Brandt's apartment.

The five story classicistic building with its carved stone cherubs above a domed entryway was exactly the type of building to house such an ultra-conservative organization as the WMF. However, Janet could not imagine it housing a computer modern enough to do the calculations she needed. She hoped Brandt hadn't overrated the machine, and that it would be able to perform the chaos calculations she'd developed for her dissertation. She conjured an image of what she would need.

Brandt had told her his computer was a Cray XT5. She recalled a Cray XT4 she had seen at the University of Nebraska, a fat round column that clustered an ultra dense packing of circuit boards. Around it had been nestled a dozen terminals. She would need uninterrupted access to one terminal. Perhaps she might even ask for a computer technician and another terminal to help her.

As they walked to the elevator, several people spoke good morning to Brandt. He pressed the button for the lower basement, then pressed his thumb against a security reader. Only then would the elevator allow them access.

The elevator doors opened to a room that stretched the entire length of the building. It was filled with row upon row of identical jet black towers stacked the entire length, each with Cray's signature purple stripes splashing their way to the floor. Janet blinked. Each black monolith represented a million times the computer power that landed a man on the moon. And there were over a thousand of them, their subdued humming whir belying the pure mathematical power hidden within each. At one end of the room was an orchestra pit occupied by several tiers of stadium style seats of terminals all facing the massive theater sized screen that showed every possible bit of economic data from around the globe. Along the sides, television monitors plastered the walls with news broadcasts playing in a Babylonian cacophony of languages.

This wasn't a computer lab, it was an economic battle center.

As they entered, the team of twenty technicians rose to greet them. A squat dark-haired older man came up, offering his hand.

"Ms. Thompson. I am Jeremy Blathstrom, Operations Manager. I am very pleased to meet you."

He was the only one wearing a three piece suit, an indication of his authority over the facility. His handshake was limp and his palm was cold. Janet glanced at the thick glasses sitting on the man's hawk-like nose. Huge bright blue fish eyes blinked back at her.

"Oh, um, hi," Janet said. "Which terminal can I borrow, Mr. Blathstrom?"

"Ms. Thompson, the entire center is yours," he said, making a sweeping gesture with his arm across the expansive room. "You may have any terminal you wish. And please, call me Jeremy."

"Oh. Okay." Janet made friendly smile at the little man. He tilted his head in a polite bow and revealed a large bald spot on top of his head. For some reason this made Janet think of Dr. Jones. She stood there awkwardly, not knowing what else to do.

"Ms. Thompson," said Jeremy, looking up at her, "may I say how impressed I am by the chaos algorithms you developed in your dissertation?"

"How did you get it?"

"Our information sources are very extensive. We've already loaded your algorithms into the machine, and have tied in the WMF databases. How would you like us to proceed?"

Janet was caught completely off guard. She swallowed hard. Was this one of Brandt's tests, poking and prodding to see how she would react? She expected to run a few rough projections as she had done for the Zimbabwe model. This was so very different. This machine was vastly more powerful than anything she had ever seen, never mind used. In front of her the team stood waiting for her orders. Behind her were the rows of black sentinels, their cooling fans whirring, waiting for her to send a burst of life through their massive silicon brains.

She had no idea what to do.

"Janet," Brandt spoke, his head wagging from one monitor to another, "the Zurich stock market has been open for only an hour, and it's already down five percent. Things are falling apart quickly. You need to tell the team what to do."

She had been teleported from Tulsa into a world-wide war zone, and suddenly she was expected to be the commanding general. The staff was all looking at her, expectant faces hovering for instructions on what to do next. Forty eyes bore down on her, assembled in this room for one solitary purpose, to wage war under her command. Brandt stood, his arms crossed, longing to prove her wrong, ready to take the mantle from her if she could not rise to the moment.

Janet's mind went blank as panic gripped her.

# CHAPTER ELEVEN

"You can do it Salty," her father's voice echoed in her head. "You landed the jet. You can do this." Salty had landed the jet, but only Janet was able to program the Cray.

"You can do it, Janet," she heard her mother say. "Yard by yard, life is hard. Inch by inch, life is a cinch. Break it into pieces, and solve them one at a time."

Janet took a hard gulp as she summoned all her mutual strengths.

"Okay Jeremy, what'll this baby do?" she asked, exuberantly rubbing her palms together to lather up her courage.

It took him a moment before he understood this strange American's meaning. "Ten peta-flop," he answered.

That was faster than the super-computer at the Los Alamos National Laboratory. She was in command of the most powerful computer on Earth. Her mouth went dry. Brandt waited for her to fail. He wanted to prove to her that she was out of her league, that her calculations couldn't measure up to his experience. That she wasn't good enough without him. But she was good. He'd said so himself. She'd worked too hard to let go of her ideas so easily.

"Alrighty then, ten quadrillion calculations per second. That'll do for now," she said in mock bravado. Raising her voice to the group she said, "Everyone, gather around. Here's the game plan. We're going work in three steps. Step one is to run off some baselines. We'll take old data from yesterday, run a projection out, and see how well it matches with what is actually happening today."

Janet gestured by spreading her arms out like bird's wings.

"That'll allow us to fine tune the algorithms. With the algorithms secure, step two will be to run up a prediction of what Zelman will do next. We'll gather operating data and wait to see if we are right. We won't block him at that point. Instead, it will prove we can predict and preempt his next move."

She glanced over at Brandt, who stood frowning at her.

"For step three we'll set the trap. We'll predict his next move, and snapo!" She snapped her fingers for emphasis. "We'll have him."

Everyone nodded acceptance. Everyone but Brandt.

The group's attention was still riveted on her, waiting for detailed instructions. She scanned the faces. Stalling for time to think.

Break it into pieces. Solve them one at a time. Yes.

Gesturing with hand chops in the air, she divided up the group into smaller teams.

"Okay, you three, load up the data as of twelve hours ago, you, you and you set me up with the pseudo-code template. Which one of you is the best statistician?" An older woman with tightly curled hair and African skin meekly raised her hand. "What's your name?"

"Clair."

"Clair, you run a simultaneous regression analysis on the chaos code. The rest of you, gather in with Jeremy and me to plot out the projection sequencing. Okay, people, let's do it!" she said, clapping her hands together to get the groups moving.

"What are you doing, Janet?" Brandt asked with a scowl.

"We're going to use yesterday's data and predict what is happening today."

"Why?"

"To prove we can use today's data to predict what will happen tomorrow. Why do you ask? How would you do it?"

"I wouldn't waste time playing with numbers in your step one through twenty seven," he said with searing contempt. "Run your projections and act."

"Brandt, that wouldn't work. I have to be sure before I take action."

"Bah. You're wasting time."

What was going on with him? Did this have anything to do with last night? It had better not.

"Look, who's in charge here, you or me?" she fumed with stony determination.

"Bah," he repeated as he stomped away.

Within an hour the behemoth computer had been configured to crank out Janet's data. It shifted into a high-pitched hum as it projected multi-colored economic trend-lines that inched across the massive screen. Dot by dot they crept along as the huge machine pulverized trillions of pieces of data from around the globe. Second by second, half of the computer predicted what it thought should have happened while the other half compared it to what actually had happened. Point by point the mammoth machine displayed Janet's results on the screen.

At first the prediction dots started to appear in near perfect correlation to what actually happened. Then they started to deviate, and then drifted apart. The predictions were useless, and sighs of disappointment speckled the room.

"Hang tight, people," Janet coached as she punched in tweaks to the equations. The massive screen went blank, and then fresh new lines appeared. The new line series still deviated, but were much closer to real world events.

"You've done it," said Jeremy. "It's close enough to start collecting data to predict his next move."

"No. It's not good enough," said Janet. "Let's try a small sub-model."

She clacked on the keys, making more changes in her equations.

Jeremy came to peer over her shoulder. Janet's small desk terminal displayed the results. Jeremy's head made slow bobbing nods as the data lines went up, then down in unison with actual events. A smile swept across her face.

"This is good," Janet murmured. "Let's run with this on the big screen."

"I'll get the changes right in. One moment," chirped Jeremy with excitement, and the technicians burst into a flurry of action.

Again the massive screen went black. The trio of trend lines returned. This time Janet's latest changes matched the projection dot for dot. Slowly they inched across the screen. Finally the last dot appeared, falling exactly over this morning's live data.

They had done it. They had built the ultimate crystal ball that could predict the future. And it worked! A thrill slid across Janet's brain. Months worth of work had been accomplished in mere hours and her years of work had been validated. The room erupted in cheers.

"Hold on people," said Janet. "It's not time to celebrate yet. This is just the first step. Let's keep it running forward and see if we can gather enough data to spot Zelman's next move."

"Finally," Brandt miffed.

Janet ignored his petulant comment. She glanced up, the British FTSE 100 index was down twenty percent. The world was unraveling. Stay focused on the projections she told herself. Everyone sat transfixed on the data screen, watching for splits in the two trend lines. One real data, the other Janet's calculated predictions.

There was nothing for the humans in the room to do but let the machine grind through its calculations. Janet's fingers drummed the desktop. Clair chewed on her lower lip. Jeremy paced the floor, his shoes tapping an incessant clop, clop, clop. Brandt showed signs of impatience, shifting from a stiff crossed-arm stance to rocking back and forth on his heels as he drew his hand through his hair.

This hurry up and wait cycle was wreaking havoc on everyone's nerves, including hers. The market data continued its downward trend. The red numbers of percentage points lost rose higher and higher. But they could only watch.

"Brandt, if we could just warn everyone about what is really going on they would know not to fall for Zelman's ploy. If everyone would just calm down, everything would be fine. We wouldn't need to run projections at all. Zelman's plan needs to feed off of fear to make the markets collapse."

"Now you are getting it right. Direct action. Do you want to warn them or should I?"

"If I could, I would," Janet absently spoke, not realizing Brandt's propensity to make things happen.

Brandt started making phone calls while Janet and Jeremy stared at the massive screen that showed the world economy from every angle possible.

"Okay Janet, the BBC Financial NewsHour is willing to do a live interview with you."

"What!?"

"You said you wanted to warn people. You'll be on live broadcast around the world before twenty five million people. Here is your chance. Say what you need to and stop Zelman's plan from working."

"I'm watching for Zelman's next move in the market. This is no time for me to go to some TV station."

"No need. We have a remote camera set up right here. They want to start in two minutes. Run to the ladies room to freshen up. You will be seen by millions."

"But Brandt..."

"No time to argue. Go!"

Janet ran to the ladies room and looked in the mirror. With only ninety seconds to go, she pulled back her hair and wound it into a tight bun, applied fresh lipstick, brushed off her beige business suit, and dashed back. She darted onto a stool Brandt had set up in front of the impressive computer screen.

"Janet, while you're talking, keep your eyes focused right there." He pointed high up on one wall to a glass lens surrounded by a slim white box with a small red light on it. "And Janet," Brandt added, straightening her suit coat and elevating her chin, "please, no academics. Just be calm and smooth. Remember Roosevelt. Your job is to put oil on troubled waters, not teach graduate level economics."

"Dr. Thompson," the unseen British voice boomed from a speaker, "we are live in three..."

"It's not doctor."

"...two, one. With an exclusive special interview we are live from the World Monetary Fund headquarters in Zurich along with Chief Economist, Dr. Janet Thompson."

Janet's peripheral vision caught her own image flashing up on a dozen monitors around the room. She looked impressive, poised and professional, with the super high-tech computer screen behind her. The tiny red light was now blinking. She tried to concentrate on looking only at the lens in the white box.

"Dr. Thompson, what can you tell us about the sudden, dramatic downturn in stock markets world wide?"

Janet cleared her throat with authority. "As you can see from the screen behind me, my team has been analyzing world wide data and has come to the distinct conclusion, that the downturn has no basis in reality. Rather, it is being manipulated to create an artificial downturn."

Brandt winced at her comment.

"Are you saying that the markets are being sabotaged?"

Brandt mouthed No-No and swung his arms crisscross to tell her not to say that. Her eyes darted from him back to the bright red light on the camera.

"Uh, no. Our macro-economic models based on chaos theory have outlined a number of possible scenarios to which we are applying regression analysis to delineate."

Brandt slapped his forehead in exasperation, and turned away.

"Could you explain that in layman's terms?"

No, thought Janet. I really can't.

"We don't know for certain, but we think someone is trying to destroy the general economy for economic gain. Perhaps to short sell."

Brandt buried his face in his hands.

"That sounds quite serious, Dr. Thompson. What is your advice for our investors?"

"Rest assured, the economy is sound, and stock prices will soon return to normal levels. My advice? Do nothing. Sit tight, and let the markets to what they need to do."

"Difficult advice to follow when prices are falling so rapidly. Thank you, Dr. Thompson."

The red light at the side of the camera turned off. She had blown it. Big time.

"Brandt Mahler!" she screamed, deflecting her embarrassment to Brandt. "Why did you tell them I was Dr. Thompson, and that I was Chief Economist?"

Snickers chortled around the room.

"Do you think there is one person on this planet who would listen to you if they announced you as Janet Thompson, inexperienced teacher trying to finish grad school? No. And why didn't you do what I said? Be calm and reassuring, I said. Instead you spew techno-blab. You just scared the life out of everyone. Whose side are you on? Zelman is laughing so hard his sides are splitting."

She thought of Zelman laughing at her. Where was he? He could be anywhere, a half a block or half a planet away. Anywhere from Auckland to here in Zurich, it didn't matter. But he knew exactly where she was. She imagined him sitting in some dark underground bunker his face lit by the blue glow of his computer screen, his mouth open wide in abject mocking laughter. This was so not fair. But she doubted fair was in Zelman's rule book.

"It's not my fault if the audience is too stupid to understand what I am saying," she said in defensive humiliation.

"Wonderful. The audience is stupid. Next time why don't you just tell the stupid ones to turn off their TVs first. That way you will only scare the smart ones!"

"Fine, I will!" Janet fumed. "And don't call me doctor again until it is true."

She turned back to the screen. The world was depending on her, and she failed. This wasn't like failing a test in school, something she'd never done anyway. Millions of people needed her to do her job. No, it was billions of people. People she would never meet, faces she would never see. But they had seen her.

Flashes of color on the TV monitors shifted her attention away from her angst. "Let's see if my pathetic little speech did any good."

Janet watched with mounting horror as the trend-lines nosed down even more steeply, just as Brandt's experience predicted. Brandt snorted his disapproval and stalked away.

Janet sat, intent on the monitor, pretending she was unperturbed. She focused on a single number, the total change in the value of stocks world wide. She watched as the penalty price of her stupid misstep ticked up until, in less than a minute, it crossed a billion dollars. Much more than her equally unwitting Thompson Accord had saved Zimbabwe.

A billion dollars in one minute. How many people could be fed with a billion dollars? Unlike the calculations in her dissertation, this was not theoretical money out of some distant economy. This was real money out of real pockets. This was millions of times worse than her worry and complaint to Brandt over their extravagant meal on the yacht.

A billion dollars. And still climbing. Janet pinched the bridge of her nose. Her stomach flopped as if the weight of responsibility was an anvil she'd swallowed.

Her phone rang. If it was Zelman she wasn't going to answer. But it wasn't.

"Rashid," she answered with tense warmth. "I'm surprised you called."

"I thought you might need a little bit of friendly support after your BBC interview."

"Support? What I need is some of Brandt's non-alcoholic beverage to dull my embarrassment."

"Well, you shouldn't be embarrassed. You did very well for a first interview."

"But I destroyed over a billion dollars in market value. I feel like a fool."

"Don't take yourself too seriously in this business, Janet. Markets go up, markets go down. The only fools are the ones who take credit for the ups and blame others for the downs. Besides, what you said was correct. You must let it go at that."

"Thank you, Rashid."

"You are welcome, Janet. Good luck. Especially with Brandt."

"What do you mean?"

"I've known Brandt since he was a boy, and his father and grandfather. The Mahlers are an intolerant sort. They have to be. Mistakes cannot be permitted. Too many people are dependent on them." Rashid drew in a breath. "He likes you, Janet."

"Why do you say that?"

"Because I noticed the look on his face when he looks at you. There was a glimmer that I've never seen before. But there was more. He is afraid of you."

"Afraid? Of me? Because of my paper?"

"No. Because you are the first one to truly pull at his stubborn heart."

"Oh."

"Janet. It is not easy living in Brandt's world. He is alone. True friends are not possible, but perhaps true love is. Good luck with the remainder of today."

"Thank you, Rashid."

"You are welcome."

Janet sat back in her chair, soothed somewhat by the kind hearted call that she desperately needed to restore some of her self-esteem. She was especially grateful for the unexpected insight into Brandt. His moodiness of this morning was becoming clearer.

Her eye drifted to the TV monitors. One showed riots in Cairo, another crowds of angry protesters in Bangkok. Civilization was crumbling. Then her gaze froze on images of green army tanks with red stars moving toward the Azerbaijan border.

"Brandt!" she croaked out in near panic. He looked up and his jaw dropped. He immediately stepped to a speaker phone.

"Nikolai," Brandt greeted, trying to sound jovial and friendly.

"Brandt," the man said in heavy English, "I couldn't wait for your old girl friend to come to her senses. With stock markets failing, I must secure Russia's best interests."

"I understand," Brandt intoned, hiding the panic in his voice that only Janet could hear. "I think you are right. Let me talk to her again. If I can get the Transnov pipeline opened, you could claim victory without your tanks."

"Yes," the seasoned man answered. "I could also claim victory with my tanks."

"But that will only drive oil prices up."

"Oh, that is shame. I hadn't considered how Mother Russia could spend all that extra money."

Brandt closed his eyes, focusing all his energy to his most powerful weapon, his voice.

"Nikolai. You know better. That will only trigger further recession in Europe and America, and ultimately drive oil prices even lower. Your gains will be short lived."

"Yes. I know that. You know that. My comrades do not."

"Nikolai. Give me an hour."

"Yesterday, hour was easily given. Today it is not. Rome is burning."

"Nikolai. Please."

"Call me in one hour," the man snorted.

Brandt closed his phone and pressed his finger tips to his temples. Janet's phone rang.

"Anton. Why do you keep calling me while you and I are fighting?"

"You are the only one who is fighting. I'm just sitting here having the time of my life." There was a deep throaty laugh on the other end of the line.

"Oooo. I hate you!"

"No, you don't. If you did you would have thrown my hat away a long time ago."

"The whole world is falling apart and it's all your fault."

"You really need to learn to stay focused, Ms. Thompson. You still haven't solved my riddle and you're running out of time."

"Ooooo!" she screamed as she threw her phone across the room. It skidded along the floor and thudded against a wall.

She crossed her arms and hunched down to her monitor trying to concentrate. She glanced at the self-absorbed Brandt pacing, trying to solve the Nikolai and Andy problem. She turned back to the data screen, begging it for answers. Jeremy quietly picked up her phone, and dropped it back into her desk.

Staring with no particular focus, her eye caught a small flicker in the data. Honed by long nights of watching her little computer in Tulsa simulate counter manipulations, the tell-tale signature in the data on the screen jumped to her attention.

"Brandt, come look at this," Janet called.

In a few long strides Brandt stood behind her, looking at the screen.

"Look at PBEC."

Brandt watched as the giant holding company's operations deviated from their projections, then fell back into place only to curve upward again.

"What am I looking for?"

"Look at the way the data is bobbling. First a lot of up and down activity, then a slow upward arc. That is the signature of a stock being counter-manipulated. In about two hours PBEC is going to tank. Looks like Rashid was right."

Brandt just stared at the data, his eye blind to what she could so clearly see. Still, he believed her.

"Damn," he said. "I can't solve two problems at once!"

"You call Andy. I'll work PBEC," she said.

"Right." He pulled out his phone.

"Jeremy," she called, "insert this tweak into the algorithms."

As Brandt talked to Andy trying to avoid another war in the Caucuses, Janet keyed in several equations that simulated a PBEC counter-manipulation.

People scrambled, loading in the changes. Then silence. Nothing to do but wait as the Cray re-created yet another new cyber reality within its silicon world and displayed its colored dots to the people waiting in breathless anticipation. One dot, then another. Slowly the machine blazed through unfathomable troves of data, trawling to find Zelman's secret moves.

"It's looking good," Jeremy drawled.

"Hush," scolded Janet, "not yet."

The dots continued.

"No, it really is looking good," Jeremy repeated.

The room hung in breathless silence as the last few dots appeared. Just one more...

"Yes!" the normally sedate Jeremy cheered, the staff joining him.

"Okay, this proves it," Janet agreed. "Zelman is counter-manipulating PBEC. But we have a long way to go yet. Jeremy, let's run the simulation ahead a few hours into the future."

"I'm putting in the commands now," he said, still bent over his keyboard.

Everyone held one collective breath as the machine churned more mountains of data. The projected data line moved ahead of the real-time one. It progressed along uneventfully. Janet could hear Brandt's footsteps and Andy's muffled angry voice spewing Russian expletives on the other end of his cell phone. He resumed standing behind her to observe the display. The huge screen's lines arced down, predicting PBEC crashing at the opening bell of the New York Stock Exchange.

"Janet, we have to stop it," Brandt whispered, his hand over his phone.

"No. Not yet. This is not his big move. I told you, PBEC itself is not enough to bring down the American economy."

Andy's volley slammed to an abrupt silence and Brandt closed his phone.

"What did Andy say?"

"She won't budge. She said Nikolai can bring his tanks. Janet, we have to stop PBEC from collapsing. It's the only way to stop Zelman."

"No. We must *not* stop PBEC. Didn't you hear me? This isn't Zelman's big move. We need the data on PBEC's collapse to predict what he'll do next." Janet stood up and called to Jeremy, "Keep a close eye on PBEC's real-time data, we need to capture exactly how the crash happens."

Jeremy nodded without taking his eyes off the screen.

"You're giving up a chance to get Zelman!" Brandt barked.

"No, I'm not! I'm making sure the one chance we have will be foolproof." Janet didn't want to look at Brandt's anger. She sank back onto her chair and stretched out her hand. "Gimme your phone," she rudely demanded, not pausing for civility or decorum. "Let me talk to Andy."

Brandt dialed up Andy and handed Janet the phone. Before Janet could speak, Andy started scolding again in Russian. Brandt stepped away to talk to Jeremy. Janet waited a moment, giving Andy a chance to vent.

"Andy, it's Janet."

"Oh. What do you want?"

"I was going to ask you the same question."

Andy was silent.

Janet continued. "I don't think your decision not to open the Transnov pipeline has anything to do with Nikolai or Russia. You want Brandt back."

"Okay, miss American money wizard. Prove you're right. Give up Brandt."

"He's not mine to give. That can only come from him."

"Walk away from Brandt, and I reopen the pipeline."

Yesterday she was walking out on Brandt for nothing. Today she was offered world peace for the same. What a difference a day makes.

"Andy, I know you think you love Brandt. But there is something you must love more. The people of your country, your heritage, your family dynasty. If Nikolai makes his move you will sacrifice all that. You can't stop his tanks. Nikolai has nothing to lose by rolling right over the STC, taking your people and their future with him."

"Then I will weld the Transnov valves shut. I will blow up the pipes."

"Don't be stupid Andy. Nikolai knows every bolt in the entire length of the Transnov the way you know the STC. He wouldn't hesitate to squat on the STC and use it as spare parts to fix the Transnov. Is that what you want?"

Andy didn't answer.

"Brandt will be so disappointed in you if that happens."

Silence.

"Then he will be mine," Janet sneered.

Andy hung up with a huff. Bingo. Janet hated to manipulate people with lies, but war must be avoided. Then she realized it wasn't a lie.

"Janet, I've got the Federal Reserve chairman on the phone. He wants us to stop PBEC from crashing," said Brandt, his eyes narrowing in challenge.

"No way. We need this data. It's more critical than PBEC itself."

"Janet, you can't just blow off the Fed Chair."

"I just did!" she snapped.

Brandt glared, his face turning red. He spoke a few more words to the chairman on the computer center's phone, then angrily snatched his cell phone back from Janet.

The second hand of a big analog clock slowly ticked off time. Jeremy stood ready to turn on the computer's data capture as soon as PBEC started its tumble. The room was deathly silent. Except for the hum of the Cray, the room was as a quiet as a cathedral full of monks under a vow of silence. Janet jumped when Brandt's phone rang.

"It's for you." Brandt handed her the phone.

She slapped it shut.

"That was the Secretary of the US Treasury," Brandt admonished with a stern frown.

"I don't care!"

She went back to staring at the monitor. In fifteen seconds it would be three thirty Zurich time, nine thirty New York time, the opening bell of the New York Stock Exchange. She stood, eyes transfixed on the screen. The second hand on the clock ticked forward in excruciating slowness. Then it clicked to vertical. Immediately, PBEC stock took a nose dive, exactly as she predicted. Janet waved to Jeremy to start capturing the live crash data for PBEC.

"Yes!" Janet spoke in victory.

"This is wonderful," Brandt scolded as he watched the financial bridge between Arabs and Americans crash and burn. "You just helped Zelman drive the Dow down another thousand points."

"Jeremy, use the PBEC crash as the search template for Zelman's next move."

Jeremy nodded admiration for Janet's strategy.

With stony determination she plunked herself down and pulled out her hair bun. She rapidly tapped the keys, searching with the captured data looking for Zelman's next move. The staff, idle for the last hour, zoomed into action as they loaded her updated equations into the machine and recalibrated all the previous data. She noticed the strain on their faces. All her calculations, all her focus was concentrated on one thing, zeroing in on Zelman's next target. Her fingers flashed, and her eyes darted as the machine bent to her will, disgorging its secret caches of data. The machine must guide her to the one in a billion answer. Or the world would collapse.

And it would be her fault.

"Look at this," Janet said to Brandt and Jeremy. "This is it. This is the big one. It mimics the PBEC crash lines so closely." She pointed to CBSH, the gigantic London bank. "Look at its curves. Does Zelman have any control over it?"

Brandt wouldn't answer.

"None that I know of." Jeremy responded.

"This is the big one, the one we have to stop."

"How much time?" Jeremy asked.

"According to my equations, about an hour."

Brandt's phone rang.

"It's for you," Brandt said.

"Who is it?" Janet asked, afraid of one too many unpropitious moves.

"The president."

"Your Dad?"

"No. Your American president. You blew off the Fed Chair and the Treasury Secretary. Now they are bringing out the big guns."

"Oh." Her confidence shattered as she took the phone. "Hello," her voice cracked.

"It is good to speak with you again, Ms. Thompson. I've heard you are doing some great work there in Europe."

"Uh, thank you, Mr. President."

"I hope you intend to put an end to mess soon, Ms. Thompson."

"Yes, Mr. President. I'm doing the best I can."

"I'd like to know if I can help you along. What can you tell me about the current situation?"

"We have projected the collapse of CBSH in an hour. I believe it is the trigger we must stop."

"Consider it done, Ms. Thompson."

"Mr. President," Brandt broke in, "may I ask what you intend to do?"

"Issue emergency credit to the Bank of England for immediate injection into CBSH."

"No way, that's stupid," scolded Janet forcefully, ignoring the protocol due his office. "You can't do that. It will cause an inverse reaction, drawing more money out of stocks. That is exactly what Zelman wants. It will make the crash of CBSH even worse."

Holding her breath, Janet listened to empty silence. Did she just insult The president? Had she actually scolded The President of the United States? Tell him that he couldn't do what he wanted?

# CHAPTER TWELVE

"Brandt, what do you say?" The president asked, ignoring Janet's transgression. "My advisors tell me that this is what I must do."

"Mr. President, I have to agree with Janet. Something as heavy handed as issuing emergency credit will likely backfire."

"Mr. President," Janet continued with more control, "inflectives must be handled delicately. CBSH will collapse because it is being manipulated to look unhealthy. The only way to counter the threat to CBSH is to make it look healthy, to restore confidence in the stock itself."

"A Rooseveltian appeal?"

"You're smarter than I thought, Mr. President," blurted Janet. "Oh sorry, that didn't come out the way it seemed. I meant it-"

Throat clearing interrupted Janet's fumble recovery.

"I'm not sure I could pull that off in any case. Hold on. I may have something else."

As the president considered his options, Janet ventured a slow, silent breath. She didn't dare look at Brandt.

"My friends, I have an ace up my sleeve that I think will do rather nicely. Keep your eyes on CNN."

The call disconnected. Brandt closed his phone and looked at Janet. She expected an angry reprimand. Instead his blue-grey eyes blazed pure joy.

"Did we just agree on something?" he asked.

"I think we did!"

In a wave of pure relief, Janet threw her arms around Brandt's neck and kissed him as the staff looked on and burst into applause. Cheek to cheek the couple turned and smiled to the group.

"Okay. Back to work," she said to Brandt with a pat on his back. "I'm curious to see what kind of ace he had up his sleeve."

Janet bent over the computer terminal, one eye on the creeping stock line, and one on the TV monitor tuned to CNN. Brandt drew over a stool and sat nearby. The importance of what they were doing still hung over her, but some of the crushing tension was gone. With the US President behind them, and Janet and Brandt now working together, they couldn't fail. She looked over at Brandt and they gave each other a knowing smile.

The markets continued their downward spiral. Twenty minutes later CNN announced a late breaking headline. The face of the news anchor appeared in the center of the TV monitor, then zoomed out as two new faces panned in on either side, Nikolai and Andy. Janet blinked at the uncharacteristically happy faces. It was as if they were two old friends reunited after years apart.

"Representatives from Russia and Azerbaijan have just announced an historic oil transport agreement that will open the long idle Transnov pipeline. Nikolai Brosnarov, what does this agreement mean to the troubled world economy?"

"It brings increased amount of oil at stable prices, and much needed hope to people around world that Russia will do all she can for world peace and prosperity."

"Anechka Topnazarov, how do you view this breakthrough?"

"The people of Azerbaijan are happy to join hands with the people of Russia to do what is best for all peoples around the globe."

Brandt and Janet faced each other and slapped high five.

"Did the president do that?" Janet asked.

"I doubt it. I think you must have hit the right chord with Andy. But I tell you, I would not want to be around Andy tonight. She will definitely not be in a good mood."

The two new friends were barely off the screen when the old familiar face of Warren Bloomberg, the infamous soothsayer of the finance giant Appalachian Gateway appeared on CNN announcing his intentions to buy up as much stock in CBSH as possible.

"This is what the president was talking about," Brandt commented. "This trick is what saved the stock market crash of 1909."

"Yeah, but it didn't work when it was tried in 1929."

CNN switched to a survey of market news, then cycled back to Nikolai and Andy.

Anxious for their plan to work out, Janet and Brandt watched for the market to respond to the two pieces of good news. It was now seven o'clock in the evening. Janet glanced around the room. Shoulders hunched over keyboards. Hands tried to give resting spots to drooping chins. The hurry up and wait cycles throughout the day were taking their toll on the staff.

At last the computer traces showed activity. CBSH stock took a serious downturn. The room was silent in hushed horror. Only the sounds of the fans cooling the straining computer circuits broke the silence. The CBSH line fluctuated up again and then down.

"You should have stopped PBEC. It's too late for CBSH," Brandt lectured.

Janet glared back at him. How easily their earlier camaraderie evaporated. The muscles in her neck and shoulders began to pull taut with a burning pain. She rolled her neck in a futile effort to quell the anxiety that descended over her. She looked around the room again. Jeremy's brow was furrowed. Clair sat with her knuckles in her mouth. Brandt's gaze flicked across the screen with iron concentration. They all sat breathlessly watching the trend-lines wobble up, teasing them for a moment, then down again.

"Oh, God," Janet groaned. "I can't stand this."

The lines moved up again, then leveled. Up, then down and then up again. Janet closed her eyes, and unable to withstand the tension of waiting, took several deep, cleansing breaths. When she opened her eyes again, CBSH was in a full upturn. The trend kept climbing. Janet waited for the curve to dip, but it struggled upward, and so did the spirits within the room. Even Brandt seemed relieved.

"Janet," he said, "I think you did it after all."

Other market indicators started to march up. A rising tide floats all boats. Within an hour a solid market wide rally took hold.

Brandt handed Janet the phone.

"It's your friend."

"Zelman?"

"No your American one," said Brandt, pressing a button to put him on speaker phone.

"Thank you, Ms. Thompson," the president said. "Your expert judgment saved the world financial system from catastrophe."

"It wasn't just me. There are a lot of people here to thank, especially Brandt."

"Yes indeed. Thanks to Brandt and to your entire team. All of you have done a fantastic job."

"Thank you, Mr. President. I'm sorry for being rude earlier."

"Not at all, Ms. Thompson. You did what needed to be done. When you get your degree, give me a call. I think an Under Secretary of the Treasury would be a good job for you."

"Ha, ha..." Janet started to laugh, then caught herself. He'd sounded serious. "Ah, thank you, Mr. President."

"And Brandt, are you still willing to follow through with your earlier suggestion?"

"Yes, Mr. President."

Janet looked quizzically at Brandt who shook his head in dismissal.

"Good," the president stated, "then good afternoon, or rather in your case, good evening."

The line went dead.

"Yee-Haw!" Cowgirl screamed. "Now we can celebrate!" The entire room broke into applause. There was a pop, then a wet splash as Jeremy poured champagne over the head of the fledgling heroine. As the fuzzy liquid poured over Janet's head, Brandt's face cracked into a broad smile. He took Janet into his arms and kissed her, merging himself into Jeremy's sudsy champagne. When he finally released her, she went around the room, slapping high fives and shaking the hands of everyone.

As the laughter died off, she looked at her weary staff. It had been a very long day. Everyone was exhausted.

"Thank you, everyone," Janet spoke. "You all did a fantastic job. I can't say it enough."

Jeremy looked around the room judging the expressions of the staff.

"Frau Dr. Thompson, we all think you should stay," Jeremy coaxed. "You should run the center. We want you as our boss."

"I think so also," Brandt said.

"Thank you all very much. That is very kind of you all, but I don't have my degree yet."

"You left Tulsa to complete your field research. Tell me you haven't accomplished that," Brandt prompted. I'm sure your Dr. Jones can make accommodations to let you defend your thesis from Europe."

"I don't know. I mean, I should get back to Tulsa. Besides, what would the boss say?"

"Herr Dr. Mahler is the boss," Jeremy said.

"Yes he is," Brandt spoke of himself, "and he already stated his opinion."

"We'll see," Janet evaded, a soft smile curving her lips.

It was after ten o'clock when Janet and Brandt emerged from the WMF building. The streets were packed with people milling about enjoying the warm breezy evening. Janet still wore her cowgirl hat, wondering if it had any value now that Zelman was defeated. As they strolled, she took it off and looked at it. They walked up to the metal railings of a stone bridge that crossed the River Limmat. She debated if she should simply toss the hat into the river. Not because she hated Zelman, but she no longer needed the hat. She didn't need to solve Zelman's riddle. The whole episode, and Zelman too, was now in her past.

Was this a past to hold on to, or forget?

Brandt gazed at her with affection as she stared at the hat and made her choice. Holding it like a Frisbee, she went to throw, but stopped. Despite the diabolical things Zelman did, there was something alluring about the man. He was quick to condemn her actions if he thought she was going the wrong way. He pushed her buttons and prodded her to do her best work. She hated that, hated that he thought he could get whatever he wanted out of her. But then again, he protected her, warning her whenever there was trouble.

Huh. That made him a lot like Brandt.

Janet smiled wryly, looked at Brandt's contented smile, and put the hat back on her head. Brandt threaded them along the river.

"Some experts claim Zurich is the most livable city in the world," Brandt spoke. "It's nights like these that make me think they may be right."

Couples of all ages were scattered about. Brandt guided their stroll to a small outdoor cafe. They sat at a tiny round table. The waiter brought their menus and Brandt ordered wine.

"You were amazing today," Brandt said.

"Yeah, well I lost it a couple of times. Especially when you kept handing me those high powered calls."

"They didn't seem to faze you. It took a call from the president to get you to talk."

"I know. I thought 'Oh my gosh. I just blew off the Fed Chairman and the Treasury Secretary. Am I allowed to blow off the president?' I think I even called him stupid. I mean, do I have the right to do that? Is it legal for me to tell the president to go jump in the lake?"

Brandt laughed. "You are the only woman that I know of who would worry about how the tell off the president of the United States!"

The waiter brought their wine.

"The important lesson from today is that your theories worked. As I have been trying to point out, you still need experience and judgment. But you did stop Zelman and save the world from another Great Depression." He raised his glass. "To Janet Salty Solterra Thompson, the ordinary girl from Oklahoma who saved the world."

They clinked glasses.

"What about you Brandt? How do you feel talking to the president of the United States?"

"I've known John for a number of years. I first met him when I was fourteen and he was still a senator. He spent the weekend at my family home. He even tried to teach me baseball. Rather unsuccessfully, I might add."

She should have known.

Her phone rang. She stepped away from the table to talk.

"Jan, I just saw you on the news again. What the heck are you and pretty boy doing over there?"

"Oh, not too much."

"I see what you mean about him picking new clothes for you. You looked fantastic."

"Huh! I'll have you know I selected those myself yesterday in Brussels." Janet beamed.

"Wow, I'm impressed. And not just with the clothes. I don't know what you said, but you looked great saying it. I believed you, even if I didn't understand it."

Janet glanced again at Brandt sitting at the table. Roosevelt was right, she thought.

"Marcie, I need some more advice."

"Sure thing. What about?"

"I'm trying to understand Brandt."

"I'm listening," Marcie replied.

"How weird is it for a guy to name his dad as his best friend? Maybe even his only friend."

"Depends on the situation, I guess. If you're referring to Casanova, then it probably makes sense. People who are that rich and privileged are often isolated, too."

"But how can that be? He's so connected to ordinary people and their problems."

"Is he? When have you seen him with ordinary people?"

"Now that you mention it, I guess I haven't. Unless I include myself."

"Tssk Jan, you are anything but ordinary. Don't ever forget that. If he can't see that...wait, don't tell me. He made his move."

"Yeah, well it might have been more of my move."

"I'm listening."

"Anyway, the morning after, I woke up and poof, he was gone. He was in the kitchen reading the paper. He barely even said good morning."

"Was there a problem, I mean, the night before?"

"No. It was perfect. Better than perfect. That's what I don't understand. I mean, why would he just ignore me?"

"How was he during the day today?"

"We fought like cats and dogs, but then we made up, I guess. Or maybe it was just the ups and downs he was responding to and it's all in my head. I don't know. I don't know how he really feels."

"How is he now?"

"Well, after the president congratulated us he's been fine."

"You spoke with the president? Which president?"

"Of the United States. Nice guy."

"Oh my God, Janet! I can't believe it. The president!"

"Marcie, stay on topic here. So now Brandt is fine, all bubbly and romantic. What does that mean?"

"It means he's happy after rubbing elbows with the president."

"No, that can't be it," Janet huffed. "They are personal friends. He was a house guest at Brandt's family estate. Marcie, are you listening to me? Talk to me about Brandt, not the president."

"Sorry," Marcie replied, dazed by the events. "Maybe Brandt is more of a playboy than we thought, and it was just another night for him."

"I don't think so, Marcie. I don't think that is the answer. God, I hope it's not."

"Then it might be just the opposite. He wasn't used to feeling what he felt, and it was too much for him. Maybe he needed space to think things through. That would explain his moodiness through the day."

"Yeah. That might be it. Rashid said the same thing. Or it could be the pending war in the Caucuses or the imminent collapse of the world economy."

"Huh?"

"Nothing. Thanks for the insight."

"Yeah, sure," Marcie replied in bewilderment.

"Love, ya. Bye, Marcie."

Janet returned to the table and the waiter came for their order, so she quickly looked through her menu.

"I don't know what any of these things are. Everything is in German."

"Would you like me to order for you?"

"Yes, please."

He ordered chateaubriand and specified how it should be made. Janet struggled with the unsophisticated part of her that didn't know how to order food in a Swiss restaurant. Brandt was raised from birth to this life. Speaking with the US President or the Fed Chair was just an ordinary event. Moving within the circles of power was more than commonplace for him. He was the circle of power. For her it was an uncomfortable learning experience.

"Brandt," she said after the waiter left, "I'm still an ordinary girl. I don't think I could continue to compete with all of this." She gestured in a vague way with her hands.

Brandt put his wine down and looked her directly in the eyes. "You don't have to. It's not a competition. All on your own you waltzed into the computer center, took it over, and saved the world. Within minutes the staff viewed you as their boss and gave you their unwavering loyalty. You weren't trained for that. You had to invent everything from scratch. Just like your chaos algorithms or how to handle a president, you created your own world in your own way. I don't know of any other person who could do the things you have done."

He continued to hold her with his eyes, approving of the woman he saw. And she wanted his approval. His attention. His love.

"Brandt, why were you so distant this morning? I didn't expect to wake up alone."

"I woke up in the middle of the night, and couldn't get back to sleep."

"Were you worried about something?"

"I don't know. I felt crowded, trapped."

"Crowded by me?"

"I'm not sure."

"You couldn't have felt crowded by me. You held me all night."

Brandt shrugged and sipped his wine.

"Brandt, was our night together so ordinary that you didn't care?"

Brandt looked stung by her question.

"No, that is not what I felt. I can't explain it. I loved being with you. I want to be with you again." A smile moved across his face and he chuckled. "Did you like the look on Nikolai and Andy's faces on CNN?" he asked.

Janet debated if she should bring him back on topic, but decided not to. He was uncomfortable with talking about his feelings. He needed his space and she would give it to him. She wasn't about to become a needy girlfriend, desperate for continuous confirmation of his feelings.

"Yeah," she laughed. "I think both of them are suffering from face cramps right now."

"I love that about you," he said, comfortable again with his distance.

Her eyes sparkled as she nodded for him to continue.

"Your sense of humor, your insight, your sense of justice." He smiled, then looked down at the table cloth, then back up to her eyes. "But that is not what I admire most. It is the one portion of your complex personality that I think has been left out of your life. Solterra. The beautiful, sexy woman that remains hidden, only coming peeking out in brief moments that drive me absolutely crazy."

The intense sincerity of his words thrilled her. Even if he couldn't talk about his own feelings, he could talk about her. Tell her what he liked about her. A surge of passion clouded her head. She could not find the words she needed to respond. When he looked at her that way she could believe anything. Believe in a future together with him.

She slowly raised her wine glass and let its rim touch her lips. She rolled the smooth glass over her lower lip in liquid leisure. Her tongue slithered out and tasted the cool glass. With languid slowness she closed her eyes, then ever so slowly opened them. Brandt's eyes locked onto her mouth. Tipping the glass up, she took the very slightest of sips, letting the dark liquid slide into her mouth.

Brandt's lips parted. Half closing her eyes, she let the heady flavors linger before swallowing, then leveled her eyes on his. He let out a long huff of pent breath. Their food arrived, but Brandt couldn't pull his eyes from Solterra's face.

She tilted her head down, letting her long silky hair spill over her shoulders. Then with a delicate flick of her head, she tossed back the wayward locks. She squinted her eyes to devilish slits that pierced his unwavering stare and she smiled because he hadn't yet flinched. But he was about to.

Fork in her left hand and knife in her right, she cut away a sliver of beef from her plate and put it to her lips. Parting them with her tongue, she slid the morsel across her tongue, into her mouth and slowly started to chew. The muscles in Brandt's neck twitched. Each motion of her jaw was highlighted with a slow and deliberate pursing of her lips. With torturous seduction, she swallowed. She cut another bite and then another.

Brandt was unable to focus on his own meal. She could sense hunger rising within him, but it wasn't for his food. It was for her. His eyes moved from her mouth to her eyes. She put down her fork, and let her eyes bore into him.

Folding her hands together, she leaned forward. "And so, Herr Dr. Mahler, do you still believe that Solterra is really so hidden?"

His eyes moved over her features, drinking her in. They dwelled on her eyes, then nose, then mouth and chin. She tilted her head to one side, presenting a profile. His gaze moved up the left side of her face, took in her ear and stopped on the glimmering sheen of her strawberry hair.

"You are the most spectacular woman I have ever met."

Without touching his meal, he stood and led her out of the cafe.

A very short while later the thick metal door closed, then appeared to slide down as the apartment elevator slowly rose. Solterra looked into Brandt's eyes. Stepping one inch closer, she placed her arms around his neck, pulled him down, and gently touched her lips to his. She didn't kiss him. Instead she slowly brushed her lips back and forth across his. When she gently bit his lower lip his arms clasped her waist. With her lips she grasped his lower lip and pulled, then released. He moaned a low growl. She repeated this on the left side of his lip. Then she placed her lips squarely on his, and kissed him. Hard. He groaned with the sensation as he pulled her up against him.

The door opened and she stuck her leg out to keep it open. Drawing him into the hallway, she maintained the kiss for as long as she could. He broke away to unlock his apartment door. She whirled him inside, shut the door and flipped the bolt shut. Tugging at his shirt and pulling him to the bedroom made her erupt in teasing giggles that she couldn't control.

He made a broad grin as he pushed open the bedroom door and groped for the light switch. But she stopped him, nudging him into the room, pressing him against the wall and locking her lips against his. She pulled his suit jacket down off his shoulders, and let it fall to the floor, then tugged at his tie and threw the half undone loop across the room as she attacked the buttons of his shirt. Soon the shirt joined the tie on the other side of the room. He reciprocated with a counter attack on her suit coat and the zipper of her skirt, then the hooks of her brassiere were snapped undone.

She pulled him around, then pushed him onto the bed. With slow deliberate motions she unveiled the lower half of him and gave it plenty of attention with her hands and mouth. He fisted his hands into her hair and let his wordless voice express his enjoyment. Slow delicious torture. She could deliver it as well as he could. But she wanted more of him. All of him.

Rising, and meeting his eyes, she smiled down at his half-closed lids. "Brandt," she crooned. "You are delicious."

"Mmmm...Solterra..." he said barely able to part his lips to speak.

She straddled him. Stretching her legs out one at a time she stroked the smooth softness of her thighs against the taut muscular contours of his legs. He moaned and put his hands on her breasts. She let him massage with his fingers as desire built inside her. Leaning down, she grasped his wrists and lifted his hands away from her chest. She pinned his arms to the bed and sank down onto his hardness. He slid into her with perfect precision. Holding him captive, she writhed over him, thrusting her hips against him and withdrawing only to crash back down onto him. Slow is better?

"Solterra," he whispered in a hoarse voice.

"I'm here, Brandt," she answered. "I'm here..."

"Let me..."

"No," she giggled, squeezing his wrists tighter when he tried to move his arms.

He gave up resisting and let his head back onto the bed with a low moan. His sculpted chest was covered with a sheen of sweat now and his breath was coming up in heavy heaves. Solterra vaulted up and down over him, bringing him closer and closer to a tremendous orgasm. Her own desire sprouted, grew and blossomed. Never before had she felt the depth of power she could call up from somewhere inside her being. Her soul? She bent and covered his sweet mouth with hers, drowning his moans with her tongue. Faster and faster she rocked until they both shuddered and gave themselves up to the climax of passion.

Solterra crumpled, sprawling over the spent Brandt as his chest rose and fell in gulping, grasping heaves. He murmured something that fell against her ear as a hot wave of breath. But she couldn't make out what it was.

"What?" she muffled half against the pillow.

He heaved a while longer, then made no more sounds except a long, contented sigh. Weak as a lambkin, she let him drag the light coverlet over them. After a few more moments she regained her breath. She slid off his body and snuggled up next to him.

"Brandt?"

He made a soft snore. Solterra kissed the shoulder she leaned against, letting her lips linger on the heated skin. She lifted her head up to look at him, but her lids were welded shut. With a sigh that matched his, she let her head sink down onto the soft chest of curls and gave up trying to open her eyes.

Janet awoke with Brandt lying warm against her back, his heavy arms wrapped around her in a protective hug. She shifted to face him.

"How long have you been awake?" she asked.

His eyes glistened and he seemed about to smile. "Just a short while. I love to look at you, to watch you as you sleep."

She nuzzled into him, a wave of contentment washing through her. This felt good. It felt right.

"Are you hungry?" he asked. "I'll make you breakfast."

"Mmmmm...not yet. I don't want to get up."

"I'll have to find something to tempt you out of bed."

"Such as?"

"Do you like to ride horses?"

"I'm from Oklahoma. Of course I do."

"Since we have saved civilization, and have nothing else to do, let's make a day trip to Graumauer."

"Graumauer?"

"My family's estate. Dad hasn't been home for a while. I'm sure Mom is bored, and would love to meet you."

"Meet your mother? As in 'meet your mother'?"

"That is usually what meeting a person means."

"Brandt, in the States that has a different meaning."

"Interpret it as you will. Do you want to go?"

# CHAPTER THIRTEEN

"Okay," she hesitantly replied.

He threw back the single quilt and stood. He was indeed a handsome man, especially dressed as he was. Playfully, Janet stuck one leg out from the cover, then a second, then slowly wiggled out while Brandt gazed with open anticipation as each inch of her emerged.

"You are so beautiful," he said, pulling her to her feet and enveloping her in his arms.

He guided her to the shower, and started the water to warm it up. Still sleepy and content, Janet let him draw her under the sensuous cascade. It fell across her back until he tipped her head and sluiced steamy water over her hair. Lathering a handful of shampoo, he began working his fingers into her scalp. He started just above her forehead, then slowly kneaded his way back over her head and down her neck. His fingers stroked through her long hair, gently touching her back after emerging from the last of her hair. He edged her back under the water and massaged the shampoo from her hair.

Filling his hand with body wash, he gently worked over the skin of her forehead, nose, cheeks and chin. He cupped his two hands together and worked around her neck, over her shoulders then down her arms. Flaring his fingers through hers, he soaped her hands, his thumbs working circles in the palms of her hands sending electric shivers along her skin. Time disappeared from her consciousness as his hands slid under her arms, over her breasts and belly.

He crouched down and placed her left foot onto his right leg, lathering and lingering over the sole of her foot. With exquisite slowness, he worked his fingers between her toes. Sensation streamed right through to her core, making her twist her hands together to keep from moaning aloud. The process was repeated for the other leg, then he turned her around and soaped her buttocks. He swept his hands simultaneously down her legs and over the backs of both knees. She groaned as pleasure surged through her, weakening her. He stood, and finished her back, turned her around, and placed his open mouth over hers while rinsing the suds off her with his roving hands.

With a shudder she recovered herself. Now it was his turn. She filled her hands with shampoo and stretched up to work her hands into his dark curls. Giggling, she let the sight of her jiggling breasts titillate him as she wiggled her fingers through his hair. Soon he was blinded by the glacier of suds she let foam over his face. She continued to shift her body, caressing with her torso, arms and leg and letting his imagination fill in the blanks his eyes could no longer complete.

Placing her palms on his cheeks, she massaged his face. Her thumbs moved over his eyes and brows, kneading across his forehead as her fingers worked his ears. She let her hands slide over his chin, then continue their magic on his neck. His neck muscles tightened in pleasure as he faced upward. His eyes were still closed tight against the soap, but his skin could sense every minute detail of her motions. With hands spread wide she moved across his chest and arms, then she brought her hands together to focus on his groin. A sigh rumbled through his chest.

Re-soaping, she stooped and wrapped her hands around the sinews of his legs, stroking up and down their long taut length. Rising, she finished his back, working her fingers into the muscles that quivered under her touch. At last she moved him under the water, unshackling him from his soapy bonds.

He turned off the water, picked her up, and carried her dripping back to his bed. The whole world disappeared again and there was nothing and no one in it but them. Together.

When she awoke, she heard Brandt up and moving in the kitchen. She couldn't find a bathrobe to wear, so she opened his closet and picked out one of his shirts. The sleeves hung past her finger tips, and the tails hung to her thighs. Perfect. She'd roll up the sleeves and see what he thought of that.

For a moment Brandt stood frozen at the sight of her. It wasn't a lustful stare. It was as if he contemplated her as a woman. Then he shook free of her spell.

"What are you doing?" she asked.

"Making breakfast."

She eyed the tiny plates and meager offerings.

"Oh, no you don't. Not one of your skimpy European breakfasts. A croissant and a scoop of goo. Sit down. Let an American cook a decent meal for once."

His face broke into a broad smile as he sat and watched her start. She opened the refrigerator and checked several cabinets. Reaching high into a corner cabinet on tip toes, her shirt tails hiked up her legs. Turning, she caught his admiring stare. She paused flirtatiously, locking eyes with him, enjoying the sensation that she could turn the head of the most eligible bachelor in Europe.

Slowly she came down off her toes, and the shirt slid back to a more sedate position, but still Brandt's eyes didn't leave her. She had trouble turning her attention from Brandt back to cooking. After a few minutes of hunting and trying to read labels, she'd identified European versions of everything she needed for the All American breakfast of pancakes, ham, and eggs. Soon she was cracking, stirring and frying while Brandt sat motionless watching her lithe body move around his kitchen in nothing but his shirt.

When she finally placed the hearty meal in front of him, she sat down. He smiled and leaned to give her a kiss. After taking a bite from the pancake and a scoop from the scrambled eggs, he nodded his approval and pointed at the opened newspaper. Brandt chuckled at a political cartoon in the newspaper he had been reading before her entrance.

"What's so funny?" she asked.

"A cartoon about you."

He turned it for her to see.

"Cirque Du Saltei" the caption read, mimicking the famous European circus Cirque Du Soleil. The background showed her starring in various circus acts. In one she held a golf club, the ball's trajectory bouncing off of Brandt's head. Another showed her vaulting from a jet, its nose stuck like a dart into the ground, she blowing kisses. A third depicted her lassoing a wad of runaway money. The last was her singing into a microphone while swinging her jacket over her head. In the foreground she was a ringmaster in a cowgirl hat so oversized the back of the brim touched the ground.

"What am I saying?" she asked Brandt.

"For my next act, I light the world on fire."

They both burst into laughter and Janet admired the sparkle of pure fun in his eyes. How could she have ever been irritated with him? She simply could not remember how that was possible.

"I wonder how the stocks are doing," she asked just before sinking her teeth into forkful of pancake.

He slid the remote to her.

"Turn on the TV and find out," he said with a mirthful glee in his eye.

"What?" she asked looking at his smirk. "You know something."

"Perhaps. And it might be the last peg in Zelman's coffin. Finishing him for good, so he'll never rise again."

She flipped on the TV to see an excerpt from a speech the US president had made while they slept.

"There is one world economy, we all share it, and it is very real," the president spoke.

"Hey, that is your line," she said.

"Shhh," he scolded, "listen."

"And so I am pleased to announce a Second United Nations Monetary and Financial Conference to be held in Bretton Woods in America, the site of the first conference held over seventy years ago. Just as the first conference ended the scourge of the Great Depression, the second conference will continue that mighty work. The answer to our economic woes is international cooperation. I have asked the conference to be led by Dr. Brandt Mahler of the World Monetary Fund."

Janet's jaw dropped. "You did it! You convinced him to go along with your economic policies."

"Actually it was Zelman. Without the fear that Zelman inspired in everyone, this wouldn't have happened."

"I'm so proud of you, Brandt!" She threw her arms around his neck and kissed him while he beamed like a school boy who had just won the spelling bee.

"This is just the first step. The first conference in 1944 was difficult to negotiate. This will be even more difficult. Also it must be maintained. Don't forget the Bretton Woods system collapsed in 1971 due to US policy changes. But I am very hopeful."

"I am very hopeful, too," said Janet.

\*\*\*

Janet and Brandt sat side-by-side and hand-in-hand riding the S-Bahn train through the lush rolling hills outside of Zurich. Janet didn't want to let go of his hand, so warm in hers. She shouldn't keep kidding herself that a relationship with him could work, but she couldn't help dreaming about it. With a sigh she shifted her gaze to the many modern square industrial buildings that seemed to coexist so easily with brown barns and brown-and-white daubed cows. The hills gave way to small pre-alpine mountains. The landscape here was spectacular.

They disembarked at Einsiedeln where a Mercedes sedan was waiting for them. A tall man stood poised at calm attention beside it. White hair and thick brows set off by a distinguished mustache defined his age. His ruddy complexion and sturdy frame made him look like an ancient king, prepared to receive visiting dignitaries. He made a silent nod at Brandt as they approached.

"Friedrich, Grutzi. Wie geht's? Janet, this is Friedrich."

"Vellcome, Fraulein Janet," the gentleman spoke in halting English. "Please forgiving of me. I am speaking yet not so goot English. Happily I meet you."

"I am pleased to meet you, Friedrich."

Friedrich's brows quirked upward for a moment as if evaluating her. Then his gazed lightened, and he exhaled as if able to breathe for the first time in a long while.

"Friedrich is indispensible. He has been working for my family his whole life."

"Ya. I am working my whole life mit this family. Graumauer is my life. Auch my father and grandfather. My son Gustav, too. May he work mit you, ya?"

"Friedrich!" Brandt scolded. "She is just visiting."

"She is goot for us here, ya? I think so. Nicht wahr?"

Friedrich held the door for Janet while she pulled off her cowgirl hat and slipped in, leaving her to ponder the meaning of his words.

"What is he talking about, Brandt?" she asked as Brandt slid in next to her.

"Don't mind Friedrich. He thinks his sole purpose in life is to protect Graumauer and assure its dynasty."

"What does that have to do with me?"

Brandt didn't answer except to shake his head and wave off the question. Friedrich was probably one of those doddering old servants who couldn't be pensioned off, just put up with. Rich people have their problems, too.

The car moved away from the station, giving Janet a view of the quaint village surrounding them.

"What is that church?" Janet asked pointing to a monumental building just a few blocks across the picturesque town.

"That is the Monastery. I went to middle and high school there."

"It looks very old and imposing."

"Well, it is old. It dates back to 681."

"Wow, over three hundred years old?"

"No, no. Add another thousand. It's thirteen hundred years old." He gestured as they passed one of the buildings. "This building is new, only three hundred years old. Friedrich, please drive along the Schmiedenstrasse and then down the Hauptstrasse."

"Yes, my pleasure, Mein Herr."

Friedrich seemed very happy to show Janet the town and the cloister. While Brandt pointed out the highlights and provided background information, Friedrich's eyes kept darting to the mirror trying to gauge Janet's reactions.

"As a school, the Monastery stresses music and language. I was particularly poor in the former, but strong in the latter."

"How many languages do you speak, Brandt?"

"Let's see, if you count Latin, Ancient Greek and Swiss German, eight fluently and another four with some difficulty."

"I can't imagine that."

"America is the center of the world, and when you stand so close to it you can't look outward very easily."

Living in America did seem isolating, but only since she'd left Tulsa. Janet's eyes continued to scan the town and the Monastery, her mind trying to run the centuries backward. Not much seemed to have changed. Except for a car here and there, some electrical fencing around a cow pasture and a few modern-looking homes, it could still be the year 691.

"Many of these town building are hundreds of years old, too. Some are over five hundred years old. Switzerland has seen much less warfare than the rest of Europe, so more of our old treasures remain."

Friedrich drove slowly, giving Janet the chance to absorb her fill of the lovely scenery and the concept of the time warp this place seemed to be in.

"The Monastery is also famous for breeding horses, dating back over a thousand years."

The buildings of the town abruptly ended at the boundary of the Monastery. Behind the edifice was nothing but steep rolling hills, with the green undulations interrupted by the occasional dot of a farm house. In the far distance, the jagged peaks of the Alps were just barely visible over the green hills. The top of the last hill was surrounded by woods and centered on it was a building that from this distance appeared to be a castle.

"What is that old building up there?" Janet asked pointing.

Brandt and Friedrich exchanged glances.

"That is Graumauer," Brandt replied.

They finished their quick tour of the town and Friedrich headed south.

"We are basically following the Alp River for which the Alps are named."

Twisting roads cut through the rocky hillsides, breaking out into expansive views of woods and meadows

"These meadows are also ancient. It takes months to get a permit to cut down even one tree. The community here is very protective of its lands and natural resources."

The paving gave way to gravel and led finally to Graumauer. The front of the estate was ringed with gray stone walls that went on forever past the green lawns and paths and faded into the distant tree-covered hills. The main house, also of gray stone, lay at the apex of the teardrop drive. The center of the teardrop held an ancient walnut tree.

The first floor of the house was of fieldstone. It was topped with a Tudor style upper floor of dusky plaster between the wooden framework. Two short side wings angled out from the center section, cupping the curve of the drive. A balcony spanned them, protecting the twin carved wooden entrance doors from sun and rain. Red and blue bric-a-brac decorations framed the brown tile roof.

Friedrich held Janet's door as she emerged and stepped to the entrance, gaping up at the extraordinary façade like a tourist. The old servant held his breath looking for her reaction to the building.

"You are liking the house, ya?" he asked.

"Yes I do. Why does it have an English Tudor upper floor?"

"It is actually a Swiss style, Riegel House," Brandt explained. "Riegel being the wooden timbres between the plaster. The upper floor was originally stone, the same as the lower, until Napoleon's cannons did some redecorating."

The main door opened, and out stepped Brandt's mother, the undisputed matron of the estate. Her short silver-gray curls framed a beautiful yet stern face. Even though it was mid-day, she was formally attired in a gray suit with vertical pinstripes that accented her slender figure.

The two women eyed each other for a moment while Friedrich nearly turned blue with anticipation.

"Brandt, it is good to see you. I worried when I heard you had several adventures recently," the matriarch spoke at last, ignoring the dejected Janet.

"Yes. We most certainly have. Mother, this is Janet Thompson, from America."

"I see," the cold woman replied without stepping forward. "Janet." The woman's wooden stance and cupped hands made Janet feel like a school girl who had been caught in some juvenile prank. "I am pleased to meet both the glamorous American Cowgirl, as well as the new WMF Senior Economist." The woman's disapproving stare bore down on Janet.

Friedrich's eyes darted back and forth between the two women in near panic. He cleared his throat, prompting Janet to provide a polite answer.

"Yes, well. I am pleased to meet you too, Mrs. Mahler."

Brandt's mother turned her back to Janet and stepped into the house without offering her hand.

"Please come in. But, I must insist, don't start swinging your jacket over your head."

"Uh, yes, Mrs. Mahler."

"I give you permission to call me Adelheidis."

"Yes, of course, Adelheidis." Under her breath Janet asked, "Why am I here, Brandt?"

"You're doing fine," he replied without answering her question.

Friedrich looked as if he'd swallowed his tongue.

A huge foyer lay inside the double doors. On either side twin curved stairways reached to a landing above that presumably led to the private quarters.

They moved into a posh library. Tall bookcases lined the walls, broken up by huge windows that gave a sweeping view of an enormous star-patterned herb garden. Janet glanced at the shelves that rose from the floor to the ceiling. A narrow cherry-wood ladder gave access to those shelves that would be out of reach. The volumes were organized by category, but the category titles were mostly in German. Each book bore an alphanumeric catalog label on its binding.

"So many books," commented Janet, amazed that anyone would have taken the time to catalog their own books. She thought only she did that.

"Many, many years ago this was a lending library. Before the days of our modern public libraries. My great, great-grandmother, a previous matron of Graumauer, devoted her life to collecting and organizing it," said Adelheidis, gesturing to offer Janet a seat.

"It is very impressive. It looks as well stocked as a university library."

"Indeed. The collection here is in many respects superior to the one at the University of Zurich. We have volumes both older and in better condition. Occasionally I am asked to grant permission to eminent European scholars to have access to certain volumes here that the university does not have."

"It was fortunate that your ancestor was such an avid book collector."

"It was her contribution to Graumauer." Adelheidis gestured for Janet to take a seat.

"And so do you continue to collect books?" asked Janet, latching onto a topic she knew something about.

"No, I do not," Adelheidis spoke, taking a seat of her own. "The collection has stagnated since my great, great-grandmother's time. It is a tradition that each matron of Graumauer, when she inherits, chooses a field in which to specialize and develop resources. My mother was a world-renown botanist who built the extensive greenhouses and designed the herb garden. My grandmother recorded folk songs and translated the lyrics from a number of local dialects. My own interests have been in horse training and land conservation."

"What a wonderful idea," said Janet, now at a loss for how to continue.

The present matron simply nodded her head. She seemed at ease in her matching seat by one of the windows. But she had positioned Janet facing into the bright sunlight. Shifting against the stiff leather seat and blinking into the glare that framed Adelheidis' face, Janet steeled herself for the coming interrogation. She shot a pleading look to Brandt.

Brandt stepped between them and gazed out at the garden. "Is Captain Wilbraham still visiting, Mother?"

"No dear. He's gone back to Ireland."

"I thought he was going to stay and work with the three fillies of his that you started."

"They were well on their way. None of them showed exceptional promise. He wasn't in any hurry to do the work of breaking them in himself. They will probably be relegated to his stud farm. I'm going to ship them back to him in a few months. There wasn't really much for him to do, so I sent him along." Adelheidis made a vague wave of her hand.

"You should have urged him to stay. He's a fine old gentleman, full of hilarious tales of his days in the British army. He could have kept you company."

"Yes, that's true, but I've already heard all of his army tales. You'll have to forgive me if I grow tired of entertaining retired cavalry officers and ex-racetrack trainers whose only interest in life is in recounting their personal achievements. If they think their stories are so compelling, they really ought to sit down and write their memoirs, instead of bothering me with their nonsense."

Brandt turned at the melancholic tone in his mother's voice.

"Are you well, Mother?"

"Yes Brandt, I'm very well. I do miss having your company. It's turned lonely here ever since you set up your apartment in the city."

"I know. I'm sorry I haven't been home as much as you'd like. I know that Dad hasn't been home much either."

"He's been home. Home in Munich."

Brandt reached to squeeze his mother's shoulder. She patted his hand and gestured him to sit. He chose to place himself to the side, between the women but out of the direct line of fire. Janet could expect no help from him at this point. She waited for Adelheidis to throw out the first volley.

Friedrich brought tea, setting it down on a low table between the seats. Steam rose up from the white porcelain teapot in swirls that matched the twists in Janet's gut. She could feel Adelheidis' gaze riveted on her. The woman ignored the tea and continued to stare. Janet's mind raced in circles, scrounging for common ground where, clearly, there was none.

Janet flicked an errant strand of hair from her brow. On the other hand sometimes the best defense is a good offense. This was Anton's Heidi, the woman he was still in love with, the woman stolen by Valter. It wasn't much ammunition to work with.

"Do you like my hat?" Janet spoke, deciding to preempt logic and shoot from the gut.

"It is quite - interesting. I've seen it before on you."

"Brandt's Uncle Anton left it for me on the slopes of Kilimanjaro."

"Anton?"

"Yes, Anton. A very interesting man. Don't you think so?"

"Yes. Interesting is a word that does describe my brother-in-law. And you, Janet, what do you think of him?"

"I don't know. He is terrifying, charming, horrible, and glib all at once. I wish I could understand him."

"I don't think that is possible."

Listening to Adelheidis' no-nonsense tone, Janet imagined few things were possible here until Adelheidis declared them to be so. Janet fidgeted in the glare from the window, uncomfortable in the heat of the woman's stare. Mentioning Anton hadn't disturbed her in the least. Would she budge if she knew he still loved her after all these years? She couldn't speak about that in front of Brandt.

"Janet, would you kindly pour the tea?"

"Yes Adelheidis, sure."

Janet reached to the tray and set a delicate, rosebud-covered cup onto one of the matching saucers. She lifted the porcelain teapot and filled the cup. With restrained care she offered it to Adelheidis. But the woman would not take it.

"I would like some cream and one sugar, please," said Adelheidis.

"Oh, of course."

Janet lifted the creamer and dripped in a small amount. Much more would overflow the cup. She eyed the sugar cubes in the tiny bowl. Fingers were definitely improper. Ah, there were sugar tongs on the tray. Keeping the cup level in one hand, Janet dropped a cube into the cup, splashing tea into the saucer. When she reached for a teaspoon and stirred the mixture to dissolve the sugar, Adelheidis softly cleared her throat.

Janet glanced at the woman's thin lips and narrowed brow. More tea spilled into the saucer and Janet slowed her stirring to contain it. Adelheidis made a barely audible sound of disgust. Janet set the spoon back on the tray and offered Adelheidis the teacup. This time the older woman took it, but she was not at all pleased. A little spill of tea shouldn't bother anyone. Janet had no clue what she'd done wrong, but it was too late now.

"Would you like some tea, Brandt?"

"No thank you, Janet."

Janet poured herself half a cup and sipped, trying to maintain an air of poise as she did so. Adelheidis remained silent, so Janet tried to think up sociable topics. She came up empty. She hadn't socialized recently with anyone but professors and fellow doctoral students.

"How did Graumauer get its name?" Janet asked, finally coming up with a topic. "Does it have some special meaning?"

"It has no special meaning," answered Adelheidis.

"Oh."

"Graumauer translates literally to 'grey wall'. It is simply the name given to it by the people."

"What people? The people who built it?"

"No, the people here in the community. Of course the name was conferred upon it many hundreds of years ago."

"I see," said Janet.

She snorted out a short laugh at her unintentional imitation of Brandt. She'd only been with him for five days and she was already picking up his habits. She darted her eyes to him, only to see that he was frowning. This was getting nowhere. Time to grab the bull by the horns.

"Do you like to ride horses?" Janet asked.

"Yes."

"Good. So do I. You have a stable right outside and Brandt mentioned the possibility of a ride."

The matron sat motionless, calculating a response. "Yes," she agreed at last. "We will ride."

The three of them stood and headed for the door with Adelheidis leading the way. Brandt detained Janet a short way behind his mother. Irritated, he whispered a hiss of words into Janet's ear.

"Janet, what are you doing?"

"Making my way, American style."

"Janet, you come with me," Adelheidis spoke with cool command. "Brandt has work to do. Don't you Brandt?"

"Yes, of course. Work." Brandt faltered for a moment, trying to invent something that desperately needed his immediate attention, then he gave up and simply walked away.

With precise clipped steps the woman led Janet to a small guest room. "You may change here."

A moment later Friedrich brought Janet a European form-fitting riding suit that obviously had been pre-selected by Brandt. The servant looked at Janet as if wanting to say a thousand words, but he held his tongue and walked away. Janet mumbled to herself at the oddness of Europeans. Or maybe it was just this family. She changed, but decided to opt for Zelman's cowgirl hat instead of the black felt riding helmet with its pert black bow in the back.

When she was finished changing, she emerged and finding the long curving hall empty, let herself outside behind the building. Standing in the sunlight, she could almost feel that woman's burning eyes staring at her from some unknown part of the house. How long would she let Janet cool her heels? Finally, Janet stepped toward the stable and stood waiting just outside the broad doors.

"Please Father, in English, so no one will understand," came an unfamiliar voice from inside the stable.

"I am saying, I am thinking she is the one, Gustav." It was Friedrich's voice. "This Fraulein Janet will be next the matron von Graumauer. I am knowing it. I can feel it. She will be your next – how are you saying it? - boss."

"You were wrong before, Father."

"I never am saying Fraulein Anechka is the one."

"No, long before that, when you told me how you knew that Fraulein Adelheidis would love Herr Zelman."

"I am not wrong."

"How can you say that? She married Valter."

"There is things you does not know, Gustav."

"What do I not know?"

"Frau Adelheidis and Herr Valter are sleeping in separate rooms always. They never are sharing the same bed."

"That cannot be. Brandt is proof."

"Brandt came before. Valter is agreeing to marry her to preserve the family dignity, but she is never accepting him."

# CHAPTER FOURTEEN

"But who...?"

"As I am saying Gustav, I am not wrong then mit Herr Zelman. I am not wrong now mit Fraulein Janet."

"But then, why did Fraulein Adelheidis not marry Herr Zelman?"

"Herr Zelman was too wild to be Master of Graumauer. He would not do. She loves him, but could not marry him."

"She sacrificed her love for Herr Zelman for her love of Graumauer?"

"This family's purpose in this life is Graumauer and all it stands for. As is mine, and yours."

"Father, you are so old fashioned."

"You will learn, Gustav. This American is the one. You will learn."

Janet heard Friedrich leaving the stable so she quickly backtracked a few steps and pretended to be just now walking from the house. Friedrich smiled at her in sheer joy as they passed each other. Inside the stable she found Gustav currying one of the horses.

"Hi."

"Hallo, Fraulein Janet. My name is Gustav."

"I am glad to meet you, Gustav," Janet said, extending her hand.

"Oh, my hands are dirty."

Janet grabbed his hand, and shook.

"Now, mine are too."

Gustav's eyes sparkled as she released him.

"Gustav. You are Friedrich's son, right?"

"Yes, I am."

He watched her approach a horse. The tall bay-colored animal startled for a moment, as if sensing something they couldn't. Janet reached to stroke his nuzzle and spoke soothingly to the animal, who quieted, and let her approach. She picked up a brush and started to curry the horse.

"What is this fellow's name?"

"He is called Salzig."

"Salzig. I like it. What does the word mean?" Janet asked as she made soft strokes of the brush against Salzig's neck. The horse responded by nickering and nibbling her shoulder as she worked.

"In English, it means Salty."

Janet halted her brushing and stared first at Gustav, then at the horse. She shook off a shiver that passed over her shoulders.

"He likes you. I've never seen him respond this way before. You are absolutely the first person that he has liked, Fraulein Janet."

Gustav's voice rang hollow in Janet's ears. A dizzy, airless sensation of floating enveloped her, detaching her from the moment and transporting her to another moment. Blinking, she looked around the stable - at the walls - at the timbers - at a spider busily weaving its web in one corner. A thousand puzzle pieces clicked together. Janet sighed in a contented way and after a moment casually resumed her brushing.

"I like you too, Salzig," said Janet.

Several minutes later Janet caught sight of Adelheidis coming through the broad stable doors.

"Ah, there you are, Janet. I thought you had become lost." Adelheidis lifted her chin and set her gaze at Gustav. "We are ready, Gustav. Bring these two animals out." Adelheidis spun on her boot heel and strode away.

Janet picked up a thick saddle pad, so white it seemed as if it were either brand new or had recently been bleached.

"Come, Janet!" Adelheidis' commanding voice pealed through the stable aisle, making Salzig startle and throw his head back.

"Easy, Salzig," said Janet, stroking his neck.

Gustav relieved Janet of the saddle pad and nodded at her to go. His gaze followed her as she joined Adelheidis in front of the stable.

"I hope Janet, that you will enjoy the Graumauer manner of training and riding which my ancestors have developed over a number of centuries and which is far superior and refined compared with the crude methods used by your American cattle drivers."

"I'm sure I will enjoy this ride very much, Adelheidis."

"Very good."

Janet took in the expanse of green lawns, framed by orderly white fences ringed with tall, stately trees and bounded by the ever-present high gray walls. A small group of horses grazed on a distant hilltop. This land, this place, she was drawn to it. She could feel it taking possession of her, welcoming her. This was more familiar ground to Janet than having tea in an extravagant library.

"You have a very lovely piece of property here, Adelheidis. You must be very pleased with it."

"I am most pleased and proud of my ancestral home. Valter has been a good master. Someday, Brandt will be. If he finds a wife. Someone worthy of Graumauer."

Janet swallowed at the obvious dig. What would it take to prove worthy of Graumauer? "It is so beautiful here, and so close to Zurich. It must be convenient for you to go shopping."

"I almost never go into the city. My work is here with the horses and the community."

"You don't enjoy going into the big city?"

"There was a time when I did. A long time ago. Before my son was born."

The clip clop of hooves made the women turn. Gustav led the animals to them. He looped the reins of one over his arm and positioned himself to boost Adelheidis into the saddle. As he boosted her up, Janet unlooped the reins and tossed them over her horse's head. She stuck a foot in the little, European style metal stirrup and swung up onto the horse's back.

Adelheidis made a sound of disgust. "Now Janet," she said, barely suppressing her distain, "you must allow me to instruct you in how to mount properly. There is a proper way to do everything with horses."

"Sure, Adelheidis," said Janet. "You just tell me what to do."

Either Janet's legs had gotten longer, or the stirrups were far too short. Janet struggled with the skimpy European stirrups for a few moments, then gave up and shook her feet loose. She'd ridden without stirrups many times. She picked up the reins in her left hand and pulled them across the horse's neck to make him turn. Instead, he bucked and half-reared.

"Yee-haw! I knew I could squeeze a little life out of you, Salzig!"

"Janet, please! Our horses have been expertly trained in the Graumauer riding style. They will not understand your reining cues."

"Oh, okay then."

Janet sat forward and let Salzig have his head. She clucked to him and gently set the reins against his neck, first on the left and then on the right. After a few turns, Salzig learned to obey her cues. He stopped trying to rear and settled down.

"Well. That will never do," said Adelheidis, trotting off along the graveled path.

Janet pressed her legs against Salzig's sides, urging him to catch up with Adelheidis. When she was beside the woman, she spoke. She couldn't let this opportunity pass.

"So, what is it that makes you stay away from the city?"

"Nothing in particular. I simply realized that I no longer enjoyed the frantic and uncertain pace of life. There were things there I needed to get away from."

"Like what?"

"The noise, and the crowds. The constant unsettled buzz."

"And Anton?"

Adelheidis' lips formed a thin line. There was a long pause and the older woman did not answer.

"He told me he still loves you."

Adelheidis slowed her horse to a walk and Janet followed suit, coming alongside the older woman.

"What can you mean?"

"He said he'd always beaten Valter at everything, except what was the most important to him. His Heidi."

Adelheidis' eyes were fixed on the path ahead, but Janet could see the faint tremble of her lower lip. A trickle of tears ran down her face.

"He's really Brandt's father, isn't he?"

The older woman looked behind to assure herself they were alone. Then her face contorted as thirty years of denial unraveled at last. Unable to speak, she nodded her head in affirmation. She looked so vulnerable, so willing to let Janet lead the way. Then she straightened, lifted her chin and forced the tears to stop.

"You," she croaked, "you are sworn to secrecy. Promise me."

"I promise. I promise I won't say a word to anyone about it."

Adelheidis made a contented acknowledgement. But, a pang of guilt shot through Janet's gut, knowing her hat had transmitted every word. Then again, perhaps this small gift to Anton would offset his stinging loss of yesterday. Who knows how Anton might behave after being so badly beaten by Janet.

"You should tell Brandt. He must suspect the truth."

"My son reveres me. The one thought he would never be able to contemplate is the truth. Valter has been a wonderful father to him and I am grateful for that. I could never take that away from him. Not now. Not ever. I will never tell him the truth." The woman fixed her sternest gaze on Janet. "And neither will you."

Janet nodded her agreement. "And what of Anton? You still love him, don't you?"

"Yes."

"Why? Why didn't you marry him?"

"What kind of life could he have given me? I was alone, my parents had me very late in life and both had passed away by then. Graumauer was wholly my responsibility and the family obligations to the Monastery and community along with it. I could not hand it over to Anton. He did not want the responsibility. He did not understand what it meant to me, or what it would mean to my son. To our son."

Adelheidis lifted her head and with a subtle swish of her gloved fingers swiped the streaks of tears from her cheeks.

"I think I understand. It must mean a lot, having inherited Graumauer from your mother and grandmothers."

Adelheidis drew a deep breath. "It is far more than that, Janet. I inherited it from the very first matron of Graumauer, Marguerat. It is a duty and a privilege that goes back nearly eleven centuries."

"Wow." Janet couldn't help but be impressed. "Brandt said some of the Monastery buildings were old."

"They predate Graumauer, but not by much. Marguerat lived in the tenth century. She was the daughter of the local ruler. When her father died suddenly, she was an orphaned heiress and went to live at the Monastery for protection. A knight of high birth, cousin to a German prince, and younger brother to another, traveled through on pilgrimage to Spain. He met her at vespers one evening and fell in love. He persuaded the monks to permit him to take her to wife. He was devoted to her and built Graumauer for her. He was a great patron of the Monastery and brought horses from all over Europe to enhance the breeding program."

"Graumauer breeds horses?"

"No, Graumauer was never involved in breeding. That was always done at the Monastery, until recently when it moved to Avenches. It was the medieval knight who began the Einsiedler training program here, for which Graumauer is still famous. The Graumauer training facility," she said, gesturing toward an enormous arena and paddocks through the trees, "specializes in dressage and jumping, but I will also start young horses if they look promising." They slowed to admire the view, then continued to walk along the path. "Graumauer has produced a number of Olympic champions," said Adelheidis, her voice proud.

"Amazing. It must take a lot of hard work to keep it going."

"Indeed it does. I could not do it alone. Valter has been a great help to me. He was always here when I needed him, fulfilling his civic duties wonderfully, for example, being here for the blessing of the horses every September. It is hard for him to be at home here now that he is EU President. He must maintain his residence in Munich, but the people here love him all the more for his work in the EU."

"And Anton could not have filled that role?"

"I did not think so. He was always off on an adventure, never home, never with his feet on the ground. He was not suitable for Graumauer."

"But suitable for you?"

Adelheidis' eyes darted back and forth debating the answer to this, the most important question of her life.

"Yes."

"Tell him."

"I don't know how."

"Perhaps it is easier than you might think."

Adelheidis shook her head, but Janet nodded back, feeling the snug band of the hat that was still firmly set upon her head. The stiffness in Adelheidis' face began melting away. She sniffled a few times and swiped at her nose with a handkerchief. After a few moments, she reflected back Janet's smile.

"You sometimes find love in unexpected places," said Janet.

"And it is not easy to know whether to trust it or not," said Adelheidis.

"Why are you still with Valter if you love Anton?"

"I could never disgrace my family. I would die first before I let that happen. Valter was kind enough to agree to help me in my distress and need. And he has honored my boundaries as well. He is a wonderful man. I could not disgrace him now after all he has done for me."

"If somehow you could be with Anton, would you?"

"And destroy Valter's and Brandt's image of me? Never. My dignity is larger than my love."

"Is it?"

"No. But I could never leave Valter as long as I am alive."

"So, you will live unloved?"

"You just told me I am not unloved."

Janet stared at Adelheidis, wondering at the kind of love Anton and Adelheidis had. How could Adelheidis have made the agonizing choice to leave Anton and yet still be in love with him after so many years? Had Anton become the ruthless man he was because of losing Adelheidis?

Adelheidis sat straight in her saddle, her eyes scanning the girl before her. Janet sat tall and still, letting the matron pierce and probe.

"Who are you Janet? I saw you when you landed the jet. I saw you singing on YouTube. I saw you on the BBC. I see you now. Which is the real you?"

"I don't know. Five days ago I did. I knew exactly who I was. And I knew I needed more than what was on offer in Tulsa. After all that has happened, I no longer know who I am."

A knowing smile broke across the matron's face.

"You will. Soon, you will."

Ahead of them was a section of low fence. Adelheidis clicked her tongue, and her horse broke into a gallop and gracefully sailed over. Janet followed, but without her feet in the stirrups she had to pull up short, and trot around the obstacle. Adelheidis had turned to watch. Janet made a dismissive shrug of her shoulders as she came up to her.

"I like you Janet. I like your honesty and I might even come to admire your American swagger. But don't discount our old European ways entirely. Now, let me show you how to jump a fence properly."

"Oh, I'd like that, Adelheidis."

"Good. First, I insist that you wear a helmet, especially when you are just learning." The older woman removed her helmet and offered it to Janet, who doffed her cowgirl hat and gave it to Adelheidis. The hat looked good on Adelheidis. If only Anton could see this!

"Now, to jump properly you must learn how to hold yourself in a half-seat position."

"Half seat?"

"This is the name for the position you use when you are getting ready to jump. Lift your seat bones out of the saddle and push your weight into your legs."

Janet watched Adelheidis riding beside her. She leaned down to shove her feet into the stirrups and tried to match whatever the older woman did. It felt as if she was unbalanced.

"Lean down, Janet. Push your weight into your legs for balance."

Janet pushed harder and her body felt more solid and steady as they walked. Adelheidis urged her horse into a jog. Janet bounced, but maintained her balance.

"Good!" said Adelheidis. "You will be a quick study."

"Thanks!" Janet puffed out in a single nervous breath.

Ahead was another section of low fence. Janet could now see that paths had been cut through the woods and fields for cross country jumping. She looked to Adelheidis for guidance.

"Don't look to the side, or down. Just try to keep your balance and sit still as the horse takes off. Your body automatically swings forward with the thrust of the horse's body. Allow your horse's head and neck as much freedom as they need to stretch toward the fence."

"Okay."

"Keep your lower legs underneath you, with your weight down through your heels, so you can absorb the shock of landing."

"What if-"

"You'll do fine."

Adelheidis increased her pace to a lope. Salzig joined in the pace, falling behind Adelheidis' mount. He seemed to know just what to do. Adelheidis went over the the fence. Janet let Salzig manage the approach. She focused on holding her legs under her body. With a sudden whoosh, they were up and over the jump. Janet bounced when they landed, but Salzig's smooth recovery kept her in the saddle.

"Wow! That was fun!" Janet exclaimed.

"Fairly good, Janet. You don't have good control, but Salzig is guiding you along. He seems to have taken a liking to you. But I don't understand why. He's not usually so cooperative. Let's go up this way. There's a series of low fences in this direction away from the paddocks."

Janet patted Salzig's neck in thanks. He proved himself worth his oats as Adelheidis led Janet over dozens of fences, coaching her position and performance until she was breathless with the thrilling exercise. Jumping fences was something she'd never imagined doing with the cow horses she usually rode.

"That will do for now," said Adelheidis.

"Awww. I could keep going. I'm not tired," said Janet.

Adelheidis smiled. "Perhaps not, but Salzig will be. He is badly out of shape."

"Why is that?"

"It's his own fault. He is usually so bad-tempered that he rarely gets the exercise he needs. I'm very surprised that he's behaving so well for you."

"I think he's just wonderful. He's very responsive and seems to know exactly what I want."

Adelheidis made a gracious nod as she continued along a wooded path. "We can ride along here at a walk until the horses are cool."

They continued riding side by side in silence. Janet welcomed the summer breeze, with its warm, grassy flavor. Thick brush crowded the ground beneath tall trees. Sunlight dappled the trail through the overhead foliage. The trees were leafy green and full of rustling leaves, but that was the only sound Janet heard. Didn't they have any birds here?

Janet's phone rang, startling Salzig for a moment. Adelheidis' mouth twisted in disgust at Janet's rude manners for leaving her phone on. Janet's pulled Salzig up and dropped behind Adelheidis.

"Anton," Janet whispered. "Why are you calling now?"

"Turn the horses around and head back to the house."

"But, Anton, wh-"

"Turn around! Now! And don't look back. You don't want to see this."

Janet looked up, and saw a sparkle of sunlight glint off something in the thick foliage of a magnificent tree ahead of them to the side of the trail. A sniper?

"Adelheidis, let's turn around." Janet could hardly keep the panic from her voice.

"But why? We haven't finished cooling the horses."

"We can cool them this way, back toward the house. Besides, it would be rude if I left Brandt for too long," Janet spoke rapidly as she turned Salzig.

"Oh, very well," Adelheidis sighed, turning her mount around and passing Janet to take back the lead.

With her back now to the sniper, Janet could almost feel his cross hairs on the back of her neck. She fought the urge to dig her heels into Salzig's side and gallop back to the house.

Between the unhurried thud of hooves she heard a muffled pop. She braced for the all too familiar whiz of a rifle round buzzing by her head. Instead she heard a faint grunt, then a distant thud, like a sack of potatoes hitting the ground.

"What was that odd sound?" Adelheidis asked, turning in her saddle.

"What sound? I didn't hear anything," Janet feigned.

Janet's heart was leaping as she trotted up to Adelheidis. She settled in alongside the older woman, preventing her from stopping and investigating further.

"Adelheidis, I want to thank you for teaching me how to jump."

"You are very welcome, Janet," said Adelheidis, turning her attention back to the trail toward the house. "You have some skill with a horse. I could teach you a great deal more."

"Thanks, Adelheidis, but I'd like to return the favor by teaching you a bit. Let me show you how to neck rein."

"I don't see the use of that method."

"You never know what sorts of odd skills might come in handy one day," replied Janet. "Let me tell you the history of it. You see because cowhands needed to have one hand free for roping, and so forth, they trained their horses to respond to having the reins laid against their neck on one side or the other."

"Yes, I noticed you trying it earlier. It doesn't look as if it gives you very firm control."

"Well, it doesn't really, but there are times when you have no choice. You have to just trust your horse to understand what you need to do." Janet paused, thinking if that was also true of Anton and Brandt. Then she took both the reins in one hand. "Now, just follow me. I'll show you." Adelheidis pursed her lips, but she followed Janet's movements as they turned the horses down one trail after another, winding their way back to the house.

When they reached the stable, Brandt was waiting for them. He stood in bewilderment as the two women approached, chatting comfortably side-by-side. His mother was wearing Janet's cowgirl hat, holding the reins in one hand, her legs dangling free of the stirrups. Janet was wearing his mother's helmet and riding in proper European style.

"Brandt!" Janet enthused with a wave of her hand. "I've been learning how to jump!"

Friedrich, breathless, jogged up to join Brandt. A tear ran down Friedrich's face as he watched the women approach. He swiped it away and added a streak of dirt to his cheek in the process.

"Friedrich," Brandt admonished, "your jacket is soiled."

Brandt hurriedly brushed fresh soil off the man's coat before his mother could see. He turned back to Janet with an expression of alarm.

"Is everything all right?" he asked Janet.

"Of course, dear," Adelheidis replied. "Come, Janet. Let's go in and have a proper tea."

The moment they dismounted, Gustav gathered the reins of the horses and led them away. Janet removed her helmet and offered it back to Adelheidis. She received her cowgirl hat back in return.

"I'll be with you in a few minutes. I just need to stretch my legs. I didn't realize jumping was such a workout."

"Janet," Brandt said. "I'd like to talk to you."

"Come dear, walk me into the house," said Adelheidis, latching onto Brandt's arm and drawing him away toward the house.

Janet shrugged at Brandt and gave him a little smile. She walked around behind the stables, then spoke to her hat.

"What was that all about, Anton?"

Her phone rang.

"I called to warn you as soon as my man found the sniper."

"Were you calling to save me or Adelheidis?"

"Both."

"I'm not sure if I should thank you, or blame you."

"Definitely thank. Mirza is as frustrated with me as she is with you. By the way, thank you for Heidi and for Brandt."

"You're welcome. After I kicked your butt yesterday are you still in the mood for destruction?"

"Destruction can be very liberating in the right circumstances. And you must know by now not to think that I am so easily defeated."

"I'm not sure I believe you." Janet paused. "You need to talk to her, Anton."

There was a long silence.

"Anton?"

"I don't know how."

"You, the man who can stop the planet on its axis, can't make a simple phone call?"

"No."

"You love her that much?"

"Yes."

"I don't understand you."

"Heidi was right. You never will. Thank you, Janet."

"Anton, how long will Mirza keep this up?"

"I told you. You only need to survive one more day. But you must solve the riddle. Then my Midnight will be complete."

He was gone.

With an uncomfortable shrug, Janet crossed in front of the broad stable doors just after she saw Friedrich dart inside. Peeking through the door, she saw him brushing off spots of mud and burrs from his coat and pants.

"Where did you learn to shoot like that?"

Friedrich startled and looked up.

"I am sorry. I am not understanding you." Friedrich feigned.

"I think you understand very well. Very well indeed. You are Zelman's man."

His eyes lit as he scanned her, the white brows closing down over narrowed lids. Then his face softened and he smiled.

"You must understand, Frauline Janet, I am working only for Graumauer's benefit. Herr Zelman is helping me when I am asking of him."

Janet stared at the man in disbelief. She placed her hands into her pockets and contemplated the ground at her feet, dragging lines in the dirt floor with the toe of her boot.

"I don't want to seem ungrateful, Friedrich. You saved my life. It's not something I can ever repay."

Friedrich made a gracious nod, but said nothing.

"I've faced some unusual circumstances in the last few days, but I never would have expected a connection between you and Zelman. He keeps turning up like a bad penny."

"Please Fraulein Janet. You must be understanding. Herr Zelman is not a bad coin. He is a goot man. Not for Master of Graumauer, no. But Master for Frau Adelheidis, without doubt, yes. He is paining for many years to be staying away. I am very much respecting of him. I am helping to him, telling him of Adelheidis."

"I understand. You need to protect Graumauer and Adelheidis."

"And now you." He smiled at her. A benign, fatherly smile.

"How well do you know Zelman?"

"He will do anything for protecting Adelheidis."

"But would you trust him on something that didn't involve Adelheidis?"

"I am not knowing. I am not thinking of anything outside of Graumauer."

"Think, Friedrich. If everything, everything in the world depended on Zelman, would you trust him?"

"I am reading in the newspapers of Herr Zelman many times. They are saying he is a very bad man, and perhaps this is goot not trusting him. He is very clever."

"So you don't think he could be trusted?"

"I am thinking the newspapers are right for not trusting to do business with Herr Zelman."

Janet sighed and her fingers tightened against her palms. Zelman could not be trusted. There was plenty of evidence to prove it, she just needed to ignore the few times...

"And yet," the old man continued in a quiet voice, "he is a man who can be trusted. In his person, he is a goot man. He is never doing harm to any people."

"How can you be sure, Friedrich. How do you know?"

"I am knowing this, Fraulein Janet, without being able to explain it. Herr Zelman can be trusted."

"After all the games, the dangerous games he has played with people's money and lives. You still think he can be trusted? Trusted with things other than Adelheidis and Graumauer?"

The old man's eyes bore into Janet without wavering. "Yes."

# CHAPTER FIFTEEN

"That is not at all logical."

"Perhaps not, but it is still so. Fraulein Janet, you are keeping this secret of today with me, yes? I am knowing you are. In the same way I am knowing to trust Herr Zelman, I am knowing that I can trust you."

Janet shook her head. "I never thought I would weigh evenly with Zelman on a scale of trust. But yes, Friedrich. I will keep the secret from today."

Friedrich sketched a bow at Janet and strode past her, hurrying toward the house. Janet took a deep breath and slowly followed after him. When she arrived inside the library, Friedrich was helping Adelheidis pull her boots off.

"Come, Janet, sit. Fresh tea will be ready in a short while."

Janet sat next to the matron.

"After we take our tea, you must spend some time with Brandt."

"I would like that. What does Brandt like to do while he is here?"

"You should ask him yourself," Brandt boomed as he entered the room with a servant woman close behind.

The woman set down the large tea tray she carried. Friedrich dismissed her with a smiling nod and bent to serve Adelheidis, but with a subtle nod and turn of her hand, the matron instructed him to serve Janet first.

"Okay, so what do you like to do when you are here, Brandt?"

"Parasailing."

"What?"

"Parasailing. Want to try it?"

"I don't even know what it is. Tell me about it."

"No. Seeing and doing are better than telling," said Brandt. "We'll go right after tea."

\*\*\*

Brandt loaded what looked like an oversized hiking backpack into the trunk of the Mercedes. He glanced back her, an impish glee in his eye, but said nothing to Janet about them. She would just have to wait to see what he had in mind. As Friedrich drove them along a dirt road to the top of grassy hill, Janet admired the distant clusters of brown tile roofs below them, surrounded by huge patches of green. The town of Einsiedeln splayed out before them with the Monastery nestled safely at the base of the series of higher hills to the south.

Friedrich's eyes kept darting to the mirror to look at her with abject relief that he had saved her from the sniper. His entire life's purpose was to save her and secure the future of Graumauer. Save her or capture her? A bird trapped in a gilded cage, is that his vision for her? She would be the matron of the estate, able to anything she pleased, anything but live her own life. The posh walls of the Mercedes began to close in.

As they rode along, she could tell Brandt was looking at her, but she didn't let herself turn to look at him. The coldness of the bed yesterday morning haunted her. Slowly she realized she didn't want Graumauer, didn't want Brandt's money or fame. She wanted the one thing she couldn't have, Brandt himself. She couldn't give in to those feelings because it wouldn't work. She could marry him, but still not have him. The real Brandt was not anything any woman would ever have. Even with that realization, Janet was too weak to face having to get over him.

Look what happened to Adelheidis and Anton. Adelheidis had made the right choice. Even though they loved each other, Anton was not ready. He was too wild, too full of adventure to settle down and give himself to her. The same for Brandt. The world needed him. More importantly, he needed the world. Would his phone ever fall silent? Would his jet ever go without use? If they ever did, he would shrivel and die of boredom.

But that would never happen. He would woo her, and marry her, and abandon her. A bird trapped in a gilded cage. Janet wouldn't be able to spend years apart from someone she'd allowed herself to fall foolishly in love with. Not when they were clearly so far apart on the social scale. This was not her world. Tulsa was. He probably wouldn't even keep in touch after she went home.

When Friedrich reached the barren top of the wind-blown hill, Brandt jumped out of his side of the car and came to hers, reaching in for her hand to bring her out of the car. She couldn't resist returning his grin. She had to admit she liked being doted on. At least sometimes.

There were two parasails already in the air. From each of the brightly colored parachutes hung a person effortlessly gliding along a ridge line, held aloft by windy updrafts of mountain air. As Janet scanned the slope she saw a guy bumping along the ground in a rough downward run dragging his parachute along the grass. With a sudden tug, his parasail was flipped from the ground, filled with air and lifted him up and away from the hill. Her eyes couldn't believe the improbable sight when a gust caught his parasail, and he rocketed upward. She had never seen anything like this.

Janet drew a deep breath to steady herself. She was no coward, but this looked dangerous.

"This has become very popular here in Switzerland. We have some of the best terrain and wind conditions in the world for parasailing."

Brandt pulled a parachute out of the trunk, placed it on the ground and tugged at the binding cord. The red and white parachute unfurled onto the ground, its bright colors a match for the Swiss flag. He spread the long thin parachute over the ground, carefully arranging its tangle of lines in perfect straight order.

"Zip up your jacket, Salty. It gets cold up there," he said as he handed her a white helmet.

The wind made it difficult for her to put on her helmet. She had to gather and twist her hair and tuck it inside the helmet, making the helmet snug. She could barely snap the multiple catches of the chin strap. When she was done, Brandt gestured at her jacket. She zipped it up to her chin.

Brandt planted a clumsy-looking harness across her shoulders and she slid her arms into the straps. From the back of the harness hung a puffy sling. When he drew the straps between her legs and snapped them all together securely across her chest, she felt as if she were in a straight jacket bound for the psych ward. Probably she should be. This looked precarious and she had no idea what she was doing. She should have at least read up on this first.

Her heart skipped and skittered faster as she watched him place the chute harness over his shoulders, and pull the straps between his legs. She glanced down the steep side of the hill where a path had been laid bare between stands of trees. They were going to jump down that cliff? As he stepped toward her she opened her mouth to protest and put a stop to this. He ducked behind her, and in one quick snap attached his harness to hers.

Helpless against his weight and the constrictions of the harness, she made a low groan as they faced into the stiff breeze coming up the hill.

"Here we go!" shouted Brandt with excitement in his voice.

He flicked his arms, jerking the parasail off the ground. It plumped with air, boosting them upward. Janet's legs scrambled to connect with the ground again. For a breathless moment they seemed stuck, the chute twisting behind them, threatening to turn and drag them along the ground over the hill. Then their feet lifted off the ground, and they slipped down the hill as if were made of ice. The wind, much cooler than it had been at Graumauer, whipped Janet's cheeks. As they flew down the slope gaining speed but no height, she wriggled and leaned, trying to force their weight away from the ground.

"We're going to scrape the ground!" she shouted.

"Don't do that! Be still!" Brandt shouted back.

Brandt threw his weight opposite to hers. Hanging in front of him with no access to control the chute, she was powerless. They jerked and jounced first to the right, then to the left. Suddenly the ground sped away from them. Brandt leaned down and to one side and Janet plummeted with him as he steered them into open air. Janet rocked her legs as the chute swooped and dove, then just as abruptly, they rocketed upward. They gained altitude fast and again Janet was forced motionless. Brandt's gloved hands lowered toward Janet's shoulders. In each one was a strap attached to a control cord. He alternated tugs at each cord to maneuver and catch as much air as possible. The chute leveled and hung a moment before wafting downward like an autumn leaf on a windless day.

"How are you doing?" he asked, leaning over her shoulder and purling warm breath against her ear.

"Okay now."

Janet was relieved that the leg straps held her in a comfortable sitting position. She had imagined dangling precariously, bouncing and leaping like a puppet. Instead, she was comfortable, as if she was sitting in an airplane, except there was no seat and no airplane.

When Brandt guided their chute back toward the hill to catch more updraft, Janet squealed in protest. She didn't like being just a passenger. As the chute drifted to within a few feet of the hill, she drew in her legs and arms, preparing for a crash landing.

"Hey, don't do that!" Brandt shouted.

Brandt threw his weight to one side and yanked at one of the cords, wrenching the chute backward. Catching the updraft at the last moment, they gained altitude and swung away from the hill. Rising above the crest, Brandt made a big lazy circle like a hawk. They gained hundreds of feet in a few moments. The broad view was astounding. The sprawl of the tan and grey town, the green fields and the ordered squares of the Monastery buildings were clearly visible below. Brandt turned, heading away from town toward Graumauer. They approached from the front of the estate. The dark green leaves of the walnut tree formed a perfect ball of foliage in front of the gray tile roof of the main building.

The rush of noisy air quieted as they skimmed over the estate in a graceful glide.

"You don't need to be afraid, Janet. And don't fight me so much. Lean with me when I lean and we'll be fine."

"I'm not afraid, and I'm not fighting you. If you weren't so abrupt we could work together," she fired back. "Just give me a little warning, would you? I hate having no idea what you're going to do."

They sailed high over the wrought iron gates then turned to the right and circled over a white fenced meadow with several horses. The horses all bolted away from the alien chute except one. It looked up at them, and Janet recognized Salzig. The sight of the horse was calming. Her anger at Brandt's criticism cooled.

The two aerialists looped around behind the stables and over the sandy practice paddocks and mirrored duck pond.

"Graumauer is so beautiful," she said to Brandt.

"Yes. I love my life here. I don't come back often enough."

Brandt continued their slow turn, following the brook that spilled from the duck pond. They were losing altitude. Brandt finished the turn and continued along their previous path away from town headed toward the higher hills to the south.

Brandt expertly guided the chute parallel to a steep ridge. The upwelling of air caught the chute and boosted it skyward. Janet was now able to echo Brandt's moves as he sought out the best updrafts.

"Look at the altitude we are gaining," he said, pointing to an altimeter strapped to his arm. "We are almost a thousand feet higher than when we started."

In the distance, the white angular peaks of the Alps were distinct against the horizon.

"Do you want to try something fun?"

"Uh, sure..."

Brandt maneuvered away from the ridge, then turned around, and flew directly at it. Janet let out a scream just as the updraft caught them, and hurled them skyward. At the height of their rise, the updraft ended in turbulence. They bounced in the rough air. Brandt pulled hard on the right control cord, swinging them out severely to the side. Knowing that he planned this, Janet leaned with him this time. They hurtled upward while the parasail dove down until their bodies were horizontal with it. Janet squealed in delight. Brandt yanked at the other cord, and they swung downward, swaying like the pendulum of a huge grandfather clock, down under the parasail, then up to the other side. Janet's movements mirrored his.

"Yee-haw!" Janet yelled at the exhilarating acceleration and the thrilling sensation of weightlessness at the top of the swing.

Brandt gradually leveled out, and glided away from the ridge.

"Want to do that again?"

"You bet!"

Again they repeated the acrobatic maneuver. Janet now had a feel for what to do with her weight and how to move her body to complement Brandt's moves.

When she screamed out her delight this time, she felt his deep laugh right through the harness and her clothes. Right down to her bones.

They sailed out high in the air, and flew toward the monastery. After circling the town, they headed for Graumauer. He made one final circuit around the main house. The teardrop drive, the stable, the paddocks, the fields and trails, all revealed their perfect symmetry. A regularity that was not as apparent from the ground. Graumauer had been carefully crafted for a higher purpose, to be a hidden focal point in the order of civilized life.

"Noblesse oblige," she spoke softly to herself.

Flying into the wind, they hung motionless over the sloping ground in front of the house and dropped by degrees. Their landing was soft and light as Brandt jogged them to a halt. The chute collapsed behind them.

With a click of metal, Brandt undid their straps and freed them from their harnesses. Janet spun around, threw her arms around his neck and kissed him. He wrapped his arms around her, deepening the kiss. The heat of his body warmed her reddened cheeks, and penetrated into her being.

Adelheidis stood in a window watching as the couple floated down from the sky. A wistful smile came to her face. Her eyes focused on her son, yet seemed to look past him to another man who once stood in that place many year before. Then she looked to Janet, also seeing another young woman of long ago kissing the adventurous young man of her dreams.

She looked down at the gold and ruby band on her finger, turning is slowly over and over. It had been her mother's. And her grandmother's. And her great-grandmother's. She gently pulled. After so many years it refused to come off. Then she gathered her will and strength and pulled harder. With a painful pop it came off. The skin underneath was red and bruised, but also fresh and alive. This ring was her life. It was much more than her half marriage to Valter, it was her devotion to Graumauer. She looked around her, drinking in the world that had owned her for three decades. Then she looked back out at Janet, and focused on the younger woman's hands. Yes, this ring would fit her finger very well.

Never again would the ring go back on the finger of Adelheidis Mahler.

The couple stumbled through the main door into the ornate foyer, laughing and carrying on about their adventure. Friedrich met them at the center of the room, beaming broadly.

"Dinner will be in one hour, Herr Brandt. May I get you or Fraulein Janet an aperitif?"

"Thank you, Friedrich. We will both have a small glass of Peppermint Schnapps after we have changed."

"Jawohl."

Brandt led Janet up the stairway that curved to the left then down the hall to her room. To her surprise, the room was very modern, painted in breezy pastels with white-washed furniture that looked like it belonged in a windswept seaside cottage.

"This room is beautiful," Janet said, easing into the room with steps as light and airy as the room itself.

"My mother can be quite stern at times, but also very contemporary in her style. She has a perennial liking for seaside themes."

"Odd for someone so steeped in Swiss culture."

Brandt laughed. "Yes. I think in her next life she will live by the sea."

Friedrich had already placed Janet's suitcase on her bed for her. Her clothes from earlier in the day were hanging in the closet, the door of which had been left ajar for her to see. A formal-looking bright blue dress and high-heeled shoes were laid out on the bed.

"Your bath is here," Brandt indicated, pointing to the equally bright bathroom decorated in seacoast theme. "Take your time getting ready. The blue dress will look great on you. I'll meet you downstairs on the rear patio when you are ready." Brandt stepped from the room and closed the door.

Janet checked her watch. Marcie would be on her morning break between classes.

"Hey, big sister," Marcie answered. "You do anything interesting lately?" There was a light chuckle that followed Marcie's prompting remark, as if she expected to be entertained with more fantastic tales.

"What a day I've had. I'm at Brandt's family estate. Brandt's mother taught me how to steeple jump horses, and Brandt and I just returned from parasailing around his home town."

"Jan, Wow. I'm having trouble keeping up with everything that you're doing. But even more wow, Brandt took you to meet his mother? That sounds like he is getting serious about you."

"Yeah. I mean he hasn't come out and actually said anything, but Marcie, things are getting weird."

"How so?"

"There is this guy, Friedrich, the head butler. I overheard him telling his son that I will become the next matron of Brandt's family estate."

"What? Has Brandt said anything?"

"Like I said, no. But his mother started giving me a history lesson about the family dynasty. It was like she wanted to train me to take over."

"Whoa. How'd you feel about that?"

"I think he brought me here to see if I would fail at impressing his mother. He changed his whole attitude when I didn't. But now I feel trapped. The place is beautiful. And I fell in love with a horse named Salzig. But his family, they are so - I don't know - Swiss. They are all a bunch of uppity-ups, and I'm not. I feel so out of my own."

"How has Brandt been acting?"

"The same. At times condescending, other times attentive and romantic."

"But you said he irritates you."

"Yes, but I don't think he means it to be irritating. He means it in a positive way."

"Irritating in a positive way. That's an interesting spin on things."

"Marcie, there is just something about him. The way he kisses me, for example."

"Go on."

"When he holds me, I don't know. It's not like anything I've ever felt before."

"Oh, boy. Jan, what am I going to do with you? I told you to be careful. You are letting your this guy take over your life. I think he is sounding more like a control freak than anything else. He tells you what to wear, what to eat, what to drink. Next thing you know he'll be telling you how to hold your glass."

"He already did that."

"See what I mean? And it sounds like his mother is doing the same thing to you."

"I know, but..."

"Look. I give up," Marcie said, anger overtaking her bubbly voice. "I've told you what to do, but you keep doing the opposite. You are going to get burned, big time, and I am not going to stand five thousand miles away and watch it happen. Do what you want. I don't care."

"No, Marcie," Janet pleaded. "I know you're right. I'll head home in a few days."

"That is what you said a few days ago. And every day that goes by you get in deeper and deeper. Tomorrow. If you don't, then don't call me."

The line went dead.

Marcie had never scolded her like that. Their normal mother-daughter roles had reversed. Janet hung her head and wanted to cry. But the tears would not come. She simply stared at the floor not knowing what to do. She stood and took her hair brush from her bag and started to comb out the tangles made by parasailing. Marcie was right. This fairytale world was not meant for her. Assistant professor in Tulsa wasn't either. Somewhere in between was a place where she could find herself, a place where she fit.

She looked at the bright blue gown Brandt had set out for her. He was picking her clothes again, and telling what to drink. Even Friedrich and Adelheidis wanted her to mold herself to their purposes. With a huff, she changed into a dark purple satin gown she had picked out in Brussels instead. She looked in the mirror. Staring back was a princess from a Disney movie. A princess waiting for the clock to strike Midnight and for it all to end.

And it would end. She was sure of that.

Even Zelman said so.

Blinking to see properly through the haze of light tears, she glided down the stairs to the back patio where Brandt was waiting.

His eyes brightened at the sight of her, then his brows furrowed.

"Are you okay?"

"Yeah, fine. Why?"

"Your eyes."

"Must be too much wind from parasailing."

He nodded acknowledgement.

Janet turned her head and swiped away the moisture at the edges of her eyes.

Friedrich brought their schnapps.

"To Graumauer," Brandt toasted. Janet, grasping the tiny glass with her fist wrapped around it, clinked back, making a dull thud.

"No, Janet. Hold it like this so it will ring," he corrected.

Control freak, Janet thought as she tried to lighten her grip. But the glass slipped and only Friedrich's fast reflexes kept the minty liquid from perfuming the table. Cinderella never spilled her drink.

She put her schnapps back on the tray and crossed her arms in frustration.

"Are you sure you are okay?" Brandt asked again.

"I said I'm fine."

Brandt put his un-sipped glass back on Friedrich's tray and signaled for him to go.

"What happened to the blue dress?" he asked.

"I like this one better."

"But I picked..." He was cut off by her withering glare.

"Janet, Brandt, here you are," Adelheidis spoke in a pleasant but formal voice. "Come, let us have our dinner."

Brandt stood and offered his arm to his mother. Adelheidis reached to take it, but she hesitated, turned and invited Janet to take it instead. Janet, too, hesitated, feeling herself being drawn down a path Marcie had told her not to go. She swallowed, and put her arm through his. Adelheidis patted Brandt's arm in satisfaction. The matron led the way to the dining room. She held out a chair for Janet, who was overly aware of the fact that Adelheidis had just sat her at the head of the table, and to what that might signify.

"What are we having?" Janet asked.

"Hirschbraten," Adelheidis answered. "How do you say it in English — deer meat."

"Oh."

Friedrich served their plates and wine. Brandt, for the first time since meeting her, did not propose a toast. Should she make one? A tense silence descended over the table.

Janet sliced into the meat and put a small bite into her mouth. She'd never tasted venison before. It tasted gamey, like old beef, and the texture was waxy.

"Janet," Adelheidis began, "did you enjoy your parasailing?"

"Yes. Very much. I never knew you could fly a parachute that way."

"Einsiedeln is truly a special place. I have loved it here and I'm sure you will, too."

Steel jaws were creaking shut on her. Janet nodded, trying not to let the walls close in on her, wincing away the flavor of her second bite of venison. The liberal dollop of red sauce hadn't improved the taste. She reached for her wine and took a hearty sip. Was Adelheidis making a grimace at her manners?

There was a long silence filled only with the sounds of silver on china. Friedrich leaned to refill Janet's wine. He gave her a mild smile along with a nod of approval before resuming his place behind her chair. He hadn't taken his eyes off her since she'd been seated. Uncomfortable heat built at the back of Janet's neck. She could feel him watching her. Like the sniper's crosshairs had been.

Janet pushed her nearly full plate away.

"Do you not enjoy the Hirsch?" Adelheidis asked.

"Oh, it is fine. I'm just not very hungry."

She lifted her wine glass, gazing through the pale liquid at Adelheidis as she spoke.

"I have a wonderful kitchen staff here, but I have been unhappy with the chef from time to time. He favors French methods and dishes, while I prefer German ways. Of course, you must always feel free to make your own choices in staff."

Change the kitchen staff? This was too much. The walls began to move, inching in on her. Her head began to swirl as a salty flavor came to her mouth and her stomach rolled.

"I hope you will excuse me," said Janet. She stood and walked to the door, leaving her puzzled hosts staring at each other.

She stepped into the foyer and closed the door behind her. Placing her cool palm on her hot forehead she leaned back against the door and took several deep cleansing breaths. Better move before someone followed her.

She walked to the closest stairway, and placed her hand on the long sweeping banister. The door to the library was open. Its warm glowing light beckoning. She glanced back to the dining room door. No one was following. A few quick steps brought her into the former interrogation room.

The chairs that she and Adelheidis had sat in earlier had been pushed back to their normal places. Adelheidis had been so cold during her grilling. Was this what they were asking of her? To become a stuffy matron stuck in a beautiful cage in the foothills of the Alps? Adelheidis had sacrificed everything to fill a role that Janet could not imagine playing. That was no more appealing than being trapped in Oklahoma, teaching undergrads.

Janet looked up at the books, so neatly labeled and cataloged. The room smelled of old leather, ancient lambskin parchment. Her mind drifted back to her apartment, to her own small collection of books. She had dreamed of someday having a library just like this one. In her dream she would carefully document and label each and every volume with care, and would beam when a worldly scholar asked permission to use her collection. Here it was. Hers for the taking.

Janet ran her fingers along the bindings. They thumped over the irregular soft leather. They stopped on one, and she pulled it out. It was in English, a memoir of a cavalry soldier. She placed it under her arm, and left the room.

Back in her bedroom, she changed into her long night gown and snuggled herself comfortably in bed to read. The book was a pompous narration of the glories of battle, and Janet quickly tired of it. It simply wasn't her type of book, too pedantic, too self righteous and self-serving. Just like Graumauer. Not something for a girl from Oklahoma.

There was a knock on the door.

"Janet," came Brandt's voice, "may I come in?"

"You will anyway, so you might as well."

Brandt sheepishly stepped into the room, and sat on the edge of her bed, leaving her as much room as possible.

"I'm sorry if we came on too heavily. It's, just well, everyone likes you so much."

"Brandt, that is not it, and you know it," she scolded. "I am just a plain girl from Oklahoma. I like your mother very much, but I am a world apart from her. You all seem to think I can just waltz into this place, and in a couple of hours become the next Adelheidis Mahler. Well I can't. It is not me. It is not who I am. Period."

"What makes you think that?" Brandt replied obviously trying to backpedal a retreat.

"Friedrich gawking at me, your mother giving me the detailed history of Graumauer, practically giving me the operating handbook for the place, telling me I should change the kitchen staff. And you. 'Hold the wine this way, move that way, wear this, drink that.' I'm tired of it, Brandt. I want to be me. I wish I could go back to being Janet Thompson from Tulsa, and not the girl who tags along with Mr. Wonderful. Maybe the other three and half billion women on the planet would jump at the chance, but not me. Okay? So back off!"

Brandt sat unmoving, unaccustomed to such a personal rejection. Then he stood, and walked to the door.

"Hey," she said, guilt piercing her heart. "I'm sorry. Come back, sit down."

Brandt didn't seem to know what else to do but comply.

"I really need to go back to Tulsa."

Brandt stared at her. She could read the deep pain in his eyes. There was no smugness there.

His face simply went blank.

She reached over, putting her hand around his neck.

"Come here."

She pulled him over to her, resting his head on her shoulder. She turned off the light, and gently rocked the wounded man.

*** 

Janet awoke, her head lying on Brandt's chest, her long hair veiling its muscular contours. Slow steady breathing rocked her up and down in gentle rolls. His arms were folded over her back, holding her with the gentle clasp of a child with his precious toy. Still fully dressed in their clothes from dinner, he'd held her all night.

She pried herself away without waking him, and checked her watch. Five AM, ten PM in Tulsa. Marcie would still be up. Janet slipped into the bathroom, and holding the door handle down, quietly closed the door.

"Hey, Jan," Marcie answered. "I'm sorry about what I said last time. Whatever I said, ignore it. You have to find your own way. I shouldn't have told you what to do. Even if it means you will get hurt. Plus the estate does put a nice new spin on things."

"No. We are not going to even go there. The only reason I would stay with Brandt Mahler is because I love him, not because he has money."

"And do you?"

"Do I what?"

213

"Love him."

"I broke off with him. I'm coming home."

"That's not what I asked. Do you love him?"

Janet didn't answer.

"Oh my God," Marcie exclaimed. "You do! I knew you would fall for him, just because he's so different from you. Ha! And I also know why you broke off with him. You can't face the uncertainty of love. Even if you found the man of your dreams, you'd find something to complain about."

"No. It's his constant criticism."

"Yesterday you said his criticisms were positive. Today you're saying you're breaking off with him because of them. Sounds to me like he was testing you to see if you could fit in his world, and you passed. Jan, you're the one who wanted a bigger world. And now that a bigger world is within reach, you've got cold feet."

"Marcie, you're wrong!"

"Am I? Oh, okay then, tell me this: why did you change your mind so quickly about Brandt?"

"I, uh. Ooooo, I don't know!" Janet slapped the phone shut, leaned with her head back against the door, and pressed the heel of her hand against her forehead. She let out a low groan of exasperation.

"Janet? Are you okay?" Brandt called.

"Oh, leave me alone!" she snapped.

# CHAPTER SIXTEEN

She heard Brandt open then slam the door out of her room. The sharp thud and its anger reverberated against her head. Hot tears filled her eyes and ran down her cheeks. She buried her face in her hands and sobbed. This was way too much stress. The wave of events bore down on her, overwhelming her in a breathless wall of confusion. Being in love was only part of it. She didn't want to give up Brandt, but she didn't want to give up herself either.

Survive one more day, Zelman said. She couldn't do it.

Lifting her head to pull in short breaths, she caught her reflection in a full length mirror. That woman was not her. Where had Janet Thompson gone, and how could she find her?

The answer was so simple: go home. All she needed to do was ask Friedrich for a ride to the train station. Maybe he'd help her get a train ticket to the airport.

Simple. Easy. Cowardly. Marcie was right. Admit it. That's what she was, and that's how she would be.

She stepped into the bedroom and pulled out her plain clothes from Oklahoma and started to dress. She'd leave with nothing she hadn't brought. There was a sedate knock on her door.

"Frauline Janet," Friedrich spoke. "Please forgive of me. Herr Mahler, Brandt's father, is calling. The Tokyo Stock Market is crashing. He is needing you and Herr Brandt to stop it. He is sending a helicopter to take you back to Zurich immediately."

Why were these people bothering her? There was nothing more she could do. She'd run all the computer simulations she could two days before. If they hadn't worked, then it was clear they'd only made Zelman stronger. Let Brandt handle this situation. Zelman was his uncle. No, his father. His own father!

"Frauline Janet. Please, you are hearing me?"

"Yes, Friedrich. I'm getting ready now."

She finished dressing in her old clothes, stuffed her passport, wallet, and phone into her pockets. She left the suitcase with her new clothes in the middle of her bed, and stepped to the door. Only what came from Tulsa would go back to Tulsa. Just one exception. She grabbed Zelman's hat and turned out the light.

As the helicopter made its clamorous landing on the lawn the horses in the paddock bolted and ran. All but one. He stood and watched Janet as she climbed into the helicopter. They locked eyes. What did Janet want from this life? He put his nose in the air and made a shrill whinny. She turned away and closed the door.

She sat next to Brandt, his lips pursed tight and his arms crossed over his chest. She watched Graumauer and Salzig drop away into the gray morning mist.

"We'll use the SBU rooftop helipad near the WMF building. We can take the tram from there. It'll be faster than getting a driver," said Brandt with stern command.

Janet looked at Brandt. His anguish of last night had turned to anger this morning. Even over the helicopter headphones, the sharpness in his voice was unmistakable. She should apologize again. Try to make him understand. But would it help?

"I told you your way wouldn't work," he grumbled through clenched teeth as the city approached.

Janet's lips parted and she stared agape at him for half a second. "Excuse me, what did you just say?"

"I said I told you your senseless plan wouldn't work. You should have listened to me. I have the experience."

"I didn't see you rushing to push your plan through. In fact I don't think you even had a plan. You had no idea what to do during the crisis, except to blame me. I at least did something. Don't you dare start Monday morning quarterbacking me."

Brandt's face contorted into a scowl, but his reply was cut short by the helicopter landing. They ran down the single flight of roof top stairs and took the elevator to the ground floor. A blue and white tram was in front of the SBU building. They dashed to the tram just as its doors were closing. Brandt jammed his finger into the big circular door button and the doors opened.

On the tram they sat across from a little girl of about five and her mother, each dressed in matching blue dresses. The mother was reading a magazine.

The bright-eyed girl held up her doll for them to see. Brandt ignored her and turned his head to look out the window.

"Mein Kind ist krank. Sie hat eine Temperatur. Sehen Sie?" the little girl said to Janet.

Janet glanced at Brandt, but he offered no translation. Janet shook her head at the girl, but she was still holding out her doll, apparently for Janet's inspection.

"I don't speak German," Janet answered with a smile, trying not to let the girl see her anger at Brandt.

The girl's eyes lit up.

"I am speaking English," she proudly boasted. "My child is sick," she said pointing to her doll. "She has a temperature. See?"

Janet reached out and felt the doll's forehead.

"Oh yes. She is sick. She is lucky she has such a good mother to take care of her."

The girl beamed.

"My name is Emily."

"My name is Janet."

The tram slowed, and the recorded announcement declared the Zurich Bahnhaben stop. The four of them stood to get off. Brandt let the woman and child off, then he urged Janet before him. She could still read anger in his eyes. She stepped off the tram into the sunlit morning.

"You're a coward," Brandt said on the sidewalk. "You're afraid you screwed things up. Too afraid to stay and clean up your own mess."

"You're right," Janet said pushing a pointed finger into his chest. "I am not staying. Not because I screwed up, but to get away from your arrogant, condescending taunts. I've had enough!"

A man intently watched the quarrel from the opposite side of the street. Stepping around the protective corner of a building, he pressed speed dial on his cell phone.

Janet never felt the blast wave that slammed into the four of them.

***

"Janet," she heard her mother call, "time to wake up."

"No, I want to sleep."

"Time to wake up."

Out in the kitchen she heard her mother's tea kettle, its loud piercing whistle demanding attention. She opened her eyes.

The area was filled with caustic sulfur smoke. There was no tea kettle. The piercing sound was Emily's screaming. Thick, dark blood covered her right thigh. Crumpled adjacent to her was the girl's stunned mother, shaking and fighting to regain consciousness. Brandt lay still, unconscious, his left arm bent unnaturally behind him.

Janet shook her head, her ears ringing. She leaned toward Brandt and checked his pulse. It was strong, and he was breathing. Emily continued screaming, her mouth open wide, showing all of her tiny white teeth framing the pink of her mouth. All of a sudden the little girl's scream stopped. She stared with fright at Janet for a moment, shuddered once, then her little body went limp.

She was bleeding to death.

The bleeding had to be stopped. Now. She'd be dead before the paramedics arrived. Janet looked around for something to use as a tourniquet. When she got up on all fours to scrounge around, Zelman's hat fell in front of her. In a flash of insight she saw the black ribbon stitched around the brim. She tore at the ribbon, ripping away hunks of felt as she went.

Winding it once around the girl's tiny leg, she crossed the ends and cinched it tight. The bleeding stopped. Janet leaned over the girl's ashen face. Please let her still be breathing. Janet laid her hand on the girl's chest. She felt nothing. CPR, what where those rules? She covered Emily's nose and mouth with hers and breathed into her.

The air filled with the high-low wail of European sirens. Approaching fire trucks. Firemen jumped off, oxygen masks in place. One knelt next to the girl and started asking Janet muffled questions in German. Janet just shook her head. They motioned Janet back and lifted Emily onto a stretcher. The girl's mother was kneeling on all fours trying to raise her head and see what was happening to her daughter. The woman's head lolled down as another fireman bent to speak to her.

Janet stood up and gazed down at the girl. She was so still, her little hand clutched the doll's arm in a stiff pose.

She couldn't be dead. She just can't be dead. Please.

Janet followed the girl's stretcher to the ambulance just as a news truck pulled up. A TV cameraman jogged up to her, making a motion with his hand on his head. He'd seen her tattered hat and recognized Cowgirl. A big lens loomed into her face.

"Cowgirl! Yee-haw!" the camera man shouted.

Janet grabbed the lens and pushed it aside. The heavy camera slammed down onto the concrete. The camera man shouted something in anger, but Janet ignored him.

She saw Emily's mother being carried on a stretcher to another ambulance.

"No, over here! Keep them together." Janet called, with urgent gestures. They didn't listen.

Running up to the mother's ambulance crew, she herded them toward the other ambulance. She must keep mother and daughter together. Janet got in the ambulance with them. Through the open ambulance door she saw paramedics inflating a protective collar around Brandt's neck.

Head injury? Spine injury?

She looked to Emily, then Brandt. Who needed her more? The decision was made for her when the doors closed and the siren screamed its way through the gathering crowd.

The medics put an oxygen mask in place and started an IV in the girl's arm as the radio squawked doctor's instructions. Sirens continued to clear the way as they hurtled down the streets toward the hospital.

"It was me they wanted," Janet said to herself. "They got her instead." Damn Zelman and his horrible plan! Friedrich was an idiot to say he could be trusted!

Rage surged in her veins as she thought of Mirza and her nameless pawns who so desperately wanted her dead. Funny, she thought, Mirza had far more confidence in her abilities than Brandt did.

The ambulance swung to a halt in front of the Emergency Room entrance. Doors flew open. Bedlam descended. Frantic for facts, the nurses and doctors mistakenly thought Janet was the girl's mother and kept peppering questions at her.

Finally she was able to explain the mother-daughter connection as their two gurneys were pushed into the building. The mother's gurney was driven off to the right into a ward treatment area. Emily was diverted down a side hall and through a set of double doors. Janet hurried alongside the girl's gurney as they raced their little patient into an elevator. The staff let Janet cram into the elevator with them. It seemed an eternity for the elevator to rise to the operating room level. Then the doors opened, and the staff and gurney surged forward en mass. A nurse blocked Janet's way as the furor headed into the operating room.

The nurse spoke German in a firm tone and pointed to a small waiting area. Janet hesitated. She needed to know that Emily would be okay. After insisting on compliance by guiding Janet to a seat, the large woman retreated to a nurse's station located at one side of the narrow hall.

Abrupt silence slapped Janet as she stood alone. The only sound was the continued ringing in her ears and the solitary nurse clacking computer keys, her sole intent to plow through the mountain of paperwork the emergency had just generated. Janet's clothes were in tatters, even the hat. She looked like an impoverished bag lady. She pulled apart a long tear on her jeans. Numerous slashes and cuts made it look like she'd been attacked by a wildcat. Every inch of her ached. But she was okay.

She hadn't seen Brandt come in. Would they have taken him to a different hospital?

"Excuse me. How is the little girl, Emily?" she asked the nurse.

The nurse didn't even look up, she only muttered something in Swiss German.

With her hat in tatters and without Brandt by her side, Janet's new found identity was lost. She had been plummeted backward a week into the role of unrecognized Janet Thompson. Dressed in her dowdy clothes from Tulsa, she was back to being a nobody from nowhere.

Her cowardly wish from yesterday had been granted.

Janet wandered away from the nurse's station. One corner of the small waiting room held a cluster of plain wooden chairs with a silent television. Not knowing what else to do she sat and fidgeted. She turned on the TV and changed the channel to CNN in English. The unhelpful nurse looked up, said something unintelligible, and shaking her head in disgust returned to her paperwork.

The New York rally that Janet's computer efforts created had been short lived. The Asian markets were in freefall. The European markets had only been open for a few minutes, but they were already down over five percentage points.

Zelman!

Instead of him walking into her trap, she had walked into his. How many billions had he made yesterday as puts and calls bounced back and forth across the globe? All the patient sweat in the computer lab, her elegant equations backed up by real live data and interventions sanctioned by the President of the United States. Nothing had mattered in the end. She felt like a fool, all alone, adrift in an ocean she had no right to have played in. This was not where she belonged. Back in the classroom in Tulsa, that is where she should be.

She checked her watch. Marcie and Professor Jones would be asleep. Yes, wallet, phone and passport were still there. Her passport cover was scuffed but the inside was still pristine. Flipping through the pages, she grimaced. Every single one was blank. Nine countries, and not one stamp. There was nothing to show for her trip but bruises, cuts and scrapes. And one very broken heart.

She'd be on the airplane before either Marcie or Brandt woke up. She stood and walked to the elevator. The elevator door opened before she got there. An orderly pushed Emily's mother in a wheel chair into the waiting room. She was bandaged and bruised, but otherwise okay. The orderly joined the nurse in the drudgery of paperwork.

"Emily is still in there," Janet said.

Emily's mother looked up, her foggy eyes trying to focus on Janet.

"You're the woman from the tram. Are you the one that saved my Emily?"

Was she? Or was she the one that caused her injury? Janet decided to nod yes.

"Thank you." The woman scanned around the room, still dazed by the day's events. "The doctor told me she was going to be okay."

Janet nodded acknowledgement.

The woman's gaze came to rest on Janet's hat. "Oh, you're Cowgirl! And you're hurt!" the woman said, finally retrieving enough wits to see Janet's injuries.

"No, I'm fine."

"Nurse," Emily's mother called. "This woman is hurt." The recalcitrant nurse didn't respond. "Sie ist Cowgirl," she said trying to gain some attention.

Before Janet could stop her, the nurse turned. A moment later there was the flash of a camera in her face.

"No, I'm not Cowgirl," Janet said, holding up her hands to block another blinding flash. "Not anymore." She got up and left the room and hobbled down a flight of stairs emerging into a hallway.

It would only be a matter of moments before there would be more cameras. She looked up and down the empty hall seeking escape. Then she saw him, Brandt, on a gurney being wheeled out of an elevator. She was too far away to judge his condition. He appeared to be un-moving. However, the three staff with him didn't seem concerned as they guided his gurney into a room. She held back, waiting, nervous that her Cowgirl identity would be rediscovered. Several minutes later, all three of the staff emerged from the room, the last one closing the door behind her.

As soon as they were out of sight, Janet stepped forward and entered the darkened room. Brandt was sleeping peacefully, his head partially wrapped in bandages, one arm in a cast, the other receiving an IV drip. She looked at the IV bag and read its label. A sedative. Brandt would rest painlessly until the doctors decided to let him wake him up.

"I'm sorry," she said, gently stroking his hair above his bandages.

"You should be," came a sharp woman's voice from the door.

Janet whirled around. Andy stood there, feet spread in an angry stance, hands on her hips. Behind her was a man. His plain gray suit and the coil of wire hanging from his ear bud told her he was Andy's bodyguard.

"What are you doing here?" Janet demanded.

Andy didn't answer. With a dangerous look in her eyes the woman scanned Janet, taking in her untended wounds and tattered hat. She leaned toward her bodyguard and spoke in rapid fire Azeri. The man nodded and stepped out, closing the door behind them.

Andy stepped forward, tossing her head to throw back her fall of blonde hair. She stretched out her arm, pointing an accusing finger at Janet.

"I was about to ask you the same question. How dare you come here after what you did to Brandt! Look at him. This is all your fault."

"My fault? This isn't my fault. Mirza and Anton have been after us for days."

Andy stopped before Brandt's bed. She shook her head at the sleeping man. Janet leaned closer, protectively shielding Brandt.

"Zelman has been after you for days, Janet? I don't believe it. I know about you and you're connection to him. You have been using Brandt to help Zelman destroy the whole world economy. You planned this to destroy the evidence. Why else would you be so willing to give him up?"

"What are you talking about? You are insane."

"Am I? Look at Brandt and that innocent little girl. Their injuries are extensive. Look at you, hardly touched, not even needing a doctor. You must have known of the bomb and used Brandt and the girl as shields."

The door swung open. In stepped the body guard followed by two Zurich polizei. The guard pointed to Janet standing with her hand still on Brandt's head.

"Stop her!" Andy desperately pleaded, instant tears pooling in her eyes.

The policemen moved toward Janet.

"Los! Weg von ihm," the lead man ordered.

"What?"

"Get away from him. Now!" he barked in English.

Janet reflexively put her hands up.

"Come with us," the polizei spoke.

"No. Why? I'm not leaving Brandt."

"You are Janet Thompson, yes?"

"Yes, I am."

"You are under arrest," the older man said.

Stepping toward Janet, the junior man unsnapped the small belt case that held his handcuffs. He pulled Janet's wrists together and to clamp the handcuffs over them.

"No. You can't arrest me." She pulled away. "You can't. What am I being charged with?"

"It's all right, Janet," Andy spoke sweetly, wiping at her false tears. "You had better do what they ask. You won't be allowed to hurt Brandt ever again."

The two polizei wrestled the cuffs on to Janet and pulled her toward the door. She clamped her teeth down against the pain of her injuries, refusing to cry out in front of Andy.

"Don't worry, Janet." Andy spoke with a velvety voice, stepping up to Brandt's head and running her long manicured nails through his curly hair. "I will take good care of him. He is mine now."

"Oooo! You!" Janet screamed. "You set this up!"

The polizei didn't give Janet a chance to react further. They yanked her out through the door and pulled her to the elevator. She didn't even know why she continued to struggle against them. Her basic instinct was to get back to Andy and tear her apart. The blonde might win a beauty contest now, but Janet was certain she could take her out of the running in the future. The police had to manhandle her through the lobby and out to their waiting black and white car with its fluorescent red stripes sloped across both sides.

During the short ride to the station, Janet managed to gain control of her irrational senses. Within minutes of arriving she was sitting on a cheap plastic chair alone in a sterile interrogation room, its harsh, overly bright fluorescent lights glaring in her eyes. Her hands, stiff and sore in her lap, were still clamped into the handcuffs. Her back ached and the cuts and bruises on her legs stung and throbbed.

The door opened and in stepped a corpulent man in his mid forties dressed in a wrinkled brown suit. Behind him followed a robust uniformed polizei matron, similar in age, her face even less sympathetic than the man's. She stood in one corner, arms crossed, watching with unblinking eyes. Janet rose from her seat.

"Please, Ms. Thompson, sit down," the man spoke in good, but accented English.

"No. I'd rather stand."

"Sit!" the man ordered.

Too weak to maintain her false bravado, Janet complied.

Another man stepped into the room. He was wearing a white lab coat, carrying a small kit box. He placed his box onto a small stainless steel table in one corner, and removed a bottle of solution and gauze pads.

"Hold out your hands, please."

She did. He placed the gauze under one hand, sprayed a solution over it, and then wiped her hand. He repeated this with her other hand, then placed the gauze back into the kit box. He handed her a paper towel, and left the room.

"Ms. Thompson," the brown suited man continued, "I am detective Gumbarri. I will be asking you some questions."

"What if I refuse to answer them?"

"That is certainly an option," he said with a smile. "An option I recommend you do not use." He opened a file folder and took out her passport. "How did you arrive in Switzerland?" he asked flipping through its unstamped pages.

"I flew in with Brandt Mahler on his jet two days ago."

"Did you not pass through immigration control?"

"No. We landed at a private hangar."

"That is a serious offense of Swiss law," he stated. "Surely you realize this?"

"No, not really," said Janet. "Brandt must have gotten diplomatic clearance or something."

"From where did your flight originate?"

Janet made a small guffaw. The less she said, the better. "Brussels."

Gumbarri held up the empty passport, leafed through the empty pages and held up his hands in a questioning gesture. "I have to question that, Ms. Thompson."

"Look. You must have seen my landing in Brussels. It was all over the news. I wasn't trying to enter Belgium or Switzerland illegally."

"So it would appear," Gumbarri replied slowly. "However, appearances can be so very deceptive, can't they Ms. Thompson?"

"If you don't believe me you can ask Brandt Mahler."

"I may have to do that, but I will have to wait until he wakes up from his injuries. Why were you there in his room at the hospital?"

"Because I was hurt in a bomb blast."

"You don't appear to have suffered great injury."

"No. I was lucky."

"Luck or planning? Did you plan this bomb?"

"No."

Janet turned her head to the side. She wasn't going to answer any more questions. She could see where this was going. Gumbarri waited a moment, then cleared his throat and resumed questioning.

"And how did you arrive at the hospital, Ms. Thompson?"

"By ambulance."

"And which doctors did you see?"

"I didn't see any doctors."

"You were hurt, went to the hospital in a city ambulance, but you weren't treated by any doctors? Why?"

"I needed to stay with Emily. A little girl who was hurt in the bomb blast."

"And how do you know this Emily?"

"We met on the tram."

"So you had just met Emily when you set the bomb off."

"Yes. No! I didn't set off the bomb. She was bleeding to death. I saved her life."

"You took advantage of the little girl's injury to get access to an ambulance that was going to the hospital."

"No. I was trying to help."

"If you wanted to help with the little girl, then why were you found in Dr. Mahler's room?"

"I was with Dr. Mahler before the bomb went off. I told you, we had been traveling together."

"Why were your hands on Dr. Mahler? Did you intend to kill him?"

"Oh, this is ridiculous."

She turned her head and didn't answer. The thought of sedatives made Janet wonder if Brandt was being kept sedated for reasons other than just waiting for his shock to wear off. What if he was more badly injured than it seemed? What if he didn't wake up? He could be in a coma for months, years. She dropped her head trying desperately not to burst into tears.

Gumbarri's cell phone rang, and he spoke briefly, then closed it.

"Can you explain why your hands tested positive for explosives?"

"What?" asked Janet, lifting her head. "I was in an explosion."

"What is your connection to Anton Zelman?"

"He's been following me."

"So you have a connection to him."

"No. I don't have a connection to him."

"Then why was he following you?"

"Mirza ul-Beg has been trying to kill me."

"You said Anton Zelman has been trying to kill you. Now you say it is Mirza ul-Beg?"

"Yes."

"I see," Gumbarri spoke in doubt. "How long have you had this connection to ul-Beg?"

Janet's mind began to swirl.

"What plans did you make with your friends to arrange the bomb?"

She shook her head at the man.

"If you tell us who they are, it will go more leniently with your own case. Tell me one name. One contact you have."

Somewhere in her logical brain, Janet knew better than to answer such leading questions, so she said nothing more in response to them. She used the next few moments to block out images of Brandt in his hospital bed with Andy leaning over him.

"I want to call the US consulate," she said.

"Go ahead."

"But I need a phone."

"Yes. That would be a problem, wouldn't it?"

"Where is my cell phone?"

"It is being held as evidence in a crime."

"Then you must provide me with a phone."

"Only if you are under arrest."

"If I'm not under arrest, then remove these." Janet lifted her hands and rattled the cuffs.

The man shook his head.

"You have to charge me or let me leave."

"No, we don't. We can hold you under administrative restraint for twenty four hours. Perhaps even longer with a judge's approval."

"I'm not answering any more questions until I speak with the US consulate."

"I see," Gumbarri intoned again. He spoke in Swiss German to the matron. She stepped to Janet and motioned for her to rise. Janet did not.

"Ms. Thompson, you are to go with Officer Mueller."

"No."

Gumbarri nodded to Mueller. She took Janet by one arm, and without even straining, lifted her from the seat, and forcibly pushed her to the door.

"We will continue this discussion later," Gumbarri spoke as Janet was led out of the room.

Mueller took Janet into an elevator that went down several floors. She led Janet out into a dark hallway lined with small cells. The matron pushed Janet into a cell. She unlocked and removed the cuffs, then lifted Janet's arms to remove her belt. Amazingly she let Janet keep her hat. Mueller then locked the door behind her leaving Janet alone with her thoughts and fears.

# CHAPTER SEVENTEEN

The cell was lit by a single stark bulb behind a heavy protective plastic shield. Janet paced in limping steps around her tiny new world, then sat on the bare mattress of her bed. Visions of Andy standing on the tarmac outside of the Lear in Azerbaijan, her two fists on her hips in defiance, flooded Janet's memory. This move of hers was to have been expected. Andy was certainly a pro at this. Could Andy have a connection to Mirza? No, Janet thought, all Andy wanted was Brandt. But why should Janet even care? What difference did it make? She was leaving Brandt, if he was going to recover, that is. The police would soon clear her. They were only doing their job. Soon she would fly back to Tulsa. That was all Janet wanted. That was all Andy wanted.

Janet should be back at the computer lab, fighting to stop Zelman's plan. Why bother now? It was pointless. She was no match for Zelman. The more she struggled, the stronger he became. She looked around the cell. It felt oddly protective, a safe haven from the storm of what was happening outside. A protective cocoon where she could escape responsibility of what was happening to the world.

"This is where cowards end up," she spoke out loud to herself.

She placed her face into her hands. Only a few tears came. She was even too tired to cry.

The sound of a key clinked through the tiny cell, and the door opened. Silent and expressionless, Mueller motioned for her to follow. They moved up a flight of stairs to a clerk's desk. The clerk handed Janet her purse, passport, wallet and belt, then held out a pen for her to sign a form.

"Where is my cell phone?"

"It will continue to be held as evidence in a crime," the clerk replied waving the pen for her signature. Janet signed and Mueller led her to the front door.

Outside the station a crowd of reporters was gathered at the base of the station's steps. As she emerged into the glaring light of day they recognized her and surged forward.

"Why did you try to kill Brandt Mahler?"

"How long have you been a terrorist?"

"How did you smuggle in the bomb?"

"How were you able to infiltrate the WMF?"

Janet turned around, trying to retreat back into the protection of the station, but Mueller blocked her way with crossed arms. Janet swung back to the crowd and finding no other options, moved forward. To her surprise, the reporters kept at an arm's length distance.

'Keep the Mirza problem quiet. It's amazing how fast notoriety can turn to leprosy,' Anton had warned her.

The reporters seemed afraid of her, afraid her terrorist leper's touch would contaminate them.

"How does it feel to be an American working against your own country?"

Janet gritted her teeth at the comment. Where should she go? The airport. That had been her goal since she had woken up this morning. Woken up to the reality of where she belonged. Now was her chance. But how to get there? She looked over the bantering heads of the reporters, seeking out a tram. There were none. Of course not. Zurich was in lock down, all because of her. No wonder everyone was acting this way. She looked for a cab, but again, none. Could she walk to the train station? Which way? Were the trains even running? Or the planes? Her eyes darted left and right, desperate for a way out.

Then she saw him. A beefy man, standing beside a limo, his eyes calmly locked onto her. He nodded ever so slightly and opened the rear door of the limo, inviting her to enter.

He could be one of Mirza's agents. They were everywhere. Gut instinct told her to move toward him.

She passed through the crowd of reporters, who parted like the waters before Moses as he crossed the Red Sea. An invisible bubble formed around her. Even the reporters' screeching became muted as she floated in an isolated stupor toward the limo. A thousand sparkles illuminated around her as flash cameras popped and glass eyed video monsters hovered surrealistically around her as she floated forward. They stood back and let her get to the limo alone.

"Director Zelman would like to speak mit you," the driver said in a low tone.

Janet sighed in relief, letting out the tense breath she'd been holding. She slipped in, and as he closed the door, she slumped back against the seat. He walked around the car, and took the driver's seat. The glass eyed monsters had swarmed around the car inches from the windows. The driver calmly started the engine and carefully eased through the throng, until he was clear, then he accelerated.

"I don't have my cell phone to talk to him," Janet said.

"Director Zelman would like to speak mit you personally."

"Did he arrange my release?"

The driver didn't answer.

Fifteen minutes later they were waved through a security gate at the airport. The airport guard blocked the few paparazzi that had followed them on scooters. Far out on a distant side leg of the tarmac an imposing private jet sat isolated in the morning sun. He was here. The man himself.

Despite all the bizarre things Anton had done since she had known him, she found herself looking to him for answers, for protection from the storm raging around her. And relief from the storm raging within her.

She remembered Zelman's strong handsome face from the Zimbabwe billboard. In those few short days her mental image of him had grown to monstrous proportions of both evil and good. Now she would meet the real man, not just a flitting voice on the other end of the cell phone.

She imagined him as an older version of Brandt, strong, handsome, in control. He probably had the same wry smile, the same gesturing twist of his hands. Brandt's features would be evident in the lines of his face and the shape of his fingers. In his dazzling eyes.

As she stepped into his aircraft she removed and held her tattered hat to clear the low door. Inside, her nostrils were slapped with the mephitic odor of antiseptic and harsh chemicals. She knew this smell, the same as her father's advanced cancer ward, the smell of hovering death. At the far end of the cabin was a hospital bed containing the hollow shell of a man, as decimated as her father had been. An array of electronics surrounded him and tubes dripped a toxic brew that kept him half alive. His every pore oozed the pungent odor that flooded the cabin. A gray stubble of whiskers covered his face, the skin too paper thin for shaving. His sunken eyes looked up from sallow gray eye sockets.

"Ms. Thompson," his voice cracked, "you seem surprised. Am I not the very image of a man with the strength and vitality to destroy civilization as we know it?"

"Why?" Her question was vague, but he knew her meaning.

"I don't make the rules, Ms. Thompson. I just use them. Life is a game that I intend to win. Quickly."

His attending physician came up to her with a triage kit, and began daubing her cuts.

"Stop it," she demanded.

"Ms. Thompson, let the doctor do his work."

She frowned, but didn't protest as he started again.

"Anton you can't do this. What about all the people you've hurt? What about the destruction you caused in Zimbabwe? You can't want that to happen to the rest of the world. What about the millions of people who are about to lose everything they own? What about Emily?"

"Ms. Thompson, you know better than to ask that. I didn't cause any of those people to be hurt. And in fact, Emily's shrapnel was intended for you. That is why you are feeling so guilty right now. You told her mother you saved her life, but you didn't tell her that it was you who put her in harm's way."

"Don't you dare blame me!"

"Ms. Thompson, you knew who was after you, yet you went prancing around in public wearing the most recognized hat on the planet like a beacon saying 'aim here'. You knew better."

Janet's mouth hung open. The man was incredible. "Look, you enticed me here under false pretenses. I didn't ask for any of this."

"No? Would you care to see the news clips of you blowing kisses to the world? Your cartoon was correct. You wanted to light the world on fire. And you have."

"You are the one who played with fire, but you made sure it was someone else who got burned. You've been dipping into the world economy for years. But you put the blame on others. It's Mirza or other bankers or the recession. 'I didn't do it, someone else did!' You're to blame for the current recession. You're just another kleptocrat, another off-Wall Street banker who rules by stealing. But that wasn't enough was it. You wanted more. You couldn't stop your financial gluttony."

His eyes narrowed to angry slits.

"I didn't invent the sixty trillion dollar Credit Default Swap market. I didn't turn a blind eye to forty trillion dollars of overleveraged hedge funds. Valter and your fellow economic analysts did. So I used them. No,

Ms. Thompson. It wasn't me who caused the recession. It was you and three hundred million other greedy Americans."

"Don't you blame America. We have the most responsible economic policies of any major country in the world."

"You are right, it was not just Americans. Look at the data, Ms. Thompson. Zimbabwe would have fallen much harder than it did without me. It was once the bread basket of Africa. I didn't create its destruction. I used it. And it will rise again. Because of me. The few billion dollars I pulled out of its economy is nothing compared to what its growth potential is. I call it an investment. You're the modern soothsayer, predict what would have been. Prove me wrong. Run your precious calculations and make the projections on your fancy computer."

"Are you saying you engineered a rapid recovery into the Zimbabwe economy?"

He nodded.

"The economy is self correcting," he said. It goes down. It goes up. But people don't like the downs, so they block them. And the pressure builds. Then the next cycle is worse. And the cycle after that worse yet. The Great Depression was nothing, Ms. Thompson. Nothing compared to the pressure fault that has developed deep in the core of the economy. The answer is simple. Take your medicine now, or take more later." His lips formed into Brandt's wry half-smile.

"Are you suggesting that I do nothing? Let the recession destroy the world economy, and let it burn itself out?" She stared into his vacant eyes. "No," she continued, shaking her head. "If your natural correction means mankind returning to live in caves, then I can't allow that to happen. I have to find another way."

"Ms. Thompson, all you've done so far is treat a few symptoms. Let it go. Let nature take its course."

"What about the American economy?"

"When Rome's time was done it simply went away."

"And left twelve hundred years of devastation behind it."

"Some things take time, Ms. Thompson. Trust me, it is the best way."

"You are horrible. How could I ever trust you?" she asked.

"Oh, you know you really shouldn't. You were right. I am a bad penny, truly." He started to chuckle and gagged, then cut short a cough.

Janet bit her lip as another stitch went into her wounds.

"What about Adelheidis?"

The gray blue eyes that looked back at her were without doubt Brandt's. And they still had enough life to express how he felt about his Heidi.

"You caught me on that one, Ms. Thompson. I didn't expect that."

"Are you going to go to her?"

"It's a bit late for that, don't you think." He gestured to his tubes. "I have hours, not days. Midnight is almost complete."

"What about Brandt? Is that why you've helped Brandt? The jet, the computer, helping Andy with the pipeline?"

"Yes and no. Yes because I suspected Brandt was mine, but I wasn't certain until yesterday. No, because I would have helped him anyway. He is one of the few people smart enough to use those items wisely. He is like me. He uses his experience and intuition instead of mathematics. Like me. I didn't need a computer to outfox your computer. Just my wits."

"What about me? Why did you get me involved in all this?"

"I suspected you might help Brandt do what was needed. The Thompson Accord is proof I was right. And no, I'm not done with you yet."

"You don't own me."

"I most certainly do. Bought and paid for."

She glared at him.

The doctor began putting away his triage kit.

"I've enjoyed our conversation, Ms. Thompson."

The body guard approached.

"What is the super-inflective, Anton? What is Midnight?"

"Your fancy computer didn't give you the answer? I'm so surprised."

Janet's jaw tightened as his insults mounted.

"Ms. Thompson. You are smart. You have a brain. Use it instead of your computer. The answer is in your hands. I've already given it to you."

Her glare turned to bewilderment.

"Good Day, Ms. Thompson."

The body guard escorted her to the cabin door.

"You can't justify what you are doing, Anton."

"No? I just did." As she stepped through the door, he added, "I've carefully taught you all the rules, Ms. Thompson. Use them."

Outside the air was cool and clear. Janet pulled in a long breath and exhaled a long huff, purging her lungs of the toxic cabin fumes. Anton was full of answers, all of them of the wrong kind. He was very good at rationalizing his maniacal deeds. Where was her answer, the one she'd gone in there looking for? 'The answer is in your hands', he'd said. Janet sighed and placed her tattered hat back on her head. This was the last day she had to find Midnight. Could she do it?

Alone?

As the driver closed the limousine door, she heard the jet engines whine to life. The aircraft nosed up off the runway before she'd even cleared the security gate.

"Vere vould you like to go, Ms. Thompson?"

"WMF building please."

\*\*\*

A short while later the limo driver opened the door in front of the WMF. The guards gawked as she calmly walked up to them, though her knees were ready to buckle from both anger and worry.

"I need to get into the computer center."

"You are not on our entry list," the head guard retorted.

"Then call Jeremy."

The guard didn't move.

She reached into her empty pocket.

"I'm calling Brandt."

The guard held up his hand and dialed Jeremy. A few moments later Jeremy emerged from the elevator.

"I'm sorry, Ms. Thompson, but I cannot let you in. Security has been tightened. I have to follow protocol."

"Jeremy, it wasn't me who set off the bomb and you damn well know that. And then Anechka Topnazarov set me up to get me out of the way so she could get to Brandt."

"I'm not certain I can believe you."

"You must have met Anechka. You know what she's like."

"Yes. Nasty woman."

"I have new information. We need to get on the Cray and stop Zelman. Now let me in." She stood glaring at him. "Jeremy, you said you wanted me to head the computer lab. Now prove it."

He stood for a moment, not knowing what to do. Protocol stated he should not, but these were not times for following protocol.

"You haven't heard anything about Brandt's condition, have you?" she asked. "I wasn't at the hospital long enough to find out. I only saw him briefly after they'd sedated him."

Jeremy's face relaxed and he let his shoulders sag. "All I know is that they are waiting for him to wake up before they know for certain. Head injuries can be tricky."

Janet nodded, letting out a long sigh. "Are you going to let me in?"

"Yes," he said as his shoulders slumped further. They walked toward the elevator. "Janet, you are a mess. Where have you been? I couldn't find out anything about you at the hospital. They had no record of you being admitted. I saw the news clips of you leaving the police station, but then you disappeared."

He swiped her into the computer center. The staff froze in amazement as she stepped into the room.

"I've been to the mountain. But I don't know where the stone tablets are."

Jeremy just stood looking at her in bewilderment.

"Load up the Cray with the simulations of the Zimbabwe economy from my dissertation. I'll give you a few new tweaks."

She sat down at her desk as if she had run the center for years. Everyone snapped to comply with her instructions.

"May I ask what these new tweaks are for?"

"I need to look for recovery modes."

"You want to see how many decades it will take for the Zimbabwe economy to recover?"

"There may be a rapid recovery mode in the Zimbabwe economy."

"What is your mathematical basis for that?" Jeremy asked.

"I don't know." She breathed a sigh of exasperation. "I really don't know. But if it did, it might mean that we don't need to find an inflective to stop Zelman. Things might spontaneously recover after a crash."

"That makes no sense at all."

"I know, but we need look to be sure about this because Zelman never lies."

Jeremy just shook his head in puzzlement. As the staff scrambled to enter her instructions, Janet sat at her desk and contemplated what Zelman had said. He had told her to give up the computer simulations. That he had already given her the answer. What had he given her besides a lot of grief and false leads?

She dialed Dr. Jones.

"Hello," came his distracted voice.

"Dr. Jones, I need to talk."

"Janet? I'm just about to start a class. This is not a very good time for talking."

"I've met with Zelman."

"Oh. That is very nice."

"I think Zelman gave me more clues as to what Midnight is. You might be able to help me figure out what he meant."

"Ahh...Hmmm..." the elder man answered, suddenly interested in a puzzle. "And what did he say?"

"He said to use my right brain creativity instead of left brain computer programs."

"Well, that does seem to make sense. The super-inflective would, by definition, be far too small to be noticed by your algorithms. And the human brain is far more capable of dealing with uncertainty than any computer."

"Then how will I find the super-inflective?"

"Did he give any more specific clues?"

"Yes. He said he had already given me the answer. That the answer was in my hands."

"What was in your hands when he said that?"

"Nothing, just my hat."

Janet's jaw dropped. She stared at the inside band of the cowgirl hat lying upturned on her desk. The words on the label jumped out: Midnight by the Tulsa Hat Company.

Breathe, Janet. Breathe.

"Dr. Jones, Midnight is the Tulsa Hat Company."

"Oh yes, I know of them, over on Third Street."

She googled the company. "Their website says they're the pride of America. The smallest company on the NASDAQ."

"Well, Janet, this makes sense to me. That would make them the smallest publicly traded company in America. Small enough to be a super-inflective. I think you have it."

"Jeremy," she called out. "Who owns controlling interest in The Tulsa Hat Company, code name THAT on the NASDAQ?"

"I've never heard of them," he said as he queried his databases. "It is - well here's a surprise. PBEC is the majority shareholder."

"Did you hear what Jeremy said, Dr. Jones?"

"Yes. Good. Now I can go back to my class knowing the problem is resolved. Good day, Janet."

The abstract man couldn't comprehend that the fate of the world still hung in the balance. As far as he was concerned the puzzle was solved.

"Why the interest in such a small company?" Jeremy asked.

"Because the Tulsa Hat Company is Midnight. It is Zelman's super-inflective. If it is destroyed at just the right moment it will cause a loss of faith in the very symbol of America, the cowboy hat."

"Tulsa Hat? I can't believe such a small company could have any impact what so ever."

"Look, I can't explain it in mathematical terms. I just know it is true. My gut tells me that Tulsa is the trigger, the last straw. It will cause the final bit of capital flight Zelman needs to reach the critical mass threshold and trigger the terminal implosion of the US economy. I can't rely on Zelman's invisible recovery mode. I have to stop him."

Jeremy's blank stare bore down on her. With all his technical mastery, he couldn't accept the significance of the tiny hat company as Zelman's Midnight. Now Janet knew what it was like for Brandt. Did he always work off of these gut feelings that he couldn't explain?

She looked up at the big screen. "How are the Zimbabwe recovery mode projections going?" she asked him.

"They are nearly done, but I'm afraid there is no recovery mode. Your model is showing just a fraction of growth after a long period of stagnation interspersed with periods of turmoil."

Zelman lied!

He hadn't set up the Zimbabwe economy to make a rapid recovery. There was no recovery. The computer projected years of hunger and civil war. A wave of nausea swept over her. The same was about to come true for America.

He duped her again. Fooled her into believing that if she simply left him alone, everything would turn out for the best. His nostrum, his cure for the world's ills was as trustworthy as he was.

Then a more chilling thought swept over her. What if he hadn't lied? What if he actually believed it, but he was wrong. The great Anton Zelman couldn't be wrong. This wild roller coaster economy must have a driver, a person who knew what was happening. It couldn't just be careening out of control, headed for who knew what. Back in Harare she believed he was pure evil. Then as she grew to know him, Anton seemed benign. Now he was asking her to believe he was good. But she had always believed he was infallible. What if he was wrong, out of control but not knowing it? That was far more dangerous to deal with than the sinister Zelman she thought she knew.

How to stop him? Tell the president? Go on worldwide television and warn everyone. Out-fox him with the world's biggest computer?" Nothing was of any use. No matter what she did, she couldn't stop him.

Think, Janet. He never lies. What else did he say?

He never did actually answer her questions. He merely nodded. That could mean anything. In typical Zelman fashion, he hadn't lied, but he hadn't told the truth either. The man was exasperating. How could Adelheidis ever fall in love with him, let alone maintain that love in silence for a lifetime? What did she see in him? Janet knew the answer because she felt it, too. There was good in Zelman. If only Adelheidis could have shared her life with him, he never would have turned out this way.

But he still needed to be stopped.

"Jeremy, we need to find a way to counter Zelman's move on Tulsa Hat. Let's start by simulating this," she said reaching to her keyboard to type in the equations. "No, wait." Her eyes darted back and forth, her fingers frozen over the keyboard.

"What is the matter?" Jeremy asked.

"The Cray." She looked back at the black columns that formed the monstrous machine. She took off her hat and stuffed it in a drawer so Zelman couldn't hear. "The computer is bugged. He's been watching our every move."

"What? Impossible."

"Believe me. If we run a simulation of the hat company, it will tip off Zelman on how to counter our move. We need to run a false simulation, one that would double cross Zelman, fooling him into saving the company, and triggering an American recovery."

"How can we do that? We need the Cray to calculate the double cross. With Zelman watching, we can't do that. If we don't use the Cray we will never be able to calculate the double cross."

"Damned if we do, damned if we don't." Janet's mind raced. Then she started typing.

"What are you doing?"

"I'm writing the equations for a foreign company buying up Tulsa Hat stock. The ploy will work because with PBEC tanking, anyone jumping in to buy up stock will be welcomed as good news. However, my equation will falsely show a strong negative market reaction to a foreign buy out of an American icon. When he sees it, Zelman will jump in to be that foreign company. However, in fact, such a move will save the super-inflective company by protecting the stock from the on-going PBEC collapse."

"But, how can we test your theory? We won't know your equations will work until after we run the simulation. Then it will be too late. Zelman will already have seen the results. How do you know they will work?"

Janet thought of Brandt. "By my experience and intuition." And a lot of luck. With a flurry of keystrokes, she wrote the Trojan equations.

They loaded up the Cray, and ran the projections. They watched as the colored trend lines showed the results of her hidden lie. Just as she predicted, the data lines took a nose dive. The worst possible time for the buyout would be just before the closing bell of the New York Stock Exchange. But, the initial impact would be minimal. The real damage would occur when the Tokyo Stock Exchange opened three and a half hours later. Janet did a quick mental calculation. That would be midnight Greenwich Mean Time.

She had indeed found Midnight. Midnight had been a 'what' and now she'd made it into a 'when', too.

There was nothing left to do but wait for Zelman to take the bait. The New York Stock Exchange would open in an hour and half. Would her slight of hand trick be enough? Her gut told her she needed more.

"I'm going over to the hospital to see Brandt," she told Jeremy.

"The trams are all shut down," he explained. "This is Zurich's first terrorist attack, and the city is in turmoil. The hospital isn't far. I'll walk with you."

"Thanks, but no. I need some time alone," she said, retrieving her hat from the desk drawer.

Jeremy drew a simple map for her and placed a WMF cell phone in her hand. "I'll call you if anything happens here," he promised.

She stepped from the cool marble of the WMF into the hot afternoon sun. Unlike the bustling night she walked these streets with Brandt, this afternoon the city was deserted. The people of Zurich were gone. The most livable city in the world had simply disappeared. The perennially vibrant city was in hiding. All because of her.

As she walked, Janet thought about Zelman. After all the harm he had caused, there was still not enough evidence to arrest him. If he had pulled his money out of SBU before the collapse, they would have had him. But he didn't. He was more clever than that.

He must have hundreds of billions of dollars pulled from other stocks to bring them all down so far, leading the market into a freefall. All that money could be hidden away in a thousand secret accounts, a technique the Swiss themselves had perfected. All perfectly legal. With a touch of his finger, he could release that money and ensure the recovery of the markets. Or he could sit back and do nothing and just watch as the world collapsed. Which would he choose to do? That is, if his mind was not already made up.

All the shops and restaurants were shuttered, the streets empty, except for an occasional police officer patrolling a critical corner. They eyed her with harsh skepticism. Was she just an errant stranger in their eyes, or did they recognize her as the hated Cowgirl. It didn't matter.

Who could talk to Anton, convince him to change his mind before it was too late? There were only two people she could think of that he might listen to, his Heidi and herself. She was easy, he had been eavesdropping on her for five days. He had listened in the hospital as Andy set her up and had her arrested. He listened to the police interrogate her. He was listening now, to her footsteps as she walked this very moment. She could simply speak, and he would listen. But what could she say that would convince him? Nothing. He enjoyed manipulating her too much. Maybe she could threaten him. Tell him Valter would hunt him down and arrest him. Anton would laugh. He was dying. He had hours, not days. Judging from his condition, she suspected the number of hours was in the single digits. You can't arrest a dead man.

Getting Adelheidis to talk to him was more difficult. They would have to meet face to face. That was as unlikely as Zelman saving the world on his own. But if she could bring Adelheidis and Anton together, for just a few minutes, would it change him? Could Adelheidis melt his cold heart and save the world? Why even bother with such futile thoughts.

Tears of frustration pooled in her eyes. Her mother would have the answers. She always did. Janet looked toward heaven for answers, but found none.

She wanted to hate Anton. Yet, there was something about him that appealed to her. He was inventive and very clever. He had figured out how to use inflectives even before she had come up with the theory and the mathematical equations that describe them. And even though her simulation proved that he had lied to her about recovering the economies he destroyed, her heart told her to believe he would. That somehow, someway, Anton was ultimately a good person. She was only one of two people on the planet that thought that. Two women, two foolish hearts. Perhaps Adelheidis wasn't so very different from herself after all.

She walked into the hospital and asked for Brandt. This time the staff recognized her, and refused to let her pass. A security guard approached, ready to toss her onto the street.

"Is he awake? Tell me that at least," she asked in irritated frustration.

The receptionist checked her monitor, "Yes," she said with a huff. "He is awake."

"Then call him."

"Come along, Cowgirl. Out you go," the guard said in disgust, taking her arm and leading her to the exit.

"Wait," the receptionist said, phone in hand. "Herr Dr. Mahler would like to see her."

Surprised, the guard let her go. She stormed into the elevator and he was right behind her. He followed her all the way to Brandt's room. She peeked into the darkened private room.

"Don't let her in," Andy's voice spoke up. She was gesturing at the guard to take Janet away.

"Why not?" Brandt asked in bewilderment. He looked to the guard. "It's all right," said Brandt. "She can come in."

"Did she tell you?" Janet asked Brandt.

"Tell me what?"

"What she did to me earlier today?"

Brandt stared back in bewilderment.

Janet turned on the TV and flipped through several channels.

"You don't need TV on, Brandt," Andy protested grabbing at Janet's remote.

Janet pulled the remote away as a news clip of her emerging from the police station came on. Brandt's jaw dropped as he watched.

"You were at the police station? How did that happen?"

"Ask her," Janet replied, pointing an accusing finger at Andy.

"Brandt, I can explain. I was trying to protect you from getting hurt."

"What did you do? Have her arrested?"

"She wasn't arrested, she was only detained."

"Andy! I can't believe you would do that."

"You shouldn't trust her, Brandt. You've only known her for a few days. You've known me for years. How do you know she's not responsible for everything that's been happening?"

"I know, that's all. Andy, I just know."

"You don't know anything right now. You've injured your head. You're not thinking straight. You haven't been thinking straight ever since we broke up."

Silence. Brandt's brows furrowed. He looked from Andy to Janet and back.

"Brandt! She's dangerous. She's working with your uncle. They want you dead. She has some secret connection to him. I know it."

"Don't be ridiculous, Andy."

"It's not ridiculous. Brandt, think about it. How else would your uncle have known so much about what you are up to?"

A tug of guilt pulled at Janet for wearing Zelman's hat.

"Uncle Anton knows everything. He always has. I'm used to that."

"No. It's her. She's been plotting with him all along. She set you up. She set off the bomb. On purpose. To kill you. Brandt, never, ever has Zurich been bombed by terrorists. Who else would do that?"

# CHAPTER EIGHTEEN

"Is that what you said to get the police in here? Did you tell the police Janet was responsible for the bomb?"

"She'd do anything to help Zelman with his plan. She's not the innocent American teacher she appears to be. Her Cowgirl act is the same as Zelman's lies."

"Andy, get out of here."

"Brandt, no."

"Get out, I said."

"Brandt...I opened the pipeline."

"I know."

"I did it for you. For you, Brandt. I called Nikolai myself and told him. I did it for you."

"No, Andy. You did it for yourself. Everything you do is for yourself."

"That's not true. I love you, Brandt. And you love me too!"

"No, I don't love you. And you don't love me. You may think you do, but you have no idea what love is."

Silence.

Andy sidled up to the edge of Brant's bed. She leaned down to him. "You don't know what you are saying, my love. Your head has been injured. I'll take care of you now. Now and forever."

Brandt looked at Janet. "My head is fine. It's my heart that hurts."

"Oh dearest," crooned Andy. "I can fix that. Let me help you."

"No Andy. It's over between us. You have to accept that. And you have to leave. Now."

Andy leaned over Brandt, wrapping her arms about his chest in a huge, demonstrative hug. Brandt turned his head away from her kisses.

"Get off me." His voice was muffled under Andy's suffocating hug.

Janet grasped the back of Andy's shirt, fisting up a sheaf of blonde hair. She yanked hard. Andy shrieked and wriggled against Brandt, clutching him to her.

"No! No, Brandt. You don't know what you're saying."

A loud steady beeping filled the room. Andy's wiggling had accidentally tripped off the nurse's call button.

The nurse came trotting into the room, followed closely by the security guard. Janet let go of Andy's hair, but the nearly hysterical woman wouldn't move off of Brandt.

"Andy!" he groaned as she leaned all her weight on him. "Get off me! Off!"

The security guard grappled with Andy for a brief moment. He managed to catch her arms behind her back, twisting until he got her up off of Brandt. He clasped her in a bear hug and drove her toward the door.

"Brandt! Don't let them do this! You love me!"

The nurse leaned to the bed, shutting off the incessant beep of the call button and the alarm of the blocked IV drip. Brandt breathed a sigh of relief as the door slammed shut behind Andy and the guard. Andy's cursing voice could be heard echoing in the hall.

The nurse silently finished timing Brandt's pulse. She straightened the blanket over him, smiled and stepped away to the door. As it opened Janet caught a glimpse of the security guard standing toe-to-toe with Andy's bodyguard.

There was a loud crash as Andy knocked some metal bedpans to the floor. Then there was silence. Andy's voice, speaking in staccato Russian was followed by the sharp sound of spitting. The hospital security guard jumped back to avoid the next round of spittle.

Andy lifted her head and stalked past the guard, trailed by her bodyguard.

Janet turned back to Brandt. He was craning his neck to watch Andy stride away. When Brandt shifted his gaze back to Janet, she couldn't help erupting in light chuckles. He joined her.

"Hey," she said affectionately. "I should leave too, so you can get some rest."

"No, don't go. I had a very restful nap, thanks to Mirza. How about you? I was worried sick until I talked to Jeremy a short while ago."

Janet stepped closer and sat on the edge of the bed. "Yeah, sorry. The little girl needed help..."

"I checked on her before I talked with Jeremy. She's going to be fine. And her mother, too."

"I'm glad to hear that."

"You saved her life."

"I endangered her life. And many others besides."

"And you saved many others besides. Don't even try to keep count, Janet. It's not possible. In your heart, in your gut, or whatever you want to call it, you must know you tried your best to solve the problem. And it wasn't even your problem to begin with."

"I'm still trying to solve the problem."

"Trying to figure out what Midnight is? Too late, isn't it?"

"No, I've got that one."

"You've got it? What is it?"

"The Tulsa Hat Company."

"The company that made Zelman's hat. You have to be kidding me. I don't believe it."

See pulled off her hat, showing Brandt the Midnight label. "Oh, it's true." Her eyes darted around the room. She stepped to the bathroom and dropped in the hat so Zelman couldn't hear.

She explained her deceitful equations and Zelman's counter-move. "He told me to let the economy do its thing and the Zimbabwe economy would recover. But Jeremy and I ran projections and couldn't find any recovery. He lied. So I tricked him."

"Something is not right, then. He never lies. He called you to tell you that?"

"No. I met him. He told me-"

"You met him?" Brandt interrupted. "Where?"

"In his private jet at the airport."

"Is he still there? Maybe Dad can arrest him."

"No, I'm sure he's gone. Brandt, we still don't have enough evidence to arrest him."

"I think we do. We don't have direct cause and effect, but we have enough statistical linkage to convince a jury he is guilty. Certainly enough to issue an arrest warrant and stop him temporarily."

"We might not need to. He's dying, of cancer. The way he looked, all hooked up to life support, I don't think he has much time left, less than a day."

"What? I didn't even realize he was sick, but I haven't seen him for a long time."

"It is too late. We can just let him go. It's over."

"No, he still needs to have justice served. If we could find out where he is, then Dad can arrest him."

Brandt grunted in pain as he tried to shift into a more comfortable position. Janet leaned forward and tenderly helped him. Their eyes met and his face broke into his signature cocky smile. She smiled back. Brandt drew in a deep breath, then slowly exhaled.

"Janet, I know I'm not what you're looking for. Whatever it is, it's not me. I wish I was, because for the first time in my life I've fallen in love."

Gulp. She wasn't prepared for this. "What, you were never in love with Andy?"

"No." He shook his head, then let it ease back against the pillow. "Lust, yeah, I had plenty of that, at least at first. I even tired of that after a while. She's a firecracker with a short fuse. Far too caustic and demanding."

"Oh, Mr. Do-things-my-way doesn't like having someone else call the shots, eh?"

"Janet."

"Okay, sorry. I don't think I could stand being around her for long either."

"You, on the other hand: smart, sassy, and sexy. Wow. The perfect combination. And you were sweet and polite, sort of charmingly vulnerable, and very willing to learn. I put you through a lot."

"Brandt, you thought about all this logically?"

He closed his eyes briefly. "Yeah. Funny, huh? That's why I couldn't sleep after that first night together, I guess. Then I realized none of those things mattered anyway. I'm in love with you simply because I am. No reason, no logic, no purpose. I just love you."

Janet stiffened on the edge of the bed. Her throat was clutched tight and she couldn't reply. She smiled weakly.

"I'm sorry about what happened at Graumauer," he said. "To be honest, I never considered your feelings after I'd come to terms with mine. The arrogant, overly assured part of me simply assumed. You were right. Any other woman would have jumped at the chance. But I had to fall in love with the one woman who wouldn't. If you could ever find a way to forgive me I promise you I will never do that again."

"Oh, I forgive you," she breathed, swallowing hard. Have it out, Janet. All out in the open. "I forgive you for Graumauer. That I can understand.

246

But for all the rest. All of what came before. The needling, the insults, the pressure..."

Brandt made a ragged sigh. "Janet, from the moment I first saw you I knew you were different. You had a fresh, in-your-face sincerity that I had never experienced before. But, I also knew you were so green, so theoretical that I thought you would get killed. I wanted to protect you. To do that I had to make you grow up very fast. The only way I knew how to do that was the way the brothers at the Monastery taught me, by correcting your mistakes. Harshly, if necessary." His eyes found hers and dwelled there, searching. "You're alive right now because I did that. I am glad that I did. But, I am also sad, because in the process I lost my chance to win your love. And now you are lost to me forever."

His smug smile was gone. It its place was a new smile, open, vulnerable, and hopeful.

"Oh Brandt, you didn't lose. I love you too. I don't know why, but I do. We're opposites about a lot of things and we clash. I don't care. No matter what else happens, I want to be with you. Come hell or high water."

"Janet, do you really want this? Me?"

She puffed out a chuckle. "I'm going to have to go with my gut instinct here because I can't make sense out of it. Logic and mathematics can only solve some of the world's problems. People do the rest. And of all the people in the world, you are the one I want to be with. Forever."

He glanced down as his chest heaved, but he didn't speak. She stroked his arm.

"I am not taking no for an answer, Brandt Mahler, so don't think you are going to send me running back to Tulsa. After all I've been through with you I'm not going to let you go."

She bent her head down to him, letting her forehead touch his cheek.

"I had never seen anyone like you in my entire life," she continued. "You were a shining knight from a fairytale. A perfect hero sent to rescue me. You simply couldn't be true. I had to find the flaws that would make you into a mere mortal like me. Then along came Andy. Wealthy jet-set beauty queen, with a very sharp edge. There was no way I could ever compete with that. I also knew I couldn't compete with you and all your sophistication. So I didn't. I ran away instead. You were right, I'm a coward."

She swiveled her head and kissed his cheek.

"I know now that I don't need to compete, because cooperating is so much more fun."

She lifted her face to meet his and mirrored his wry half smile. She leaned in and kissed him, and stroked her lips over his face.

"I love you, Brandt."

"Janet, I love you."

"My name's not Janet," she intoned, "or Salty," her voice throaty and deep. "For you, it's Solterra."

They both laughed, soft and low. Then she placed her hands on his cheeks and kissed him. A kiss he returned with equal passion. He lifted his free hand and clasped it over her shoulders, pulling her down to deepen the kiss.

"Ahem...Ms. Thompson," a nurse interrupted. "There is someone to see you at the nurse's station. It's urgent."

"Oh, sure." She looked to Brandt and he nodded for her to go, closing his eyes and maintaining a contented smile.

Janet grabbed her hat and stepped out of the room immediately recognizing Zelman's body guard standing in the hallway.

"Ms. Thompson, please follow me."

"Uh, sure. Why?"

He didn't answer. She followed him to the elevator and rode to a floor with a private ward. There, in a tiny side room was a bed with a man in it. A man covered in tubes and wires.

"Anton?"

As she approached him the same ghostly stench of poisonous chemicals assailed her nostrils. He'd obviously deteriorated in the few hours since she'd last seen him. Tubes in his throat prevented speech, but his hand was taped to a special voice enunciator keyboard. His fingers flashed over the keys.

"Ms. Thompson, welcome," the metallic computer voice spoke. "I see you ran your simulations."

"You know I did. You lied. There is no recovery mode."

"Ms. Thompson, Brandt is right, you are very inexperienced. You forgot one important item in your projections."

"What?"

"Your own Thompson Accord."

A look of shocked humiliation spread over her face. He was right. She hadn't included that piece in her recovery model.

Her face hardened. "Then why? Why did you do it?"

"It's all a game, Ms. Thompson. In a few hours I will be the world's first trillionaire. He who dies with the most toys, wins."

"What about all the people you have hurt?"

"As I told you before, I haven't hurt anyone. All I did was rearrange the economic landscape and make it better."

"Better? How can you say that?"

"The world economy was headed for a massive bubble. Several years ago I decided I had to fix it, using what you later called inflectives. Had I not done that, your doomsday outcome would really have happened. I surgically lanced the boil, and let out the infection, so the economy could heal itself. Tomorrow ask Rashid if the derivative and CDX markets are still threatening the world. Oh, by the way, I also made buckets of money doing it."

"Fine. So, why did you need to bring me into all of this?"

"I needed you to distract Mirza, to make her think I was fighting with you when in fact I was fighting with her. She loves me, and she wants to kill me. I can't let her do that."

"You endangered my life? You dangled me in front of her rifles so I would take the bullets not you?"

"Not at all. When she ransacked your apartment her instructions were for them to kill you first and take your computer second. I barely got you out of there in time."

"You could have simply warned me."

"What fun would that have been? Besides, you are too head-strong to have listened. Admit it."

He made a grotesque chuckling sound around the tubes in his throat.

"That is why you said you owned me."

"As I said, bought and paid for. And you have been such fine entertainment, too."

Janet's nostrils flared. "You used me!" She clinched her fists.

"Yep. Like a puppet on a string."

"What you did was wrong. You can't use me or the millions of other people you've used."

"Ms. Thompson, to state the obvious, I most certainly can. And I most certainly did."

"You can't break the law just because you want to. You can't play God."

"But, I did. And a fine job of it, if I may say so myself. Better than what He would have done," he said, pointing a trembling self righteous finger toward heaven.

"You are disgusting!" she sneered. She turned to leave the repugnant man.

"Please tell, Valter to hurry. I don't have much time." He belched that same hideous laugh around his breathing tubes.

She stormed out of the room, headed for the elevator with full determination to turn him in.

Then she stopped.

That was exactly what he wanted her to do. That's why he said in the jet earlier that he wasn't done with her yet. He wanted her to be his little messenger girl to Valter so he could pass Go and collect his trillion dollars. She was tired of his games and manipulations, of being used as a pawn in his global chess game. She wasn't going to fall for it. No. Not this time.

Then her logical mind kicked in. He needed Valter's arrest to protect him from Mirza's wrath when he restored his money back into the economy. Despite her own personal feelings, she should do everything she could to help him, because helping him would help the world and hurt Mirza. Janet believed what Valter had said about Mirza losing interest in her after Zelman was gone.

But what if Zelman didn't put his money back into the economy? What if the SBU collapse really had wiped him out and he had no money? He would have to suck up the rest of PBEC's assets to recover his money from Mirza. In the process he'd destroy economies worldwide. And again he'd need Valter's unwitting protection to keep the wolves from his door. The only way to win against him would be to not have him arrested.

She dialed Jeremy.

"Jeremy, what is Zelman's net worth?"

"Hold on, that should be easy." She heard a clatter of computer keys. "It coming up now. Huh. This can't be right."

"What?"

"The computer calculates that he is bankrupt. In fact his debts are mounting. By tonight he will be the world's poorest man. This can not be. Let me run the calculation again."

"Don't bother, Jeremy. Thanks."

A dying man fantasizing about the glory of his dying empire. His bravado was lies, all lies. Or worse, self delusions. Have him arrested or not? It all came down to one simple question. Did she trust him to restore the economy?

Glancing into a patient's room she caught a TV news report. The New York Stock Exchange had just opened. Even from her position in the hall it was clear what the charts on the TV were saying. Today was worse than the Great Depression's Black Tuesday. America was collapsing. Not just the economy, but the country itself. Her gut twisted in anguish. Even if he took the bait of the Tulsa Hat Company, he had no money. Midnight was useless. Or was it? Her heart still spoke of trust in the withering man.

She walked back to Brandt's room. Valter and Adelheidis were sitting by Brandt's bed. Adelheidis was holding his hand. Valter's hand rested on Brandt's arm. The statesman rose to greet her.

"Janet, I'm so glad to see you. I've been so worried," he said, giving her a fatherly hug. "Brandt and I have been talking. I need to apologize for my brush off in Brussels. I didn't realize how important you are in my son's life."

She smiled at Valter and patted his back as he let go of his hug. She turned her smile to Brandt's mother, but Adelheidis was ice cold. After what she said to Brandt last night, Adelheidis wasn't buying her reconciliation. The welfare of Brandt and Graumauer were not negotiable. Janet stepped toward Brandt, but Adelheidis stepped to block her.

"I believe the United States is in that direction." Adelheidis' eyes seared into Janet's as she pointed a demanding finger toward the door.

"Mother," said Brandt.

Janet looked to Brandt. The man who could face down the Russian Army wasn't willing to step into this battle, or maybe he just didn't have the energy. Janet was on her own again. Adelheidis trusted Zelman. So did Friedrich. That spoke volumes. But not enough to convince Janet. She needed to test Zelman to see for herself.

"Adelheidis, could you come with me for a moment?" said Janet in a firm, but polite tone.

"Why?" The entrenched woman crossed her arms in defiance.

She'd landed the jet. She'd programmed the Cray. Time for action.

"Just come with me," Janet demanded, pulling the older woman out of the room with a squeal of protest.

She drew Adelheidis into the elevator before the astonished woman could react. She pushed the button for the private ward. Nothing happened.

"Anton, let us up," she said to no one in particular. Adelheidis looked at Janet in consternation. A second later the elevator started. When the doors opened, the bodyguard motioned them to Anton's room. Adelheidis stopped in shocked disbelief when she saw Anton and recognized who he was. She turned to Janet.

"Adelheidis, this is it. This is your last chance to talk to him. Your last chance to tell him the truth. I don't have anything to prove to you. Not anymore. I'm in love with Brandt and he's in love with me. You can't change that. Not now. Not ever."

Adelheidis blinked. She bit her lip and cautiously inched forward to the man whose eyes were locked on to the one treasure this world had withheld from him. Placing her fingers into the few remaining threads of his once thick hair, her eyes filled.

"Anton. Why couldn't we have found a way? There must have been a way. Did it have to come to this?" She leaned down and kissed him on the cheek, one of the few places not covered by tubes.

A single tear formed in the dying man's eye, and rolled down his cheek. Janet closed her eyes and let her instincts tell her what to do.

"You win, Anton," Janet said rolling the dice that held the fate of the world. "I'll give you two a chance to talk, then I'll tell Valter where you are."

For a moment there was a spark of gratitude in his reddened eyes. Then he turned to his Heidi.

Janet closed the door behind her and walked to the elevator.

Brandt and his father were chatting in the hospital room, watching the melt down on TV with worried eyes.

"Where is Mother?" Brandt asked.

"She'll be along in a minute."

The room was deathly quiet as Janet stepped to Brandt and took his hand while they watched the American economy crumble. There was nothing to do. No action to take. Nothing could be done but watch and wait. The clock slowly inched toward Midnight.

The three looked up as Adelheidis stepped into the room, a wistful smile on her face. Her gaze lingered on Brandt. In her eyes were a thousand motherly stories of what Brandt meant to her. Her gaze paused only for a moment on Valter, then shifted to Janet. She nodded, giving tacit approval of the young woman holding her son's hand. Then she sat down, folded her hands, and closed her eyes.

Janet lifted herself away from the drowsy Brandt. She whispered into Valter's ear. His eyes widened, and they stepped outside for a private conversation.

# CHAPTER NINETEEN

The ten o'clock nightly news was about to start. All stations were poised for the latest sensational live story. The ward outside of Anton Zelman's hospital room was crowded with television cameras.

Valter stood pompously talking with reporters, his arm proudly around Janet's shoulders.

"It was Dr. Thompson who saved the day. She has been stalked and terrorized by Anton Zelman for a number of days, but she never gave up the hope that all her suffering would result in justice being able to be done for this evil man."

The same reporters who badgered her a few hours earlier were now eager to laud Europe's restored heroine.

"How long have you worked for the CIA?"

"Do you have direct contact with the American president?"

"Will you able to save the world economy?"

"Where did you get your hat?"

Janet was again a celebrity. At least for today. The reporters pressed forward. No longer afraid of her leprosy, they peppered her with questions. She stood in her battle torn clothes and hat, the heroic soldier fresh from the trenches, smiling proudly as the flash cameras popped.

With her famous wink to the reporters she whispered out of the corner of her mouth, "Valter, we haven't much time."

Valter nodded and his eyes were bright with anticipation. Armed with an arrest warrant, and live before fifty million households, he entered the room.

The shriveled man on the bed could barely move as the glare of camera lights burst upon him. He was nearly invisible among the intravenous lines and respirator tubes that tenuously held him from falling into the pit of death.

"Anton Zelman?" the president boomed with operatic bravado.

The man could not speak with the tubes in his throat. He meekly nodded.

"You are under arrest for..." the EU president's words were cut short by the wail of monitors as they crashed to flat line. All the cameras zoomed in for a close up of Anton's face. Janet took his hand. With a shudder, he made two last grunts around his throat tubes. His eyes burst open, looking to heaven, then he surrendered to the ultimate justice, his hand cold and limp in hers. Doctors and nurses pushed past the reporters and worked, franticly trying to resuscitate him.

Despite their heroic efforts, Anton Zelman died.

"What did he say?" Valter asked Janet.

"He said 'Yee-haw'."

So fitting, Janet thought, that he should have the largest audience for a live death in history. She closed her eyes, imagining tomorrow's cover of The Sun or Le Monde. Anton's face looking to heaven. Who else but Zelman could pull that one off?

Was he a hero or a villain? Janet couldn't decide. But he certainly drank every drop of life and died on his own terms. Whether he was roasting hell or resplendent in heaven was not something any mortal would ever know. The tortures that drove him were now behind him, his adventures were complete. He had finally achieved the ultimate freedom. He could finally rest.

She felt sorry for the man. He had wanted to die the wealthiest man on earth, the world's first trillionare. Instead he died bankrupt, the world's poorest man. He wanted to outlive Mirza. Perhaps he even wanted to save the world. None of his goals were accomplished. The brilliant Anton Zelman died a defeated and broken man.

She scanned the room. She was the only one crying.

***

Janet sat with Adelheidis and Brandt in his hospital room. The TV was tuned to CNN. With a sixty percent drop, the NYSE was about to close on the worst day in its long history.

"And finally, some good news," the CNN anchor announced. "Dr. Janet Salty Thompson, American economist and world wide celebrity has just purchased controlling interest in the Tulsa Hat Company. Stocks in the smallest company on the NASDAQ immediately sky rocketed as investors jumped to be part of the least amount of good news."

It took her a moment to realize Zelman had bought the stock in her name. A dead man's last gift. Why? Who cares? He'd taken the bait, that's what mattered. Or did it. The inflective was too late. It was as worthless as yesterday's news.

Janet switched the TV to a financial talk show, Big Bucks. She had clicked into the middle of a segment on her, the TV backdrop a close-up of her Marilyn Monroe wink from Brussels.

"Looks like Thompson knows what she is doing," one of the commentators enthused. "She is making a killing. Her stock value is skyrocketing. The numbers don't lie, she has make over ten million dollars just in the last ten minutes. This is outrageous. What a greedy witch. This is a crime!"

"What did he just call me?" Janet raged. "I'm not greedy. I didn't do any of this."

"Shhh," Brandt extolled.

"Greedy witch is right," the other commentator cackled. "But hey, she is my kind of criminal. Give me some of your witchcraft, baby. Let's hear from one of our callers. Len from Seattle, you're on Big Bucks."

"You are absolutely right. The Wichita Witch must have planned this months ago."

"Wichita! I'm from Tulsa."

"Shhhhh."

"Look at these companies," the caller continued, "American Dynamics, United Entertainment, Hospitality Hotels, all skyrocketing. I'll bet you dollars to donuts she is the reason."

"What do we do about it?" the commentator asked.

"Buy!"

"Right on, brother!"

Janet clicked the remote to off.

"I didn't buy stock in any of those companies," Janet protested. She pulled out Jeremy's cell phone. "I'm going to call and straighten them out."

"Janet. This is your Midnight super-inflective at work. Their avarice is causing a rally. Let it do its work."

"But it is my reputation they are trashing."

"Janet. In last twenty four hours you've gone from saint to Satan and back. Don't worry about it. Besides, let Salty have some fun with this."

Janet gave him an open mouthed look of indignation. Then a slow smile spread across her lips.

"You're quite the woman."

"How so."

"You don't even care that you just became a multi-millionaire."

"You know, I didn't even think about it."

She turned the TV back on, and changed to a more reputable channel. They watched as the New York closing bell rang, and all transactions came to a crashing halt. The world would be in financial slumber for three and a half hours as time slowly inched forward to the Tokyo opening.

"Janet, you triggered a rally in New York," Adelheidis assured.

"A rally based on pure greed. Everyone thinks I'm a liar and a cheat, trying to make a quick buck. I don't want to be known for that."

"Janet, you've created hope for a recovery. Noblesse oblige. You did your duty. Let's not worry how you did it."

A nurse walked into the room, pushing a cart.

"I think it will take more than my computer tricks and avarice to trigger a lasting recovery," Janet replied.

"You're right," the nurse said, pulling out a gun and pointing it at Janet. Everyone froze. The nurse pulled off her cap, letting her long black braid fall.

"Mirza," Brandt muttered.

"Janet," Mirza spoke in slow metered tones. "We meet at last."

Janet said nothing, her eyes transfixed on the weapon in her opponent's hand.

"Mirza," Brandt broke in, trying to negotiate a peaceful settlement. "What are you doing? Surely you don't think you can simply walk in here, shoot Janet, and walk out."

"I have no intentions of walking out. The Economic Jihad is nearly complete. Anton is broken and dead. My job is almost done. I have just one more detail to finish, and my life's work is complete."

"But why shoot Janet?"

"She is the one person whose meddlesome interference could stop me. The one person whose brilliant mathematics could rival my own." Mirza swaggered up to the frightened girl. "The great Dr. Salty Thompson," she sneered. "Shaking in her shoes." Mirza shook her head in disapproval. "I'm disappointed. I thought Anton had better judgment than

256

to pick someone like you. I guess Anton was sicker than he realized, his mind was going. Oh well." She lifted the gun toward Janet's head. Janet squeezed her eyes shut.

"Mirza, don't," Brandt pleaded.

"Don't worry Brandt. That is not why I am here. I have no intention of shooting Janet." Mirza turned her gun toward Adelheidis.

"You," Mirza sneered. "For years I didn't know who you were. The invisible woman that my Anton was in love with. I wanted him, but could never have him, never once, because of you. But now I have you." She ran the cold steel barrel of the gun under Adelheidis' chin, and around her neck.

Adelheidis braced herself, preparing to die, trying to maintain dignity, trying not to tremble.

"Mirza," Brandt calmly pleaded. "Think about what you are doing."

"Oh I have. I've thought about this for years, preparing my life for this moment. But again, don't worry Brandt. I won't shoot your mother." She pointed the gun at him. "I intend to shoot you, and make Adelheidis and Janet live with the pain of watching you die for the rest of their lives." Mirza looked to the two women. "And I do hope you both have long, long lives to suffer through."

Janet's mind raced, trying to find a way to save Brandt.

"Janet and Adelheidis, you have ten seconds to say good-bye to Brandt." Neither woman moved. "Nine," Mirza said, executing her countdown. "Eight."

Adelheidis looked to Janet. Both women understood the hidden message, and what must be done.

With a scream Adelheidis jumped toward Mirza, lunging for the pistol. Janet dove between the gun and Brandt, blocking Mirza's shot. Mirza tried to shoot, but couldn't get her gun around Janet's body. Adelheidis grabbed Mirza and the two women wrestled with the pistol clamped between them. Janet leapt forward, forcing her hand into the space between them, groping for the deadly cold steel. The two women wrenched around, pulling Janet's arm out. Then came a sharp report, as the pistol fired. Searing agony swept across Adelheidis' face, as her knees buckled, and she dropped to the floor.

Mirza spun around, pointing the gun toward Brandt, and then her eyes rolled back into her head as a scarlet plume of blood spread across the chest of her white uniform. The gun rolled from her hand, fell and clattered across the floor. As she began her long topple toward the floor, Mirza's index finger pulled against the missing trigger again and again in a desperate attempt to complete her goal. A smile of satisfaction came to her lips as her imagination completed the scene her eyes could not fill. Then she hit the floor, motionless save the twitching of her one finger. Then that stopped also as the pool of blood spread under her.

"Adelheidis," Janet pleaded as she scrambled to the matron, searching for the still invisible gunshot wound.

"My heart, my heart." Adelheidis mouthed as nurses burst into the room.

"Heart attack," Janet screamed to everyone. "She's having a heart attack."

In mere moments another nurse broke through the door with her crash cart, followed by a doctor who pulled the defibrillator from the cart while the nurses pulled at Adelheidis' elegant blouse. He peeled the protective papers from the paddles and pressed them to her chest. He nodded agreement with the computer readout on the monitor. Her heart had stopped.

"Zurückweichen!" the doctor called out and the nurses pulled back. Then his thumbs reached forward and pressed the two red buttons on the paddles and discharged the defibrillator into her chest, pounding the woman from the floor. A moment of stunned silence followed, as the monitor searched for a heartbeat. Then the rhythmic beep of a sinus heartbeat started. A quick hoist by the team of four, and Adelheidis was on a gurney and whisked out. The still-bleeding Mirza was lifted on to another gurney, her beautiful smile frozen on her face. Janet followed in pursuit of Adelheidis.

A short while later Janet and Valter paced outside of Adelheidis' Intensive Care Unit cubicle as Brandt was wheeled in. Janet ran to him wrapping her arms around him.

"I can't believe they let you come down here,"

"They had no choice. I threatened to take back this wing of the hospital," Brandt chuckled. "How is she?"

"I already told you, the initial indications are very positive," Janet replied. "They're still running tests, but they think she will make a full recovery."

"Thank God," Brandt spoke. "And Mirza?"

"Gone."

"How about the stocks?"

"We don't know. Jeremy says the projections are very dire. Even with a late New York rally, it doesn't look good. It is nearly two o'clock here in Zurich. Tokyo is about to open. If they continue the decline, Jeremy projects food and fuel shortages within a few days. There is a TV in the waiting area just outside the door. Come on, let's watch."

She wheeled him to the television and sat next to him. CNN showed images of the riots that had already started around the world. Hand in hand, they waited for the opening bell of the Tokyo Stock Exchange.

"What does your gut tell you, Janet?"

"I don't know. Zelman died broke. Even if he wanted to help, he has no money. That, and being dead doesn't help his cooperation." Janet let out a slow sigh. She squeezed Brandt's hand. "I just don't know."

The fate of the world teetered in the balance. Janet thought of the people who ran the hat company. They would have no idea of their importance. They were probably washing supper dishes and helping their kids with homework. Neither did the millions of people around the globe waiting for Tokyo to open. They were biting their nails, waiting to see if the world would be quietly blasted back into the dark ages. They didn't have a clue of the importance of America's smallest company. Or about what was going to happen. Neither did she. The second hand ticked forward. In excruciating steps it moved toward the twelve mark. Three more steps, two, one.

Midnight arrived.

The news cameras zoomed in on the digital readout of the Nikkei225 index. In excruciating stillness, nothing happened. Then a gut wrenching downtick. Then another. Janet's heart sank. Mirza had won.

Then an uptick, then another, then a jump. The camera panned back. Indicators across the board ticked upward as a buy American wave swept through the Tokyo exchange, and a tsunami of cash poured into American stocks. Her phone rang.

"It's Rashid," she said. Rashid's earnest words echoing in her mind. She couldn't take credit for this upturn any more than she should lament the previous losses.

"Rashid, how are you?" Janet enthused, holding the phone for Brandt.

"I am well. Very, very well. I have two interesting bits of news to share with you. First, Anton Zelman just went from the world's poorest man, to the world's wealthiest, the world's first trillionaire. Second, world wide funds of Credit Default Swaps and Hedge Funds have been wiped out. They are gone."

"How is that possible?"

"When Anton's assets went negative, he took Mirza's accounts with him. They were loaded with those toxic assets. Mirza unwittingly saved the economy."

"Did Anton do that on purpose?" Brandt broke in.

"I can't tell. I guess we will never know. However, Janet's moves are being credited for saving the economy."

"Thank you, Rashid."

"You are welcome." Rashid paused. "Brandt, stay close to Janet. She will protect you," he quipped mocking his previous advice to Janet. "Good-bye, my friends."

"Talk to you later, Rashid," Janet bubbled.

"You did it, Janet!" Brandt said as she closed her phone.

She shook her head. "Naw, I didn't do anything. And who knows what might happen tomorrow. I don't even care, as long as I have you."

He swept her into his one good arm.

"I love you," he said.

"And I love you," she returned between his kisses. Then she pulled back an inch. "Brandt, what will happen to him? You know, what is left of him?"

"Dad and I are his only family. We will give him the funeral he would want." He paused, staring into space for a moment. "I'm going to miss him. He was never there, and yet he was always there."

Janet started to cry. "I will miss him too."

*** 

A cold gray fog hung over the massive funeral as the Mahlers stepped from the Zurich cathedral. Dignitaries from around Europe stood in quiet respect for this reclusive person they knew so little about, but whose fame and notoriety had spread across the world. Security was extremely tight. The police buzzed about in their black and white cars and scooters, constantly checking the IDs of the droves of reporters and cameramen as they angled for the best photos and stories.

The Mahlers stood on the top step of the Cathedral's long, steep stairway. Janet wore a black wool suit with mid-calf hem. A delicate black veil hung over her eyes and half covered her face.

Brandt stared at the ground, unable to speak, unable to cry. Even in his moment of grief he was handsome, one arm in a black sling that matched his perfectly tailored black double breasted suit and reminded the world of his recent brush with death.

"It all happened so fast. I still can't believe it," he murmured.

Valter put a comforting arm around his son. "No one can. She was a good mother."

Brandt stiffened as the military honor guard wheeled the casket of Adelheidis Mahler from the cathedral sanctuary. At the head of the wide stone stairway they stopped, and with crisp military precision lifted her and carried her down to the hearse below. Friedrich had to turn away, his pain greater than even when his own wife died.

Janet looked at Brandt through her veil, and saw him pinch the bridge of his nose to fight back a tear as the cameras zoomed in on the tragic, handsome face. She could now understand how he needed to grieve twice. A public grieving in full view of cameras and millions of people, not an act of pride or bravado, rather a claiming of his proper responsibility to the people. Private grieving had already come and more of it would come later. Right now, the public needed him.

Janet placed her left hand strategically on his shoulder, showing her ruby and gold engagement ring to the world, the one Adelheidis had so recently relinquished. She knew a thousand women were biting their knuckles in envy. Like Brandt, she was not being boastful or vain. It was her chosen and proper place.

Valter, the man who could lead a continent by his sheer force of will watched his son through watery eyes. What were his true feelings? Perhaps in a few years on a cold winter night sitting by the fire Janet would ask him. But for now it was not for her to know. He had done his chosen duty and had served Adelheidis well. Like Adelheidis, he was also now free.

The Mahlers were guided to the lead car. The press corps would only follow them half way to Graumauer. Even the paparazzi would respect the unspoken limits. There would be no photographs of the final private burial in the plot that held stones spanning a thousand years.

As the procession wound its way through the twisting Zurich streets Janet looked up and saw a tram with one of a thousand neon yellow placards that were now scattered around Europe. Plastered with her face wearing a genuine Tulsa Cowgirl Hat, it bore only two words; Yee-Haw. She thought of Zelman's words, "I've carefully taught you the rules, now use them." She had indeed learned the rules, and Tulsa Hat sales were exploding. She was a wealthy celebrity. No one could ever claim her pending marriage to Brandt was for either fame or fortune.

As the Mahlers approached the hilltop plot, the sun finally managed to burn through the haze. Friedrich had spent the last two days trimming each blade of grass by hand to assure his matron would be comfortable in her new home.

Adelheidis would rest in peace after a job well done. She maintained the dynasty that was entrusted to her. She survived the second heart attack that should have claimed her, forcing her crippled heart to beat until the mantle could be passed on to someone worthy of Graumauer. She died in peace knowing her reward for a lifetime of sacrifice was at hand.

Valter stood with Janet and Brandt for a decently respectable period of time before he hugged them both and reclaimed the limo to drive him back to Munich. The newly-engaged couple stood at the graveside for a long time before they walked slowly back down the little hill to the house.

"How about going for a ride with me?" suggested Janet. "Some equine exercise to help you work up an appetite."

Brandt made a small smile. He lifted the hand he held and kissed it. "Sure. Thanks for looking after me, Janet."

A short while later they emerged hand-in-hand and headed for the stables. Salzig whinnied recognition to the only person he would allow to ride him. Janet pulled out a saddle pad as Salzig eagerly awaited a trot around the estate. Gustav appeared and quickly saddled another horse for Brandt.

"Gustav, where's Friedrich?"

"My father is officially in mourning. He has given me full charge of his duties."

"That's a first," said Brandt. "How are you managing?"

"Oh, quite well. I was born to it, after all." He smiled at them, and hummed a little under his breath.

"Well, let me know if you need anything," offered Brandt.

Gustav nodded his thanks as he led the horses out to the mounting block. As Salzig proudly carried Janet along now familiar trails, she was soon lost in thoughts of the earlier funeral she and Brandt had attended just one short week ago.

The funeral for Anton Zelman was a small affair. He had few friends and even they didn't brave the rain that fell in the small Prague cemetery. Anton would not have wanted it any other way.

"He lived and died on his own terms," she said aloud.

"Uncle Anton? Yes, I suppose he did."

"He died the wealthiest person on earth. The world's first trillionare. He had the most toys, and won his game of life."

"You have to admit that's pretty amazing. He beat Dad - again. And yet, Dad didn't seem all that upset about it this time. He said he'd gotten something from Anton all these years. Something that Anton could never take away from him no matter how hard he tried." Brandt shook his head in puzzlement. "I don't think he meant he actually enjoyed all their fighting. I wonder what he meant?"

Janet knew the answer as she gazed at the son Valter had so proudly raised, a son Anton was never able to claim in anything but biology.

"I really have no idea," said Janet with a shrug.

"I'll have to ask him about it in a few weeks when we meet at Bretton Woods. He seemed delighted when I asked him to co-chair the meetings with me. I can still learn a lot from him."

"Yes, I'm sure you can."

"You can, too. He's got more experience than both of us put together!" Brandt shot her his signature smile. "Frau Dr. Mahler."

"Hey! You can't call me that yet. It's not true."

"But it will be. We'll be married here in the spring and then we'll fly to Tulsa so you can accept your doctorate. You were right, it will not be 'Dr. Thompson' after all."

"I don't know if I should go through with it."

"What, you're not backing out of the marriage...!"

"No way, not ever! I mean the doctorate."

"You can't still think that you don't deserve it."

"Well, it's just that I think I should defend it. You know, properly."

"Properly? You don't think Jeremy's affidavit along with all the algorithms and data he documented for the university was enough of a defense of your theory?"

"Yeah, I guess."

"You guess...? Well, if that's not good enough for you then world economies in full recovery modes have to be. Zimbabwe is going to show the world how it's done – Janet Mahler style."

Janet relented with a bouncing nod. She'd accept her degree next spring and Brandt would be there to see her receive it. Her husband Brandt. She beamed at her handsome companion. She planned to have sons. Sons that looked just like him.

Oh God! Zelman!

She hadn't thought of that until now. Her sons would have Zelman's blood, too. Well, nothing could be done about it. Brandt was who he was. And Anton had touched her in a way no one would ever be able to do again.

Janet wondered what had been said in Anton's last conversation with Adelheidis. Could a lifetime of love be compressed into a few minutes? Had he intended to recover the economy all along, or had the presence of Adelheidis changed his mind at the last moment? No one would ever know.

"Race you to the pond," declared Janet suddenly.

"And back!" shouted Brandt, urging his horse into a run.

Half an hour later they ambled back to the stables, exhausted but more content. Gustav came out to collect the tired mounts.

"Fraulein. Ah, sorry. Janet, while you were out riding a box arrived from overseas. I set it in the library for you."

"Thanks, Gustav."

Janet and Brandt went directly to the library. Seeing the return address as Tulsa, Janet eagerly opened the box. It contained a handful of valuable antique books. Brandt lifted a few of them out. Loose packing paper fluttered onto the carpet.

"These will add nicely to the collection, Janet," he said, glancing at the cataloging labels. "I didn't know you were interested in collecting private memoirs and diaries."

"There are lots of things you don't know about me."

"Yet," he said seductively, as he hooked her with his good arm and kissed her mouth.

"Yes, yet..." she murmured amongst the tangle of lips.

He released her and bent to pick up the papers that had fallen.

"There's a note from Marcie and one from Dr. Jones."

"Oh. Read them, will you?" asked Janet, rubbing dust off the binding of a scrapbook.

"'Jan, I'm so happy for you! Of course I'd be delighted to come help you plan the wedding! Just one question: what should I wear?'"

"You'll have to take her out shopping when she gets here and teach her about fashion," said Brandt with a chuckle.

Janet beamed at him.

"'Dear Janet, Thank you for the very generous offer, but I have to admit, I'm not really prepared to travel so far from home. Besides, it will take months of delightful reading to pour over the many wonderful revisions in your theory. Fascinating reading so far. I will be very pleased to see you (and meet Brandt) when you come back for graduation next spring. Take care of yourself until then. P.S. I was very sorry to hear about the death of Mr. Zelman. I would have liked to have had the chance to meet him. Regards, Dr. Jones.'"

"I wonder if Dr. Jones and Anton would have gotten along?" mused Janet.

"I don't know," answered Brandt, lifting out the remaining books to hand to Janet.

"Maybe I'll have to write a biography of him."

"Of Dr. Jones?"

"No, of your Uncle Anton."

Brandt nodded thoughtfully. "Interesting idea."

Anton had done it all. He had played life's game, and won. His last adventure had been played out. He had moved on. Heaven or hell? Whichever it was, she hoped he had finally found some kind of happiness. A wry smile came to her face thinking of the man who had bludgeoned his way into her life, changed it, and then left. She looked up at his tattered cowboy hat, poised in a place of honor over the mantle. She wished she could hear his voice one more time.

Brandt's phone rang.

"It's Thailand this time," he said, closing the phone with concern. "Want to come?"

"Sure. Let me just grab my little black dress."

# EPILOG

The newlyweds sat under the beach cabana out of the hot tropical sun as Friedrich brought a tray of drinks. He beamed at the couple he had predicted would be together. The dynasty had been transferred. His life's purpose was complete. Being here with them on their seaside honeymoon was an extra he had never dared hope for.

"Thank you, Friedrich," she said, "and thank you for agreeing to come with us."

"You are welcome, Mein Frau. This is where I belong. Now that Graumauer is having a new mistress I am glad you are asking me to continue to serve you in my old job. Thank you for inviting me to accompany you."

"I also want to thank you, Friedrich, for your excellent service in watching over Adelheidis for all those years," he said. "You were faithful until the end. You have always been so much more than just an employee to the family."

"Of course. Graumauer is my life. It is meaning so much to me to guard Adelheidis. Especially because you are in Zurich and not being there."

"Yes indeed," she agreed. "And a special thanks for saving me from the sniper."

"I am making top marksman in the army. I am glad my skills are not too old."

"Friedrich," her voice becoming more solemn. "I am sorry for your grief. It must have been very difficult for you to lose your matron."

"It is being very difficult. But being with you here now makes it all worthwhile. The dynasty has been transferred. And thanks to you, also.

You are giving up so much. You are giving up your entire old life to come here to start a new one."

She looked to her husband and smiled.

"It was worth it, Friedrich."

A look of satisfaction spread over Friedrich's face as he watched the couple, so exuberant and youthful as they exchanged flirtatious glances with each other.

"Mein Herr, may I get either of you anything else?"

He looked to his wife who shook her head no.

"I am so happy you are here to help me miss Mirza," Anton said to his Heidi.

# ABOUT THE AUTHOR

**Other books by Kat Duncan:**

**Romantic Suspense - The K-Cycle Series**
$ix Days to Midnight: http://www.smashwords.com/books/view/35415
Sunda Cloud: http://www.smashwords.com/books/view/67979


**Romantic Suspense**
Wild Rose Press: http://www.thewildrosepress.com/fiftyeight-faces-p-4366.html


**Historical Romance**
Without a Lord: http://www.smashwords.com/books/view/36804


**On Writing**
Telling Details: http://www.smashwords.com/books/view/33766


**Connect with Me Online:**
My website: http://www.katduncan.net
My blog: http://www.katduncan.net/writeabout
Smashwords: http://www.smashwords.com/profile/view/katduncan
Facebook: http://www.facebook.com/writeabout
Twitter: @Write_About
Amazon: Kat Duncan at Amazon
Goodreads:
http://www.goodreads.com/author/show/4585624.Kat_Duncan


**Cover Artist - Avril Duncan**
email: avrildc@gmail.com
DeviantArt: http://avrildc.deviantart.com